FALSE NINE

PHILIP KERR is the bestselling author
of the Bernie Gunther series, for which
he received a CWA Ellis Peters Award.
He was born in Edinburgh and now lives
in London. He is a life-long supporter
of Arsenal.

Follow @theScottManson on Twitter

PHILIP KERR

A SCOTT MANSON THRILLER

FALSE NINE

This book is for my dear friend, Jonathan Taylor

The term 'false 9' refers to a player playing in a lone-striker position who drops deep to search for the ball. The intention is to draw opposing central defenders with him and create a diversion for team-mates to move into space behind the defensive line and exploit chances to score.

Kieran Robinson

CHAPTER 1

Whenever I want to feel better about life I go on Twitter and read some of the tweets about myself. I always come away from this experience with a strong feeling about the true sporting character and essential fairness of the great British public.

> You're a useless bastard, Manson. The best thing you ever did was resign from this football club. #Cityincrisis

> Did you really resign Manson? Or were you sacked like every other overpaid cunt in football management? #Cityincrisis

> You left us in the lurch, Manson. If you hadn't quit we wouldn't have that stupid bastard Kolchak in charge and we might not be 4th from bottom. #Cityincrisis

> Come back to the Crown of Thorns, Scott. Mourinho did it. Why can't you? All is forgiven. #Cityincrisis

I suppose you think that what you said about
Chelsea on @BBCMOTD was clever, you stupid
black cunt. You make Colin Murray look good.

Most @BBCMOTD pundits are the walking dead.
But if Darryl Dixon ever needed to put a crossbow
bolt in a someone's eye, it's yours.

Just because you've been on the cover of GQ
doesn't mean you're not a black bastard, Manson.
You're just a black bastard in a nice suit.

We miss you, Scott. The football is rubbish since you
left. Kolchak hasn't a fucking clue. #Cityincrisis

When are you going to explain why you quit City,
Manson? Your continued silence about this is
damaging the club. #Cityincrisis

I'm only on Twitter because my publisher thought it would help to sell more copies of my book before Christmas. There's a new edition out in paperback with an extra chapter about my short reign at London City. Not that it says very much. I'd already signed a confidentiality agreement with the club's owner, Viktor Sokolnikov, which forbids me from saying why I left the club, and mostly it's to do with the death of Bekim Develi. Or at least as much as I can say about that. The new chapter had to be read by Viktor's lawyers, of course. Frankly, it's really not worth the paper it's written on and all the tweets in the world aren't going to alter that fact.

I'm not a fan of social media. I think that we'd all be a lot better off if every tweet cost five pence, or you had to put a postage stamp on it before you sent it. Something like that. Most people's opinions aren't worth shit, mine included. And that's just the reasonable ones. It goes without saying that there's a lot of hate on Twitter and a great deal of that hate is to do with football. Part of me isn't surprised. Back in 1992 when a programme cost a quid and a seat no more than a tenner, I expect people were a bit more forgiving about football-related matters. But these days with a ticket at a top club like Man U costing six or seven times as much, you can forgive the fans for expecting a bit more from their team. Well, almost.

The funny thing is that while I never pay a lot of attention to the nice things people tweet about me, I can't help but pay attention to the insults and abuse I get. I try not to but it's hard, you know? To that extent, Twitter is a little like air travel: you don't pay it much attention when it's going well, but you can't help but pay attention when it's going badly. It's curious but there's a small part of me that thinks there's an element of truth to the unpleasant tweets. Like this one:

> If you were any good, Manson, you'd be at another club by now. But for the death of Joao Zarco you'd still be picking up cones.

And this one:

> Deep down, you always knew that the boots you were wearing were much too big for you. That's why you fell, you stupid fuck. #Cityincrisis

Then again, just occasionally you read something that seems to have something interesting to say about the game itself.

> You never understood that the purpose of passing is not to move the ball but to find the free man.

And perhaps, this one, too:

> The trouble with English football is everyone thinks he's Stanley Matthews. Don't dribble the ball, run with it; run to provoke.

For anyone who calls himself a football manager, being unemployed is probably your default position. Losing your job – or leaving it because you find it's just untenable – is as inevitable as scoring a few own goals if you're a good number four. As Plato once said, shit just happens. It's always painful to leave a football club you've been managing but the high rewards for success mean there are also high risks for failure. It's the same with investment; whenever I see my financial advisor for lunch he always reminds me of the five levels of risk appetite. These are: Averse, Minimal, Cautious, Open and Hungry. As an investor I would describe myself as cautious, with a preference for safe options that have a low degree of risk and may only have a limited potential for reward. But football is very different. Football is all about the last level: if you're not risk-hungry you've no business being a manager. Anyone who doubts that should look at the colour of Mourinho's hair or check the lines on the faces of Arsène Wenger and Manuel

Pellegrini. Frankly, it's only when you've lost your job that you can truly say you've made your bones as a manager. But let's face it, today's managerial pariah can quickly turn into tomorrow's messiah. Brian Clough is the best example of a manager who failed badly at one club only to succeed spectacularly at his next. It's tempting to imagine that Leeds United might have won two European Cups, back to back, if only they'd kept faith with Clough. In fact I'm sure of it.

Even so, it's hard being out of football management. It wasn't so hard during the summer, but now that the season is well under way I just want to be on the training ground with a team – even if I am just picking up the cones. I miss the game a lot. I miss the lads at London City even more. Sometimes I miss the team so much I feel physically sick. Right now I feel ill-defined as a person. Like I have no meaning. Etiolated. Which is a good word for what it's like to be an unemployed manager: it means someone who's lost their vigour or substance, and it also means pale and drawn-out due to a lack of light. That's exactly how I feel: etiolated. Just don't use a word like that on *MOTD* or they'll never ask you back. I can just imagine the tweets I'd get about using a word like that.

The fact is that you're only a manager when you're managing, as Harry Redknapp might say. When you're not doing it – when you're appearing as a pundit on *MOTD*, or a guest on *A Question of Sport* – you're what, exactly? I'm not sure that I'm anything at all. But here's another tweet that puts it very well, I think:

Now that you've left City, Manson, you're going to
find out that you're just another cunt in football.

Yeah, that's exactly right. I'm just another cunt in foot-ball. It's worse than being an actor who's working as a waiter because no one knows when you're a 'resting' actor. But when you're a manager who's out of work the world and his fucking dog seem to know about it. Like the bloke who sat beside me on the plane to Edinburgh this morning.

'I'm sure you'll find another job in management soon,' he said, encouragingly. 'When David Moyes was sacked from United I knew that it wouldn't be long before he was back at a top club. It'll be the same for you, mark my words.'

'I wasn't sacked. I resigned.'

'Every year it's the same old game of musical chairs. You know, Scott, I think people should bear in mind that it takes time for a manager to turn things around when a club is not doing well. But if you give a manager that time, then quite often he'll prove his gainsayers wrong. Nine times out of ten, the manager's just the scapegoat. It's the same in business. Take Marks & Spencer. How many CEOs has Marks & Spencer had since Sir Richard Greenbury left in 1999?'

'I wouldn't know.'

'The problem there is not the manager, but the whole retail business model. The fact is that people don't want to buy their clothes where they buy their sandwiches. Am I right, or am I right?'

Looking at my travelling companion's clothes I wasn't too sure about that. In his brown suit and salmon pink shirt he looked exactly like a prawn sandwich but I nodded politely and hoped for a moment when I might get back to reading Roy Keane's riveting book on my Kindle. It never came and I got off the plane wishing I'd thought to wear a cap and a pair of glasses, like Ian Wright. I don't need glasses. And I don't like caps. But I like chatting about football with strangers even less. Looking like a cunt is a lot better than spending a whole flight talking to one.

It was very strange being back in Edinburgh after so many years away. I ought to have felt more at home here – after all, it was the place where I'd done the larger part of my growing up – but I didn't. I couldn't have felt more alien or out of place. It wasn't just the past that made Scotland seem like a foreign country to me. Nor was it much to do with the recent referendum. I hadn't shared the Scots' dislike of the English as a boy and I certainly didn't share it now, especially since I'd chosen to make my home in London. No, there was something else that made me feel separate, something much more personal. The truth was I'd never really been permitted to feel like a proper Scot on account of the colour of my skin. All of the kids in my class at school had been freckle-faced, green-eyed Celts. Me, I was half black – or, as the Scots used to describe me, 'a half-caste' – which was why I'd been nicknamed Rastus. Even my Edinburgh schoolmasters had called me Rastus and although I wouldn't ever have shown it, this hurt.

A lot. And it had always struck me as amusing that the minute I arrived at a school in England – with a Scots accent long since scraped off the bottom of my shoe – my nickname should have become Jock. Not that the boys of Northampton School for Boys weren't racist, too, but they were a lot less racist than their Scottish counterparts.

I'm lucky in that I have a seat on the board of my dad's company to fall back on, but that certainly didn't stop me from putting myself around a bit to see what was out there. My agent, Tempest O'Brien, was firmly of the opinion that it was important for me to see as many people as possible.

'It's not just your achievements that make you eminently employable,' she'd told me, 'it's you, the whole GQ package. You're one of the most articulate and intelligent men I know, Scott. Christ, I nearly said in football, but that's not saying much, is it? Besides, I think it's crucial that people see you're not just sitting back and living off your earnings – which according to the newspapers are substantial – as a director of Pedila Sports. So it's important you play that down. If people think you don't need to work then they'll try to buy you cheap. So the first place I'm going to send you is Edinburgh. There's a job going at Hibs. No one is going to try and buy you cheaper than a side in the Scottish Championship. I know your father was a Hearts man through and through but you should go and talk to them because it's a good place to start. Better that you should make your mistakes and hone your interview skills there where it won't matter than somewhere more important where it will, like Nice, or Shanghai.'

'Shanghai? Why the hell would I go to Shanghai?'

'Did you see *Skyfall*? The Bond movie? Shanghai is one of the most futuristic cities in the world. And the place is just rolling in money. It might be good experience for you to work there. Especially if they start buying football clubs in Europe. And the rumour is they're looking to do just that. The Chinese are a can-do people, Scott. Can do and will do, probably. When the Russians get tired of owning clubs or when the rouble finally collapses and they have to sell out, who are they going to sell to? The Chinese, of course. Within twenty years the Chinese are going to be the world's number one economic superpower. And when China rules the world, the capital of that world is going to be Shanghai. They started building a new tram in December 2007, and it was open less than two years later. Contrast that with Edinburgh's tram. How long did that take? Seven years? A billion quid spent on it and still they're bitching about fucking independence.'

The tram – which was supposed to run from Edinburgh Airport to a stop just across the road from my hotel – was out of action that particular morning; a power cut, they said. So I got the bus. It was an inauspicious start. And Tempest was right about something else, too: they were still bitching about independence.

I checked into the Balmoral Hotel, ate some oysters at the nearby Café Royal and then went down Leith

Walk towards Easter Road to see Hibs play Queen of the South. The ground and the pitch were better than I remembered and I guessed there were between twelve and fifteen thousand there – a big difference from the record attendance of sixty-five thousand in 1950, when Hibs played their local rivals Hearts. It was a cold but beautiful afternoon, just right for a game of football, and while the home side had the better run of the play for most of the match they were unable to take their chances. Paul Hanlon and Scott Allan both went close and Hibs lost a chance to go level on points with a side they ought to have beaten with ease. The Queens looked happy to have come away with a point in a goalless draw that did not please the Edinburgh fans. Jason Cummings was about the only player who impressed me when his swerving thirty-yard shot was saved by the Queens' goalkeeper Zander Clark, but it was a less than memorable game and on the evidence of what I'd seen, Hibs, who were more than ten points adrift of the league leaders, Hearts, seemed destined to be spending another year out of the SPL.

I went back to the hotel, ordered some tea which never came, had a hot bath, snoozed my way through the football results and *Strictly For Morons*, and then went around the corner to a restaurant called Ondine, where I'd arranged to meet Midge Meiklejohn who was one of the club's directors. He was an affable man with a large head of red hair and green eyes. In his lapel was a Hibs crest which served to remind me just how old the club actually was: 1875. And of course this proud tradition was a major part of the club's problem. Of any old club's problem.

We talked generally about football for a while and drank our way through an excellent Sancerre before he asked me what I'd thought of the game and, more importantly, Hibs themselves.

'If you'll forgive me,' I told him, 'your problems aren't on the pitch but in the boardroom. You've had how many – seven? – managers in ten years? Who've probably done the best that could be done, in the circumstances. The manager you've got is doing a great job, and things aren't going to get any better until you address the fundamental problem which is that football clubs are like regional newspapers. There are simply too many of them. Prices are going up and readership is declining. There are too many papers competing for too few readers. The same is true of football. There are too many clubs competing not just with each other but with television. Your gate today was maybe twelve thousand, while some of your players are on two or three grand a week, maybe more. Your wage bill must take two thirds of your gate. Which leaves running costs and the bank. Your business is dying on its feet. Full-time football is just not a viable option for you or, for that matter, for nearly all of the Scottish clubs, bar two.'

'So what are you saying? That we should just give up?'

'Not at all. But the way I see it you have two choices if you're going to survive as a club. Either you do what some Swedish clubs do – clubs like Gothenburg – with most of the players taking part-time jobs as painters and decorators. Or there's what a French philosopher speaking about something else calls "the detestable solution". A solution which makes total business sense but which will have the supporters crying out for your head, Midge, and everyone else on your board.'

'What's that?'

'A merger. With Hearts. To form a new Edinburgh club. Edinburgh Wanderers. Midlothian United.'

'You must be joking. Besides, that's been considered before. And rejected.'

'I know. But that doesn't mean it's not the right solution. Edinburgh isn't Manchester, Midge. It can barely support one good team, let alone two. You use the assets of one club to pay off the debts and build a future for them both. It's simple economics. The only problem is that tribes don't like economics. And Hibs and Hearts are two of the oldest tribes in Scotland. Look, it worked for Inverness Cally Thistle. In less than twenty years they've merged two failing clubs and gone from the Scottish Third Division to being second in the SPL. The case for a merger is irrefutable. You know it. I know it. Even they know it – the supporters – in their heads. The only trouble is that they don't think with their heads, but with their hearts. If you'll pardon the expression.'

'These people aren't like other people,' said Midge. 'They know how to hate and more importantly they know how to hurt. I'd probably have to seek police protection. Leave the city. We all would.'

'Then to quote Private Fraser, you're doomed. Doomed, I tell ye. It's the same for most of the clubs in the north of England. It's history and tradition that are holding them back, too. There's this singularity called the Barclays Premier League that deforms everything that comes close to it and which is sucking everything in English football into its mass. The big clubs get more successful and the poor ones disappear. Who wants to go and pay twenty quid to watch Northampton Town get stuffed when you can support Arsenal in the comfort of your own home? That's the physics of football, Midge. You can't argue with the laws of the universe.'

'It's only a game,' said Midge. 'That's what these bloody people forget sometimes. It's only a game.'

'But it's the only bloody game as far as they're concerned.'

I went back to the hotel to watch *MOTD* but it hardly seemed worth it since the matches were all Scottish ones. Not that there would have been any English Premier League matches anyway because of international duties, which meant I was at least spared watching Arsenal throw away a three goal lead, as they'd recently done against Anderlecht in the Champions League. That had grieved me a lot less than it might have done. The fact is that since I started to watch football with the eyes of an ordinary fan I've come to appreciate something genuinely beautiful about the beautiful game. It's this: learning how to lose is an important part of being a fan. Losing teaches you – in the words of Mick Jagger – that you can't always get what you want. This is an important part of being a human being – perhaps the most important part of all. Learning to cope with disappointment is what we call character. Rudyard Kipling had it almost right, I think. In life it helps to treat triumph and disaster with equal sangfroid. The ancient Greeks knew the importance that the gods placed on our ability to suck it up. They even had a word for it when we didn't: hubris. Learning how to suck it up is what makes you a mensch. It's only fascists who will tell you anything else. I prefer to think that this is the true meaning of Bill Shankly's oft-quoted remark about life and death. I think that what he really meant was this: that it's character and sand that are more important than mere victory and defeat. Of course you couldn't ever say as much while you're the manager of a club. There's only so much philosophy that anyone can take in the dressing room. That kind of shit might work on centre court at Wimbledon but it won't wash at Anfield or Old Trafford. It's hard enough to get eleven men to play as one without telling them that sometimes it's all right to lose.

CHAPTER 2

Tempest O'Brien was one of only three female football agents in the game. The other was Rachel Anderson who'd famously – and successfully – sued the Professional Footballer's Association when she'd been forbidden entry to the PFA dinner in 1997, despite being a FIFA-registered football agent. It was Rachel who'd broken down barriers in the game for people like Tempest who I'd appointed as my agent just before I went to work with Zarco at London City. Before becoming a football agent, Tempest had worked for Brunswick PR and the International Management Group. She was clever, very good-looking and made everyone she met feel as though they were as smart as she was. Football might be less racist than it used to be but as the likes of Andy Gray and Richard Keys demonstrated in 2011, it's still a bastion of sexism. I should know; sometimes I'm a bit of a sexist myself, but as a black man in football management I felt it was my duty to help break down some barriers by giving Tempest the chance to represent me. I've regretted it only once. We were at the Ballon d'Or awards party in Zurich a couple of years ago, both staying at the Baur au Lac, and we almost went to bed together. She wanted to, and I wanted to, but somehow good sense prevailed and we managed to finish the evening alone and in our own rooms. She looks a bit like Cameron Diaz so you'll have a pretty good idea of why – at the time, anyway – I regretted not going to bed with her as any man might have done. Tempest's second idea was a job at OGC Nice.

'Actually,' she admitted, 'I'm not one hundred per cent sure that there is a job and maybe they're not sure themselves. They're French and they play their cards pretty close to their chests. Besides, my French isn't that good so I can't read between the lines of what's been said. Your French is much better than mine so I expect you'll suss out what the true state of play is there. But it is Nice and they're a league one side so it won't do you any harm to meet them and for them to register that you're tailor-made for a job there. If not now then perhaps in the future. I can't imagine a more beautiful place to work. They're suggesting they meet you in Paris because they're playing PSG this Saturday. It ought to be a good game. Anyway, take Louise. Stay somewhere nice. Have lots of sex in an expensive hotel.'

It was all good advice and my girlfriend, Louise Considine, didn't need much persuading. A detective inspector with the Metropolitan Police, she had plenty of leave due to her and so it was that we caught the Eurostar to Paris early one Saturday morning in November.

'You don't have to come to the game, you know,' I told her. 'If I were you I'd go shopping at Galeries Lafayette, or go and see the new Picasso Museum.'

'Well at least you didn't tell me to go and buy myself some expensive lingerie,' she said, rolling her eyes. 'Or to go and get my hair done. I suppose I should feel glad about that.'

'Did I say something wrong?'

'What kind of girlfriend would I be if I left your side for one minute this weekend? I want us to sleep together, bathe together, and go to the football together. But I have only one condition. And it's this. That you leave your awful pyjamas at home.'

'They're silk,' I protested.

'I don't care if they once belonged to Louis XIV. I like to feel your bare skin against me in bed. Clear?'

'Yes, Inspector.'

The train was full of people heading to Paris for some early Christmas shopping and these included some boisterous football fans who spotted me in the international departure hall at St Pancras and struck up with a chorus of,

'You left 'cos you're shit, You left 'cos you're shiiiit, Scott Manson, You left 'cos you're shit.'

Which wasn't so bad, all things considered. I've heard a lot worse about myself than that. Besides, I was the one who was travelling to Gare du Nord with a beautiful blonde on my arm, even if she was a copper.

'Does that bother you?' she asked.

'Nah.'

'Good. Because these days I'm only empowered to arrest people who are on Twitter. Going after real thugs and criminals is no longer a proper and efficient use of police time.'

'I can almost believe that.'

'It's true.'

On arrival we checked into our hotel and went straight out again to have some lunch. Even in Paris there are times when food has to come before anything, although that wasn't quite the way Louise saw it.

'*Soupe à l'oignon* is just the thing to have inside you before a match,' I said. 'Not to mention a cassoulet and a good bottle of Riesling.'

'I can think of something else I'd like inside me,' said Louise. 'As soon as we've finished lunch I'd like you to take me back to the room and fuck the arse off me.'

And so after an excellent lunch we went back to the hotel; there was just time to fuck the arse off her before catching the Metro from Alma Marceau to Porte de St-Cloud.

I liked going to a football match on the Metro. No one recognised me and it was like being an ordinary fan again – even in Edinburgh I'd had a few smart remarks on the way down Leith Walk to Easter Road. The PSG fans in the Metro carriage certainly smelled real enough; it was like a bar in there. But they were well behaved and I saw no sign of the hooligan element that was supposed to exist at PSG and which, in 2006, had resulted in one fan being shot dead by the Paris police following a racist attack on a supporter of Hapoel Tel

Aviv. Millwall might get off on the fact that no one likes them but it has to be said that no one dislikes them enough to shoot them dead. Not yet, anyway.

Outside the Parc des Princes there were more cops on the streets than there were lovers' padlocks on the Pont des Arts. They looked like they meant business, too. Most of them were armed and dressed for a riot which seemed less than likely: it wasn't Nice but Marseille – currently topping Ligue 1 – who were PSG's most bitter rivals.

'They're not taking any chances,' said Louise, 'are they?'

'Every time I come to Paris it seems there are more coppers than there were before. I think if you're looking for a job in France the gendarmerie is probably the best place to start. It seems the French government doesn't trust the people.'

'Can you blame them?' It was just like Louise to speak up for another country's police force. 'Between 1789 and 1871 they had five revolutions in this city. Sometimes it seems that there's a demonstration every other weekend. The French are an obstreperous lot.'

'In an English-speaking world there's a lot to feel obstreperous about. I admire their determination to hold on to what makes them French. We could do with a bit more of that in England. Maybe learn a lesson from the Scots. Have a referendum about whether we want to kick them out of Great Britain. Something like that.'

'Have you thought about joining UKIP?' she said.

Olympique Gymnaste Club Nice Côte d'Azur was eleventh out of twenty in Ligue 1, and Paris Saint-Germain was second. Nice, founded in 1904, was the older club by seven decades and doing rather better than the fire sale of players in the summer might have led us to expect. Paris had not lost a football match since the beginning of the season and while I'd come to France looking forward to seeing Thiago Silva, David Luiz and Zlatan Ibrahimovic in action for PSG, it was the Parisian number nine, Jérôme Dumas, who impressed me the most. He was as quick as greased lightning and just as unpredictable, with a left foot that was as sweet as any I'd seen; the player he reminded me of most was Lionel Messi. It seemed strange that there was a rumour he was for sale. He was full of running and might have scored had there been more of an understanding between him and Edinson Cavani, nicknamed 'the matador' on account of his flamboyant style on the pitch. Zlatan might have scored the only goal – from a penalty – but the Parisians did not convince and, after the goal in the seventeenth minute, unaccountably PSG took their foot off the gas which left the initiative with the Niçois, who looked unlucky not to come away with a point.

We went back to the Plaza and had a quick shower before going out for dinner.

The following morning I left Louise in bed and went down to breakfast with Gerard Danton, who was one of the directors at OSG Nice. He was a handsome, well-dressed man in his forties and I was glad I'd decided to take Louise's advice and wear a blue blazer, a shirt and a new tie from Charvet that she had bought me the day before. We spoke in French. It's a language I love to speak although my Spanish and German are better.

'This is a nice hotel,' said Danton. 'I've not stayed here myself. I usually stay at the Meurice. But I think I prefer this.'

'My girlfriend would probably agree with you. And of course it's very handy for the Metro.'

He frowned, as if he didn't quite understand why someone staying at the Plaza could think the Metro to be at all important.

'I took the Metro to the match,' I added.

'You took the Metro to Parc des Princes?' He sounded surprised as if he'd never considered doing this himself.

'Quicker than the car. It took me no time at all. Besides, I like going to a match on the Metro. In London I can't do it. Not for the present, anyway. I'd get too much stick.'

He glanced out of the window into the hotel court-yard. 'What's that they're building out there?'

'It appears to be an ice rink.'

Danton shivered. 'Paris is too cold for me,' he said. 'I prefer the south. I take it you've been to Nice.'

'Many times. I love the Riviera. Especially Nice. It's the only part of the Côte d'Azur that feels like a proper city.'

'With all the problems that brings.'

'Not all. You've got the nicest climate in Europe. Spain and Italy are too hot. Nice is Goldilocks. Just right.'

'Tell me. Why on earth did you leave City? You were doing so well there.'

'I loved the club, it's true and I miss it more and more. I suppose I was an idealist. You might say I believed in a certain style of football. And perhaps I was not pragmatic enough.'

That's a very diplomatic answer.'

'I'm afraid it's the only one you're going to get. Really, it's best I don't say any more. Since Tony Blair and George Bush diplomacy has a habit of sounding like a lie.'

'Very well. What did you think of our football?'

'The first half an hour was difficult for you. They wouldn't have got that penalty anywhere but the Parc des Princes. But Grégoire Puel organised his players very well and you endured the storm, which was mercifully brief. Frankly, they allowed you back into the game when they should have closed it down. If you play with the same intensity you showed in the second half you've a good season ahead of you, Mr Danton. Given that you were missing some key players I thought you made a very good game of it. They were lucky to get three points.'

'And yet, we've had just one point in our last four matches. How can we put things right? What is the best way forward for Nice? What's going wrong?'

'In my opinion, nothing. Nothing at all. It's just that you don't have Qatari money to throw around like confetti on the likes of Cavani, Ibrahimovic, Luiz, Silva, or Dumas. PSG have bought their second place, just like Manchester City have bought theirs. If you had any one of those players things might be very different for you. Do you have a spare thirty-five million to buy Jérôme Dumas? Because I hear PSG might be looking to offload him in January.'

Danton shook his head. 'We've had a difficult summer. We had to reduce our wage bill quite substantially. We couldn't afford that price.' He shrugged. 'Nobody can, unless they have an Arab or Russian daddy to buy them all the cakes they want.'

'Oil money distorts everything. Not just football. Take a look around this hotel. There are people staying here who spend money like it has no real meaning.'

'True. But it's the same at the Meurice.'

I shrugged. 'You're punching above your weight, Mr Danton. Puel is doing a good job. I'm sure I couldn't do any better than him. Not with your resources. Your goal-keeper, Mouez Hassen, made an excellent save. He kept you in the game. And if Eysseric had scored we might be having a very different conversation. In the first half the ball burned your feet. In the second you started to enjoy yourselves. I don't see much that needs to change. Except maybe that you should tell your players to free themselves a little more, and to enjoy the game. All of which makes me wonder why you wanted this meeting.'

'Window shopping. Like everyone else in Paris. Who can afford to do anything else in this city? Apart from the Russians and the Arabs.'

'Don't forget the Chinese. They may have slightly less money than the Russians and the Arabs but there seem to be more of them spending it in Paris.'

'It's not everyone who would be straight enough to say what you've said, Mr Manson. Especially when he's unemployed. That kind of honesty speaks volumes about a man's character. For the same reason I admire a man who's not too proud to take the Metro. So, I hope you'll allow me to pay for your weekend. The fact is, you've probably saved me quite a bit of money this morning. And I appreciate that most of all. Especially in Paris.'

CHAPTER 3

The best way to see Shanghai is at night when the huge, neon-lit city looks like a fabulous, black velvet-lined jewel box full of shiny red rubies, glittering diamonds and bright blue sapphires. Tempest was right. It was just like *Skyfall*, except that I wasn't planning to kill anyone. Not that anyone would have noticed, probably. I'd never seen so many people. Shanghai has a population of twenty million and it's hard to imagine that the individual has any real significance. Equally, it's hard to know exactly what's going on. Everything looks like a major metropolis but when you can't read anything very much it's easy to feel lost and out of your depth. There's that and the fact that I had a hard time telling Chinese people apart, which isn't racist so long as you recognise that they probably have the same problem with people in the West.

My host was the Chinese billionaire, Jack Kong Jia, who had contacted Tempest with an invitation for me to come and manage his football club, Shanghai Xuhui Nine Dragons, on a rolling six month contract. JKJ, as he was popularly known, owned the Nine Dragons Mining Company and was reportedly worth six billion dollars, which explained why I'd been installed in an eight thousand pound a night Chairman's Suite on the eighty-eighth floor of the Park Hyatt, one of the highest hotels in the world.

'Jack Kong Jia is supposedly in the market to buy an English football club,' Tempest had explained back in London. 'He's not just looking for a manager in Shanghai but someone who knows English football and can help advise him about that, so it would be a good thing if you and he got along.'

'Which one? Any idea?'

'Reading. Leeds. Fulham. Take your pick. Owning a football club is not for the faint-hearted, that's for sure. You might need nine dragons to give yourself the courage to do it.'

'I don't know if I want to work with another foreign billionaire,' I said. 'I worked for one before, remember? And I didn't like it.'

'Which is exactly why a six month contract in Shanghai would be a good idea. That way you can decide if you take to each other or not. Look, Scott, this guy might be the next Roman Abramovich or Sheikh Mansour and let's be realistic, it's not as if there are any other offers right now.'

'True. But it's not like I need the money. I can afford to wait for the right offer to come along. And I'm not sure this is right for me. It's not as if I can even speak Chinese.'

'I've only spoken to him on the telephone but Mr Jia speaks perfect English, so that's not a problem. And half the team are from Europe.'

I grunted. 'I keep thinking there's a club in Germany I could manage. I speak fluent German, after all. I like it there.'

'You've not been to Shanghai, have you?' she asked.

'No.'

'It's my opinion that to walk away from this would be like turning your back on the future.'

'Are you speaking from experience?'

'No.'

'Then you're guessing.'

'Call it intuition. Look, Scott, one of the reasons I was hired by you was so that I might have an opportunity in an almost exclusively male world. That means you have to accept that I'm going to think outside the box. I also have to tell you that I need to make a living and if I'm going to represent you I have to remind you that right now I'm earning ten per cent of nothing. So, please. Give this a chance.' She picked up my hand and kissed it fondly. "And do try to cheer up, Scott. Smile. Things will get better, I'm sure of it."

'All right. And you're pobably right. I'll go.'

'And when you get there don't talk yourself out of a job, the way you did in Paris. Try not to be so very honest. The current team manager, Nicola Salieri, has already resigned. Mr Jia seems to have a high opinion of you. All you have to do is go to the match and listen to what he has to say.'

Mr Jia met me in a luxurious private box at the thirty thousand capacity Yu Garden stadium where Shanghai Xuhui – wearing a blue and red home strip that looked suspiciously like Barcelona's – were hosting Guangzhou Evergrande. He was a handsome man in his early thirties with Michael Caine glasses, an American accent, a diamond-encrusted watch as big as the Queen's coronation crown and, in the lapel of his suit, a little Chinese flag. We were carefully attended by eight beautiful Chinese girls wearing smiles that were bigger than their little black minidresses. They poured our drinks, fetched us food, lit Mr Jia's endless cigarettes and took care of his large and almost continual in-play bets. He drank Krug champagne – all the time, it seemed, and not I thought because he liked it but because it was the most expensive. I restricted myself to Chinese beer – Tsingtao – because I liked it and because I wanted to keep a clearish head for business and the game in hand. But in truth we were so high above the pitch it was difficult to follow the match. The player names on the shirts were yellow and in Chinese and while they also had numbers, the programme was in Chinese too, so I had little or no idea of who was who.

'You like Shanghai?' he asked. 'Your hotel room? Everything is to your liking?'

'Yes, everything is great, Mr Jia.'

'I want you to like it here. This is the future, Mr Manson. It's impossible to be here and not to think so, don't you agree?'

'Wasn't it Confucius who said that prophecy is

always difficult – especially when it's a prophecy about the future?'

Mr Jia laughed. 'You know Confucius? That is good. Not many managers can quote Confucius. Even in China.'

I shrugged, modestly. I had an idea that there were many famous names who were alleged to have coined this saying, among them Confucius, but I had no wish to insult Mr Jia by suggesting that this was now the kind of quotation that could be found inside any Christmas cracker.

'I was very much an admirer of London City,' he continued.

'Me, too. Still am.'

'Of João Zarco and yourself. I tell you honestly that if Mr Zarco had still been alive it might have been him who was sitting here now.'

'Zarco was the best manager in Europe,' I said. 'If not the world.'

'This is my opinion also,' said Jia. 'But I also think that you are the next best thing. That if you had stayed at London City you would have achieved greatness. Of course it might turn out that their loss could be my gain.'

Mr Jia allowed one of the hostess girls to refill his glass. While she did so his hand drifted up her skirt and stayed there for a moment but she did not flinch and the smile remained fixed on her face. Evidently she was used to this Game of Thrones style behaviour. And I got the feeling that she would not have blinked an eye if I had copied his behaviour and done the same. But my hands stayed wrapped around my beer glass.

'I heard a strong rumour that your departure from City had something to do with a foreign betting syndicate,' he said. 'That you discovered that the death of Bekim Develi in Athens was connected with an in-play bet made in Russia. Oh, it's all right, I'm not asking you to confirm this rumour. This is common knowledge here in China. I like to bet myself – all Chinese people like to gamble – but I make it a rule never to bet on my own team. The bets you've seen me making are all on other matches taking place this afternoon. Principally the match between our principal rival, Shanghai Shenhua and Beijing Guoan. I tell you this so that you will know that I am not a crook. I am, however, very rich and what else can you do with money but spend it? I have a million yuan riding on the result of that match; this is about a hundred thousand pounds. But there's nothing to stop you betting on Nine Dragons, Mr Manson. Or for that matter on these dogs from Guangzhou Evergrande. Although I wouldn't recommend it. They are without their best player – Arturo. The Brazilian? Shanghai Xuhui Nine Dragons will almost certainly beat the Greens this afternoon.'

'Why nine dragons?' I asked, changing the subject. 'Why not seven or eight? Or even ten?'

'Nine has the same pronunciation as a word which means everlasting and so this is a very lucky number in Chinese,' he explained. He kept on watching the match while he spoke, the match reflecting like tiny televisions in his glasses. 'Many Chinese emperors liked the number a lot. They wore nine dragon imperial robes, and built nine dragon palace walls. In the Forbidden City you will find the number nine affects almost everything. The number nine and its multiples are also liked by ordinary Chinese people. On Valentine's Day a Chinese man will present his lover with ninety-nine red roses to symbolise eternal love. Really there's no end to the fascination we Chinese have with the number nine. I even have a number nine tattooed on my back. Just so that my wife really knows it's me. When I bought this team I wanted to emphasise great power and hope for the future. Which is where the number nine and you come in, Mr Manson. I have great plans for the future of this football club and the Chinese Super League.

'But these are as nothing beside the plans I have for English football. It is my intention to buy a famous club sometime in the next twelve months. I regret I cannot say more at this stage. But this club was once at the top of the old English First Division and it is my wish to make it so again. To that end I will need the help of a man such as yourself. We can do great things, you and I. I hope we can make a deal while you are in Shanghai. When you do there will be a signing fee of one million pounds. We will have two contracts – one with Shanghai Xuhui and one with the Nine Dragons Mining Company. This is called a Yin Yang contract and it is the way things are done in China. The contract with Nine Dragons will be the more lucrative but between them these contracts will pay you £200,000 a week. I also propose that you start work in two weeks' time. You can stay in the Chairman's Suite at the Grand Hyatt at my own personal expense. It can be your home while you are in Shanghai. This will also be in the contract.'

'Two hundred thousand pounds a week is a lot of money,' I said.

'Yes. Almost ten million pounds a year. This would make you the highest paid manager in the world. This also is a statement of my intent. The biggest club in the world should also have the highest paid manager. Of course you would not have to pay tax on this money. Chinese tax rates on foreigners are forty-five per cent. But since your country has a double taxation treaty with China you may work here for 183 days before you would pay tax. Which means that if you stay we will also make a contract for 182 days in this country. And then for 182 days in the UK. This way you will pay absolutely no tax at all.'

'I don't mind paying a fair amount of tax,' I said.

'Yes, but what is fair?' Mr Jia laughed, a heavy smoker's laugh that sounded like someone trying to start an old car. 'That's the four and a half million pound question, isn't it? At least it is in this case. Certainly there's not a government in the world where some of the people don't say that they pay too much tax.'

'Look, before we talk about such matters hadn't we better talk about football?'

'What, more words about football? Or have you had some sort of revelation about the game since last you spoke about it? On the BBC's *Match of the Day*, was it not?'

'I said a lot of things about football on that programme.'

'Yes, but unlike what usually gets said, what you said was interesting.'

'I'm glad you think so.'

Jia changed his glasses, took out a Smythson red leather notebook and flicked through the pages at some very small writing in Chinese.

"The Thoughts of Chairman Mao." Then he caught my eye and smiled. "But not really. I'm just joking. No, these are some of the things you have said, Mr Manson. Such as – let me see – yes, that sometimes you can have too many great footballers in a team. That for each of them there's a temptation to prove himself to the manager, to showboat. That too much talent can stand in the way of efficiency. This is a very Chinese way of looking at something.'

I nodded and recalled that this wasn't what the BBC had wanted to hear from me. They'd wanted to talk about there being no football managers in the BPL who are black. I'm never much interested in talking about that for the simple reason that I don't consider myself any more black than I consider myself white. I don't want to be a spokesman for ethnic issues in football. The BBC researcher had looked shocked when I suggested this and I realised – with a shock, it has to be said – that the real racism that exists in Britain today is that any amount of black in your make-up makes you wholly black. He didn't look at me as someone who was part white, but as someone who was wholly black. Any amount of blackness taints any whiteness you might have. Fucking BBC. It was always politics with them, never just about the sport. That's why I like Sky.

'You also said – what was it now, let's get this right – you said that football should always be easy but making it look easy was the most difficult thing there is in modern sport. That's true of almost anything great, Mr Manson. Just watch a film of Picasso drawing something on a sheet of paper. He makes it look so easy. He gives the impression that anyone could do it. But making it look easy is what's rare. You were so right about that. That's what I want from you. Simple attractive football.'

'Don't you want to hear my ideas for the future of this club?'

'I've read your book. I've seen you interviewed on television. I have watched you on YouTube. I have even heard you on TalkSPORT. Whenever I am in London I have been to see London City. I know your ideas already, Mr Manson. I know everything about you. How you were falsely accused of rape and imprisoned. How you were eventually acquitted. How you got your coaching certificates while you were in prison and, soon after your release, you joined Barcelona. How your ex-player father is now a successful sports entrepreneur. The apple doesn't fall far from the tree, Mr Manson. It is evident to me that you are a chip off the old block. It seems to me that you are very keen to be a success in your own right and not to rely on your father's money to pay your bills. Am I right?'

'You're not wrong, Mr Jia,' I admitted.

'Maybe I tell you my own philosophy about football. Which is also my philosophy of business. This is why

I like football. It is possible to learn lessons from football that apply in the factory and in the boardroom. My philosophy is this, Mr Manson: if you can't make a profit then make sure you don't make a loss. This is simple economics. On the pitch we express this differently but, in essence it's the same thing. If you can't win then make sure you don't lose. A draw is still a draw and a point is still a point and, at the end of the season, when it all comes down to the last game and you win the league by just one point – like Manchester City in 2014 – you still win the league.'

I nodded. I hardly wanted to spoil his story by reminding him that Manchester City had beaten Liverpool to the title by two points, but the point was well made. You might just as easily have said that if Liverpool had come back from their away match against Crystal Palace with more than just a draw – as they ought to have done after being 3–0 up – then they'd have won the title. Football contains more 'what-ifs' than a script meeting at Warner Brothers.

'I should also tell you that you will have a budget of three hundred million yuan to buy any new players you see fit to buy for Shanghai Xuhui. This also will be in the contract. This is also part of my philosophy: you get what you pay for.' He found another cigarette and waited for one of the girls to light him. 'Of course I am aware that Shanghai is not yet an important part of the footballing world. But Shanghai money will be. And soon. I'm sure I don't have to tell you that success in football is all about money. Sadly, the days of Nottingham

Forest winning the European Cup without big money to spend on top players are behind us. There is no longer any room for romance in football. It's money that talks today, not flowers and chocolates and a manager with a nice turn of phrase. You want romance, there's the FA Cup. But everything else is about money.'

'I agree. I wish it wasn't true. But it is.'

We talked for a while longer and then, when the match was over – Shanghai Xuhui won the game 2–0 – he offered me a tour of the Yu Garden stadium the following morning.

'I'd rather not take you in there now, so soon after the match,' he explained. 'Nicola Salieri has agreed to delay the announcement of his resignation until a new manager has been appointed. So, call your agent, Miss O'Brien. Discuss it with her tonight. But I'll expect your decision in the morning, Mr Manson.'

CHAPTER 4

Two weeks later, after a blissful Christmas holiday with Louise in Australia at the Tower Lodge in New South Wales, I was back in Shanghai.

It wasn't just the money that had persuaded me – although that was persuasive enough. It was the chance to be in at the beginning of something important in English football. He'd dropped a few broad hints about the club he was thinking of buying which sounded to me a lot like Leeds. I hoped it would be Leeds. Leeds was the only big club that really deserved to be back in the Premier League. After all, they had been one of the original twenty-two clubs that had voted to form the Premier League. And I could see no real reason why, with the right amount of investment, Leeds – the sleeping giant of the Championship – could not be the great team they had once been. It had worked for Manchester City. Elland Road was already the second largest football stadium outside the Premier League, with almost 38,000 capacity. That was bigger than White Hart Lane.

At Pudong International Airport I was met by an Oddjob-type driver and one of Jia's beautiful PR girls, who escorted me back to the Hyatt. The girl's name was Dong Xiaolian and she spoke perfect, unaccented English. In the back seat of Jia's Rolls-Royce she told me of the schedule of events that lay ahead of us that day. It all sounded very exciting but even before the car was moving things started to go wrong. She handed me an email from Tempest sent to the hotel which confirmed what I suspected: that the million pound signing-on fee had still not been paid.

'In the afternoon we have a press conference at the hotel with all the major Chinese media,' explained Dong. 'I will be your interpreter. I have a Master's degree in English literature. I am self-employed and you should regard me as being at your personal disposal while you are in Shanghai. At least until you can find a full-time interpreter. Which I am also prepared to do. I will do anything you want me to do, Mr Manson. Anything at all. Anything. You will only have to ask.'

'There is something,' I said. 'I haven't been paid. There was a signing-on fee of one million pounds which hasn't yet appeared in my account. It was supposed to have been paid by the time I arrived here in Shanghai.. Which is disturbing, to say the least.'

'I shall speak to Mr Jia about this immediately we get to the hotel,' said Dong.

'Thank you.' I glanced over the schedule she had given me. 'What's this here?' I asked. 'A medical? I'm going to manage, not play.'

'Before you start work you must have a medical examination to make sure that you don't have Ebola or HIV.'

'You've got to be joking.'

'Don't worry, it's standard practice for all African men who wish to work in China.'

'I'm not African,' I said. 'I'm British. Or, to be one hundred per cent accurate, Scots-German. On my passport it says that my place of birth is Edinburgh. That's Edinburgh in Scotland, not Edinburgh in South Africa. And I'm certainly not going to have a test for Ebola and HIV. You can forget about that for a start.'

'A black man who comes from Scotland? This is a subtlety that Chinese people and more importantly the Chinese authorities will not understand. The tests are mandatory, I'm afraid. Chinese people think all black men have Aids. And now Ebola, too. It will be necessary for you to obtain a work permit in China to show that you are not a health hazard.'

'This is insulting,' I said.

'Nevertheless, it is the law. All foreigners but especially blackies who play for Chinese football clubs have to be tested. Please understand that I don't think you have Aids or Ebola. I should certainly not be sitting in the car with you if I thought you had Ebola. Not for one minute. Nor should I have offered to sleep with you if I thought you had HIV.'

I shook my head. 'Did you offer to sleep with me?'

'Of course. That is what I'm paid to do.'

'Why?'

'As well as being an interpreter I am also an escort. And don't worry, I had an HIV test yesterday, so you could be quite sure I am one hundred per cent healthy. I will show you the certificate when we get to the hotel.'

'There won't be any need for that, Dong. Look, I don't want there to be any misunderstanding between us. I think you're very nice but the only service I require from you will be to interpret for me at this press conference.'

'Are you sure? I will give you a very great deal of pleasure.'

'I think there has been a mistake. I have a girlfriend back in London. She trusts me – more or less – not to misbehave when I am away from home. You understand?' I wasn't sure that this was actually the case; Louise and I had never discussed the issue of my fidelity or hers, but I wanted to get past this embarrassing situation with the least offence possible.

Dong nodded. 'Pity,' she said. 'I find you very attractive. For a blackie. I never had one before. They say once you've had black, you never go back, yes?'

'Well, you'll just have to wait a while longer for that pleasure. With me it's all strictly business, all right? No hanky-panky.'

'What is hanky-panky?'

'Never mind. You just see what's happened to my money, all right? And please don't ever refer to me again as a blackie. I don't know where you obtained your degree in English literature but this is a very offensive way of describing someone who is black.'

'I apologise. I meant no offence. Frankly I thought it was a term of affection. Like Frenchy. Or Jerry. Do Germans mind being called Jerries?'

'That's different. Blackie isn't as bad as some other words perhaps, but it's still racist.'

'But surely you know by now that all Chinese people are racist by nature.'

'I'm beginning to.'

'Perhaps I should tell you that most nightclubs in Shanghai are a no-go area for blacks. The doormen assume they are all drug dealers and forbid them entry.'

'That won't be a problem for me, Dong. I don't much like nightclubs.'

'The players do.'

'They won't be going to nightclubs either, Dong. I tend to believe that sportsmen should treat their bodies with respect. This means no smoking and no drinking.'

Dong laughed. 'But everyone smokes in China. Especially sportsmen.'

'So I noticed.'

I didn't say much more until we got to the hotel but once there things swiftly went from bad to worse. The Chairman's Suite I'd had the time before was no longer available. They offered me a standard room with an en-suite bathroom which was a long way from the Presidential Suite with its own kitchen, dining room and the best view in Shanghai. When I rang down to reception they told me this was the only room they had; then they asked me how long I would be staying as the room was booked for only two nights. Even more perplexing was the discovery that I was paying my own hotel bill. By now I was beginning to feel as if I'd made a serious mistake, but it was only when I spoke to Dong and asked her to have Mr Jia call me that I began to think that something was seriously wrong.

'I don't understand,' she said. 'Mr Jia is out of town. His secretary says he was called away unexpectedly on business last night, to Hong Kong. And that he won't be back for two whole days.'

'So, he won't be at the press conference in …' I glanced at my wristwatch. 'In fifty minutes' time?'

'He has sent you a text to apologise,' said Dong.

'A text. Oh well, that makes everything just fine.' I looked at my phone. 'Now if I can only get some reception then I'll be able to read it.'

'But she did assure me that the money is being paid in to your account today.'

'I'll believe it when I see it.'

'We should go to Gemini now,' she said.

'Gemini?'

'This is what the Hyatt hotel calls one of its many conference rooms.'

'Seems appropriate.'

'How is that?'

'Gemini has two faces, doesn't it? Never mind.'

'It's on the second floor. All the Shanghai press and television have been invited. Already this is a big story. Apparently the previous manager did not know he was to be fired. Outside Gemini you will meet other people from the club, I think. They will introduce themselves.

One of our top television people, Yuan Ming, will be there to introduce you. She hosts the Chinese equivalent of *Match of the Day*. Our version of Gabby Logan, yes?'

I nodded, not quite sure if Gabby Logan had anything to do with *MOTD* any more but it hardly seemed relevant right now to question this.

I was on my way down to the Gemini room when Tempest O'Brien rang me on my mobile.

'I've been trying to get hold of you all morning,' she said.

'There's not much reception here,' I said. 'At least not on my phone. I hope you're ringing me to say that the money is now in my account.'

'No. It's not. I don't know what to tell you. It's not like Mr Jia hasn't got the money, either. Everyone I know in the business world says the same thing: that he's a billionaire several times over. But there's another problem, too. I had a phone call from a friend of mine who lives in Beijing. According to him you told a newspaper that Chinese referees are all crooked and don't know their offsides from their elbows.'

'Of course I didn't. Why would I do that? Especially now. Even if it was true.'

'The Chinese Football Association is pretty pissed off about it.'

'If I'd said it, I wouldn't blame them. But I didn't. Look, I'll have to call you back. I'm about to go into a press conference. I'll call you when it's over.'

Dong led me to a room at the back of Gemini where several Chinese men and one very glamorous television presenter were awaiting my arrival. The men were wearing Xuhui tracksuits and were, it seemed, part of the coaching staff, although it was rather hard to tell since none of them spoke English. All of them were smoking. We all bowed to each other politely, shook hands, exchanged business cards, and one of the men handed me a tracksuit top with the club crest on the chest and I put it on. Then we went into the conference room where we took our seats behind a long table in front of almost a hundred newsmen and women. The room was decked out in Shanghai Xuhui's copycat Barcelona colours which did nothing to restore my faith in these proceedings: I was beginning to regret my decision to work for a football team that looked very like the equivalent of a fake Rolex.

Even as Yuan Ming started to speak, my mind was in a state of turmoil about what to do. I might have overlooked almost everything – the casual racism, the mistake with my hotel room, the request for a medical examination, the absence of the club's proprietor at the press conference announcing my appointment – if the money had been paid into my account as had been agreed. That really rankled with me, especially after all Jia's remarks about the importance of money in the modern game. And finally I could stand it no longer. I interrupted Yuan Ming and announced that I'd changed my mind – that I wouldn't be joining Shanghai Xuhui after all. I spent a few minutes giving my reasons, after which the press conference broke up in some disarray and, ignoring the many questions that were being fired at me, I quickly made my exit. It all looked like that stupid commercial for Chanel Bleu when the prat with the nose says, 'I'm not going to be the person I'm expected to be any more' – or some such bollocks – and one of the girls in the audience swoons at this show of Gallic individuality.

I kept on thinking that Brian Clough had lasted forty-four days at Leeds United; I hadn't even lasted forty-four minutes.

I returned to my room where I sent an email to Tempest telling her what I'd done and spent the next half an hour booking a return flight to London. Then I poured myself a drink, drank it and lay down on the bed and told myself that this nightmare would soon be over. Maybe I'd be able to laugh it off when I was back in London but right now I couldn't have felt more depressed.

CHAPTER 5

There was a knock at the door of my hotel room. I opened my eyes and stared out of the window at my Standard Room view. It wasn't much different from the view in the Presidential Suite except for the fact that there seemed to be a little more cloud at this level. Then again, maybe that was just my outlook on the day. Cloudy with a chance of aggro.

'Go away,' I shouted. 'I'm trying to sleep.'

There was another knock and this time I picked up my iPhone and with the help of the translation app, I shouted the Chinese equivalent, '*Likai*! *Likai*!' It sounded more polite than 'fuck off', which is what I felt like saying. My love affair with China was definitely over.

'Mr Manson?' said a man's voice. 'I need to speak with you on a matter of grave importance.'

'If you're from the newspapers you can sod off.'

'I am not from the newspapers, Mr Manson. I promise you. Please, can we talk? Just for a minute. I can assure you that it will be to your advantage.'

The man's English was good enough to persuade me that the least I could do was answer the door and hear him out.

I slipped off the bed and opened the door to reveal a Chinese man in his late forties. He was wearing a pair of jeans, sunglasses and a black leather jacket; around his neck were several silver necklaces and on his thin, bony fingers was a selection of grotesque rings. He looked like a Chinese version of Keith Richards.

'Scott Manson?'

'Yes.'

'Forgive me, Mr Manson. In the circumstances I know this will sound like a very strange question, but have we ever met before?'

'It's you that's knocking on my hotel room door, remember?'

'Please, if you could just answer the question. Before just now, had we ever met before?'

I thought for moment. 'No, I don't think so.'

'You're quite sure about that?'

'What is all this? You're not a policeman, are you? You sound like a policeman.'

'No, I'm not a policeman. But please. Just answer the question.'

'No, I'm sure we haven't met before. I think I might have remembered the necklaces and the rings. Not to mention the David Beckham aftershave.'

'Too much?'

I shrugged. 'Depends if you like it or not. As it happens I don't. I think it might have been made by the same people who made his whisky. It's all alcohol and not much else.'

'Perhaps you're right.' The man smiled. 'So then. Let me introduce myself, Mr Manson. My name is Jack Kong Jia. I own the Nine Dragons Mining Company.'

He paused for a moment to allow this information to sink in. Which it did. I felt a huge weight start to descend on my head. It reminded me of a time when I'd had a kick-about for a telly programme using one of those old leather footballs with laces. It had been waterlogged and when you headed it the thing was like a bloody cannon-ball. When you play with a ball like that you wonder how any of those lads on *Gillette Soccer Saturday* can manage to string two words together. Maybe that's the real reason ITV ended *Saint and Greavsie*.

'Since you admit that we've never met before, you'll also admit that I couldn't possibly have hired you to be the manager of the Shanghai Xuhui Nine Dragons football club.'

'I don't understand. You say that you're Jack Kong Jia?'

'I don't say it. I *am* Jack Kong Jia. Yes, that's correct, Mr Manson. I am he. I can see you still don't believe me. Let me prove it to you.'

He handed me his passport and after my initial surprise that a Chinese passport should be in Chinese *and* English I felt my heart sink as I saw that his name was indeed Jack Kong Jia. The passport also said that he was a businessman, and that he was unmarried.

'So who was guy I met before?'

'Did he show you his passport?'

'No.'

'Then it may be that we shall never know. But if I might come in for a moment then perhaps we can find an answer to these and other questions.'

'Yes, sure. Please. I think you better had.'

Inside my room he collected the remote control off the bedside table and switched on the television. 'Let me show something. Just to banish any further doubts you might have about who I really am.' He searched through the channels. 'As it happens,' he added, 'I'm currently on the Bloomberg Channel, on a series called *Market Makers*, talking about the uncertain future of the Chinese economy and our very overvalued stock market which is in line for a correction. Yes. Here we are. I am in conversation with Stephanie Ruhle. She's rather attractive, don't you think?'

I watched for a moment – just long enough to realise that he was probably who he said he was – and then handed him back his passport.

'You begin to see the problem,' he said, switching off the TV.

I nodded. 'Shit, I knew there was something wrong the minute I got off the plane. I was supposed to have been paid a signing-on fee which never arrived.'

'In business I always say that the only thing you can trust these days is the money. A man's word is worth absolutely nothing next to the certainty of a CHAPS transfer.'

'And there was to be a medical, too.'

'A medical?' Jack Kong Jia laughed. 'For you? This is not necessary for a manager. Even for a player this would be possible to fix. Frankly I can fix anything here in Shanghai. Especially a medical. I should know.' He grinned. 'I have a minor heart condition – a hole in the heart – that somehow never shows up on my regular health check. Although everyone now knows about this.'

'I'm wise after the event on that one, I'm afraid. Look, I don't get it. Why would someone want to make me look a fool like this? In China?'

'Not you, Mr Manson. This isn't really about you at all. I'm sorry to disappoint you on that score. This is all about me. Someone has gone to a great deal of trouble to impersonate me and embarrass my company. You're just the fall guy in all this. Which I very much regret as I was an admirer of yours when you were managing London City.'

'But I went to the club,' I said. 'We watched a match against Guangzhou Evergrande in a private box. I had a tour of the Yu Garden stadium the next day. I even met some the players. It all seemed so plausible.'

'The box was probably one of our top executive hospitality packages. The one with the hostess girls? And the Krug champagne?'

I nodded.

'As for the private tour of the stadium, with a player-meet, this costs five thousand yuan. About five hundred pounds. No, you've been had, Mr Manson. And had good, too. The man hired to impersonate me was an actor, probably. A man with some ability, it seems, since I don't assume for a moment that you're a complete idiot.'

'Fuck,' I said.

'Exactly so.'

'If he's an actor then perhaps we can trace him. He's committed fraud.'

Mr Jia – the real Mr Jia – smiled a smile of pity. 'There are twenty million people who live in Shanghai,' he said. 'Even if we could find him, what would be the point? The damage is already done.'

'But why? Why would someone do this?'

'Oh, it's simple enough. You see, I – my club – was about to hire two new players from English clubs to come and play for us in a few months' time. At the end of your season. These two players – who are household names, I might add – they may have been finished in your Premier League but they would have been paid top wages and would, almost certainly, have given us the edge over all our rival teams. Not to mention some significant marketing opportunities. However, your press conference has put paid to that, I imagine. No one in their right mind is going to sign for Nine Dragons when the evening newspapers print the story about you walking out on us before you'd even started. Even for a hundred thousand pounds a week. You were very eloquent, Mr Manson. Your signing-on fee was not paid. Your accommodation arrangements were dishonoured. There were some calculated insults. Racism. Those new players who would have come are black. No, I'm afraid it all makes us look as if we're not to be relied on for a moment. Wouldn't you agree?'

I nodded. 'But who would do something like that?'

'This is Shanghai, Mr Manson. Back in the mid-nineteenth century this city gave its name to a slang word used by seamen which means to steal, borrow, kidnap and not bring back, but frankly little has changed since then. There's a lot of sharp and underhand work that goes on here which passes for normal business practice. Ethics and business do not yet go hand in hand like they do in London's square mile.'

'I wouldn't be too sure about that.'

'Oh, I accept that things are not perfect in London. But however imperfect they might seem to you, Mr Manson, by comparison this place is the wild west. There are regulations but they are not enforced and if they are, a bribe can easily fix things. Being a wealthy man – one of the wealthiest in Shanghai – it's fair to assume I have my share of enemies, not just in business, but also in the world of football. Sportsmanship is not something that we have yet learned to appreciate here in China. There is winning and not much else. A top four finish may be good enough for Arsenal but it is not good enough here. In Chinese we have a saying: second place is just a sore loser's word for failure.

'No, if I had to guess, I'd say it was one of my Chinese Super League footballing rivals who have tried to scupper our chances of hiring top European talent. Most likely Shanghai Taishan who are our most bitter opponents. I might almost say "Forget it, Jack, it's Chinatown", except that I'm afraid I can't forget this. I'm sorry to tell you that we'll have to call another press conference where you admit your mistake. Tomorrow. Here in this hotel. In the same conference room. You can leave the arrangements to me. There will be loss of face but this is the Chinese way. To admit you were wrong. You can tell everyone you were duped and then eat some shit. Just make sure you don't say something like "all Chinese look alike". That will only make things worse.'

I shook my head. 'He didn't look like you,' I said. 'Then again, we weren't sure what you look like. There are no pictures of you on Google.'

'As much as possible I try to remain out of the limelight, Mr Manson. My appearance on Bloomberg was a first for me. '

I walked to the window and stared out at the awful landscape of skyscrapers and neon signs. If this was the future then they were welcome to it and, for the first time since walking out on London City in Athens, I wished I hadn't been so principled. I missed London and I especially missed the lads in my team, which was still how I thought of them. It was the first Saturday in January. City had a derby against Arsenal and I would have been picking my first team players and preparing my pre-match talk. This was the time of year when any manager in English football came into his own – when it really mattered what you said and did. It's the hardest job in the world to motivate players who are knackered from too much football and know they're risking injury because of the midwinter madness that prevails in the English game. It can't be denied that there were too many fixtures between Christmas and New Year.

The Germans manage to close down for forty days, which makes a lot more sense than what we do. Even the football crazy Spaniards and Catalans manage to take thirteen days off.

Only in Britain did the clubs and more importantly the television companies treat the game like it was some kind of pantomime. The show must go on, and all that bullshit. Perhaps this had been all right back in the day when the game was played on mud at a snail's pace – as at the Baseball Ground in 1970 – but these days the pitches were as fast as billiard tables and it's speed that causes most of the injuries in the modern game. Of course it was the injury to me and my reputation that ought to have been occupying my thoughts now. I was going to be a laughing stock. Viktor Sokolnikov's newspaper – his latest toy – would make sure of that.

'And if I don't?'

'I'm afraid I must insist. And more importantly for you, my lawyers will insist upon this, too. A top English firm. Slaughter & May. I imagine you've heard of them. Mr Manson, I sincerely hope you can understand just how generous I have been already, in coming to you in person like this to explain your unfortunate mistake. I could have placed the matter in the hands of the police and alleged a criminal conspiracy to defame both me and my company. And you would almost certainly have been arrested. But a public apology will be enough for now. Afterwards, when the dust has settled, we can discuss how you can make the matter up to me. It may be that there's some sporting service you can yet do me.'

I nodded. 'Very well. Look, I'm sorry. I really don't know what else to say right now. I'm not usually lost for words. Perhaps when I stop feeling like a complete idiot I'll be able to think of something.'

'Perhaps it would help if I had my lawyers draw up a statement for you to read tomorrow. I shouldn't like you to say nothing at all out of sheer embarrassment.'

'Yes. That would help. You've been very gracious about this, Mr Jia. I can see that now.'

'Thank you.' He paused. 'You're sure you can do this?'

I nodded. 'Oh, I'm used to looking like a complete twat in front of the television cameras. Why did we lose? Why didn't we play better? Why did I make such a stupid mistake? When you're a football manager, sucking it up – it sort of comes with the territory.'

CHAPTER 6

Trying to avoid the English newspapers, I spent the next
two weeks staying with my parents, at their chalet in
Courchevel 1850 and Skyping Louise, who was busy
anyway with her police work. Thanks to the Russians
Courchevel is one of the most expensive resorts on earth
where a simple omelette in a restaurant can cost as much
as thirty euros. I skied – badly – read a lot, drank too
much and watched the telly. My dad calls it a telly;
actually it's more like your local cinema, with a high-
definition screen and projector and short of standing in
your technical area, it's probably the best way to watch
football that has ever been invented.

The only downside is having to listen to Gary Neville,
who doesn't seem to have a good word to say about
anyone and just isn't very personable – as you might
perhaps expect of a defender. I should know. I'm not
very personable myself. Sometimes I make Roy Keane
look like a game show host.

'I don't think it's right,' said my dad, 'that you can
stop playing for a top team and then be allowed to

comment on top team matches. There's a clear risk of bias. One week you're United's most loyal player, and the next you're Sky's pundit and commentator? Piss off. Yes, you bring expertise to the commentary team but you can't just put away the feelings of rivalry and animosity you have for Arsenal or Manchester City, nor the opinions you have about certain players. It's like asking Tony Blair to take charge of *Newsnight* and then have him ask George Osborne about Conservative economic policy. It can't be done fairly. To my mind there should always be a cooling-off period. At least a season before you're allowed on the telly.'

'So put it in a Tweet,' I told him.

'And stay off Twitter, will you?,' added Dad. 'You don't want to put your foot in it again. Leave that to Mario Balotelli.'

In a place like Courchevel, avoiding the press was easy enough but avoiding the comments about me on Twitter was more difficult, especially as with nothing better to do with my time it was becoming something of an addiction.

> Seems as if chinks have same problem as white people. They can't tell one dozy black bastard from another. #Manson's-fuck-up

That was fairly typical. But some of the comments were actually quite funny.

> Confucius say, better the Russian devil you know than the Chinese devil you don't. #Cityincrisis

What do you call a retarded Chinese football
manager? Sum Ting Wong. Or Scott Man Son?

My dad lives very well, it has to be said. His ski chalet
is looked after by the local Hotel Kilimandjaro; they
supply a chef and other hotel services which means you
don't have to do anything when you're there. But my
dad could see I was becoming restless and one morning,
as we walked along to the ski lift, he told me he'd had
a call from a friend of his who was on the board at
Barcelona FC.

'Tell me, son, when you were working for Pep
Guardiola, did you ever meet a vice-president called
Jacint Grangel?'

'I expect so. But I don't honestly remember him right
now. At Barcelona they've got more vice-presidents than
Ann Summers.'

'It seems that he's got a job for you. It's not a management or coaching job. It's something else. Something
temporary. But something potentially lucrative. And
which he said requires your special skills. His words,
not mine.'

'Like what?'

'He wouldn't say on the telephone. But I've a shrewd
idea of what's going on. Look, I've known Jacint Grangel
for thirty years and I can honestly say he's not a man
who would waste your time. Besides, you can speak
good Spanish – even a bit of Catalan – so I reckon you
can look after yourself down there.'

'I don't know, Dad.'

'You're wasting your time here, you know that, don't you? And you can't hide forever. You fucked up. So what? Football is all about fuck-ups. It's what makes the game interesting. You fall off the horse, you get back on.'

'Supposing it's not a horse you get back on, but a donkey?'

'Only one way to find out. Get your arse to Barcelona. They'll pay your expenses. And you'll get to see the best team in the world play football. I'd come with you myself but you'll do better on your own. You can make up your mind without your old man there to sway you one way or the other. Don't want you blaming me for what you end up doing.'

'Maybe.'

'Come on. Why not? You always liked it in Barcelona. The women are nice. The food is good. And for some reason they seem to like you. They're what you have to bear in mind. Not the bastards who hate you. There are people who want you to fail. You have to say "fuck them" and then shit on their heads. You have to rise above yourself, Scott. That's how success is measured.'

CHAPTER 7

The Princesa Sofia Gran Hotel is located in the west of Barcelona and is but a stone's throw from the famous Camp Nou. It's not the best hotel in the city – the Princesa has all the charm of a multi-storey car park and I much prefer the art-deco charms of the Casa Fuster nearer the city centre – but it is where FC Barcelona conducts a lot of its commercial business. If you hang around the hotel's vast, rather Saudi-looking lobby long enough you're almost certain to see someone famous from the world of Spanish football. From my chilly suite on the eighteenth floor I had a splendid view of Camp Nou which, from this altitude, looked smaller and less impressive than I remembered. It's only when you're inside the stadium that you can appreciate how it can accommodate almost a hundred thousand spectators. In 1993 the pitch was lowered by eight feet which helps explain this footballing *trompe-l'oeil*; and even now there are plans to remodel the stadium and increase capacity by 2021 to 105,000 at a cost of six hundred million euros. Nothing seems to be beyond the ambitions of this club or the Qataris who help to bankroll it. And why not? If you're ever in Barcelona you should check out the FCB museum; it's only when you see the trophy cabinet that you can begin to understand where the club's ambitions are founded.

There's more than one football club in Barcelona – RCD Espanyol has a large and enthusiastic support, especially among those who are opposed to Catalonian independence – but you wouldn't know it while you're there. Almost the whole city wears FCB's *blaugrana* colours and everyone you speak to seems to support the club. Virtually the first thing you see as you arrive in the ultra-modern airport terminal is the FC Barcelona shop where, among other club merchandise, you can buy yourself a doll as big as a football boot that resembles your favourite player. In their plastic boxes these have the look of illustrious, embalmed corpses. The Luis Suarez doll is especially like a cadaver from a Mexican catacomb, while Lionel Messi's figure wears a rictus smile as if he's not quite sure if his lawyers were serious or not when they told him how much previously avoided tax he now has to pay on undeclared income.

'They want me to pay how much? You're joking, surely? Did you really say fifty-two million euros?'

'Er, yes.'

By all accounts, that's not the end of the affair, either. It seems that Messi may have to stand trial, with the possibility of going to prison, which is at least one way that Real Madrid can be absolutely certain of *el clásico*.

It was a cold Sunday night when I walked out of

the hotel down to Camp Nou to see a match against Villarreal. I caught a quick glimpse of some of the players arriving in the black cars given to them by club sponsors Audi, whose four-ringed logo is in prominent evidence at the entrance to the club with the result that any match at Camp Nou has the air of a cut-price Olympiad. Still, to my mind these Audis look better to the paying public than Lamborghinis and Bugatti Veyrons. Black means business and a German saloon or Q7 exudes an air of common sense which is sorely lacking in the luxury car showrooms these footballing superstars have at home. And there's one other good thing about driving a more modest car like an Audi: it's less likely to arouse the envy and spite of the Spanish tax authorities.

I had a ticket in the central grandstand which entitled me to as much free cuttlefish and Cava as I could eat and drink in the hospitality suite. At €114 a seat there were plenty of locals doing just that, although I could see little or no evidence that any of this hospitality extended to anyone wearing the yellow of Villarreal. I'm not even sure any of them were in the stadium, and certainly no one expected them even to score a goal up against the sheer firepower of Messi, Suarez and Neymar – no one except me, perhaps. Villarreal has a good record against FCB and hadn't lost a match since November. I necked a quick San Miguel and, keen to avoid the eye of anyone who might remember me from my time at Camp Nou, I went to take my seat.

The minute I felt the glare of the green, heard the buzz of the crowd and caught the smell of the newly sprinkled grass in my nostrils I felt my stomach tighten as if I had been putting on the shirt myself. It's always like this. I expect there will come a time when I feel different near a football pitch but hopefully those days are still as far off as my Zimmer frame and hearing aid.

My seat was almost on the touchline and very close to the dugout of the FCB *técnico* Luis Enrique Martínez Garcia. At this level the pitch at the Nou seemed vast and with this number of people cheering on their team it was almost laughable that anything the manager might say during the course of the match would ever be heard by anyone other than the fourth official or the other manager. Really it's just for the benefit of the fans, or the TV cameras; when you see José Mourinho performing in his technical area think Laurence Olivier in *Richard III*; and certainly his theatrics are sometimes worthy of an Oscar or a Golden Globe. In spite of the fact that he looks a bit like Roy Keane, I like and admire Luis Enrique who's probably the fittest guy in football management having competed in several marathons and ironman challenges. And not just me: back in 2004, Pelé named him as one of the top living footballers.

The match kicked off at nine – only in Spain could a match be played at a time when many Englishmen are very sensibly thinking about going to bed – and straight away there was Messi, right in front of me and looking smaller and frankly much less happy than the doll wearing the number ten shirt I'd seen at Barcelona Airport. His twinkle-toes were working better than his smile, however, and he reminded me of Gene Kelly tap-dancing his way through *Singing in the Rain*, or Fred Astaire in *Top Hat*.

A lot is made of the rivalry that exists between FCB's Messi and Cristiano Ronaldo at Real Madrid. And I'm sometimes asked, who is the better player? Which one would you have wanted to come to a club that you were managing? The truth is they're very different players. The taller more muscular Ronaldo is a consummate athlete, while the five-foot-six-inch Messi is more like an artist. Ronaldo seems more arrogant, too, and I can take or leave his strutting *torero* act that he puts on when he scores a goal. It's like he expects the ears and the tail of the bull he has vanquished to be given to him. Me, on the rare occasions I ever scored a goal, I always looked around to thank the guy who'd passed me the fucking ball. It just seemed like good manners. You pays your money, you take your choice.

Reading the match programme I half-expected to see Barca's newest striker, Jérôme Dumas – reportedly now on loan from PSG – among the reserves at least, but there was no sign of him as yet. I was, however, delighted to see a match with Barca's leading three scorers – Messi, Neymar and Suarez – leading their attack. It was all shaping up to be an exciting evening, as it's not often you get a chance to see three of the best players in the world in action at the same time.

The game started with Villarreal in possession but Messi's skilful moves managed to put Barca back in command and Villarreal showed quickly that ultimately they lacked the balance, intensity and speed of the Barca team at its best. But Barca too were misfiring. Suarez had three early goal-scoring chances with only one on target – a point-blank salvo turned away by Villarreal keeper Asenjo after just thirteen minutes. Number 16, Dos Santos, missed three scoring chances, again saved by Asenjo. With such chances coming, the Barca supporters waited patiently for a goal, but after half an hour of play, things did not go their way. Villarreal's Gaspar unleashed a left-footed blast that looked destined for the other side of the field until Tcherychev deflected the ball past Barca keeper: 0–1 to Villarreal.

The goal had a predictably unsettling effect on the Barca players. Their energy disappeared, the team looked demoralised. The crowd fell silent. And the responsibility to get Barca back in the game fell again to Messi. One minute before half time he seized his chance. His searching pass found Rafinha in the area whose shot was saved by Asenjo, but the rebound fell to Neymar who banged it in without a moment's hesitation.

Having equalised, Barca returned in the second half transformed. They pressured and threatened, proving why very few other teams cause so much disarray in opposing teams on and off the ball, both in defence and attack.

Nevertheless, Piqué's defensive mistake allowed Villarreal's Giovani to take advantage and assist Vietto's strike, to make it 1–2 to Villarreal in the fifty-first minute. Camp Nou went silent again as if the crowd realised that the Yellow Submarine wasn't going to go down easily. Just as the silence was becoming even more uneasy, both Suarez and Messi were denied before Rafinha scored the equaliser. 2–2. The cheering *culers* had just taken their seats when, in the fifty-fifth minute, Lio Messi let fly with a beautiful curving shot from outside the penalty area. With little or no room for the strike it seemed like the kind of goal that perhaps only Messi could have envisaged, let alone scored. 3–2 to Barcelona.

The last half-hour saw Barca nervously protecting their lead, and slowly they wore the other side down. Near the end Rafinha was substituted and, feeling very cold – as the evening progressed the night grew colder and so did I, I'd forgotten must how cold Barcelona can be in winter – and irritated with what looked like an obvious attempt on the part of Barca to delay the game, I tweeted something stupid about how he was being taken off because it was his period. It was the same sort of Cranberry Juice Joke that's in Scorsese's film, *The Departed*. But at the time I thought no more about it.

The match finished. Villarreal had lost for the first time since November. But for Barcelona the win – which left them four points off Real Madrid at the top of La Liga – seemed typical of their lacklustre season: the flashes of brilliance were few and far between and they made it look hard work. As we would have said in England, they 'won ugly'. But they still won so most of the crowd went home happy. Frankly, I thought Villarreal – who had a goal disallowed for offside – were very unlucky not to go home with a draw.

The next day – which was no less cold – Jacint Grangel took me to lunch at the Drolma Restaurant in the Majestic Hotel – one of the best in the city. To be honest it's a little grand for my taste. I prefer somewhere more authentically Catalan, like Cañete in the older part of town. (Whenever I'm there I think of Hemingway; I've no idea if he ever went to Cañete but there's a big ibex head on the wall that makes me think he'd have liked the place.) But then again I wasn't paying. Drolma's chef, Nandu Jubany, is considered to be the great genius of Catalan cuisine and it's easy to see why; I'd forgotten just how good lollipops of foie gras with white chocolate and Porto reduction can taste.

When I arrived at Drolma with Jacint there were others already seated at the table; three men, each wearing a sober blue suit with a shirt and tie. That's the thing about Barcelona; everyone dresses well. No one would dream of turning up for lunch at a place like Drolma wearing a tracksuit and sports shoes. A lot of the time I look at players and the way they dress and think they need a good slap. There was another vice-president from Barcelona called Oriel Domench i Montaner, but I was surprised to be introduced to Charles Rivel, from Paris Saint-Germain, and a Qatari called Ahmed Wusail Abbasid bani Utbah. At least I think that's what his name was. It's possible the guy was just clearing his throat.

We spoke in Spanish. I can manage a bit of Catalan – which is an interesting, almost hermetic combination of French, Spanish, Italian and awkward-squad bloody-mindedness – but Spanish is easier for me. It's easier for everyone who doesn't speak Catalan. Catalans are very proud of their language and rightly so; under General Franco they had to fight very hard to keep their culture alive. Or so they'll tell you. The same is true of the football club. Or so they'll tell you. In 1936 Franco's troops shot dead the president of the club, Josep Suñol, and to this day he is known as the 'martyr president'. That sort of thing tends to put English opposition to the people like the Glazers and Mike Ashley in the shade. And perhaps it also explains why this club, which was founded by a group of English, Swiss and Catalans, is considered to be *més que un club* – more than a club. FC Barcelona is a way of life. Or so they'll tell you.

This is going to be an interesting lunch, I thought, as the waiter poured the wine; I couldn't imagine what they wanted to speak to me about. For a brief moment I wondered if it might have something to do with what had happened in Shanghai – if perhaps these three groups of people were looking to invest with Jack Kong Jia and wanted the opinion of someone who'd actually met him. By his own admission, Jia was someone who avoided publicity.

'I believe you saw the match that PSG played against Nice,' said Charles Rivel, from PSG. 'At Parc des Princes.'

'Yes. It was a bit like watching Arsenal grinding out a one–nil victory. I thought Nice deserved a draw more than you guys deserved a win.'

This was also true of the match between FCB and Villarreal but I kept that particular observation to myself.

'I'm not sure that's fair,' said Rivel. 'If Zlatan hadn't hit the woodwork in the first fifteen minutes he might just have scored one of his best goals. The way he controlled the ball, turned and then took his shot was superb. For a big man he's incredibly light on his feet.'

'Nevertheless, he missed. And by his own standards that's just not good enough. What does he say in his book? You can be a god one day and completely worthless the next. That's especially true in this city. He took his foot off their neck. That's how it looked to me.'

'You've read his book?' asked Jacint.

'I try to read all of the books about football, although sometimes I ask myself why. And while I start them all, there's hardly ever one I finish. Including Zlatan's book. In my opinion his wasn't a good book. I think he's a good player. Just not much of a writer. No worse than the others, perhaps. Like most of these books there were few insights into the game. But it was a shrink's casebook.'

'It's true,' said Oriel. 'They ought to have called that book *The Ego has Landed.*'

'Perhaps he should have hired Roddy Doyle to write it,' said Jacint.

'I think Henning Mankell would have been more appropriate,' said Rivel. 'They're both Swedes, after all.'

'We could use Kurt Wallander now, perhaps,' murmured Ahmed. 'Given the situation.'

'I don't think Ibra was very fair about Guardiola,' said Oriel.

'We're not here to talk about Ibra,' said Rivel, 'but someone else. Another PSG player.'

'Wouldn't it be better to have Mr Manson sign a confidentiality agreement first?' said Ahmed.

'I don't think we need to worry about that with a man like Scott,' said Jacint. 'His word is good enough for me.'

'Can we depend on you to treat this matter with confidence?' asked Rivel.

'Of course. You have my word on it. In case you hadn't noticed, gentlemen, I've been rather keen to avoid the press of late.'

'Is that working?' said Jacint.

'How do you mean?'

'Have you checked your Twitter account?'

'Not today.'

'It seems you made a tweet about Rafinha that has some of your female followers in a rage.'

'I did?' I shrugged, not really knowing to what Jacint was referring. 'I'll check it later.'

'What we're here to talk about – well, right now, it's probably the best kept secret in football,' said Oriel.

'Now I really am intrigued,' I admitted.

'First of all, we should say that we think you're a talented young manager,' said Rivel. 'In spite of recent events in China. Which could have happened to anyone, really.'

The Qatari nodded. 'It's very difficult to know what's happening when you're in Shanghai.' He laughed. 'At least in Qatar there are only two million people. That makes things a lot simpler. Unless it's something to do with religion. And Sharia law. And women's rights.

And the 2022 World Cup. Then things can get very complicated.'

I smiled, liking him for that.

'Your reputation as a young manager and coach is one thing,' said Jacint. 'But it seems you have also gained something of a reputation as a problem solver. It's now a well-known fact that it was you and not the Metropolitan Police who solved the mystery regarding the death of João Zarco.'

'And the death of Bekim Develi,' added Oriel.

'I'm sure that you know I can't comment about that.'

'You can't,' said Rivel. 'But the Athens police can. They've dropped some very broad hints that you were of great assistance to them in their inquiries.'

'It's your skills as a private detective that we need now,' said Jacint.

'And for which we are prepared to pay,' said Ahmed.

'Whisky, Tango, Foxtrot,' I heard myself murmur. *What the fuck?*

'Handsomely,' added the Qatari.

'Really, gentlemen, I have no skills as a detective,' I insisted. 'As usual, this is just the press exaggerating what happened. Anyone would think I was Sherlock Holmes in a tracksuit. Hercule Poirot with a stopwatch. The Kurt Wallander of the touchline. I'm not. I'm a coach. A manager. And right now it's a football club I need, not an interesting case. Give me a squad of players and I'll be as happy as Larry. But don't ask me to play the copper.'

'Nevertheless, you understand football and footballers,' said Rivel. 'In a way that perhaps the police do not.'

'There's no perhaps about it,' said Jacint. 'I can't speak for how things are in Paris, but it's quite impossible to be objective about football here in Barcelona. There's too much emotion involved.'

'I think the same is probably true in Paris,' said Rivel. 'Besides, the French police aren't exactly known for their closed mouths. Just look at what happened to Francois Hollande. And before him to Dominique Strauss-Kahn. This story would be on the front of *L'Equipe* in no time.'

'Gentlemen, you're wasting your time. I've really no interest in crime. I don't even like the goddamn books. All those stupid boring detectives with their drinking problems and their failed marriages. It's all so very predictable. My idea of a good case is one made by Louis Vuitton.'

'Please, Mr Manson,' said Ahmed. 'At least hear us out.'

'Yes, Scott,' said Jacint. 'Please. Listen to our story.'

'All right. I'll listen. Out of respect for you and this club, I'll listen. But I'm not promising anything. I'm telling you, it's football I want to play. I don't want to play cops and robbers.'

'Of course,' said Oriel. 'We understand. But more than anyone perhaps you understand footballers. The pressures. The mistakes. The pitfalls. You might not quite appreciate it yourself, Scott, but you're in a unique position in football. In quite a short period of time you've made yourself quite indispensable to any European club who needs a special kind of help. You speak several languages...'

'And, more importantly than that, you speak the players' language, Scott,' added Jacint. 'Players trust you in a way they wouldn't trust the police. They're young men, some of them misfits and even delinquents from quite difficult backgrounds. Men like Ibra. He was a punk and a car thief, wasn't he? If any of our players or perhaps those of PSG are going to confide in anyone it probably won't be some nosy cop with a tape recorder in his hand. It will be you, Scott. You've done time in prison. You've been falsely accused of something. You don't much like the police yourself.'

'True,' I said. 'Although I seem to be getting over that. My girlfriend, Louise, is a detective with the Metropolitan Police.'

'So much the better.'

"Perhaps it's her you should be speaking to." I knew I wished I was.

The waiter came and took our order. And it was only after we'd eaten our the starters and tasted the wine that Jacint returned to the subject that was preoccupying him and the other three men.

'I expect you've heard that Jérôme Dumas has been taken on loan by us from PSG,' he said.

'Yes,' I said. 'I was surprised. I think he's a good player.'

'He never really clicked with us,' said Rivel. 'I don't really know why. He's a talented player. But there was something in his head that was not quite right for us. It works like that sometimes. Torres worked at Liverpool but he never worked at Chelsea.'

'Dumas came to Barcelona,' said Oriel, 'and then he went on holiday. Because he was on loan we'd agreed to honour his existing arrangements. We had yet to present him to the fans at the Nou Camp. Which is why we've managed to keep the lid on things so far.'

'He had an injury which meant he couldn't have played anyway,' said Jacint.

'He picked up a groin strain in the match you saw, against Nice,' said Rivel.

'He certainly looked like he was trying harder than anyone else in the team,' I said.

'Nothing too serious. He just needed rest, that's all.'

'So what happened? I mean, what's he done?'

'He was supposed to report for training at Joan Gamper on Monday, January the nineteenth,' continued Jacint, 'but he never showed up.'

Joan Gamper was the name of Barca's training facility, about ten kilometres west of the Nou Camp in Muntaner; strictly off-limits to the press, everyone in Barcelona referred to it as 'the forbidden city'.

'And there was no sign of him at the hotel where we'd put him in the best suite until he could find somewhere to live.'

'The same hotel as you,' said Oriel. 'The Princesa Sofia.'

'FCB called us,' said Rivel, 'and we went to his apartment in Paris, but there was no sign of him there, either. Since then we've been in contact with the police on the island of Antigua where he went on holiday. So far they've turned up nothing. It seems that he arrived on the island but there's no record of him leaving again. Of catching a flight back to Paris, or Barcelona. Or anywhere else, for that matter. We've phoned him. Sent emails. Texted him. Called his agent. He's as baffled as we are.'

'Who is it?'

'Paolo Gentile.'

I nodded. 'I know Paolo.'

'In short,' said Jacint, 'Dumas has disappeared. Which is where you come in. We want you to find him.'

'For a fee,' said Ahmed. 'You might even call it a finder's fee.'

'He's only been gone two weeks,' I said.

'In the life of any other man of twenty-two, that's not much. But the fact is, he isn't any other man. He's a footballing star.'

'For once,' I said, 'the newspapers and television could surely help. It's difficult to be missing when the whole world is aware of that fact.'

'True,' said Jacint, 'but this is no ordinary football club. It's owned and operated by the supporters, which means they trust us and are rightly very unforgiving when things go wrong. As we see things it's up to us to try and fix the problem before we are obliged to announce that we may have a problem. That's what the Catalan people expect of Barca. No excuses. But perhaps, in the fullness of time, an explanation.'

'There's also the public relations of the situation to consider,' said Oriel. 'It may have escaped your attention but things are difficult in Spain right now. The economic situation is dire. Twenty-five per cent of the country is unemployed. Losing a player we're paying one hundred and fifty thousand euros a week for just looks bad. We can ill afford that kind of adverse publicity when the average wage is just seventeen hundred euros a month.'

'It's not just that,' said Jacint. 'When there's so much going wrong in the lives of our supporters the one thing they need to be absolutely sure of is that all is well with their beloved football club. That we are still the best in the world.' He shook his head. 'The best football team in the world doesn't lose an important player like this. They expect us to make sure our overpaid superstars can at least steer their Lamborghinis to the training ground.'

'I don't know how things are in London but for most of these guys Barcelona is why they get up in the morning,' said Oriel. 'It's why they can feel good about themselves. Their whole world view is affected by how the team is doing. You start to rock that boat and things could get very choppy indeed.'

I nodded. '*Més que un club*,' I said. 'I know.'

'No, with respect I don't think you do,' said Jacint. 'Unless you are Catalan it is impossible to know what it is to support Barca. This club isn't just about football. For a great many people the club is the symbol for Catalan separatism. Barca has become even more politicised than when you were last working here, Scott. It's no longer just the *Boixos Nois* – the crazy boys who are in favour of breaking away from the rest of Spain. It's virtually all of the *penyes*.'

The *penyes* were the various fan clubs and financial groups that made up FCB's highly idiosyncratic support.

'If the Spanish government agree to allow us a referendum, then this football club will be the epicentre of that move for independence,' said Jacint. 'But those who are opposed to an independent Catalunya will try to exploit a situation like this to pour scorn on us. To accuse us of mismanagement; if we can't be trusted to govern a football club then how can we be trusted with the government of Catalunya?'

'Which means that this is about much more than just a missing player,' said Oriel. 'Nothing must interfere with our drive to be given our own referendum. Like the one you Scots had.'

'Tell me,' said Jacint, 'as a Scot, how did you vote in the referendum?'

I shrugged. 'I may be a Scot but I wasn't allowed a vote because I live in England. Those people aren't interested in democracy. And I have to tell you that I'm not in favour of Catalan independence any more than I was in favour of Scottish independence. In this day and age it makes a lot more sense to be part of something larger. And I don't mean the EU. Go and see how things are in Croatia if you doubt that. As part of the old Yugoslavia, Croatians used to mean something. Now they don't mean anything at all. And it's worse if you're Bosnian. They're not even part of the EU.'

At this point the conversation started to become an argument about independence movements and it was Ahmed, who managed to steer the discussion back to the subject in hand: the disappearance of Jérôme Dumas.

'We will pay all your expenses to look for him,' said Ahmed. 'First class, of course. And a flat fee of a hundred thousand euros a week deductible against a fee of three million euros if you do manage to find him.'

I nodded. 'That's very generous. But supposing he's dead?'

'Then your fee will be capped at one million euros.'

'Supposing he's alive and he doesn't want to come back?' I shrugged. 'I mean, clearly he's disappeared for a reason. Perhaps he sneaked off to Equatorial Guinea to see the African Cup of Nations. For all I know, he even went to play. Stranger things have happened.'

'I never thought of that possibility,' admitted Ahmed. 'Perhaps he's got Ebola. Perhaps he's in a field hospital awaiting rescue. Holy shit, that might explain everything. You know he's not the only player who's gone missing since that tournament.'

'Dumas is not black African,' said Rivel. 'He's French-Caribbean. And as such he's eligible to play for France.'

'Have you considered the possibility that he's been kidnapped? Footballers make good victims. They're overpaid, asset-rich and wayward. They don't always do what they're told and most of them figure they're too tough for bodyguards which means that they're easier to snatch than most rich kids. When I was in the nick I had a bunch of cons come to me with a scheme to kidnap a top Arsenal player. There are some bastards out there who'll do anything for money'

'If that's what this is then we've received no demand for ransom,' said Jacint.

'Nor has PSG,' said Rivel.

'But you are certainly empowered to negotiate a release if it turns out that this is what's happened,' said Ahmed.

'Then suppose he's just had enough of football?' I said. 'Maybe he's burned out. That can happen.'

'Your fee is still one million,' said Ahmed. 'The three million euro fee is payable only if Dumas plays. Needless to say that his failure to play at all for FCB will have financial consequences for PSG.'

'We won't get paid,' said Rivel.

'If he's had enough of football an important part of your job would include persuading him to come back home,' said Oriel. 'That's another reason we want to hire you. To talk him round if he's got cold feet.'

'Let's say I do take this job. How long should I keep looking for?'

'Until the end of this month,' said Ahmed. 'Four weeks. Six at most.'

'Ideally,' added Jacint, 'we should like the player back in time for us to play him in *el clásico*, on Sunday, March the twenty-second. If he could feature in the match against Madrid, it will be as much as we can hope for.' He shrugged. 'As you may remember, Madrid won the last classic, three–one, in front of their home fans.'

'We were robbed,' said Oriel. 'Not the first time, of course.'

'They came from behind after Neymar gave us the perfect start, with a goal after just four minutes.'

'They had a penalty which should never have been given,' said Oriel. 'It was ball to hand, not hand to ball as the law states. Gerard Piqué was unfairly penalised. It was the sheer injustice of this penalty that affected our team.'

I nodded, smiling. Nothing changes very much in a rivalry like the one that existed between Madrid and Barcelona. But it was perhaps the only rivalry in which one side had forced the other to play, at gunpoint. For many, the hatred that now existed between Madrid and Barcelona had not existed at all until that game, in 1943. Madrid won the game 11–1, which makes you wonder about the team talk at half time. What did the manager say to his team?

'On second thoughts, you'd best let these Spaniards beat us, lads, or they're liable to shoot us, like they shot Lorca. If they can shoot a poet these fascists can certainly shoot a football team.'

'Will you do it?' asked Jacint. 'This club will be forever in your debt.'

'And ours,' added Charles Rivel.

'I don't know,' I said, wavering a little.

I like Barcelona. I like Catalans. I just didn't want to turn into football's Inspector Clouseau.

I got up from the table.

'I'm going to the men's room. So give me a few minutes, to think about it.'

'If it's a question of money...' said Ahmed.

'The money's fine,' I said. 'No, I'm just wondering if you'd come to Pep on his year off and asked him to help you out like this, what he'd have said.'

'Pep's not an intellectual,' said Jacint. 'You're the one who went to university, not him. All he knows is football.'

'Maybe that's where I've been going wrong,' I said. 'Anyway, university doesn't mean much nowadays. You can get a degree for staying in bed and watching television. What I meant was that Guardiola has always been very single-minded. A man with a plan. Total football of the kind he learned under Cruyff doesn't seem to accommodate what you're asking me to do. Other clubs might get the idea that I'm less interested in playing 4-4-2 than in playing the amateur sleuth.'

'You're a clever man, Scott,' said Jacint. 'Maybe a little too clever for this game. But you'll always be part of the Barca family. I think you know that.'

There are times – usually when it's someone paying me a compliment like that – when I look down at my feet as if I expect to find a ball, and the fact is that sometimes I still don't know what to do when I see there isn't one. I swear when I first stopped playing football I used to wake up at night and look around for the ball. Especially when I was in the nick. It's like I don't know what to do with my feet. As if they're at a loss without a ball to kick. Like a soldier without a rifle, I guess.

I went to wash my hands. Along the way I glanced at my phone and saw from the Twitter feed that some women were calling on me to be sacked after my joke about Rafinha coming off the pitch during the game against Villarreal because he had his period. The fact that I didn't have a job didn't seem to have registered with my critics, many of whom had tweeted to tell me I was a sexist pig and every bit as bad as Andy Gray, and so I dismissed them from my mind.

Besides, it seemed rather more important that the manager of another Premier League side had just lost his job. I didn't kid myself that I was about to walk into another big club soon. Not when there were men like Tim Sherwood, Glenn Hoddle, Alan Irvine and Neil Warnock all looking for a new job. In truth I'd already made my decision about what I was going to do. Jacint had reminded me, subtly, that Barcelona had taken me into their family at a time when I was recently out of prison, and anyone else might have given the matter of my employment a second thought. I owed the Catalans something for giving me a chance when no English club had been there for me. And now that I came to consider the matter in more detail, it seemed that I owed them, big time.

Besides, without a ball to kick, what else was I going to do with my time?

I came back to the table.

'All right, I'll do it. I'll look for your missing player. But let's get one thing clear, gentlemen. Let's assume for one minute that I am as clever as you say I am. Then you'll forgive me if I tell you the real reason you want to find Jérôme Dumas and are prepared to pay me so handsomely to do it. Which has only a little to do with everything you've mentioned. I mean, that was nice and it all sounded very plausible. Even romantic. I like the idea of Barcelona as the political heart of Catalunya.

But as a reason for paying me to try to find Jérôme Dumas discreetly? It's bullshit.

'The real reason you want me to find Dumas is mostly to do with the FIFA transfer ban on FCB that took effect at the end of December 2014.'

This was the ban that was imposed as a result of FCB having breached the rules regarding the protection of minors and the registration of minors attending football academies.

'I assume the loan of Jérôme Dumas from PSG to FCB was specifically constructed to get around the transfer ban. Because, according to my sources, you won't be able to sign another player until the end of 2015, which means that the loan of this player assumes a much greater importance than it would normally have done. Especially in a year with a club presidential election.'

My sources were my own father, of course, but it sounded better than just coming out with 'my dad says'.

'There aren't many top strikers who get loaned between clubs like this. You were lucky to find one at this time of year. Most smaller teams are looking to sell their best players to the bigger clubs in the January transfer window. So I also assume that FCB will pay a fee to PSG at the end of 2015, regardless of whether Dumas performs or not.

'Look, I don't blame you. I'd have done the same if I'd been in your position. A ban like this because of some stupid administrative error seems quite disproportionate and typical of the high-handed way that FIFA conducts itself these days. Frankly, I think they're all a bunch of crooks. But please don't think I'm at all ignorant of what's going on here. If you hire me you hire me to find the truth, with all that that entails. I think it's best we all know what's what here. Fair enough?'

Jacint smiled, exchanged a look with Oriel and then nodded.

'Fair enough.'

CHAPTER 8

I returned to Paris to begin the search. By now the Twitter flap was a storm with the sorority calling for the FA to punish me with a fine, and given some of the things I was on record as having said about the FA, this looked to be more than likely. Tempest O'Brien told me she thought that the tweet about Rafinha was going to cost me ten grand, which works out at almost seventy-two quid a character.

Jérôme Dumas's apartment was in the sixteenth *arrondissement*, in Avenue Henri Martin, on the edge of the Bois de Boulogne. The apartment was at least four hundred square metres, on the top floor of a high-end building near the embassy of Bangladesh and, if you like that kind of thing, sumptuously designed by some modern architect. Most of the furniture looked like it was out of an old sci-fi movie about the future. I was met there with the keys by the PSG club fixer, Guy Mandel, who showed me around the place and gave me some useful background on the missing player.

'Dumas came here from AS Monaco about a year ago

for twenty million euros,' he explained. 'Bit of an attitude. But then that's not unusual. Originally from Guadeloupe in the French Caribbean. That's not unusual either, as it happens. I don't know how much you know about the place but for a tiny island with the population less than the city of Lyons, it punches well above its weight. Of the French World Cup Squad in 2006 seven were from Guadeloupe. The island is part of France, see, so it's not a FIFA-recognised country. Just as well, probably, otherwise we wouldn't have had people like Thierry Henry, Sylvain Wiltord, William Gallas, Lilian Thuram, Nicolas Anelka and Philippe Christanval eligible to play for us.'

'I never knew,' I said. 'So much great football from such a small island.'

'Not that there's a great deal of affection for France on the island itself. I believe most of the islanders tend to side with Brazil. Can't say I blame them really. France tends to call these people scum when they live in the suburbs and French only when they play for the team. I expect it's the same in England.'

I nodded. 'Perhaps.'

'They could probably have qualified for the World Cup in Brazil if we'd given them the opportunity. In other words if we – the French – hadn't blocked them from becoming a FIFA member.'

'I had no idea,' I said.

'There are probably a lot more I've forgotten who come from Guadeloupe. I only know these names because Jérôme Dumas told me about them. He was very proud of his island heritage.'

'Do you know how long he's lived in France?'

'No idea. His life before Monaco is a bit of a mystery, really.'

Comprising an entrance hall, a large living room, a second rotunda lounge of fifty square metres, several bedrooms, a superb kitchen, a gymnasium and a wine cellar, the apartment would have been any young man's dream. As would have been the Lamborghini and the Range Rover that occupied the apartment's two parking spaces. But for me it was the roof gardens that really distinguished the place; the views – which included the new Louis Vuitton Museum designed by Frank Gehry – were superb and there was a large variety of mature plants that showed no sign of having been neglected by the owner's absence.

'Who looks after this place?'

'There's a maid and a gardener who come in almost every other day. A boy who cleans the cars. A cook who prepares meals according to nutritional guidelines drawn up by the club. He had a PA called Alice, who he let go after signing the deal with FCB. Nice girl. Clever.'

'I shall certainly want to speak to her,' I said.

'All the details are on the attached file I sent by email. And she's coming over here in an hour or so to assist you in any way she can.'

'Thank you.'

'There's even an art advisor employed by a private bank who bought pictures for him. He had access to the place so that he could come in and hang pictures and position sculptures.'

'Is this one of them, do you think?'

I was looking at a painting of a pumpkin by Yayoi Kusama. I wouldn't have minded having a painting by Yayoi Kusama myself.

Mandel pulled a face. 'Not my taste. The sort of crap they hang in that new heap of mangled tin they call the Vuitton Museum.'

He was wrong about that. Like the rest of the paintings on the walls of Dumas's apartment the Kusama was much too representational ever to have found a place in the Vuitton collection of contemporary art. For one thing you could perceive what it was – almost – which meant of course that it lacked all irony and, therefore, was without significance and possibly any lasting investment value. I guessed that the private bank was giving Dumas the kind of advice he wanted to hear so that they could buy him the kind of paintings he wanted to see instead of the ones that would make him money.

'The place is on the market, of course, now that he's on his way to Barcelona. With Lux-Residence. I think they want eight million for it.'

'What about girlfriends?'

'There were lots of girls, as far as I heard. But none that caused him any trouble. No unwanted babies. No rape charges. That kind of thing. Nothing that required any help from me.'

'Anyone regular?'

'There was one girl he was seen out with more often. A model at the Marilyn Agency here in Paris. Name of Bella Macchina. Blonde, legs up to her arse, smell under her cosmetically enhanced nose – you know the type. But I don't know how serious it was. You'd have to ask her. You'll find the agency number in the attachment.'

'I will.' I glanced around the apartment. 'You'd never know that a footballer lives here,' I remarked. 'I mean, there's not a shirt in a glass case, a player award, a winner's medal anywhere.' I went to the bookcase which was all politics, art books and photography mono-graphs. 'There's not even a book about football.'

'Well, you can't fault him for that,' said Mandel. 'Me, I like a good thriller, not some shit about life in the *banlieues* and how my only way out was to kick a fucking ball. You can say all that in one short chapter.'

'Yes, I think I read that one, too.'

Mandel stepped onto the terrace and lit a French cigarette. He was a heavyset man with longish hair and an almost bifurcated nose like a pixie's arse. In his butcher's fingers the cigarette looked like a little mint that had become stuck to his hand. His huge head nestled in the outsized collar of his white shirt as if his neck didn't exist at all. His voice made Ray Winstone's Bet365 commercial sound effeminate.

'You mentioned an attitude problem,' I said.

'They've all got one of those. Name me one fucking footballer who doesn't think he's descended from Zeus. The minute they buy a Lamborghini they think it comes with a parking place on Mount Olympus.' He laughed, cruelly. 'And then they have to live with the thing and drive it. Which soon brings them crashing down to earth. There are times when I think God only invented

Lamborghinis to prove to footballers that they are mortals after all. You just try reversing his Aventador out of the garage downstairs. It's like trying to manoeuvre a grand piano.'

'But attitude was almost the first thing you said about Jérôme Dumas. So maybe he had more attitude than most.'

'Maybe.'

'How did you find him, personally?'

'When he first came to the club, it was like he was a different guy, you know? Full of laughs and jokes. It was impossible not to like Jérôme. Then something happened. I don't know what. He changed.'

'Changed, how?'

'Perhaps he grew up a little. Became a bit more serious. Took himself a bit more seriously. Too seriously.' Mandel pulled a face. 'He was too political for our tastes. Too left wing. He was always shooting his mouth off about things on Twitter that had nothing to do with football and which he ought to have left alone.'

'Such as?'

'The PS. The French Socialist Party. He gave money to the lefties which hardly endeared him to some of his team mates, none of whom much like paying Hollande's millionaire tax. I believe he also gave money to some youth groups here in Paris. And you can bet if there was a demonstration he'd have been there. He was a real hypocrite like that.'

'How do you mean?'

'We French take revolution very seriously. We don't

like people who play at revolution. For whom it seems to be a pose.'

'Was it a pose?'

'The Lamborghini lefty, that's what people called him. Mao in a Maserati.'

'Yes, I can see how that might irritate some. Is that why PSG decided to loan him to FCB?'

Mandel nodded. 'Then there were the interviews he did with *Libération* and *L'Equipe* which pissed a lot of people off and really helped him on his way out of the Parc des Princes.'

L'Equipe was a French nationwide daily newspaper devoted to sports.

'Is that in the attached file, too?'

'Of course.'

'By the way, I shall also want to see the recordings of the most recent matches Dumas played for PSG. This season and last season.'

'This season he's had one good game. That was back in September, against Barcelona.'

'That was the famous 3–2 in Group F, right?'

'Yes. He was really good that night. He didn't score himself but he had three good assists. You ask me it was that night which persuaded Barca to take him on loan. I mean, he wasn't just good in attack, he was good in defence, too.'

'I saw him in the match against Nice. He wasn't bad then, I thought. Of course I had no idea that I was going to have to pay such close attention to the minutiae of this young man's life. When you are trying to understand the man and what has happened to him it helps to see him do what he is good at.'

'Very well. I'll get you some films. Would you prefer DVDs or video files?'

'Video files. And I'll need some tickets for the next home match. You never know who I might have to sweeten up for some information. You can have them back, of course, if I don't use them.'

'Sure.'

'Now then. That article in *L'Equipe*. Read it to me, while I search this place.'

'All right. But tell me what you're looking for and then maybe I can help you there, too.'

'I really have no idea what I'm looking for, Mr Mandel. I'll only know it when I see it and even then perhaps not immediately. As so-called detectives go, I'm someone who relies on the discovery of things unsought. The forensic equivalent of penicillin. The trick to this is to realise the significance of what one has found. Which is, of course, not always immediately apparent. It's the equivalent of the goalkeeper who scores goals as well as saving them. Rogério Ceni scored 123 in his career. That's not a happy accident. It's more than that – what the English call serendipity. Since your language doesn't like to use English words, I would invite you to take *rogérioceni* as the French equivalent.'

It sounded good. And I hardly wanted to tell him that serendipity was the only thing I had in my investigative sports bag. The truth was I felt like a physio called onto the pitch to fix a torn Achilles with just a roll of tape

and a bottle of smelling salts. Really, it was pathetic
how ill-equipped I was to carry out my appointed task.

I went into the bathroom and opened the cabinet – it
seemed like a good place to start my search. You can
usually tell a lot about a man just by searching through
his medicines. Naturally there was lots of ibuprofen –
sometimes it's the only way you can get yourself down
to the training ground – and plenty of kinesio tape:
taping a sore joint *works*, especially when you're also
taking ibuprofen. But almost immediately – even before
Mandel had started to read the article from his iPad –
I had discovered that Jérôme Dumas was depressed.
In the cabinet was a bottle of one of the most commonly
prescribed SSRIs – selective serotonin reuptake inhibi-
tors. I placed the bottle beside the handbasin and
kept searching.

> Jérôme Dumas has courted the anger of Paris Saint-
> Germain supporters by stating that the fans at Parc des
> Princes have made him feel unwanted and that this has
> now reached the stage where he almost avoids the ball.
> In a frank interview, Dumas also said that it was no
> fun playing for PSG and that he only looked forward
> to away games now as there were fewer fans present
> to give him a hard time.

'Ooo, that's bad,' I said, opening a drawer. I found
a rather large toilet bag which I unzipped and rifled
through, tossing most of the contents into the bath.
'That's very bad.'

'It's really dispiriting when your own fans are the ones shouting the racial abuse,' Dumas said. 'Of course you want them to support you. But lately I've had a run of bad form when I haven't scored and they've not been very understanding. I just wish they would be a little more patient with me. You don't mind the away fans booing you. That's part of the game. But it's different when it's your own support. In the game against Nice there seemed to be one standard for me and another for Zlatan. I don't understand why there were whistles and catcalls when I missed a goal but nothing but applause when he hit the woodwork. There's a double standard here which I find baffling and hurtful.'

In the toilet bag I was surprised to find several packets of Cialis. I placed these beside the SSRIs.

'I'm sure everything will come right when I score my first goal for PSG but the longer I go without a goal the more pressure I'm going to be under; and the more pressure I'm under means the less likely I am to score. It's a vicious circle.

'At the moment I actually look forward to away games because I feel I'm going to get a lot less stick from the crowd. And I'm not the only player who feels this way. One or two of the other lads who haven't scored of late are finding it hard to deal with the high expectations of our fans. I think they should try to get behind our players a bit more and for them to offer encouragement to get things right on the pitch instead of stick when we get things wrong.

'Laurent Blanc was a great player and he's a great manager too. But I don't think he knows how to get the best out of me, yet. Frankly, we are struggling to communicate, he and I. It's not like there's anything wrong with my French like some of these Africans. At the moment there is some sort of impediment between us that stops us communicating properly. But I don't know what it is. If I make a mistake it isn't because I am lazy, which is what has been suggested and why I am talking like this. Sometimes I make mistakes. We all do. That's football. But when I miss a chance that's what people say. They're like, "He missed that chance because he was out of position; and he was out of position because he's a lazy black bastard." As a footballer you have to laugh about it and shrug it off. But lately I seem to have forgotten how. I tell you I feel really low about this.'

Jérôme Dumas was dropped from the games against Nantes and Barcelona and his provocative comments will place a further strain on his relationship with PSG fans and management. Charles Rivel, for the club, disagreed strongly with what Dumas told *L'Equipe*: 'The fans don't strike me as hard to please at all. They follow the club all over Europe. It's a very loyal support that we have here at PSG. One of the best. I haven't heard fans booing Dumas or calling him lazy. But let's be honest – this is a player who is on €125,000 a week. Yes, it's human nature to want to be loved. But it seems utterly deluded of Dumas to be complaining that people who are paying eighty euros a ticket to watch a single game are not being supportive enough. This player needs a reality check. Yes, the team should have scored more than one against Nice, but it's just paranoia on the part of Jérôme Dumas to suggest that he was singled out by the fans for an extra level of criticism.'

For Dumas the best bit of news will have been that he was picked for the game against Guingamp. This does not sound much for a player of his standing and the player's latest comments will only fuel speculation that he is on his way out of Parc des Princes and is already bound for another club. Some will say good riddance. If you compare Dumas's stats with those of Ibrahimovic and Cavani it's impossible not to agree with this reporter that, given the number of minutes played versus the number of goals scored and shots at goal, Dumas has been found wanting. It seems he has yet to learn that more is expected of the player earning €125,000 a week than the fans paying his wages. But in the warped world of modern football these spoiled Renaissance princelings seem to want it all.

Mandel looked up. 'That's it. There's a table here on the page opposite with those stats which tell the real truth. But really, what he said, it was unforgivable. Most people think he gave the interview to accelerate his transfer to another club.'

'That's certainly the way I read it,' I said. 'Then again, there's no doubt he was genuinely depressed. This is Seroxat. You don't take this unless there's a real problem.

I wonder if the team doctor knew he was using this shit.'

Mandel shrugged, collected the packet of Cialis in his enormous paw and pulled a face.

'Or that.'

'Any man of his age who can't get it up for a woman like Bella Macchina has a problem, all right. That's a better reason to get depressed than not getting the ball in the back of the net.'

'Erectile dysfunction is often a corollary of depression.'

Mandel grinned. 'Maybe in England, monsieur. But not here in France. We get depressed but we're never so depressed that we could stop fucking.'

We went into the bedroom where I quickly found a drawer full of bondage equipment: chains and manacles, collars and restraints. And it was only now that I noticed the mirror on the ceiling immediately above the bed, which I pointed out to Mandel.

'Maybe he likes fucking a lot,' suggested Mandel. 'In which case he might have needed the Cialis. Even a man as young and fit as Jérôme Dumas can require a little help now and again. I wish we'd had this stuff when I was his age. Especially if I had known what I now know, which is that you get to a certain age and you don't fuck at all. With or without Cialis.'

CHAPTER 9

Dumas's PA, Alice, provided me with several useful telephone numbers, including that of his ex-girlfriend, Bella Macchina, the Marilyn Agency model whom she called and arranged for me to meet that evening. Alice made me coffee while she and I talked in the apartment's huge and very shiny kitchen. She was a good-looking girl with short hair and glasses who somehow reminded me of Jeanne d'Arc. Perhaps it was the *gamine* hairstyle. Then again it might have been the silver cross around her neck, the silver bouclé sweater that resembled a chain-mail shirt, or the number of cigarettes she smoked, lit with a handsome vintage lacquer Dunhill she said had been a parting gift from Jérôme Dumas, the flame of which needed a little adjusting it was so long.

I explained that PSG and FCB had hired me to try and find him.

'I know,' she said. 'Mr Mandel from the club told me.'

'First of all – and I'm sure that a lot of people have asked this already, so I apologise in advance – but have you any idea at all where Jérôme might be now?'

'I had assumed he was already in Spain. That he must have gone there immediately he came back from his holiday in Antigua. Because there was no real reason for him to return to Paris. The apartment is up for sale. The agency believed it would sell more easily if he left it furnished as it is now. Only Mr Mandel tells me that there's no evidence he ever came back from Antigua. That neither of the return air tickets he bought were used.'

'I believe so. Tell me about Antigua.'

'He had planned to go there for two weeks over Christmas and New Year. It was me who bought the air tickets and booked the hotel.'

'There were two tickets?'

'He had arranged to go there with his girlfriend, Bella. But they broke up just before they were supposed to go and so he went on his own.'

'Any idea why they broke up?'

Alice smiled. 'He was like any other young man with too much money. There were a great many other women ready to help him spend it. I think she was able to tolerate that for a bit. After all, she saw a few other men herself. But with Jérôme women were like a hobby. You'd have to ask her about this. I don't feel comfortable talking about this with a stranger.'

'You'll forgive me, I hope, if some of my questions seem intrusive, but there's a time factor here. If I don't find him soon I think the loan deal with FC Barcelona could be off. Which would be bad for Jérôme. His reputation is already in the mud. This could finish him.

Clubs don't like players who take time to settle in, but they especially don't like players who disappear without a trace. It makes picking a team difficult.'

'I suppose you're right,' she said. 'So, ask away.'

'Did you ever sleep with him yourself?'

She coloured.

'I'm sorry. But I have to ask.'

'Yes. But we both agreed it was a mistake and we decided not to do it again.'

'Was it?'

'How do you mean?'

'Did he agree more than you did? That it was a mistake?'

'Yes.'

'Were you in love with him, maybe?'

'Yes,' she said dully. Alice took off her glasses and began to clean them with a tissue she'd found in the sleeve of her sweater. She was much better looking than I had first appreciated.

'Did he know that?'

'No. I certainly didn't tell him. And I don't think he was capable of knowing it in any other way. He was much too caught up in himself to have even considered the possibility. My feelings were probably quite low on his horizon.'

'When Bella said she wouldn't go with him to Antigua – did he ever ask you to go in her place?'

'He would have done if I hadn't already made it very clear that I wasn't prepared to go in those circumstances.' She tried a smile but it didn't seem to work very well. 'It's one thing to come off the bench as a player substitute in a football match, it's another thing to take another girl's place in a man's bed. Even if the sex we had was very good.'

'Why did he want to go to Antigua when he was from the island of Guadeloupe? After all, Guadeloupe is less than a hundred kilometres south of Antigua.'

'I asked him that. The reason was simple, he said. For one thing he has no family left in Guadeloupe. But the main reason he said is that Antigua has much better hotels. He was booked in to stay at Jumby Bay, which is the best hotel on the island, apparently. A villa there costs anything between ten and twenty thousand US dollars a night.'

'Christ, it must be good.'

'He could afford it.'

'I suppose so.'

'He likes expensive hotels. The more expensive the better.'

'I've heard he's a bit of a champagne socialist. Is that right?'

'You've been talking to Mandel. Jérôme's a socialist, yes, but I don't think he liked champagne very much.'

'It's an English phrase. It means that you're a hypocrite.'

'Not in France. There are plenty of socialists who like to eat and drink well here. Especially in Paris. Our president, for example. Jérôme likes the good things in life, like anyone else. Me included. In different circumstances I wouldn't mind a week in Jumby Bay and I'm a socialist. And I love champagne. So what does that make me? A hypocrite?'

'No, but you're not telling other people to wear a hair shirt and pay less attention to making money. You're not the one going on demonstrations outside the French stock exchange. Or preaching the end of capitalism to Mélissa Theuriau on French television.'

The co-editor in chief and anchor of *Zone Interdite*, Mélissa Theuriau was generally held to be the best-looking woman on French TV – a view with which I found it hard to disagree.

Alice shrugged. 'It wasn't all hot air with him, you know. He's done some good things with his money. Things he didn't like to shout about.'

'Such as?'

'There was a youth centre in Sevran to which he often gave money to pay for sports facilities. He went there sometimes to see how they were getting on. He wanted to give something back.'

'Sevran?'

'It's a suburb northeast of the Paris Périphérique.'

'Tough area?'

'Very. Lots of black kids with no future. His words, not mine.'

'What was he like to work for?' I asked.

'Thoughtful. Gentle. Kind. A bit impulsive.'

'I found some antidepressants in the bathroom cabinet. Did he seem depressed to you?'

Alice took a deep breath and smiled a gentle smile. 'This is Paris. Everyone is depressed about something.

It's how we Parisians are. From what I've seen of life in London I don't think we're as carefree as the English. Even when we drink champagne.'

'Was there anything specific depressing him?'

'His mother died about six months ago. I suppose that might have had something to do with it.'

'Here in Paris?'

'No. She lived in Marseille. That's where she brought Jérôme to live when they left Guadeloupe.'

'Any other family there?'

'As far as I know it was just her and Jérôme.'

'Anything else that might have been getting him down?'

'His football. He hadn't been playing well. And he was getting a lot of abuse from the fans for not trying hard enough. The situation with Bella also depressed him, of course. I'm not sure she loved him but I would say that he loved her. And the loan to Barcelona. That affected him a great deal, too.'

'I gained the impression that he wanted this move from PSG. That he was looking forward to it.'

'I think he convinced himself it would be a good move. But he was concerned the loan to FCB was evidence that there wasn't a club that was prepared to buy him outright. That no one else would touch him. He was worried that it meant he was getting a reputation as a player who was difficult. Someone in the French newspapers had compared him to Emmanuel Adebayor. And this depressed him too, I think.'

'Yes, I can understand how it would.'

'He was worried how he might be received in Barcelona.'

'Do you think he was the type of guy to commit suicide?'

She thought for a moment. 'I don't know.'

'Did he ever talk about suicide? The way people do sometimes? How you'd do it? Jump off a tall building. Drown yourself. That kind of thing.'

'No.'

'Because players do kill themselves,' I added. 'My own friend, for example. Matt Drennan.'

'I'm sorry.'

'I was with him the night he hanged himself. He'd been drinking, but that was nothing new. He'd been drinking too much for years and there was nothing that he did or said on this particular night that made me think he might be suicidal. At least suicidal enough to go and do it after leaving my house. But in retrospect I wish I'd treated the possibility with greater seriousness. And that's what still haunts me a little. The idea that perhaps I could have done a little more.'

'There's nothing I'm not telling you, Mr Manson, if that's what you're driving at. And if he has killed himself I won't be haunted by the idea that I could have done more for him. I did everything for him. His laundry, his dry-cleaning, I paid his bills, booked the taxis and the tables at the restaurants and the nightclubs, took out the trash – which is to say I paid off the girls who needed paying off...'

'Hookers?'

'By the bus load.'

'Hmm.'

'I answered all his mail, answered his telephone and I even wrote his tweets.'

'Yes, I was going to ask you about his Twitter account...'

'I'm afraid you won't find any clues there. I wrote all his tweets. If you look at his Twitter account you'll see that the last one was written on my last day of employment. The day before he went to Antigua. Most of them I cleared with him. The rest were retweets, or stuff I picked up in the newspapers about football that struck me as interesting. Nothing personal.'

'Well, at least that's one mystery solved.'

Alice frowned.

'I thought maybe the date of the last tweet might be significant,' I explained. 'In trying to determine if he might have committed suicide.'

'What can I tell you? France has a suicide rate that is three times higher than in Italy and Spain, and twice the rate in Britain. It's like I was telling you earlier. We're not a happy people. Maybe that's why we've had so many revolutions. There's always something that's pissing us off.' She shrugged. 'He was on Seroxat, wasn't he? Since Jérôme Dumas left Paris I've been taking Seroxat myself.'

CHAPTER 10

Paris looks its best at night. I'm not going to get stupidly Woody Allen about this but after dark the place really is magical, even a little ghostly, like one huge haunted house. Maybe it helps not seeing all the cops on the streets or the beggars in the doorways, not hearing the clamour of the traffic, not smelling the decay, but at night, when you look up and see those searchlights coming off a floodlit Eiffel Tower as if searching out enemy bombers, there is nowhere else like it on earth. Around every corner is some new aspect of the city, some new delight for the eyes, some extraordinary affirmation of the ingenuity of men. The man who is tired of London is tired of life but the man who is tired of Paris must be tired of civilisation itself. The continued existence of Paris – such an affront to so many Americans who can't adjust to its lofty indifference from ordinary human concerns – is perhaps the premier work of man anywhere in the world. The extraordinary proclamation of a beauty that never fades is especially true at night, when the lady always looks her best.

No mortal woman in Paris could have looked better than Bella Macchina, especially in the elegant setting of Le Grand Véfour – a fine restaurant in the elegant arcades of the Palais-Royal. She was tall and blonde and blue-eyed and astonishingly beautiful and – as Mandel had said – possessed of legs right up to her arse. And maybe this is the secret of why French women look so good; *they live in Paris*. Even the tramps in Paris are the best, most convincing-looking tramps you've ever seen.

Bella was every inch the model: the hair heaped on top of her head was like golden thread and her complexion as smooth and clear as milk. She wore a black, embellished suede minidress, a pair of spiked leather Louboutin pumps and carried a matching mini-spiked leather evening bag. As she catwalked her long-legged way to my table even the women in the restaurant turned around to get a better look at her. But I don't think Bella noticed. She was already smiling at me and extending a lace-mittened hand, and then allowing about three waiters to help her sit down. I guess they were in search of a view of her underwear. I know I was. These days you snatch your pleasures where you can.

'Would you like something to drink?' I asked.

'Just champagne,' she said.

I enjoyed that – the use of the word 'just', as if champagne was something ordinary and quite undeserving of the ludicrous price that Le Grand Véfour deemed appropriate for what is only wine with bubbles, after all. Not that she'd have known anything about the cost of champagne. Women like Bella Macchina know the price of nothing and the value of only the most expensive so I threw caution to the wind and told the waiter to bring us a bottle of vintage Louis Roederer, which is a favourite of mine. Cristal is for footballers – American footballers.

We chatted for a while, ordered dinner. I even tried to flirt with her a little.

'Bella Macchina. It means beautiful car, doesn't it? In Italian?'

'Yes.'

She didn't volunteer any information about her name and it didn't seem worth irritating her by asking about it. I don't suppose any of the women in France or England ever thought about it; after all, she'd been on the cover of the Christmas issue of Paris *Vogue* wearing what looked to me like a Lagerfeld parody of an SS uniform, so what did they care what her name meant in Italian.

'Jérôme used to say I was the Lamborghini of women. Difficult to drive.'

'That's for sure. I mean the car, not you.'

'Is it difficult to drive?'

'I think you'd have to be Lewis Hamilton to drive it well.'

'Lewis who?'

I smiled. What did it really matter if she hadn't ever heard of Lewis Hamilton? I find that you can forgive a really beautiful woman an almost prelapsarian level of ignorance. And I was damn sure that there were plenty of English footballers I knew who couldn't have told you who Winston Churchill was. So, what the hell? Just to be seated opposite her made me feel more attractive. It was like someone had instructed her beauty to sit on a flowery island and sing out to passing sailors in order to lure the shirts off their backs. There were no prices on the enormous menu given to her by the waiter but she knew instinctively what to choose that would cause the most damage to a man's credit card. It was as well that FCB was picking up my expenses.

I took her hand and inhaled the scent. If music be the food of love then smell and touch are certainly the hors d'oeuvres. I was starting to feel hungry.

'Nice,' I said. 'I bet you can't find that in Duty Free.'

'No. That's one of the reasons I wear it. I don't like smelling like anyone else.'

'Don't worry,' I said. 'You could eat a hamburger with extra onions and mustard and you still wouldn't smell like anyone else.'

She liked that.

We talked about all sorts of things though I really can't remember what. Opposite her I was doing well just to remember my own name and it was quite a while before we got around to talking about Jérôme Dumas. With her perfect smile faltering a little, like a flickering light bulb, she sighed, shook her head and ran her manicure over the mini spikes on her evening bag as she told me about him.

'In some ways he's a very caring man. Thoughtful. Always generous. He does a lot of charity work for UNICEF and for cystic fibrosis charities. In other ways he's the most selfish man I ever met.'

'How *did* you meet?'

'We met during Paris Fashion Week in 2013 when we were both doing modelling for Dries Van Noten and G-Star RAW,' she explained. 'We were wearing G-Star's latest untreated denim jeans. I think they liked the fact that he was so black and I was so white. So did I. And so did he. The Othello shoot, they called it. You know? Like the famous play?'

A little more familiar with the play than the brands, I nodded.

'It wasn't love at first sight. But it was something close to it, perhaps. We started seeing each other almost immediately. Like you, he's a very beautiful man. And he pursued me relentlessly. He showered me with gifts. This Cartier bracelet was a gift from him on my birthday.'

She lifted her arm to show me the solid gold band around her wrist; it had the head of a panther with emeralds for eyes and diamonds for a collar and it certainly looked very expensive.

'Isn't it lovely?'

'It certainly is.'

'We went to the shop on Place Vendôme to choose it.' Without any trace of embarrassment, she added, 'And that was the night we first slept together.'

It figured, I told myself. I didn't know how much those little baubles cost but, looking at it now, I didn't think there would be much change out of a year's wages for some regular Jean.

'I hate to ask about your private life,' I said. 'But it's important that I try to cover all of the possibilities as to why he might have disappeared. To that end I need to know how things were between you. So if I apologise if occasionally I manage to sound like a cop.'

She nodded her assent to being gently probed.

'Well, at least you don't look like one.'

'You were together for how long?'

'About a year.'

'Maybe you could tell me why you guys broke up.'

'He was seeing other women.' Bella pulled a face. 'Although "seeing" doesn't begin to cover what he was doing. And "other women" hardly explains what they were.' She shrugged. 'They were prostitutes. High-end escorts. Two at a time, usually. Jérôme liked to see two women in bed together. I hold myself responsible for that, mind you. On his birthday last summer I hired a hooker myself and had her make love to me while he watched us.'

I tried to stop myself grinning as, for a brief second, I imagined her in bed with another woman. It wasn't the kind of birthday present any woman had ever given me, but then I wasn't one hundred per cent sure I'd have been entirely comfortable watching another woman go down on my girlfriend.

'I bet that blew his candles out,' I said.

'He liked it a bit too much, actually. After that he was always inviting girls around in pairs to his apartment. It got so that I refused to go there in case I found the kind of evidence I couldn't ignore. You know, women's panties, contraceptive packets, manacles, that kind of thing.'

'Right.'

'There were two women in particular he liked to hire. From an agency that called itself the Elysée Palace. They were American twins. Blonde, very expensive and very, very tall. L'Wren Scott tall. At least six feet and taller in high heels. He called them the Twin Towers and by his account – he was quite open about it – they would do anything. With footballers you expect that a bit. I mean, they're athletes, with appetites and a culture – or perhaps the lack of one – to match. But it wasn't what I was looking for in a relationship. I'm five years older than him. And I would like to settle down and have a family, sooner rather than later. We'd even talked about me coming with him to Spain. I love Barcelona and it seemed that there might be quite a bit of work there for me. There was a strong possibility that Hoss Intropia or Desigual were going to make me the face of their new look. And there was even some talk that a top retail brand in Spain were prepared to give me my own line in underwear. Which would have been fantastic.'

'Yes,' I said. 'I'd like to have seen your own ideas on underwear.'

Bella smiled sadly and touched my hand.

'Anyway, things came to a head between us just before Christmas. Jérôme had booked a holiday for us in Antigua – just the two of us – and then I found a sex-toy under the bed. Which I was really pissed off about and which almost persuaded me to end our relationship right then and there. I took his word that he was prepared to change, that he was prepared to stop whoring and to give up all other women. But even as we were talking and he was promising to turn over a new leaf another woman called Dominique was texting him a very lovey-dovey picture of the two of them together. I couldn't believe it. It looked as if they'd been on some holiday I didn't even know about. And it really was the final straw when he lied to my face about it. So that was the last time I saw him. I'm sorry he's missing, Scott, but I've completely washed my hands of him. This is going to be a Jérôme-free year for me. I've no wish ever to see him again.'

'Then I apologise again for asking you to describe things that might be painful for you.'

'It's okay. I had a pretty miserable Christmas about it but really, I'm over him now.'

'Did he call and try to persuade you to change your mind?'

'Maybe. Yes, I should think so. But I changed all my numbers and my email address so he couldn't persuade me. And for Christmas I went back to stay with my parents in Arras so he couldn't find me at my apartment.'

'So how did Alice get hold of you?'

'I gave her my number on the strict condition that she didn't give it to Jérôme. When he got loaned to Barcelona she lost her job, of course, and asked me if I could help her find another. It's not so easy now, finding jobs in Paris. As a matter of fact I was thinking of employing her myself. She's very loyal. I like that. I think perhaps she was a little in love with Jérôme.'

'Did you know he was taking antidepressants?'

'Yes. He wasn't very good at keeping secrets.'

'Do you think he might have been suicidal?'

'No. Not him. He loved himself too much.'

'What about his mother? She died about six months ago, didn't she? A man can take that quite hard.'

'They were close. But not close enough for it to have made him suicidal. I don't know for sure. But I think he was scared about something. Something that wasn't related to football which might have been getting him down.'

'Oh? Like what?'

'I'm not sure. He enjoyed playing politics, as I expect you know. And he wasn't very popular with the police because he had said some things about them that they didn't like. Sometimes he said he thought of himself as the Russell Brand of football. Anyway, a month or two ago, there was a big demonstration about something on the Place de la Bastille. While it was happening a girl was attacked by a black guy. Almost raped. You can see it on YouTube, I think. When she described her attacker to the police she said he looked a bit like Jérôme Dumas. She didn't actually mean that it was Jérôme Dumas who'd attacked her but by the time the description was put out on police radio the police had decided it was him they were looking for. And he was arrested. It took him several hours to convince the police that he had an alibi. I was his alibi. I had to go to the station and tell them that he'd been with me at the time of the attack. Which was true.'

This all sounded very familiar and I told Bella that something very similar had happened to me.

'Anyway,' she continued, 'the police took him to the station and while they had him in custody they were a bit rough with him, I think. And when they'd finished with the rape charges they suggested his involvement with the *banlieue* gangs was a lot more than him giving money and clothes to a youth centre in Sevran. That he was actively involved with the drugs trade. Which wasn't so hard to believe if you're a white policeman in Paris. Someone like Jérôme cultivated the black gangsta rapper look. As he was leaving the station the police told him they would be keeping a very close eye on him. I think some of them were PSG fans who didn't like what he'd said in *L'Equipe*. Anyway, that's what scared him. The idea that they were out to get him.'

'Is that what they said?'

'In so many words.'

'Why didn't Mandel tell me about this?'

'He didn't know about it. Nor did Alice. No one did. Jérôme and I – we kept it very quiet in case it affected his chance of a transfer out of PSG. At the time that's what he was hoping for. He'd been linked with clubs like Arsenal and Chelsea as well as Barcelona and he thought – probably correctly – that any talk of an arrest for rape or drug dealing might affect that.'

'He wouldn't be wrong,' I said. 'English football clubs are very conservative. Especially now that the sisterhood is so very well mobilised on Twitter. The opinion of women about football and footballers used to count for nothing. Now it can be the difference between keeping your job and losing it. Big Brother is watching you, all right, only Big Brother is us, ourselves. Smartphones at the ready, we're all Big Brother now, don't you think?'

Bella nodded and smiled through that and it was clear to me that she really didn't know who or what Big Brother really was or what I was even talking about. But to be fair I wasn't that sure George Orwell had ever made much of an impact in France.

'Fortunately,' she said, 'all the story amounted to in the newspapers was that the woman who'd been attacked had given a description of a black man who looked a bit like Jérôme Dumas and the whole thing just morphed into a few column inches about how the police were so racist and stupid that they'd put this out as the description of the man they were looking for. You know – as if all black men look alike? His actual arrest passed them by.'

'Have you ever been to this youth centre?'

'Are you joking? No way. It's one thing for someone like Jérôme Dumas to go there, on public transport – when he wanted to be, he could be very anonymous, you know? – but it's something else for a tall white blonde to go somewhere like that. Don't get me wrong. I like the Metro. But in Sevran a woman like me – I'm just a mugging waiting to happen.'

'You are in that dress,' I said. 'I was thinking of mugging you myself when we left here.'

She smiled but I wasn't sure she'd understood what I meant.

'It's Miu Miu. I'm glad you like it. Miuccia Prada is one of my favourite designers. The pink shearling coat I was wearing when I came in here is Miu Miu, too. Such a clever woman. Did you know that in 2014 *Forbes* magazine ranked her in the top one hundred most powerful women in the world?'

'I didn't know that. Anyway, the thing is, I think I might have to go to Sevran tomorrow,' I said. 'What's this place called, do you know? The youth centre?'

'I think it's called the Alain Savary Centre.'

'Who's he?'

Bella laughed. 'I haven't the first idea. Someone who liked football, I expect. There are plenty of those in France. By the way, if you go there you'd best leave that nice gold watch in your hotel room safe. What is it – a Hublot? The Big Bang Gold?'

I nodded, realising at last we'd managed to find a subject about which she was extremely well-informed: fashion and luxury goods. I expect she had a master's degree from Net-A-Porter.

'It's my favourite man's watch in the world. Carlo Crocco is a friend of mine, although the brand is now owned by Louis Vuitton, of course.'

'Of course.'

Bella touched my hand again and this time she didn't take it away. She let it rest lightly on mine. 'Better still, Scott. Why don't you leave your lovely watch on my bedside table? Along with those handsome gold cufflinks, and that nice matching tiepin. And your wallet probably. That way you'll still have all your nice things safe when you come back from Sevran.'

CHAPTER 11

From Bella's apartment near Parc Monceau I took the train to Sevran-Beaudottes station where I asked in the halal butcher's shop, for directions to the Alain Savary Sports Centre.

Looking for his name on the internet, it turned out that Alain Savary was a French socialist politician and a former Minister of National Education which probably explained why Bella Macchina hadn't heard of him. Education wasn't working in France any better than it was working in England.

I was wearing some of the gangster-style clothes that Jérôme Dumas had previously left behind at Bella's apartment: a hoody, a battered Belstaff motorcycle jacket, a pair of ripped G-Star RAW jeans and a *casquette* on my head – a baseball hat with a PSG logo on the front which was oddly hateful to me. The anomalous brown Crockett & Jones shoes were my own as the Converse trainers forgotten by Dumas were too small.

My own Zegna suit was hanging neatly in Bella's closet and, as she had suggested, my gold watch was lying on her bedside table. I hadn't slept very much but then sleeping seems like a bit of a waste of time when you're in bed with a naked supermodel. A combination of champagne, red wine and good cognac, not to mention a cigarette and her insistent and clamorous love-making, had left me feeling very slightly fragile. My cock felt like it had been inside a coffee grinder. Which wasn't so very far from the truth: the woman was a James Brown dream, a real sex machine. I might almost have felt guilty about that if I hadn't had such a good time. Like the Daft Punk song, I'd stayed up all night to get lucky, and lucky was how I felt.

But for the three hundred pound shoes on my feet I hoped I looked like anyone else in that neighbourhood, which is to say jobless (40 per cent of young people in Sevran are unemployed, or so I'd learned on the internet), African (that was easy for me), tired (that was also easy after my night of passion with Bella) and poor (36 per cent of people in Sevran are below the poverty line). Back in 2005, after three weeks of rioting that ended in a government-imposed state of emergency, there had been talk of a Marshall Plan for the *banlieues*, but there was little or no sign of any money having been spent here. And it wasn't difficult to see the evidence of people barely scraping by, and sometimes not at all. The graffiti said it all: *SANS ESPOIR*, which means 'without hope', and I couldn't have disagreed with that. But for the graffiti I could have been in any London sink estate. Surrounded by 1970s neo-brutalist blocks of flats resembling monochrome Rubik's cubes, it was the sort of area where they could easily have filmed the French version of films like *Harry Brown* or *Attack the Block* and a whole world away from the eighth where Bella's apartment was situated.

The Algerian guy in the butcher's shop directed me to the Lidl supermarket, and next to it a recreation area with a rusting Christmas tree sculpture and a plastic football pitch with markings that were barely visible. A boy of about fourteen wearing a cheap tracksuit was standing there with an Adidas Smart Ball under his foot which told me something. These balls cost about 175 euros and it suggested that I might at least be close to the place where Jérôme Dumas had spread some of his cash around; that amount of money was a fortune in a dump like Sevran.

'I'm looking for the Alain Savary Sports Centre,' I said.

The boy, who looked to be of Middle Eastern origin, pointed at a low-level concrete square, covered in graffiti, that resembled the police station in *Assault on Precinct 13*.

'Be careful,' he said.

I walked down a slope and around the building to a security glass front door. Already I could hear loud music – it was NTM's *Paris Sous les Bombes* – and smell the skunk. Inside the sports centre there was little sign of sport, just graffiti and a few posters of more French rappers. I wandered into a dressing room where the music was coming from. I knew it was a dressing room because there were lockers although I suspected that none of them contained so much as an old football sock. A gang of youths was grouped there and, seeing me, one of them got off a plastic chair and came to me with a baggy of white powder already in his hand, expecting that I was there to buy drugs.

'No thanks,' I said. 'It's information I'm looking for.'

'Are you a cop?'

I grinned. 'Fuck off.'

I sat down on the edge of a Formica table and surveyed the gang who were mostly black, and in their teens, but no less intimidating for all that. But kids are like computers; you give them shit, you get shit back. So I wasn't intimidated; besides, I always feel comfortable in a dressing room. I looked around me. It was hard to see what Jérôme Dumas could have spent money on in here.

'No, I work for Paris Saint-Germain,' I said. 'The football club. I take it you've heard of them.'

'If you're scouting for talent, we're it, Dad.'

'Yeah, give us a fucking ball and we'll show you a trick or two.'

'No, I'm not scouting.'

'You're a bit old to be a footballer, Dad.'

'You're right. I'm too old now. But I used to play. For Arsenal.'

'Arsenal's a good club. Thierry Henry. Sylvain Wiltord.'

'Arsène Wenger. He's a good manager.'

I nodded. 'Know them all.'

'What's your name, Dad?'

'Scott Manson.'

'Never heard of you.'

'Yeah, well, my career was tragically cut short, wasn't it?'

'Got injured, did you?'

'Nope. I went to prison. I was banged up for something I didn't do.'

'They all say that, Dad,' said the gang's apparent leader. He was a handsome boy wearing a PSG hoody tied around his waist and a Dries Van Noten T-shirt. At least I thought it was Dries Van Noten; the satin 'D' patch had been torn off but I was pretty sure I'd seen Jérôme Dumas wearing the same T-shirt in a picture that Bella had shown me in her own portfolio.

'True,' I said.

'How long for?'

'Long enough for it to end any hopes I might have had of a winner's medal.'

'From what I hear nothing's changed at Arsenal.'

'Yeah, it's been a while since anyone there got a winner's medal for anything.'

I let that one go. An FA Cup means less than it did of old, even to those who win it.

'I remember,' said the leader. 'You raped that chick, didn't you?'

'They said I did. But I just happened to be in the wrong place at the wrong time, that's all. The police thought I looked good for it and fitted me up.'

'Yeah, we all know how that works.'

'So what brings you down here?'

'Like I say, I'm working for PSG now. I'm what you might call a fixer. I'm a guy they call on when they want something sorted. On account of the fact that a lot of footballers are just bad boys. Just like you. Right now I'm looking for Jérôme Dumas. They sent a fuck-up to find a fuck-up, you might say. Dumas didn't turn up for training and they told me to check out all his usual haunts, see if I can't find him. His lady told me he used to spend money on this sports centre. Although I really can't see the evidence of that.'

The leader laughed. 'He used to come here all right. Only it wasn't to spend money on this fucking sports centre.'

Everyone thought that was funny.

Easy does it, I thought. Best not be too direct about this. They might be chary of dropping him in it.

'Look, I won't ask what he got up to when he was here. It's none of my business. But we're worried something might have happened to the guy. That maybe he's done himself in. Gone on a bender. Lost more than a weekend, you might say. So when was the last time you saw him?'

'Couple of weeks before Christmas.'

'It's no big secret what he did when he came here to Sevran-Beaudottes, man,' said the leader. 'He used to buy his weed and blow from us.'

'I never figured him as the type to put stuff up his nose,' I said.

'The blow was for his ladies. You know, to get them in the mood for love, right? All he did was smoke a little bit of weed and hang out. He liked to talk politics. Like maybe he wanted to be one himself one day.

He wanted to hear what we had to say about all kinds of shit. He didn't just want to talk the talk, he wanted to walk the walk, too. I guess you could say he liked to pretend he was down with us. Which was cool because he was generous. Brought us clothes and trainers from fashion shoots he'd been on. Cash, too. Jérôme gave us money for all kinds of shit. He might have suggested that we use it to buy sports kit and shit like that but he knew that wasn't going to happen. For one thing, who would come here to play us who wasn't soft in the head?'

'So what *did* you spend it on? The cash he gave you?'

'Food and drink. More weed. More blow. And more than that, we couldn't possibly say. Now and again we used to arrange a big party and he'd come around and have a good time. One time he bought us all dinner at the local rotisserie. I really think he thought he could make a difference.'

'And what do you think?'

'Nah. Take more than a footballer with a conscience to fix things round here.'

'Fair enough.'

'Hey, how about some free tickets?' said the gang leader.

I smiled. 'I was wondering when you'd remember to ask.' I put five tickets on the table. 'Those are for the Champions League match against Chelsea on the seventeenth.'

'No way.'

I took out a couple of fifties and tossed them on the table.

'And get some dinner on me, right?'

I walked back the way I'd come. Only this time the kid with the smart football was playing keepy-uppy. And I stopped to watch him.

I'd seen some great freestylers in my time. There's an English guy called Dan Magness who's probably the best in the world and has taught the likes of Messi and Ronaldo a thing or two. He's known as the Keepy-Uppy King. But of course just because you can keep the ball in the air doesn't make you a great footballer. There's a big difference between a player and a performer. Being part of a team means letting someone else have a turn with the ball. I was at one club where the youth side had hired a good freestyler and he always took one touch too many. But this kid was good. In fact he was outstanding. And when you see someone as good as this kid was, it's like watching an art.

The trick to good keepy-uppy is to avoid the toes and drop the ball on the laces. It's the way I was taught to do it. That and keeping the ball close to your body. But that's just the start. I love playing keepy-uppy myself because it's a hell of a workout. When I was younger and fitter and playing twice a week my best was about ten minutes but I think Dan Magness once did twenty-six hours using just his feet, legs, shoulders and head, which is incredible. He's good but he wasn't a patch on this kid. How do I know that? I don't for sure. But I'm almost certain that Magness hasn't perfected the art of keeping the ball up in the air – I swear this is true – *with his eyes closed.* Or sprinting while juggling the ball on his knees and head. It seemed that there wasn't anything this kid couldn't do with a ball. It was like watching someone toy with gravity and make a monkey out of it.

What was more he did it all with such an economy of movement that he made it look really easy, which is the first principle of sporting excellence. Make it look simple.

'How old are you, kid?'

He stopped the ball under his foot and put his hands in the pockets of his tracksuit trousers. 'Fifteen.'

'Does the smart ball make it any easier?'

'No,' said the kid. 'The battery runs out after about two thousand kicks. But that's better than nothing when you've got no one to play with. My mum bought me it, for Christmas.'

'What about those guys in the club?' I asked. 'Can't you get a kick about with them?'

He laughed and then looked away for a moment. He was about six feet tall, with dark eyes and a long face; he was handsome in an adolescent way, but none of that interested me so much as the fact that there was a black yarmulke pinned to the back of his black-haired head, which was how I hadn't noticed it before. The kid was Jewish.

'The sports club isn't for anyone interested in football,' he said. 'And anyway, my mum told me to keep away from those guys. They're dangerous. That's why I told you to be careful, man. Someone was shot around here just a few weeks ago.'

'Is that so?'

'Not that they would ever play with me.'

'Why not?'

The kid shrugged.

'Because they're Muslims and I'm a Jew. From the Lebanon. Jews aren't very popular around here.'

'I see. Are you in any kind of team at all?'

'I was back home. But not since we got here to Paris.'

'Do you want to be?'

'More than anything.' With his toe he flicked the ball in the air the way someone else might have shrugged or rubbed his own chin. 'I just took up freestyling to fill in a bit, and work on my skills, until I could find someone to play with. But that's not so easy around here, like I say. Since the Israelis started bombing Gaza it's not so easy being a Jew in Paris.'

'From what I've read, son, it was never easy being a Jew in Paris.'

'Really?'

'Do you ever read *L'Equipe*?'

'All the time.'

'The people who started that paper, back in the 1890s, were anti-Semitic. There was this Jew, a military officer called Captain Dreyfus who was wrongly accused of being a spy and sent to prison on Devil's Island. Back in the day there was another sports newspaper that was for Dreyfus. But *L'Equipe* was formed by a bunch of businessmen and anti-Semites who thought Dreyfus was guilty. Even though he'd been fitted up for it.'

'How do you know about it?'

'Let's just say that reading about miscarriages of justice used to be a special interest of mine.'

'Shit. I'll never read it again.'

'No need. It isn't like that now. It's just football, not politics. I don't think anyone even remembers poor old Dreyfus these days.'

'If you say so.'

'Tell me, how long have you been doing freestyle?'

'About six months.'

'*Six months?* Jesus.'

There was a box of matches in the pocket of Dumas's Belstaff jacket. I tossed it to him. 'See what you can do with those.'

The kid caught the box of matches and frowned.

'How do you mean?'

'Play with the box of matches instead of the ball.'

'Oh.'

The weight shifts around inside a box of matches which makes it more difficult to juggle than a tennis ball or an orange which would have been the usual way to distinguish someone who was good from someone who was really talented.

He managed several minutes until I told him to stop. I was already thinking about giving Pierre Hélan – an old mate of mine who worked at the French Football Federation's national academy at Clairefontaine – a call. Because despite all the bollocks in football – the diving, the mind games, the stupid money – I realised that there was a big part of me that still believed in the romance of the game. Surely every manager thinks that one day he's going to do a Bob Bishop and discover the next George Best. Why not me? I asked myself, especially now that some of the spark had gone out of my own managerial career. *I think I've found you a genius*, Bishop had telegrammed Manchester United's manager, Matt Busby. I figured my eye was no less sharp for talent than anyone's.

'You're good.'

'Thanks.'

'Really good. And believe me I know.'

'You in the game then?' he asked.

'Yes.'

'What you doing around here?'

'I'm supposed to be looking for Jérôme Dumas. He's gone walkabout. I heard he used to come down here sometimes. PSG have hired me to track him down. Like one of those dogs in Périgord that sniffs the ground for a white truffle.'

'Yeah, those things are really valuable, aren't they?'

'S'right. They can fetch as much as fifteen thousand bucks a kilo. The big ones have gone for more than three hundred thousand dollars.' Was this Jewish boy the equivalent of one of those rare white truffles? I asked myself. 'Anyway, Dumas – he didn't report for training and they're a bit worried something has happened to him.'

The kid nodded. 'Yeah. I seen him once or twice. He was a good player when he was with Monaco. But since he joined PSG he seems to have lost his mojo.'

'More importantly, did he ever see you?'

'No. The fact is, I didn't like to show him my skills.'

'Why the hell not?'

'Come on. You've met those guys in the club. That's why. Like I told you, my mum told me to keep away from them because they're into drugs and lots of bad stuff. I figured that probably included Jérôme Dumas. On account of the fact that they sold him drugs. I don't take drugs. He used to come out of that club room down there with a spliff still in his mouth.'

'A bit of weed and some blow.' I shrugged. 'It's not the crime of the century. Even in football.'

'Maybe so. But he also got a gun off them. And that's not cool.'

'Do you know that or did someone tell you?'

'Someone told me. But I know it, too.'

'How do you know it?'

'Look, I'm here on this pitch a lot. Sometimes all day. I see things happening around here. I keep away from those guys and they leave me alone but in return I'm supposed to use this burner if the cops show up.' He took out an old mobile telephone and showed it to me. 'Not that they'd hear it ringing, given that their music is so loud.'

'Yeah, I noticed.'

He shrugged. 'You didn't look like a cop.'

'I'm not. I work in football. I used to manage a club in London, but right now I'm freelancing. Keep telling me about the gun.'

'Only that Dumas wasn't the first guy who came around here looking for a gun. And whenever those guys sell a gun they hand it over in a cream-coloured enamelware lunch box. To hide the fact that it's a gun. But everyone around here knows what's in those boxes. It isn't some guy's baguette. And I didn't come all the way from the Lebanon to get shot here in Paris.'

'Good point.' I looked for my watch and then remembered where it was.

'Want to go and get a cup of coffee?'

'Sure.'

'What's your name, son?'

'John Ben Zakkai.'

'And by the way, what was the name of the guy who was shot here? The one you were talking about earlier?'

'Mathieu Soulié.'

CHAPTER 12

As soon as I was back the Plaza I called Mandel.

'How good are your connections with the police?' I asked.

'Good.'

'I need you to find out all you can about a murder that took place a few weeks ago. The victim was called Soulié, Mathieu Soulié.'

'Might I ask why?'

'It's probably nothing.'

Then I changed my clothes and went out to lunch.

Paolo Gentile had flown in from Italy aboard his own private jet for our meeting at Arpège, which is possibly the best restaurant in France if you're a vegetarian like he was. The French aren't much given to vegetarianism but when they do it, it's the best. A stone's throw from Invalides, the place in the Rue de Varenne is nothing much to look at – certainly not from the outside – and there are few clues as to the eye-watering expense of the tasting menu which, at 365 euros a person, is a lot for a few bags of leeks and potatoes. But Gentile, a vegetarian who always ate there when he was in Paris, was an advert for his diet; in his handmade Brioni suits he looked more like a prosperous Geneva banker than someone who worked in football – although maybe a word like 'work' was stretching it. And he was less principled than he could have been. Anyway, he'd done well for someone who'd once owned a nightclub on the Via Valtellina in Milan.

He was returning to hibernation after a busy January buying and selling several household name players, including a couple of record winter break deals with clubs as far afield as Glasgow and Istanbul; Davey Conn's move from Rangers to Chelsea for twenty million pounds was reported to be the biggest deal in the Glasgow club's history, but the most lucrative deal struck by Gentile had been the sale of Lazio's star striker, Carlos Amatriain, to Manchester City for forty-two million quid. It was small wonder he could afford to own a private jet.

As he sat down at the table he put both his phones on mute, and from time to time when each rang, he checked to see who was calling but I'm flattered to say he didn't speak to any of them while he was lunching with me.

'You know I should be skiing in Cortina with my family,' he said. 'Instead of which I'm here with you, Scott.'

'You're protecting your investment in the former PSG number nine. There may not have been a transfer fee for Jérôme Dumas, but there will be. Eventually. Provided I can find the stupid bastard. And of course until then you're taking ten per cent of everything he makes, Paolo.

Anyway, while I was waiting for you to turn up, I calculated that you earned more than ten million quid off your commission on transfer fees in January, so you can afford to delay your holiday a little.'

'Tell me something. Are you still with that red-headed *stronza*?'

'If you mean Tempest O'Brien, then the answer is yes, she still represents me.'

'In spite of her dropping you in it with the Chinese like that? You should get rid of her right now before she does you some real damage. If she'd exercised a bit of due diligence that would never have happened.'

'And you'd know all about due diligence, you old crook.'

'I'd never have let you go there on your own like that. To Shanghai? Fuck off. It's the wild west out there, my friend. There's no way you should ever have been in Shanghai. You should be with me, Scott. If you were you'd have a new club by now. I'm amazed you're still out of work. A man with your talents, your languages, it's a crime that you're not managing a top team. Don't forget there's no transfer window for managers. I happen to know a top English club that's desperate to drop their manager. I could find you a new job, just like that.'

He snapped his fingers, which only succeeded in summoning the waiter.

We ordered, quickly.

'Let's just stick to the matter in hand, shall we?' I said after the waiter had gone. 'Jérôme Dumas.'

'How much are they paying you to find him?'

'Enough.'

'I'll give you a fifty thousand euro cash bonus on top of whatever they're paying you if you can find him. Save the boy from himself if needs be. Just get him back to Barcelona before the end of March. Will you do that for me?'

'Of course. But that Qatari guy already offered me a finder's fee if I can find the boy in time for him to play in *el clásico*.'

'Oh, I'm not worried about the match. If he plays he plays. No, I own half the economic rights in that boy and I just negotiated a deal worth twenty million pounds for him to be the new global ambassador for the fashion house Cesare da Varano.'

'Doesn't you owning his economic rights contravene FIFA regulations on agents?'

'But you're not going to tell them, are you, Scott? You dislike those bastards at FIFA almost as much as I do. No, the people at da Varano want him to start on a new advertising campaign that can be ready for Milan Fashion Week in September. That boy's going to be worth more off the pitch than he is on it. Especially since he started to become the mouthpiece of anti-capitalist agitation. Danny Cohn-Bendit in a Cesare da Varano suit. Russell Brand in a pair of football boots. That's why he has to be found. I've got a lot of other deals in the pipeline. A big cosmetics company want to make a cologne with his name on it.'

'Makes sense, I suppose. They did an Aramis, didn't they? So why not Dumas.'

Paolo Gentile laughed. 'I still have a bottle of that piss in my drawer. Every so often I have a sniff of it to remind me of my spotty adolescence. Like Proust. There's even talk of a commercial with the Zaragoza Bank. One of the biggest in Europe.'

'Did Dumas know about all this sponsorship?'

'Of course. I called him just before he went on holiday to tell him the good news about da Varano. And I might have mentioned the bank.'

'But is that how he took it?'

'How do you mean, Scott?'

'That this was good news?'

'He's a footballer. They have a limited shelf-life. You can be Peter Pan for only so long in this game. Unless it's David Beckham we're talking about these guys have got ten years at most to make their money, after which – for most of them, at any rate – it's a trip to the bankruptcy court or running a guest house in Skegness. Often both. It's an agent's job to maximise the client's earnings while he can. You know how this works. If only he'd had the sense to marry that nice girl. What's her name? Bella something. Isn't she great?'

'Bella Macchina. She's fucking gorgeous.'

'I could have turned them into the next Brand Beckham. The salt and pepper David and Victoria. That's what he wanted.'

'I can't believe you just said something like that. And to me.' I grinned. 'I'd forgotten what a fucking racist you are, you old wop.'

'Don't be so sensitive. I could probably do something

very similar for you, Scott, if you'd let me. The black Mourinho. Something like that. You're just not paying attention to who and what you are. To the value of your own brand. You're not the cleverest man in football, Scott. I am. But you do have a brain and that's unusual in this game. You're a good-looking guy, too. You could be the face of something yourself.'

'Jérôme Dumas. We're straying from the subject. Again. What I'm trying to find out is, did he feel under pressure because of all this shit? I mean, here's a kid who thinks he's Russell fucking Brand, leading the French fight against capitalism, and you're trying to turn him into the preferred tool of the big brands and the bankers, for Christ's sake. This is a boy who went on demos, Paolo. These are the people who smash the windows of banks, not plug them on the telly.'

'Which is precisely why this particular bank wanted him. To sell the idea that their bank listens to the people and gives them the service they want.'

'They all say that.'

'I know. But advertising agencies exist to help them say it more persuasively than anyone else.'

'They all say it while paying their employees big bonuses and evicting people from their mortgaged homes. Yes, I get what's in it for them.'

'You don't believe that. You're not that naïve.'

'No, of course I'm not. What I'm trying to point out is that even he might have started to feel like a hypocrite. Which creates its own pressure. The week after there's an article in *Libération* in which he's espousing Maoist revolution, you're trying to sell him as the public face of a bank. The week after that article, Jérôme Dumas gives an interview to *L'Equipe* bemoaning the fact that he's not loved by the fans. Small wonder. From what I've read online most fans wanted less politics and more goals.'

'I didn't see the piece in *Libération*.'

'Maybe you weren't paying attention.'

'I'm his agent, not his nanny. I'm there to advise him, not wipe his nose. Ever since he went to Monaco I've been there to show him that football is a business and that it's important to treat it as such. Because nobody is as smart as everyone, especially in retrospect. Right at the beginning I told him to find himself a role model from football and try to live up to this person's image, model himself on them. We went through a book I have, of exemplary footballers. And he picked another former Monaco player, Thierry Henry. Sure, I was able to tell him a few home truths about how he's perceived in the media. It was me who persuaded him to take on Alice as his PA, and to get her to start managing his social media. And to keep an eye on him generally.'

'You mean she spied for you?'

'Not in a bad way. We managed to avoid a lot of calamity tweets like that. Twitter is a bloody minefield.'

'Anything else you're not telling me, Paolo?'

'She was supposed to tell me if he started gambling again, that's all.'

'Gambling?'

'When he was playing in Monaco he got a taste for playing cards. I had to sort out some poker debts he had. Nothing that hasn't happened to a host of other players.'

'Debts to who?'

'Some bookmakers.'

'Legit bookmakers?'

'Of course legit. It wasn't anything heavy duty. Listen, Scott, I looked out for that boy. I went to his mother's funeral in Marseille. Just to make the numbers up otherwise it would have been only Jérôme who was there. That's above and beyond, you know.'

'How did he take it?'

'No better or worse than I took my own mother's passing.'

'You had a mother? I never knew.'

Paolo smiled a sarcastic smile.

'Were they close?'

'Not especially. In fact I gained the impression that there was some issue between them. I think he took against her for some reason. But I don't know what that might have been. For a man who talked about himself a lot he managed to say very little. I never gained an impression of who he really was. Or thought he was.'

'Most young blokes are like that. Especially in football. Sometimes, with all the training and the games and the media, there's no time for introspection. Most of them think inner space is the title of a movie directed by Christopher Nolan. They start playing, make money, ten years pass – as you say – and then they wake up one morning, unemployed, with bills to pay and not the first idea of what makes them tick. That's probably the one moment when you really do need an agent. Someone to counsel you on what to do next.'

'We're quite a long way from that. The boy is just twenty-two. Look, I don't have to justify myself to you, Scott. My conscience is clear. I couldn't have done more for him. If he's had some sort of breakdown I shan't hold myself to blame in the least bit. I watched his games on the telly, of course. Went to one or two when I was in Paris. Told him what I thought of his game. Believe me, Scott, I love the game. I have a season ticket at Verona. And take my word for it, you've got to love the fucking game to have a season ticket for the *scaligeri*. Tell you what – the next time you're in Italy, I'll take you to the Marcantonio Bentegodi to see a match. Preferably against Chievo – the other club in Verona. You know, I've always thought you'd be just the man to put us back where we belong. Up there with the Milans and Juventus.'

'Let me tell you something about your client, Paolo. If he did pick Thierry Henry as his role model then it wasn't working. Frankly he might just as well have picked Joey Barton or Mario Balotelli. The more I look into this kid's life the more I begin to see how close to disaster he actually was.'

'You're exaggerating, surely.'

'I don't think so. Between you and me he was using drugs and prostitutes like his two middle names were Charlie Sheen. Bella dumped him because she found a sex toy under his bed. He bought a gun off some gangsters in one of the *banlieues*. He was clinically depressed and using happy pills. And now, on top of all that, you tell me he used to have a gambling problem. It seems to me that there are two Jérôme Dumas. Maybe three. There's the Dumas who plays football for PSG and fancies himself as a man of the people and a bit of a street philosopher. Then there's the guy who's down with the gangs who likes hookers and dope and guns. And somewhere in between these two slices of bread is the advertising brand you were trying to turn him into. The black David Beckham. The face of a bank and an Italian fashion label. Talk about a false nine. This guy is the false nine to end all false nines.'

'If you say so. But we're all a mass of contradictions. This is the human condition. A hero on one day can be a villain the next. No human being can ever really hope to understand another, and no one can fathom another's unhappiness. Heroes are no longer the simple men of old – the Bert Trautmanns and the Bobby Moores. Perhaps they never were. The world is not black and white, Scott. It's always been black and grey. You sound surprised about that. And that surprises me.'

'Clue me in here, Paolo. The kid's disappeared. The cops on Antigua have looked all over the island. But there's no trace of him. And no trace of him having left the island. Apparently he checked out of the hotel – a little earlier than scheduled – paid the bill by credit card, and left. Hasn't been seen since. So where do you think he's gone?'

'I really have no idea. But I assume that's where you're going next. To Antigua. I mean, that's the logical place to begin your search in earnest.'

'I leave tomorrow. I'm following the same route he took. Flying to London Gatwick and from there to Antigua. While I'm on my way down there maybe you can persuade FCB and PSG to change their minds about offering a reward for information as to Jérôme's disappearance.'

'There's not a chance of that happening, Scott. This is commercially sensitive on all sorts of levels. I thought they made that clear already. I know I just did. Besides, the cops down there didn't want us to offer a reward. They thought it would be counterproductive.'

I shrugged. 'Can't blame me for asking. It would certainly make things a lot easier.'

'In which case they'd hardly be paying your ass a hundred grand a week to find him.' He looked around. 'You're staying at the Jumby Bay, too? Like he did.'

'Yes.'

'There's a great restaurant there. You should try it.'

'I expect I will.'

'And I should check out Guadeloupe while you're down there. That's where Jérôme was from, you know – before he went to live in Marseille with his mother – and it's only a short plane ride south from Antigua. Or is it north? I can never remember.'

'Antigua is north of Guadeloupe.'

'It should be nice down there at this time of year. I would say have a nice time but I assume you're going to be busy.'

'It's a real hardship, isn't it? Going to the Caribbean in February. But someone's got to do it.'

'If anyone can solve this mystery, I'm sure it's you.' Paolo was silent for a moment and then frowned. 'Maybe you can already tell me why he bought a gun. And from whom?'

'He bought it from some punks who hang around the Alain Savary Sports Centre in Sevran. It's one of these charming suburbs in northeast Paris. I was there this morning.'

'Not dressed like that, I hope. Or wearing that gold watch.'

'No. I went back to my hotel and changed before coming here.'

That was almost true.

'The Alain Savary Centre is the one Jérôme was supposed to be putting money in. He was giving the local youth money, all right. But it wasn't for footballs and sports kit. It was mainly for weed and blow. And the gun, of course. I don't know why he wanted that, no. Not yet. I'm going to ask the lovely Bella when next I see her. Maybe she can tell me. That won't exactly be a hardship, either. She's very easy on the eye.'

Paolo Gentile's brown eyes narrowed over the top of his wine glass; he took a sip, and then wagged a perfectly manicured finger at me. I'll say one thing for Paolo, he's probably the best-dressed man in football. *GQ*, look out.

'What?'

'Just make sure you keep your hands off her.'

'Meaning what?'

'Meaning that life is just like football; just different sets of tactics.'

'And that means what, exactly?'

'It means, my deliberately obtuse friend, don't try and fuck her. She's just a kid.'

'Nonsense. This is a grown-up woman we're talking about, Paolo. You make her sound like Lolita with a lollipop and a pout.'

'Just stay out of her pretty little pants, sport.'

'Why would you think that there was even half a chance of me getting in them?'

'Because no one ever fucks these models. Everyone thinks they're untouchable. Which means they're anything but, of course. And don't act so innocent about this. You're a dog, Scott. That's right. You've got a bit of form here, Scotty my friend.'

'What are you talking about, form?'

'For fucking other men's wives. That's what got you into trouble before, wasn't it? When you were still at Arsenal? I mean, if you hadn't been with that guy's wife, you'd never have gone to prison, would you? So, learn your lesson well, my friend, and just make sure you just leave Bella Macchina alone.'

'As far as I'm aware, Bella and Jérôme Dumas weren't married. In fact, they broke up just before Christmas.'

'Perhaps they did. But that's irrelevant from where I'm sitting.'

'Take my word for it, there's a velvet rope around a girl like that.'

'Is there? From what I heard she likes black guys. I'm telling you to make sure you're not one of them.'

'You know I hadn't thought of trying to fuck her,

Paolo. But now you've mentioned it…' I grinned. 'You've given me an idea here. Maybe no one is fucking her. Be a shame to let a nice white booty like that go to waste. Isn't that what this is about? Maybe you just don't like the idea of white women going with black men. Because believe me, the ship has already sailed on that particular vexed issue. Even in Italy.'

'It's got nothing to do with race. And everything to do with that boy's commercial future. With her commercial future, too. She may not realise it yet but there's a shelf-life for models, too. They're both of them financially much stronger together than they are apart. I figure Jérôme will stand a much better chance of getting back with the lovely Bella if no one else is seeing her. And no one would certainly include you.'

'Bollocks.' I shook my head. 'Look, I'm flattered that you even think I stand a chance with a girl like her, but you needn't worry. I'm already in a relationship. Okay?'

'I'm serious, Scott. Most men have a weakness. Mine is money. And white Ferraris. I have four now. Frankly, I don't need any of them. Most of the time I have someone to drive me. But I have a weakness for these cars. Your weakness is women. Always has been. In spite of what you say – your modest denials – women are what will always get you into trouble. So, take my advice and keep your filthy paws off that girl. She's forbidden fruit to a man like you.'

CHAPTER 13

'Have you any idea why Jérôme should have felt the need to get himself a gun?'

'My God, I'd forgotten about that.'

'You saw it?'

'He showed it to me.'

'When was this?'

'October? Maybe November. I'm not sure.'

Bella leaned out of bed, grabbed her cigarettes and lit one. She was still wearing a black corselette, black stockings and suspenders, but her tiny floss panties were long gone. Looking at her golden bare butt now and remembering with lips that were still glowing just how much time I'd spent with my head between her legs, I wasn't so sure I hadn't eaten them. That's the thing about forbidden fruit. Like the saying goes, it often tastes the sweetest. Paolo Gentile was right about that much anyway. Women had always been my weakness. I might have said they were my Achilles heel except that my feet had nothing to do with what I wanted to do with Bella. I might have felt a little more guilty about betraying Louise but I'd already managed to persuade myself that I had an out with my girlfriend on account of the fact that Bella was a Marilyn supermodel, and of course it's not every day that a supermodel with legs up to an arse you could eat your sushi off makes it clear that she wants you to fuck her brains out. That's not much of a defence. And I wouldn't like to see anyone try that in court – even a good barrister. Rumpole of the Bailey couldn't have put that one over. An all-male jury might just have bought it. Gentlemen of the jury, just look at this woman, for God's sake. Wouldn't you have fucked her, too? If you'd had the chance? Sure you would. But how many juries did you get these days that didn't have at least one disapproving battleaxe on board for the trial? The days of *12 Angry Men* were long gone.

Of course I knew that eventually I would feel guilty; just not yet.

'Want a cigarette?'

'No, thanks. I really only smoke when it means keeping someone I like company. Like last night. No one should have to smoke alone. Least of all a beautiful woman. And certainly not in this city. So, tell me more about Jérôme's gun.'

'It was a black thing, he said.'

'I'm black. And I've never wanted to own a gun.'

'A gangster thing. You know, like 50 Cent or Ice Cube. He liked to wave it around in his apartment. To point it at the mirror and pose with it. That's all. He was like a kid with it. Although sometimes he had it under his pillow. It was more of a style thing, I guess. I mean, he wore the clothes and listened to the music and, from what you've told me, he got down with the guys on the street. I think the gun was just part of all that bullshit. Like I said, this guy is five years younger than me. And it showed sometimes, you know? He liked his toys. The Lamborghini. The gold chains. The diamond panther studs in his ears. He bought them at the same time as he bought my bracelet, from Cartier. They were thirty-five thousand euros.'

'What kind of a gun was it? Can you remember?'

'I don't know. It's not like they're made by Hermès, are they? One gun is much like another to me.'

'A handgun.'

'Yes.'

'Revolver or automatic?'

Bella thought for a moment. 'I don't know. No, wait. I have something.'

She slipped out of bed and walked into the bathroom where she hauled open several drawers.

'An ex-boyfriend gave me this when I was last in the States,' she called out and I began to wonder what it was she was looking for. Another gun?

But when she returned to the bedroom she was carrying a box containing what was described as a *MAGNUMDRYER: Model 357. The authentic western gun hair dryer.* It had a pink handle and an extra large silver barrel. A novelty, obviously, but the kind that might easily get you killed.

'It was like this,' she said.

I opened the box and smiled. The hairdryer was even equipped with a white leather holster.

'A magnum?'

'Yes. Only his was black, with a rubberised handle. Not silver with a pink handle like this one.'

'No, well, you can see how that would wreck the effect. It's hard to look like an authentic gangster when you're holding a magnum that has a pink handle.'

'I don't use it,' she explained. 'It's the wrong current for France.'

'There's that, and the neighbours. Someone might think you were planning to kill yourself if they saw you put that next to your head.' I shook my head. 'Only in America. You'd think they had enough guns without making innocent objects look like guns, too. I mean, you look at this and figure that it's only a matter of time before some dumb hairdresser in St Louis gets shot for blow-drying a lady's hair. I mean that; it will almost certainly happen. Everything you can say about America – good or bad – is always true.'

'I never thought of that. But yes, you're right. Especially if you're black.'

I nodded. 'Especially if you're black.'

'You pull the trigger to operate it.'

'Just like a gun. I don't use them myself. Hairdryers, that is. But even I figured that you pulled the trigger to make it work.'

'And you control the temperature with the thing at the back.'

'The hammer.'

'The hammer, yes.'

'You know, I searched Jérôme's apartment from top to bottom and I didn't find a gun. Nor any ammunition. Have you any idea what became of it?'

'After I found out that he was keeping it under his pillow I told him to get rid of it – to chuck it in the Seine before he hurt himself. Either it went or I did. So maybe he did get rid of it. All I know is that I never again saw it.'

'What about gambling? Paolo Gentile told me that when Jérôme was back in Monaco there were some guys he owed money to. Debts.'

'I know he liked to play poker. He was always watching it on television. But he never mentioned that he'd lost any money. And as for debts he always seemed to have plenty of cash in his pocket. He usually had at least a thousand on him. I know because I was often borrowing money for a cab.'

'Tell me about his other friends. His team mates at the club. Who was he close to?'

'Nobody.'

'Yes, that's what I heard from Mandel.'

'Especially after the piece in *L'Equipe*. He trained. He played. He went home. He said that's how he preferred it. Are you going to speak to any of them?'

'No, the club want this kept as quiet as possible. It only takes one idiot with a Twitter account to fuck that up and then this is all over the newspapers.'

'I certainly don't want that. And not just for Jérôme's sake. I mean, if they start looking for him, it won't be long before those bastards at *Closer* are hanging around outside my building again.'

Closer was the celebrity picture magazine that had broken the story of how the French president, François Hollande, was having an affair with actress Julie Gayet.

'I thought you French had privacy laws to stop that kind of thing.'

'Oh, we do. But the magazines just pay the fines, which aren't much compared with how many sales a big story can put on their circulation.'

She finished her cigarette, swept the box and the novelty hairdryer onto the floor, lay back on the bed and fixed me with a steady, blue-eyed stare that could have unzipped my trousers, had I been wearing any. If I could have read her mind I think I would have said that she wanted me to fuck her again. Paolo Gentile had been right about that, too. It had been a while since anyone had fucked her.

'So, what's your next move?' she asked.

'My next move?' I rolled on top of her, pushed her long white thighs apart and nudged inside her. She gasped as I flexed my pelvis and swiftly found my way right up against the neck of her womb. 'My next move is this.'

'That's what I hoped it would be.'

Which just goes to show that when it comes to sex a man and a woman can read each other's minds pretty well, really. There won't ever be an ebook that can take the place of all that.

CHAPTER 14

On the long plane journey from London to Antigua I watched a recording on my iPad of the Paris Saint-Germain game against Barcelona in the early stages of the Champions League, last September. It was the match which PSG had won 3–2, and counted as a pretty stunning result for the French although the actual game seems to have been more immediately famous as the one when David Beckham turned up with guests Jay-Z and his wife Beyoncé, neither of whom looked as though they were much impressed with what they saw. Looking like Charlie Brown in his dorky, flat-brim baseball hat, Jay-Z couldn't have seemed less comfortable if Beyoncé's sister Solange had been sitting right behind him just waiting to give him another kicking in an elevator.

No one had expected PSG to win without the talismanic Zlatan Ibrahimovic – he had an injured heel – who must have regretted a chance to prove to his former club, Barcelona, that they had been wrong to let him leave on loan to AC Milan, in 2010. Frankly, anyone who saw the Swede's thirty-yard wonder goal for Sweden against

England in November 2012 knew that this was always a mistake. The French were also without their captain, Thiago Silva (thigh problem) and the Argentine striker Ezequiel Lavezzi (torn hamstring). And if all that wasn't bad enough, Barcelona had fired six past Granada the previous weekend with a hat-trick from Neymar and two from Lionel Messi – the little Argentine's 400th and 401st career goals. On the same weekend, PSG had struggled to get a 1–1 draw against the no-hopers from Toulouse. Even PSG's manager, Laurent Blanc, had seemed to recognise the impossibility of the task ahead of him when, in a pre-match press conference, the former French captain had spoken of Barcelona as his side's 'near masters'.

But on the night against Barcelona, PSG played out of their skins and it was plain to see that this was the match that had persuaded the Catalan side to make a mid-season move for Jérôme Dumas, because while PSG's goals had been scored by David Luiz, Marco Verratti and Blaise Matuidi, the man of the match was, without question, Jérôme Dumas. In and out of possession he had been the spirit of PSG's impressive display. Having played for much of the previous season as a holding player, the young Frenchman was moved forward into the No. 10 role for the game against Barcelona, although his workrate did not seem to suffer in the least. Brimming with two-footed invention, he was a great example to the Parisians and on several occasions he managed to turn like a scalded cat in the tightest spaces and get his team out of pressure, creating chances where none had seemed to exist before.

Dumas was equally irrepressible in defence, frequently

dropping back deep to aid David Luiz and Gregory van der Wiel, who were hard to break down, although Messi and Neymar tried hard enough. Halfway through the second half, Dumas had briefly looked tired, as if he might have to be taken off, but Laurent Blanc's decision to keep him on proved inspired when Verratti nodded in a perfectly weighted ball from the Frenchman. At times the sheer verve he brought to his work seemed nothing short of miraculous: in one fifty-yard run deep in the second half begun after he'd easily dispossessed no less a figure than Lionel Messi, Dumas dribbled, swerved, pivoted and almost slalomed, before succumbing to a hard, scything tackle from Dani Alves which would have had many a footballer crying foul, before getting up again with a smile instead of an accusatory stare of goggle-eyed incredulity at the referee.

He was like this for the whole game: an unruly, hyperactive, runaway child. Messi and Neymar – who both scored – must have wished that someone would put Ritalin in his half-time water bottle. Even Dumas seemed to recognise that he'd surpassed himself.

When the match was over Jérôme Dumas finally left the pitch with his socks rolled down his wobbling legs and wearing a euphoric grin like some footballing d'Artagnan from the pages of *The Three Musketeers*, that great French novel written by Jérôme's more famous namesake, Alexandre Dumas. On the strength of the performance I saw in this match it didn't seem too much to expect that this young footballer would soon stand alongside the writer in the pantheon of French glory.

CHAPTER 15

There are two things that strike you as your plane comes in to land on the Caribbean island of Antigua. The first is how small the island is. It's not much bigger than the city of Birmingham. The second is how like an emerald the green of the land is against the lapis-lazuli blue of the sea which seems to extend forever so that you can hardly tell where the sky ends and the sea begins. Darker blue patches of coral reefs surround the island like submerged thunderclouds and almost every inch of the meandering coast is gilded with the sand of some perfect beach. Nearer to the ground there are more houses than you anticipated and these are mostly white as if a green coat had been studded with the shiny buttons of some eco-minded pearly king. And then there is the airport, as pink as candyfloss with the name of the island helpfully spelled out in large green letters under the seven arches of the building's roof which resemble alphabetical trains sitting in a railway siding, awaiting dispatch to various parts of the island. But this is the last time on Antigua you ever stop to think about something so urgent as a train because as soon as you are off the plane life drops a rusty gear or two. Enveloped by warmth and confronted everywhere by almost fluorescent smiles, you even blink more slowly as if you'd just had a hit on a big spliff and were trying to remember your own name and something like a name actually mattered. Nothing on Antigua seems to matter all that much. There's not even a drink-driving law which – in spite of the many wines I'd sampled in Club Class – hardly mattered either since the hotel had sent a man with a car to drive me to a jetty, and from there by boat to an even smaller, more exclusive island where there were no cars at all. I might have normally baulked at seventy-five bucks, US, for a ten minute airport transfer but already I was feeling as laid-back as the fellow with cornrows in his hair who drove the boat. Besides, that's the thing about travelling on someone else's dollar: suddenly everything seems quite simple; only the best will do. If you ever win the lottery then come straight here; that's the Euromillions lottery, not the smaller, British one; two weeks at the Jumby Bay won't leave you much change from a British lottery win.

As I arrived in Antigua's airport a photographer took my picture which irritated me as I had hoped to remain as anonymous as possible. I hardly wanted to talk to anyone about being hoodwinked in Shanghai or, as the *Sun* had put it, *Manson's Chinese Fake-Away*, which I have to admit was rather good.

But I was keen to talk to almost anyone about Jérôme

Dumas. I decided to get started right away, and by the time the boat guy picked me up to take me to Jumby Bay, I'd already asked questions of the airport police and my driver. I thought the sooner I found out what had become of the guy the sooner I could get back to looking for a proper job in football. And there was something about the boat guy I liked which encouraged me to think he might be a bit more forthcoming than the cops and the chauffeur.

'Welcome to Jumby Bay,' he said. 'The island is named after a local word meaning playful spirit. It comprises just forty guest rooms and suites and a collection of villas and estate homes owned by a group of people who are all committed to protecting the environment and several endangered species that still live on the island such as the hawksbill turtle, the white egret, and the Persian black-headed sheep. Everything in Jumby Bay is *su-stain-able*.'

He said it like I should watch out where I put my dirty hands and feet but clearly he liked to talk and I hoped it might not be too much to expect if, having helped me with my luggage, and then into the boat, he also helped me with some information that hadn't been fished out of the resort's guest brochure like the local red mullet.

'It's a long way from home, isn't it? The Persian sheep, I mean. How did it get here, anyway?'

'I don't know, boss.'

'Christopher Columbus, I suppose,' I said, answering my own question. 'Along with horses and syphilis.'

'I suppose you must be right.' The boatman laughed and then clapped his big hands. 'All these years I've been saying it, and I never asked myself what a Persian sheep be doing here in the Caribbean.'

'And a black-headed one, too,' I said. 'There seems to have been a bit of a theme going on here.'

'Hell, yes. You're right.'

'When you think about it, everyone is a guest here. People brought over from Africa to cut the sugar cane – like you and me – a few Europeans, and the Persian black-headed sheep. And the tourists, of course. Strikes me as the people who were first here – the real native Antiguans – are probably long gone.'

'Never thought of it that way. But I guess you're right, boss. Where you from? London?'

'That's right. What's your name?

'Everton.'

'Like the football club?'

'That's right.'

'You like football? I assume your father did. With a name like Everton.'

'He did, that's true. He was from Liverpool. But me, I support Tottenham Hotspur.'

'I'm not sure that answers my question, but never mind. I guess it's lucky your dad didn't support Queen's Park Rangers.'

Everton grinned a big grin.

'Listen, Everton. I've come to Antigua to look for a guy named Jérôme Dumas. He was a guest here at the Jumby Bay over Christmas and New Year. A footballer from France. He's about twenty-two years old, has studs in his ears that look like diamond panther heads and a stupid big watch on his wrist like my one, probably.'

Everton nodded. 'This is the guy the police was looking for, right? The Paris Saint-Germain footballer who's gone missing.'

'That's right.'

'Sure, I remember him. Big gold Rolex Submariner. Lots of gold chains and rings. He got all the best Louis Vuitton luggage. Same as Bono. Give me a pretty good tip for carrying it all, too. Nice fellow. French, you say? Figured him for something else. Reminded me of that other fellow, Mario Balotelli. They say he's Italian, but it's hard to tell these days where a fellow is from. Me, I'm from Jamaica, originally. But ain't no work there. Just trouble. Couldn't figure him renting such a big villa at Jumby Bay given that he was on his own. Couldn't figure you out neither, until you told me what you was doing here. Most guys like you and him come with a nice girl. He didn't look like the type who was into reading and playing chess with hisself.'

'Did the island cops speak to you?'

'Naw. They spoke to the concierge, the hotel manager, and to the ladies who cleaned his villa. But not me.'

'What do you think happened to him?'

'Only a hundred thousand people on Antigua, boss. It ain't so easy to disappear in a little place like this. Even if you is black. Man with Louis Vuitton bags and diamond earrings is like a neon sign on this island, boss. He tends to stand out in the crowd.'

'The police say he checked out of Jumby Bay and went straight to the airport.'

'That's true. I took him there myself. Even carried his bags into the airport building. But he never got on the plane to London.'

'And they didn't speak to you?'

'Like I say, they is a joke.'

'So how was he?'

'He was all right, boss. Didn't seem troubled or nothing. Said he was on his way to play football in Barcelona but that he was going to be training hard because he put some weight on while he was here. I told him that this wasn't unusual, the food at Jumby being so good. Hey, make sure you try the restaurant at the Estate House while you're here, boss. Is Italian cooking. And probably the best in Antigua.'

'You talked?'

'Sure we talked. Talked a lot. He said how much he'd enjoyed himself. The usual. He said he was looking forward to coming back again.'

'He'd been here before? You said "again".'

'Yeah, I reckon he was here about a year ago. Something must have happened at the airport, I reckon.'

'Like what?'

'No idea. Like I say, he seemed fine. I walked him and his luggage into the terminal myself. I left him and his trolley at the newsagent. Reading a newspaper.'

'That's odd.'

'What is?'

'Well, most people buy a paper after they've checked

in. Can you remember which paper it was? Something French? *Libération*? Something to do with football. *L'Equipe*, perhaps?'

'Might have been. Whatever it was he didn't look very happy.'

'I see. What did he do – while he was at Jumby Bay?'

'Ain't much *to* do 'cept lie in the sun, swim, use the spa, watch TV. Jumby Bay is quiet. People come here to get away from it all.'

'What about the main island? Is that quiet, too?'

'They like to party big time there, for sure.'

'So maybe that's where he spent his time. I expect the police will be able to tell me.'

'The RPF?' Everton laughed. 'The RPF don't know shit about nothing.'

The RPFAB was the Royal Police Force of Antigua and Barbuda. I'd sent them some emails and an inspector from the Criminal Investigations Department was expecting me at their headquarters in the island capital of St John's the next day, but I was keen to get Everton's opinion of their competence, or lack of it.

'You don't think much of them.'

'The RPF couldn't find their own balls in a bird bath, boss.'

'Is there much crime here?'

'More than our prime minister would have people believe. But if you keeps away from Gray's Farm on the west side of St John's at night I reckon you be safe enough. Most folks on the island call that place the

Ghetto. It be where you go to score some weed, find a hooker, get yourself shot maybe.'

I nodded. Yep, I thought, that might be just the place someone like Jérôme Dumas would go.

'As a matter of fact, there was a murder on the island while Mr Dumas was here.'

'Oh?'

'Local DJ called Jewel Movement got hisself killed on his boat. They arrested the guy who did it, mind. Caught him red-handed. Even the RPF couldn't fail to catch him. By all accounts they found him with the body. Dead man's blood all over him. According to the cops, the case is cut and dried. Which is just the way the cops like it, of course. I never yet met a policeman who wanted to go looking for a pineapple when he already got a peach.'

'Cops are the same the world over, I guess.'

'Damn right. I wouldn't be surprised if they hang him for it, too.'

'You still hang people here?'

'When we're allowed to, by your English courts. Legal system here allows these bastards to appeal to something called the Judicial Committee of the Privy Council. Whatever that is. You ask me, it's a lot of do-gooders who don't know shit about Antigua.'

I smiled. 'You know the Leeward Islands well, Everton?'

'Like the back of me hand, boss. Got my own boat. I like to go fishing sometimes. When I'm not watching Asot Arcade Parham play football.' He shrugged. 'That's a local side. Pretty good by island standards. Like they're top of the Antigua Premier Division. But not Spurs standard, you know?'

I nodded. 'Tell me something. How easy is it to get from Antigua to Guadeloupe?'

'LIAT – that's the local airline – they operate a flight most days from St John's to Pointe-à-Pitre. A short hop. Half-hour at most. Cost you maybe eighty bucks.'

'If Jérôme Dumas did decide to leave the island, then I'm thinking a boat would be the best way to do it, undetected.'

'Oh sure. All sorts of folk come and go by boat, especially at night. Weed smugglers, mostly. Like DJ Jewel Movement. Word is he moved a bit of grass hisself, sometimes. But why Guadeloupe? Barbuda is nearer. And British, too. You don't have to show your passport there when you land.'

'Because Jérôme Dumas is originally from Guadeloupe.'

'Gotcha. Well now. Ain't no ferry service from here down to there, boss. But I could take you there on my next day off, no problem. Off the books, as it were. Guadeloupe is only a few hours' sailing away.'

'All right. It's a deal. And ask around St John's, will you? Discreetly. See if you can find out if anyone else with a boat might have performed a similarly clandestine ferry service for Jérôme Dumas.'

'Tongues sure wag better when the nose smells cash, boss.'

'True.' I handed over a couple of hundred East Caribbean dollars. 'See how much talk you can get with that, Everton. And keep the rest for yourself.'

Everton throttled back and let the boat drift towards the little wooden jetty where several porters were awaiting our arrival in what resembled a largish birdcage. A little red golf cart took me up to the main part of the hotel where I swiftly checked in and went to my suite, which lay on the other side of an antique gate and at the end of a small private courtyard surrounded with palm trees overlooking the sea. There was an outdoor garden full of frangipani flowers with a rain shower and a tub. It was hard to believe that I was being paid, handsomely, to be here. I sipped my welcome cocktail, switched on the TV and settled down to find out what sports channels they had on cable. You do the important things first, right?

CHAPTER 16

The RPF police station in St John's Newgate Street had seen better days but none of them I'll warrant since the British had left. A yellowing concrete three-storey building with iron bars on the lower windows and a threadbare flag on a crooked white pole in the front courtyard, it looked more like a cheap motel with hot and cold running cockroaches. Close by was the Museum of Antigua and Barbuda but the police station itself might easily have been one of the museum's more interesting exhibits. Everything in there seemed to move at an invisible pace, as if displayed in some dusty glass case. Just around the corner to the east was St John's Cathedral and a girls' high school and a few blocks to the west was the island's deepwater harbour where cruise ships as big as office blocks from places as far afield as Mallorca and Norway were now docked. The girls' school was on its break or its lunch hour. I knew that because through the open windows of the police station you could have heard the girls' screaming and shouting back in Palma and Oslo.

I'd seen the police inspector handling Jérôme's disappearance before – on Google Images. His name was Winchester White. There was a photograph of the island's top-ranking security officials in a meeting about something and, in the picture, it looked a lot like he was asleep. Maybe it was just an unfortunate photograph but, speaking to Inspector White, I quickly gained the impression that he was looking forward to closing his eyes again the minute I'd left his office – not least because there was a large tin of Ovaltine behind his woolly head. He wore a neatly pressed khaki shirt and a pair of matching trousers. His dark, peaked cap lay on the desk in front of him as if he'd been begging for change. Except for the fact that Winchester White was black he looked like the district commissioner from an old *Tarzan* movie. I wouldn't have been at all surprised if he'd had an officer's swagger stick.

'It's not that my employers doubt the efficiency of the RPF,' I said. 'Not for a minute. It's just that they feel they have to be seen to be doing something. In fact, the insurance company is insisting on it. I'm sure you understand how that works. Jérôme Dumas is extremely valuable to both Paris Saint-Germain and FC Barcelona. Not to mention a whole host of companies with whom Mr Dumas has important commercial arrangements to do with his image rights. My intention here is not to step on the RPF's toes but, perhaps, to provide a different perspective on exactly what might have become of him. Please understand, I'm here to assist, not to obstruct.'

This sounded good; shit, it might even have been

true. There are times when I even manage to convince myself. The UN Secretary General himself couldn't have sounded more diplomatic.

'It's not the RPF,' he said dully. 'It's the RPFAB.'

'Right. Thank you.'

'You're forgetting Barbuda.'

'No, I wasn't. I was just giving you some shorthand. So that I didn't waste your valuable time. But my mistake. I can see now that wasn't really important.'

'It's important if you is from Barbuda,' he said. 'Like I am.'

There was a longish silence while the police inspector tasted the inside of his mouth and then scratched an almost invisible pimp moustache before a short coughing fit had him hawking something up, and going to the window to spit. As he moved I caught the strong smell of sweat on his body, like the sharply sour odour of a waxed jacket, and I began for the first time to consider something of the everyday, harsh reality of his life as a policeman on a little tropical island. Against the bright sun he almost disappeared for a moment, like a character on *Star Trek*, before he strolled back to his swivel chair and sat down again amidst a cacophony of creaking wood, imitation leather and professional pride.

'Go ahead and ask your questions,' he said, 'and I'll tell you what I can tell you.'

'Are there any leads you're working on?'

'Not as such, no.'

'Have any bodies been found on the island that have yet to be identified?'

'I don't think he dead, if that's what you mean, Mr Manson. Antigua's a very safe place. Safer than London or Paris.'

'Still, there are murders here, aren't there? DJ Jewel Movement, for example.'

'Murder is rare on the island. We caught the man who killed DJ JM more or less immediately. The whole thing be cut and dried.'

'Yes, yes of course. But actually I was thinking of suicide.'

'Don't do it, Mr Manson.' He grinned. 'You're still a young man with your whole life in front of you.'

I smiled back at him. 'He was prone to depression, you see.'

'What the hell he have to be depressed about when he can afford to stay at Jumby Bay?'

'That's a good question. But of course that's not how depression works. His footballing career in Paris hadn't gone so well. Which is why he was on his way to play for Barcelona. He'd broken up with his girlfriend. And he was taking antidepressants. So, maybe he heard about a favourite suicide spot on the island. You know? A cliff. A beach with a rip tide.'

'You swim far enough you'll meet a shark for sure and then we might never find him. Only, the desk clerk at the hotel said he was in a good mood when he left. Even after he'd paid the bill, which would have depressed me. 'Sides, why go to the airport if you thinking of doing yourself in? It don't make no sense that he should do himself in if he be about to check in and go home. I don't see him packing all his bags and then going for a swim. Also, if you be going to do yourself in you generally leave something behind. Maybe not a note. But possibly your mobile phone. The rest of your stuff. But it ain't just Mr Dumas who is gone, it be all his stuff too.'

'Good point.'

The inspector sighed and waited for me to ask another question. It was beginning to seem as if in spite of my pretty speech he wasn't about to volunteer any information. And I didn't need to find a horse's head at the bottom of my bed in the morning to get the message: me and my Inspector Poirot bullshit really weren't welcome here.

'Are you working on any theories as to what might have happened to Mr Dumas?' I asked.

'Theories? Shit, yeah. Got plenty of those.'

With each reluctant answer I was also aware of the dust on the floor, the chewed pencil on the desk, the brimful ashtray, the open door which, alongside the ceiling fan, was the room's only air conditioning, and the many advantages of my own life compared with his. As he'd suggested, the bill I was very likely going to generate at the Jumby Bay Hotel would probably be as much as a cop like him made in a year. Sometimes you had to wonder how it was that more tourists in a place like that didn't come to a sticky end. Quite what the inspector would have made of Jérôme's more obviously luxury lifestyle – which was there for all to see in the latest edition of GQ that was on the coffee table in my suite – I could only imagine.

I waited for a long moment and then asked: 'Might I ask what these are?'

'I personally am of the strong belief that the man was snatched from VC Bird Airport minutes after he arrived there at the end of his holiday. That someone figure he be a man with lots of money. Like all of you folks at Jumby Bay. But unlike most of the folk who go holidaying in Jumby we happen to know he went to some bad boy clubs in St John's that is frequented by drug traffickers. For that reason we think he came up on their radar as someone who might be worth kidnapping. And that they persuaded some girl to entice him away from there. I am of the opinion that he probably be held somewhere in the centre of the island. Signal Hill, perhaps. That they be looking to deliver a ransom request when they think it a bit safer than now. And that they be keeping their heads down for fear that we be catchin' them. Fact is, I got my men searching the whole island looking for this young fellow and I am confident that we find him any day now. It's just a question of time, see? Everything on Antigua take a bit longer than it does back in England. But rest assured, sir, that if he's on the island, we will find him.'

I nodded. 'What clubs are they – the bad boy clubs you were talking about?'

'I wouldn't recommend you go to any, Mr Manson. We got enough trouble as it is with one missing tourist.'

'Nevertheless, I would like to know the names. For my report, you understand.'

He nodded. 'All right. There's a place off the Old

Road on Signal Hill that's called The Rum Runner. They smoke a lot of weed, get drunk on canita, run their whores, watch football and porn on TV. The satnav on an Enterprise Car that Mr Dumas hired showed he'd been there. He was also near a brothel in Freetown that's widely known as the Treehouse.'

'And have you questioned the people there?'

'Questioned, sure. Didn't get no answers. Didn't expect to get any, neither. RPFAB ain't welcome in they places. People tend to clam up when we start asking questions.'

'Perhaps if we were to offer a reward. Say a thousand dollars.'

'Here's the thing about rewards, Mr Manson. As I told your employers in Paris they're not a substitute for good old-fashioned police work. They waste my time. A high income on the island is thirteen thousand US dollars. People say anything in search of a reward which is as much as what you're suggesting. For a thousand dollars I myself would tell you I saw the man abducted by aliens. Ya see what I is saying? I just don't have the men to separate the time-wasters from what might be a genuine lead. So keep your money quiet, please.'

I tried another tack. 'You've considered the possibility that he's no longer on the island, of course.'

'Sure. We've been checking out private airfields, boat-yards all over Antigua. Believe me, sir, we leaving no stone unturned in the search for this man. I call you as soon as I find something. My advice to you is go back to your comfortable hotel and sit by the telephone.'

I wasn't going to do that, although he was right, of course. I was merely playing at what he was doing professionally, 365 days a year. He did it because he had to do it, in order to make a living. He knew it and I now I knew it; and, as I was leaving his office, I reflected how polite he'd been. I might easily have laughed if Winchester White had turned up in my office posing as a football manager, and yet here he was, listening patiently while I asked my very obvious questions. I felt appalled at myself and decided then and there that this was going to be the last time I was ever persuaded to play the joke role of amateur detective.

I thanked him for his time and walked out the door. In a little waiting area outside his office was an attractive, well-dressed woman in her early thirties who, seeing Winchester White, stood up, politely. A black Burberry briefcase sat on the floor by her polished black shoes. In spite of the heat her white blouse looked as clean and fresh as the tablecloth I'd had on my table at breakfast time.

As she smiled at me I realised she must have heard every word I'd said to the police inspector.

Not that there are many secrets on an island the size of Antigua.

CHAPTER 17

I went back to the hotel and found myself sitting by the phone.

It wasn't because I was awaiting a call from Inspector Winchester White – I wasn't holding my breath for that – but because I couldn't think of anything else to do. Ordinarily, in a place like Jumby Bay, I'd have swum in my private pool, sat in the sun, ordered a cocktail and read a book, probably. But that didn't sit right with me while I was taking money from the club. Especially as they weren't having the best season. And things had only been made worse by the departures of goalkeeper Andoni Zubizarreta and the club captain, defender Carles Puyol. Meanwhile there was a lot of talk on the sports pages that Chelsea would make a move for Lionel Messi in the summer. There were few who doubted that Roman Abramovich had the money and the balls to afford the £156.7 million buyout on the Argentine's contract (not including image rights and salary). Not that UEFA FFP restrictions would have permitted such a transfer. Probably. But it came as a surprise to me that Viktor Sokolnikov was also talking about trying to bring Messi to the Crown of Thorns. And the thought that I'd walked away from a great football club where I might have had a chance to manage a player who was probably the best footballer in the world left me feeling a little blue.

So when the phone did ring I thought it might be someone from Barcelona, PSG, or even a Qatari calling to enquire how things were going and if I'd yet discovered anything useful. I wouldn't have known what to say. To my relief it was just Everton – the Jumby Bay boatman.

'Hey, boss, I looked you up on the internet. You is famous. You played for Arsenal. And you managed London City. I was thinking, while you're here maybe you could come down to take a look at a youth side I work with. They call theirselves the Yepton Beach Cane Cutters. Give they a few tips.'

'Maybe. Perhaps later when I've done what I'm supposed to be doing. I'm a little busy right now. The Catalans they're anxious to have Jérôme Dumas back in Barcelona before *el clásico*. I take it you know what that is?'

'For sure. It's like the most important match in Spain, right? Listen, boss, I flashed some of your money around St John's but so far come up with nuthin'. I reckon anyone who knows anything about what happened to Jérôme Dumas is going to want a lot more than just a hundred bucks.'

For a moment I remembered the inspector's words about the effect of money on people who didn't have very much and how they might start to invent stories they thought I might like to hear. I hate it when cops are proved right.

'I think that I should be there if that happens.'

'Sure, boss. Maybe we can meet this afternoon. There's a bar on Nevis Street called Joe's. I finish work at four today. Shall we meet then?'

Minutes later, the telephone rang again.

'Mr Manson? My name is Grace Doughty and I'm a lawyer at Dice & Company. We almost met today at the police station in St John's.'

'I remember. You're the lady with the Burberry briefcase and the nice shoes.'

'You noticed that.'

'I pay a lot of attention to someone's feet. Always have.'

'I couldn't help but overhear what you were saying to Inspector White. I hope you won't think this presumptuous of me, but I wanted to offer you my firm's help in finding Mr Dumas.'

'That all depends on what kind of help you had in mind.'

'Perhaps I could come and see you at your hotel?'

I glanced at my watch. It wasn't like I had anything else to do. If nothing else you'll get a better feel for how things are here, I told myself. Besides, it always helps to have a lawyer handy when you're nosing around in foreign countries.

'No need. I'm going to be in St John's this afternoon. Besides, if you're going to help me I'd like to see what kind of front you put up.'

'Shall we say three o'clock? I'm at twenty Nevis Street.'

'I'll be there.'

The quaint colonial buildings that made up Nevis Street in St John's were Creole-style cottages with wooden pillars, small verandas and shingle roofs. As I approached the wooden steps that led up to the front door of number twenty I half expected to see a swinging seat or a rocking chair. Some of these buildings were red, some were green, a few were pink or yellow and none was higher than a lamp-post; all of them were quite dwarfed by an enormous cruise liner, several storeys high, that was moored to the pier at the end of the street, and which towered over them like a Westfield shopping centre that had come adrift from its inner-city foundations and lost its way before washing up here in Antigua. Dice & Co was located in a pink building with yellow shutters and an orange roof from which a spaghetti tangle of cables and wires led across the street to a telephone cable in front of a Seventh Day Adventist Church that looked more like a police station than the police station.

I went inside and found myself in a near-perfect facsimile of a Dickensian lawyer's office, right down to the floor-to-ceiling bookshelves filled with the *All England Law Reports*. There was a big leather chesterfield in the waiting room, a landscape picture of King John signing the Magna Carta and several portraits of geriatric English judges wearing full-bottomed wigs. All the place lacked for an English legal atmosphere was a freezing fog rubbing on the window panes.

The receptionist ushered me straight into her employer's office where the tone of the decor changed a little. There were two photographs on the wall of Grace Doughty wearing a karate suit; she seemed to hold a black belt which must have helped to persuade some of her clients to behave themselves – at least when they were with her. I expect they needed reminding, too, as Miss Doughty was a real looker. She was black but I figured she was also what is sometimes described as high yellow in that she must have had a large proportion of white ancestry. She wore a navy-blue jacket and skirt, a crisp white blouse and was as voluptuous as a Mexican bass guitar. I knew there had been another reason why I'd wanted to see her in person, and this was it.

'Miss Doughty, this is Mr Scott Manson,' said the receptionist.

Miss Doughty got up and came around her desk with brown eyes that were already sizing me up. She had the look of a woman who was destined for higher things, at least in Antigua.

'Pleased to meet you,' I said.

I was just about to shake her outstretched hand when the giant cruise ship sounded its massive horn which, on that small quiet island street, sounded like the final trumpet blown at the day of judgement or, at the very least, an irate mastodon.

'Jesus Christ,' I said, shrinking into the collar of my polo shirt. 'Do they do that very often?'

She laughed. 'Only every day. You get used to it.'

The horn sounded again and seemed to linger in the air long afterwards.

'I don't think I would. I bet the young mothers of St John's just love that.'

'This is a sleepy little place. It helps to keep us awake.'

'I guess so.'

'I've just been reading about you, as you can see.' She pointed at her leather-topped partner's desk where, on a laptop, I saw my Wikipedia entry displayed on screen. 'It seems that you and I went to the same university.'

'On an island as small as this that makes us practically related,' I said.

She laughed again. 'I think so. And I think we must have overlapped by a year.'

'I'd like to say I remember something like that, but I don't.'

What was wrong with the men on Antigua? To let a woman as fine as this one go unclaimed. She wasn't even wearing an engagement ring.

'Please. Sit down. Would you like some tea?'

'English tea?'

'What else would I offer someone who went to Birmingham University?' she said.

'You make it sound like the Old Vicarage, Grantchester.'

'It was for a girl like me. I loved every minute.'

Mrs Doughty looked at the secretary still hovering in the doorway. 'Tracy, would you bring us all some tea and biscuits please?'

'Is that where you got your LLB? At Birmingham?'

'That's right.'

'You didn't ever want to stay on in England and practise there?'

'Too cold,' she said. 'And too wet.'

'You got that right.' I smiled, liking her own smile which matched the string of white pearls around her neck and trying to keep my eyes off the Grand Canyon-deep fissure of cleavage that lay close to it.

'And the interest in karate? Where did that come from?'

'Oh that. At Birmingham, too. I was into a lot of sports there. I even played a bit of women's football. And supported Aston Villa.'

'Someone's got to, I suppose.'

'Hey, just a few years before I started my LLB they finished sixth in the table. If they hadn't sold Dwight Yorke to Manchester United they might have finished even higher. Somehow the purchase of Paul Merson never quite made up for that. He was good but never as good as Yorkie.'

I made a quick *Question of Sport* guess. 'That must be the 1998–99 season you're talking about.'

She nodded.

'At one point – Christmas – we were top of the Premier League. They'll come good again, I feel sure of it,' she said.

We chatted like this until the tea arrived but as soon as it was served I tried to bring her to the point of me being there.

'So, Miss Doughty, what makes you think you can help me find Jérôme Dumas?'

'Just so as we're clear here. You *are* looking for him?'

'It would seem pointless denying it after you heard everything I said to Inspector White.'

'And that you're acting in the interests of FC Barcelona.'

'Not just them. Paris Saint-Germain, too. Strictly speaking, he's still their player, on loan to FCB.'

'Last of all, is it your intention when you've found Jérôme Dumas to take him straight back to Europe?'

'Yes. It is. The season is well under way and he's needed to bolster their chances of winning the league. There's an important match coming up against Madrid and they'd like him back well before that so that he's truly match-fit.'

'Then I'm certain I can help you to find him.'

'That's great. But before I say "you're hired" can I ask if your certainty is based on something better than just the same kind of optimism that says Aston Villa will come good again?'

'It is. I can't be too specific at this stage but I can tell you that the help I'm offering isn't just from me. It comes from a reliable source. My client. Who wishes to remain anonymous at this stage.'

'Is this someone who's looking for a generous payday? Because I should warn you I'm only authorised to pay any kind of reward when Mr Dumas is safely back in Barcelona.'

'On the contrary. My client asks for no money at all.'

'I like him already. Do you know where he is? Mr Dumas?'

'No. I don't. And nor does my client. But he does know where he might be. To that extent you will still have to go and look for him. But at least now you'll know that you're looking in the right place.'

'I thought I was in the right place.'

'Not yet, you aren't. Look, I'm sorry to be so cryptic, Mr Manson. But you really will have to trust me on this.'

'Perhaps if I knew some more about your client...'

'And if I gave you a name, how would that help you? In fact, I can promise you that it wouldn't help you at all. It would only slow you down. And we don't want that, do we? My understanding is that you want to return to Europe with Jérôme Dumas as quickly as possible and with a minimum of publicity. Am I right?'

'Yes.'

'Then I think you have no option but to put your faith in me and my firm.'

Tracy, the receptionist, arrived back in the office with a tray bearing a teapot and china plates and saucers. Grace Doughty poured and I took a cup from her unringed hand.

'The tea is good,' I said. 'Just like home.'

'I'm pleased you like it.'

'Suppose I take your advice and don't find Jérôme Dumas. I'll have wasted my time here. Which is limited. Suppose what your client really wants is to sell me a dummy. To put me off the scent. Then where will I be?'

'But if there was any scent to be found in this case, as you put it, you wouldn't be sitting in my office drinking tea, would you?'

'Not yet, perhaps. But I've a good nose. And I can generally find my way around.'

'Oh, I can readily believe that. Thanks to the English tabloids you've made quite a name for yourself as something of an amateur detective. The sleuth of Silvertown Dock. Isn't that what the *Daily Express* called you? This time last year, wasn't it? But we both know that isn't going to work here.'

'Since you studied law in England then you'll know that the tabloids have a habit of exaggerating almost everything, Miss Doughty. They almost never allow the facts to obscure a good story. You're right. I'm not a detective. Nor have I ever been. It was more sheer luck than Sherlock that enabled me to solve the murder of João Zarco.'

'Nevertheless, someone else thought enough of those talents to send you all the way down here to look for a missing person, didn't they?'

'I wouldn't read too much into that, if were you, Miss Doughty. They had to do something. For form's sake. Not to mention for the sake of Mr Dumas. They're worried something might have happened to him. Everyone is. That's why I'm here. To make sure everything possible is being done. But no one is expecting me to work a miracle.' I paused and sipped my tea. 'Can you at least assure me that he's still alive?'

'He's alive. I'm certain of that much, anyway.'

'I see. Well, that's the best news I've had since I came here.'

'Look, why don't you give it twenty-four hours? See

what happens. If after that you've not found Jérôme Dumas you can go back to trusting your own nose. But I don't think my client will mind me mentioning that his interests are also served by the swift return of Jérôme Dumas to Barcelona.'

'Now I really am intrigued about your client.' I knew there were a few famous footballers who had a house on the island – Andriy Shevchenko, for one – but I could see no earthly reason why any of them would have been interested in sheltering Jérôme Dumas. 'All right,' I said. 'I agree. So what happens now?'

'Go back to your hotel and await a phone call.'

'You sound like Winchester White. I don't think he liked me.' I felt my eyes narrow as I looked at her. 'You two aren't in cahoots, are you?'

'Why would you think that?'

'Because he might have left the door of his office open deliberately? So that you could eavesdrop on our conversation? Because he didn't strike me as the careless type.'

'My, you are suspicious. No, he and I are not in cahoots. If you remember I wasn't actually there when you arrived. I got there after you. And I was there to discuss a quite different matter. In my experience, Inspector White always leaves his door open. Not least because it's hot and he doesn't have any air conditioning like my own office. But since you have mentioned him I should also add that my client has not shared any information with him regarding the whereabouts of Jérôme Dumas. This is an exclusive arrangement which hurts no one since Mr Dumas hasn't committed a crime on the island. So you're not likely to get into trouble either, if that's what you were worried about.'

'It wasn't. And I don't mind a certain amount of trouble.'

'I can imagine.'

'I was referring to the kind of trouble that comes with being a football manager. When you're in charge of a squad of twenty-four overpaid, oversexed, overexcited young men, shit happens. That's the real reason PSG and FCB sent me down here. Because I've been a young footballer myself. I know the game. And I know the pressures of the game. I think they thought that if I did manage to find Jérôme Dumas, I could speak his language and persuade him to come home.'

'Let's hope so. Okay. That's it. For now. I'll be in touch just as soon as I've spoken again to my client.'

'And when will that be?'

'Soon. I'll call you tonight. Will you be at your hotel?'

I nodded.

Everton was seated on the wooden steps of the bar where we'd agreed to meet, smoking a roll-up and awaiting my arrival. Seeing me, he quickly stubbed out the cigarette, dropped it into the pocket of his white shorts for later, stood up and enveloped my hand in his own leathery paw as if we'd been ghetto buddies at a barbecue.

I told him about Miss Doughty.

'What kind of a lawyer is she anyway?' he asked.

'The good-looking kind.'

'No, I meant, what kind of law does she practise?'

'I dunno. The kind that represents criminals in court, I guess. What other kind is there?'

'Is she the greedy kind of lawyer? Or just the dishonest kind of lawyer?'

'That remains to be seen. But she was kind of persuasive.'

'Oh, that kind of lawyer.'

'Yes. Exactly.'

'Well,' said Everton, 'it sure couldn't harm you to go along with what she says. Not for twenty-four hours. Man, it takes people twenty-four hours just to order a bloody taxi on this island. Strikes me you'll get further with her than I have speaking to local boatmen.'

He handed me back some money.

'Here, boss. You better have this.'

'Then you'd better let me buy you a drink.'

We went into the bar, ordered a couple of the local beers and sat in the window. We hadn't been there very long when I saw Grace Doughty walking up the street. She was carrying her Burberry briefcase.

'That's her. That's the lady lawyer I was talking about.'

'Man, that is a fine-looking woman.'

'You think?'

'When you said she was a lawyer I was thinking of someone playing on a rubber tyre at the end of a chain. But that lady is hot, boss.'

Everton was right. The woman had more curves than a bag full of footballs. If I stayed on Antigua I knew I was going to have to put my hand in that particular bag, regardless of the consequences. If only I knew what she was up to, who her client was, where this was all going. I had to find out more about Grace Doughty.

I handed Everton the money he'd just handed back to me.

'Look, Everton, why don't you follow her? See where she goes. Who she knows. It might give me a better idea of what this is all about.'

'Sure thing, boss. Anything you say. Following pretty girls – I'm an expert.' Everton stood up and drained his beer bottle. 'But you know, it strikes me that maybe she can keep you company while you is looking for this guy. You could do worse than her for female company right now. A man needs a bit of female company in the tropics. Maybe you should give her a ring and ask her to dinner at Jumby Bay. Get to know her better. Then maybe you can learn to trust her better, too.'

Everton was right about that too but nevertheless I spent the evening alone, festering with irritation and resentment at my appointed task. I felt as if I'd been left on the bench after an extended Christmas break had left a question mark over my fitness and all I really wanted to do was play football, regardless of the consequences for my hamstrings. Come to think of it, that's how I feel most of the time. It's like there's a football-sized hole in my life which I don't think anything, not even management, is ever going to be able to fill. Certainly not searching the jungle for some stupid kid who couldn't handle the pressure. If that's what had caused him to disappear. After what Grace Doughty had told me in her office I'd stopped believing that anything bad could have happened to Jérôme Dumas. I almost wished that it had.

A brick-faced couple from Birmingham eating dinner at the next table in the softly lit robbery that was being perpetrated in the hotel's swish restaurant were looking as bored as a pair of Staffordshire dogs on a chimney-less mantelpiece. They must have wondered what the hell they were doing there. I know I did. Meanwhile, an electric piano trio worked its way stolidly through a repertoire that had been inspired by the elevator muzak in an Arndale shopping centre. At that particular moment my world – the world of football – seemed to be more than an ocean away and if the chairman of Tranmere Rovers had called to offer me a job managing the club, I'd have taken his fucking arm off.

CHAPTER 18

It sounded good. The part about Tranmere Rovers. But it wasn't entirely true. Over a swift dinner with my iPad I checked my email and there was one from Qatar offering me a job working with the national side, which must have seemed urgent after their recent exit from the Asian Cup in Canberra. The 4–1 defeat they'd suffered at the hands of their most bitter rivals, the United Arab Emirates, would have been especially hard to bear for the Qataris. But try as I might I couldn't see myself doing a Don Revie and coaching football in the desert any more than I can see a World Cup being played there in the summer of 2022. Nobody can. They'd have more chance of mounting an ice-hockey tournament. But it wasn't just that. It was the way all of these Arab countries treated women. I like women. A lot. Paolo Gentile couldn't have been more on target about my Achilles heel if he'd hit it with an arrow.

Then there was an email from Tempest asking when I was going to be back in the UK. I'd been summoned to appear before the FA to face a charge of bringing the game into disrepute because of my stupid tweet about Rafinha having his period. I replied to her that I honestly didn't know when I'd be back but that obviously I'd agree to meet with them as soon as I was in London. So that was something to look forward to. If it wasn't so irritating it would be laughable.

I also had an email from Mandel in Paris. Attached was a copy of the Paris police report on the murder in Sevran-Beaudottes: a drug dealer had been found shot dead less than two hundred metres from the Alain Savary Sports Centre. There had been no arrests and there were no suspects, but there was a clue: the dead man had been found with a bloodstained satin patch in his hand. On the patch was a Gothic letter D. And I couldn't help thinking that this was the same patch missing from a T-shirt modelled by Jérôme Dumas in a magazine and which was now being worn by another drug-dealer in Sevran. All of which might have been a pretty good reason to leave Paris and not come back.

My mobile phone rang, which was a surprise since the signal was up and down like a yo-yo. It was Everton.

'I done followed that lady like you asked, boss.'

'And?'

'After we saw her outside the bar on Nevis Street, I tailed her east for a couple of blocks onto Independence Avenue, and then Coronation Avenue. She went to the local jail, boss. HMP St John's, Antigua. She was there for almost an hour, after which she went to a travel agent on Nevis Street, and then to a place in Jolly Harbour. I followed her in me own car. Jolly Harbour is about fifteen minutes' drive southwest of St John's. She lives in a nice apartment close to the golf course which is a game she plays because there was a full set of clubs in the back seat of her car. She lives alone, I reckon. There's only her name on the bell. I was about to call you from a bar in Jolly Harbour when she went out again. And I followed her all the way to the ferry dock.'

'The ferry dock. Where's that?'

'The ferry dock for Jumby Bay, boss. There's one every hour. I figure she's on her way to see you. She's on the boat now. Be there in less than five minutes, I'd say.'

'I'm not expecting her.'

Everton laughed. 'Looks like that lady has got other ideas. Maybe you is going to have some female company tonight after all, eh?'

I left my room and went down to the lobby, hid myself behind a banana plant and waited. A minute or two later Grace Doughty came in through the door of the hotel, looking a little less formal than when she'd been in the office. She was wearing a pink skirt and jeans, with a pair of matching blue, high-heeled sandals that helped to show off her shapely legs. At the front desk, she spoke to the concierge, handed him a manila envelope and headed out of the front door again. And because she was wearing heels I had plenty of time to collect the envelope from the concierge and catch her up on the pathway to the jetty.

'You were leaving the ground without shaking hands? That's an Aston Villa supporter for you, I suppose. You and Paul Lambert both.'

She frowned.

'He's the current Villa manager,' I explained.

She smiled thinly. 'I didn't want to disturb your dinner.'

'Had that. Believe me, with just my iPad for company it didn't take very long.'

'The restaurant's supposed to be very nice.'

'It is. I suppose.'

'Albeit very expensive.'

'Yes it is. Still, it's an expensive mail service you're running here at sixty bucks for the ferry trip.'

'Actually it didn't cost me anything because I said I'd be coming straight back. I wanted to make absolutely sure that got into your hands tonight.'

'Well now that you're here, why not stay for drink?'

We went into the bar where I ordered some wine. 'Thank God you came,' I said. 'Now I can justify ordering something good. It never seems worth it when you're on your own.'

'I know that feeling.'

'You live alone?'

'Divorced. Husband's a lawyer, too. Which isn't a good recipe for matrimonial harmony.'

'I think it beats marrying a footballer. I was never a good husband.'

'That's a fairly common mistake.'

'What's this?' I asked staring at the envelope.

'An air ticket, to Pointe-à-Pitre.'

'Where's that?'

'Guadeloupe.'

'Is that where I'm going?'

'First thing tomorrow morning. We both are. I felt I should accompany you. As a sign of my good faith. To help you find Jérôme Dumas. Besides, it's a short flight and I thought you might need someone along who speaks French and Creole.'

'And is this on the say-so of someone in the local nick? Your secret client perhaps.'

'So, it seems that you do have a good nose after all.'

'I like to know who I'm dealing with. Especially when it turns out to be a criminal.'

'I didn't know you were so particular,' said Grace. 'Given your own penal history.'

'Is that on Wikipedia, too?'

'Yes. It is. You've had an interesting life, Mr Manson.'

'Scott. If we're going to be travelling together we should call each other by our first names, don't you think?'

'You are going then? To Pointe-à-Pitre?'

'I don't think I have much choice. Right now, yours is the only game in town. So I may as well play along. Three points would be nice, but I'll settle for a no-score-draw. Finding out just where he is right now would be almost as good as meeting him in person.'

'Have you met him before?'

'No.'

'So why did they send you and not someone he knows?'

'I might be wrong about this but the people he's met already aren't too impressed with him. In fact, not knowing him might actually be an advantage.'

'Is that why PSG loaned him to Barcelona?'

'Probably.'

'Was he in any kind of trouble?'

'In Paris? Yes, he might have been. I'm not sure.'

The waiter arrived with the wine; I sniffed it carefully and then nodded at him to pour.

I clinked glasses with Grace affably; she tasted the wine and added her appreciation.

'Incidentally,' she said, 'it's worth mentioning that while my client may be in prison at the moment, that doesn't make him a criminal. Actually, he's on remand. That means he's innocent until proved guilty. Although to be quite frank with you that's the part of English justice that continues to elude me. You arrest a man, charge him, throw him in prison for months and months, and only then do you bring him to trial. Some of my clients have been waiting to come to trial for more than a year. That might be permissible in England where the prisons have to conform to European standards, but here, on Antigua, it's nothing short of a disgrace.'

'Believe me, Wandsworth nick isn't Jumby Bay. And it's eighteen months of my life I won't ever get back. Especially as those eighteen months might have been the best I'll ever know. I was playing for Arsenal when it happened and it doesn't get much better than that. Not for me.'

'I'd have thought management could be a lot of fun.'

'There's nothing that's as much fun as playing. Take my word for it. And it's best you do. That way I can spare you a lot of the clichés about football. I tend to suffer from those the way normal people have dandruff.'

'I'll certainly let you know if I get bored in that way. I'm the female equivalent of Head n' Shoulders.'

I opened the envelope and found an open return ticket to Guadeloupe. But that was all there was in the envelope. 'What, no suggestions for where to look? No addresses? No names? I thought that was the deal. Unless he's hiding at the airport.'

'I wish he was.'

Grace tapped her head and as she lifted her arm I caught a strong scent of her perfume, which did little to dissuade me from finding her attractive.

'They're all in here. Oh, don't worry, Scott, this little magical mystery tour won't take us long. Guadeloupe isn't very big. And it's a dump, too. Frankly, the less time we have to spend there the better. The airport is the best thing on the island. That's not a joke. If Guadeloupe was half as nice as Antigua the British wouldn't have let France have it. There's certainly nowhere like Jumby Bay on the island. It's probably the least charming island in the Caribbean and is full of French people who can't afford to go to St Barts. About the only thing on Guadeloupe which is better is the education system, which ranks among the best in the whole of France.'

'You know the island well?'

'I used to go on holiday there, for a while, when I was a child. But originally I'm from Montserrat, which is a little island just south of here. My mother was from Antigua, which is how I came to live here. What about you? What's your background?'

I told her about my Scots father and my black German mother.

'That's quite a mixture,' she said.

'I sometimes wonder where the black part of me originated.' I grinned. 'I know it's not Scotland. That's been pointed out to me more times than I care to remember. The Scots aren't exactly known for their sensitivity in matters regarding race. Or about anything else, for that matter. But now and again, I'd really like to know where my ancestors came from. Which part of Africa, you know?'

'You can't help that when you're in the Caribbean. It comes with the territory. My great-great-grandfather was white. But whether that means he owned my great-great-grandmother I'm not sure.' She shrugged. 'I'm not even sure it matters. Not any more. The slavery thing, I mean. When I lived in Birmingham I used to get pretty worked up about things like that, but not now. Life's too short. And me, I'm such a mixture of races that it would probably take the CERN particle accelerator to separate all of my atoms out and say where they came from.'

'You got that right.'

'It's ironic though. The way rich Europeans bring the descendants of the young black men they used to transport across the Atlantic to the Caribbean to work on sugar plantations, to play football in places like Liverpool, Lisbon and Lagos. Those were the centres of the European slave market.'

'Not just the Caribbean,' I said. 'There are plenty coming straight from Africa, too, these days. But it seems especially true of Guadeloupe. Half the French team would seem to hail from Guadeloupe. Why is that, do you think?'

'I think maybe you'll have a better idea after you've been to the island.'

'You know, I wish I'd met you when we were in the overlap, at Birmingham University. I might have enjoyed it a bit more.'

'I bet you did all right with the girls.'

'I was a pig.'

She smiled patiently. 'You wouldn't have liked me. I was always working in the library. Law is rather demanding in that respect.'

'I like libraries. Just because I work in football doesn't mean I don't read. I might have worked a bit harder myself if I'd known you. You might have inspired me. I think I had it rather easy in comparison with you. It must have taken a lot to get yourself there from somewhere like here.'

'I've no complaints.'

'No, you're not the type to complain. I like that, too.'

'Anything else? You're doing well. And I'm in the mood for compliments.'

'You like to hear them, I guess. But I doubt you take any of them that seriously. It strikes me you already have a pretty good idea of who and what you are. Someone else's affirmation isn't of much importance to you. And you can take that as a compliment.'

'That's three in a row. Means you get a prize.'

'Oh, what's that?'

'You get to buy me another drink.'

We talked some more, and then Grace said she should probably go.

'I'll walk you down to the ferry,' I said, signed the bill and stood up, expectantly.

'Good manners, too,' she said. 'How I've missed that in a man.'

'You can thank my mother.'

Grace stayed put in her chair.

'What's wrong?' I asked.

'I only said I should go,' she said. 'Not that I am going. There's a subtle difference between the preterite form of "shall" and the present progressive tense. Especially when it comes to sex.'

'That sounds like a lawyer's argument.'

'It is. But as it happens I'm a little easier to persuade than an English jury where you're concerned. Then again, I am biased. I didn't expect to like you. A lot.' She smiled. 'Don't look so shocked, Scott. I'm a single woman. And I'm not in a relationship. Nor likely to be either. The men on this island leave a lot to be desired. At least by me. I'm not about to share everything I've worked hard to get for myself so that I can support some lazy good-for-nothing who stays home, drinking beer and watching cricket on television all day. I have the example of my mother and my father to know that's not for me. Slavery may have been abolished but believe me, it still exists in thousands of homes all across the Caribbean. Uncomplicated sex suits me just fine for the moment. Of course, if you'd rather not then just say so. I won't be offended. Like all lawyers I have one safe place to keep the cash box and important documents, and another for my feelings.'

I sat down again and took her hand. 'Just one thing. Even if you don't always understand them you'll have to allow me the odd sporting metaphor in bed. You see, for any Englishman, football, not poetry, is the gold standard for metaphors about sex and love. Without football no Englishman would even know how to make love. And I always sing when I'm winning.'

CHAPTER 19

There were several things about Guadeloupe that reminded me strongly of France: the autoroutes, the cars, the number plates on the cars, the postal vans, the occasional Casino, and the airport, of course, which, like the road to England from Scotland, was perhaps the island's most impressively modern and inviting feature. But as soon as we left the airport and the main highways things turned more ramshackle. Nature was rampant, as if the lush tropical vegetation itself was in the process of staging some irresistible green revolution against the march of civilisation – although on Guadeloupe civilisation was less of a march and more of a slow, barefoot, sideways shuffle. Indeed, the island seemed to be trying to push mankind and all of his pathetic and unwelcome structures back into the sea from where they had originated. Palm trees grew out of abandoned buildings and bushes flourished on rooftops like hundreds of eco-friendly satellite dishes. Old wooden planters' mansions on fire with banana leaves and which were little more than tottering façades, looked like the forgotten sets from a Hollywood movie. As your eyes passed over their once elegant lines you half expected to see Stanley Kowalski appear on the street and drunkenly howl 'Stella!' with frustrated desire at one of the padlocked upper doors and windows. And if all that wasn't enough for the islanders to contend with, there was the occasional earthquake as well – the most recent a 5.6 magnitude less than two months ago.

Pavements that were greasy with dirt and cracked with the relentless heat of the sun looked like trays of toffee and were almost as sticky. Fence posts and gates collapsing because of the damp and the voracious appetites of many insects resembled driftwood that, at any moment, might find its way back into the sea that seemed never very far away. There was salt in the hot air and on almost everything else, like a hoar frost. Large pelicans wheeled across the sandy beaches like pterodactyls before dive-bombing the waves for fish and one had the feeling that at any moment a dinosaur might have lumbered noisily out of the trees, crushing several shacks underfoot before eating a small 4x4, or perhaps a dozing Rasta man. Crickets whistled away in the bushes like the wheels of a dozen rusty wheelbarrows. Dogs dozed in doorways and on street corners with only the twitch of a flea-bitten ear or the slight ripple in a ribcage to persuade you that they were not fresh roadkill.

In the central square of Pointe-à-Pitre there was a spice market that was about as picturesque as a cheap tea-towel and just as small, where none of the so-called traders seemed to care very much if anyone bought anything or not. I've seen more obvious enterprise in a hospice for the chronically ill. Here and there were a few traces of former French elegance; a fountain, the bronze statue of some forgotten Gallic hero, an ignored wall plaque; otherwise a guillotine might have seemed more in keeping with the look of the place. It was indeed like a Devil's Island without Papillon, a penal colony bereft of convicts, although the many aimless French tourists who had recently disembarked from the two cruise ships now docked in the harbour of Pointe-à-Pitre seemed as if they might have been sent there as a punishment. With their pale skins, backpacks and ugly, shapeless sportswear they had the bewildered look of men and women who were uncomfortably far from home and true justice. Certainly there was nothing attractive in the shops of this unlikely capital that might have made any of them glad to be here. Even the local graffiti seemed to lack style.

But while the island and its buildings were less than attractive the same could not be said of the indigenous people. With the exception of a bearded lady I saw eating garbage off the street and the fat hookers inhabiting the shanties on the western edge of the town, the Guadeloupeans themselves were altogether more noble in appearance. Some of them were astonishingly beautiful and looking at them it was easy to understand how it was that this island of less than half a million inhabitants could have produced such fine-looking men as Thierry Henry, Lilian Thuram, William Gallas and Sylvain Wiltord. All of the islanders spoke French but to each other they spoke Creole, which is a mixture of French and Spanish and as different from normal French as Welsh is from English. I can speak both French and Spanish and yet I couldn't understand a word of Creole – it made me glad that Grace had insisted on accompanying me. There was that and the fact that she was great in bed, which may have been the best reason why we decided to check into a local hotel and base our search from there, at least for one night.

'The Auberge de la Vieille Tour doesn't begin to compare with Jumby Bay or any of the better places on Antigua,' explained Grace as we arrived at the hotel in Le Gosier, to the east of Pointe-à-Pitre, 'but it's the best of a bad lot. Believe me, we could do a lot worse. I'm told that there are times when the food here is almost edible. Besides, it's quite close to the spot where we're going to commence our search for Jérôme Dumas.'

Built around an old eighteenth-century windmill and occupying three hectares of tropical gardens on the edge of the Caribbean, the hotel resembled one from a very old Bond movie, *Thunderball* or *Live and Let Die*, perhaps, and, in lieu of a bottle opener, whenever we were there I was looking around for a man called Tee Hee with a steel claw for an arm. I could equally have used a steel-claw-type arm for a telephone aerial as the mobile signal on the island was almost non-existent, as was the whole concept of service with a smile. The Guadeloupeans may have been a handsome people but they weren't in the least bit interested in giving customer satisfaction. In the hotel some of them were just rude.

Which drew the scorn of my female companion.

'They've got no idea how to run a hotel or a restaurant,' she said. 'Which is odd considering that this is part of France. I mean, you'd think they'd have learned a bit about food and hotel-keeping from the French.'

'Why is that?'

'Perhaps it's something to do with their dislike of the so-called Mother Country,' she said. 'They'd certainly like to be independent of France. So perhaps their rejection of French cuisine and decent hotel service is a corollary of that. Either way, I always feel rather sorry for all those French tourists who get off those hideous cruise ships in search of a good meal. You can go from one end of this island to the other in search of edible food and you won't find it. You haven't tasted really bad food until you've eaten in a local Creole restaurant.'

'I can't wait.'

We were sitting in the hotel bar while this conversation took place, having ordered a glass of fruit juice with which to refresh ourselves after the bumpy flight from Antigua.

'I mean, look at that,' she said, pointing at the hotel's hapless barman. 'It's a scandal. This island is sinking under the weight of all the fruit growing on the trees and still he's giving us fruit juice out of a bottle and then diluting it with mineral water. Because he's too lazy to squeeze a few goddamn oranges.'

'I'm beginning to see why you left,' I said.

'This place always drives me crazy. What you were saying at Jumby Bay about how it's hard to know why so many footballers in the French national team come from this island, I was thinking that it's a lot easier to understand why so few of them – if any – ever come back. Imagine if you were a hugely well-paid footballer from Guadeloupe, living in Paris. All those fine restaurants. All that lovely shopping. The beautiful houses. You'd think you'd died and gone to heaven.'

'So what's Jérôme Dumas doing back here?' I asked. 'I've seen the way he lived in Paris. And I can tell you, the guy was behind heaven's velvet rope.'

'Now that I don't know,' said Grace. 'I've got no idea why he was here. All I have are four possible addresses where we might find him.'

'Courtesy of our mystery convict?'

'Courtesy of our mystery convict.'

'That's it?'

'Not quite. My client was specific that we should visit these four locations in turn. One after the other.'

'I wonder why.'

'I think we'll have a better idea about that when we've been to the first address. Don't you think? It's a short walk from here. In Le Gosier.'

After we finished the ersatz fruit juice we walked out of the hotel entrance and went west along the road. After a short while we came to the Morne-à-l'Eau cemetery – a gated necropolis full of hundreds of tombs and mausoleums all made of black and white marble tiles and resembling a village made of liquorice. Next to this was a strangely modern church with a corrugated roof and a bright blue, eight-storey bell tower that the local fire department might have used for exercises.

As we passed the church, Grace looked at me and said, 'Do you believe in God?'

'When I'm more than two goals down I've been known to pray, yes.'

'That's not quite the same thing.'

'Depends if it works or not. When it works I believe and when it doesn't I don't. It's as simple as that.'

'Are you serious?'

'I think it's better to be absolutely sure of nothing when it comes to things such as God. I don't feel frightened by not having an answer to something like that. Generally speaking, I like not having the answers to anything important. How could we ever know that shit? This is the way things are supposed to be, I think. And this is one reason I like football so much. In football it's perfectly possible to have all answers to everything mysterious, such as why one side wins and why another side loses. To that extent football provides a perfect philosophy for life, by which I mean a theory or attitude that acts as a guiding principle for human behaviour. And it will never let you down. Unless it involves FIFA and Sepp Blatter, of course, in which case it will always let you down. But fundamentally football is a perfect way to live your life, because all "why" questions can be answered in football, as opposed to a lot of other things where they can't be answered at all.'

Grace laughed.

'I'm serious. Believe me, applying the values and tenets of football to the world in general will take you a lot further than any religion I've ever come across. You have to be a philosopher to be a manager – although not every manager knows that he is one. And you can forget Stephen Hawking. There's not one manager in football who doesn't have a better understanding of time than he does. How it expands, how it stretches, how everything in a game changes from one minute to the next.'

'I had no idea that it was so intellectually challenging. And here was me thinking that it's just twenty-two men kicking a ball around.'

'That's a very common mistake.'

We turned the corner and stopped in front of a concrete bungalow that must once have looked modern and inhabitable; now it reminded me of a caravan in January. The fuse box on the front wall was open and half of the electrics were spilling out onto the grass verge in a miniature Gordian knot of coloured wires and copper screws; the windows were untidily curtained and dirty; and the porch was home to a broken washing machine and a bale of old newspapers.

'We're here,' said Grace. 'At the first place I was told to look for Jérôme Dumas.'

'If he's here he certainly needs rescuing.'

It was impossible to know if the place was occupied or not but, undeterred, Grace opened the gate to the empty driveway and, ignoring the faded yellow front door, she went around the back with me following close behind her. By now we could hear a football match on a radio or a television, life's universal soundtrack, and I started to believe that our search was going to be a mercifully short one.

'Hello,' Grace said loudly in French. 'Is there anyone home?'

Instead of Jérôme Dumas we found a man lying on a cheap sunlounger and reading a copy of *France-Antilles*, which is the local newspaper. Seeing us in his back yard he put aside his newspaper and stood up. He was tall, thin, strong, and very very black; he looked like a length of pig-iron.

'You're not the cops,' he said in French.

'No, no. no. Nothing like that. Look, we're sorry to disturb you, but we're looking for a friend. Jérôme Dumas.'

The man shook his head. 'Never heard of him.'

'I know,' said Grace. '*Mwen ka palé Kréyol. Sa ou fé?*'

The man nodded. '*Sa ka maché, è wou?*' he said.

They continued in Creole, which meant I understood nothing about what was happening. The conversation lasted about five minutes, at the end of which Grace smiled and shook the man's hand.

'*Mwen ka rimèsié'w anlo,*' she said, and walked back the way we'd came. I followed.

'No,' she said. 'That's strike one, I'm afraid.'

'I never get that,' I said. 'About baseball, I mean. They call it a strike when they don't hit it. That's what you meant, isn't it?'

'Yes.'

'I never get that – any more than I get calling American football, football, when no one kicks the goddamn ball. At least hardly ever.'

'Well, he didn't know where Jérôme Dumas is. At

least he said he didn't. I don't know whether or not you noticed the headphones on the ground by the sunlounger. They were Paris Saint-Germain Beats, by Dr Dre.'

'I didn't see that. No.'

'Which are quite expensive, I think. At least a hundred euros.'

'At least.'

'And just the sort of thing that someone might bring a guy from Paris, as a present. Like the PSG charms key ring that was lying next to them. And the miniature PSG shirt in the acrylic glass ornament that was on the kitchen windowsill.'

'You didn't happen to see what number it was?'

'Nine, I think.'

'You see what I meant before? About me being a detective? That's Jérôme's shirt number.' I grinned. 'So much for my powers of observation.'

'I expect you were trying to get your head around Antillean Creole.'

'Maybe. I mean, I can speak good French, but I don't understand a word of Creole.'

'That's the whole point of it. It's not meant to be understood by the masters.'

'Is that why you were speaking it? So that I wouldn't understand?'

'No. I was speaking Creole so that he wouldn't feel threatened.' She took my hand. 'But I do like the idea of having a master.'

'I can see I'm going to have to be quite firm with you.'

'Oh, I do hope so, sir.'

'Where to now, Mr Frodo?'

'Back to the hotel. And from there we can get a taxi into Pointe-à-Pitre. For some lunch and then the next address on our list.'

'If that guy knows where Jérôme is then he's bound to tell him that we're looking for him, don't you think?'

'I would say that's half the point of us looking for him at the four addresses that I've been given by my client, wouldn't you?'

'In which case we might easily subvert the whole process and go to the last address on your list.'

'We could do that, yes. But then you'd only have my word that it was the last address on my client's list, wouldn't you? So, I think we'll just do this by the numbers. The way my client asked us to do this. You never know. We might incur some penalty for disobedience. And we wouldn't want this decided by penalties, now would we?'

CHAPTER 20

The Yacht Club in Pointe-à-Pitre wasn't really a yacht club but a modern-looking restaurant on the edge of an empty harbour. It certainly didn't look as if any of the smart yachts that came to winter in the Caribbean were mooring here in Guadeloupe. It wasn't much of a restaurant either and I've had much better meals at Piebury Corner, near the Arsenal, and certainly less expensive ones. Guadeloupe used the euro and while there was nothing of any quality to buy and – on the evidence of the lunch we pushed around our plates at the Yacht Club – nothing to eat either, the prices were comparable with mainland France, which is to say, expensive.

It started to rain, which didn't help my mood. The waiter came and drew down some screens to stop our table from being soaked. It seemed uncharacteristically thoughtful.

'That's the most expensive bad meal I've had in a long while,' I remarked.

'I'll remind you that you said that at dinner. I warned you not to have the Creole Plate.'

'The mobile signal's not much better.'

'No, but I'm really not surprised by that either.'

'You're not expecting much of an improvement then?'

'In the signal? Or the food?'

'Either one.'

'Not until we're back on Antigua.'

'I'm beginning to understand why you're over there and not here. You know, it's a pity. You could do a lot with this island.'

'If you were a Bond villain I guess you could. But what did you have in mind?'

'I dunno.'

'Perhaps, if they were able to prove that this was the island that Columbus discovered first, and not the Bahamas, they might get some Americans coming here. No one really knows for sure where he came ashore in 1492. If they could get some Americans then that might bring in some money.'

'I suppose so.'

'Without that it's all a question of attitude. I think there would be more money spent here if the local people looked as if they gave a shit. Until that happens, this place is going to remain a backwater. Right now the most valuable export the island has are its footballers.'

'That I can understand. Almost. But how is it that the French manage to export their ugliest tourists here? I like the French, I love the French, but these are the most badly dressed tourists you can find anywhere south of Blackpool. Anyway. How do you change an attitude?'

'Give the place its independence, probably.'

'Yes, I can see why that wouldn't ever work in France. You're talking about taking away the best chance France has of winning the next World Cup. And the one after that.'

'Not everything's about football, Scott.'

'Who told you that?' I grinned and finished a bottle of Carib, the local beer, which wasn't very good either. 'Football is, in point of fact, more important than everything. It's only when people understand this that we'll arrive at the true meaning of life and death and perhaps the universe, too. In fact Total Football is the only feasible theorem. Anything else is bound to fail.'

'I've been away from Birmingham for too long. I never know when you're joking. Or maybe I've just lost my sense of humour since I became a lawyer.'

'Now that just can't be true. After all, to support Aston Villa you need a good sense of humour.'

It stopped raining just as quickly as it had started and within minutes the temperatures were soaring again.

We left the restaurant and walked around the corner to the dock where the cruise ships were anchored. Halfway there we were intercepted by an almost toothless beggar to whom I gave a two euro coin. A row of shabby offices and shops that seemed to have gone out of business faced the dock, among them a ladies' hairdresser with several faded photographs in the window that would have deterred any woman who cared what she looked like. Grace knocked on the door and peered through glass that was almost opaque with heat and dust.

'This is one of the addresses?' I asked.

'That's right.'

'It doesn't look like anyone's been through this door in a while,' I said, observing a pile of uncollected mail inside the door.

'All the same, I think someone's in there,' said Grace, pressing her nose against the glass.

'I doubt it,' I said. 'And I'm beginning to doubt why I'm here.'

'We accept disappointment. But we don't lose hope. The thing about mounting a search for someone or something is that there's always a stage when it seems like a wild goose chase. Right up until the moment that you find what you're looking for it helps to be patient, I think. Columbus teaches us that much, surely.'

'True.'

Finally a door a few yards up the street opened and a woman poked her head out.

'*Weh*?'

The woman was black, about forty, wearing a white blouse and with a sort of blue tartan turban on her head. In the lobes of her ears were earrings that looked like two golden fly-swats and around her neck was a yellow cotton scarf that was tied into a knot above her narrow waist. Once again the conversation was conducted in Creole. I was left staring up at the huge ship which looked even more like an office block than I'd supposed; there was a viewing deck and from it I could see the three of us being viewed by a man with a telescope. I was tempted to give him the finger – I thought of the number of times I'd wanted to do something like that in the dugout at Silvertown Dock on seeing the TV cameras focused on me, usually when something catastrophic had just occurred on the pitch – but fortunately I restrained myself long enough for the conversation to be completed.

'Who was that?' I asked when the woman in the turban had disappeared back indoors.

'No luck there, either,' said Grace.

'What did she say anyway?'

'Very little.'

'It didn't sound like very little. It sounded like quite a lot for very little.'

'Mm-hmm.'

'Any of these people have names? Or does she just go by the name of Queen Creole?'

'I don't think their names are that important.'

'Maybe not. I don't know. I don't know anything right now. Maybe Jérôme Dumas was watching us from the ship. You know I wouldn't be at all surprised. If he's on the island at all it looks like the best place to stay. And very probably the best place to get dinner, too. I don't know why anyone would come here, really. He certainly didn't come home for the food, that's for sure.'

'All the same, like you say, this was his home.'

'So far that doesn't mean very much.'

'No, I mean that old hairdresser's salon. That was his home when he and his mother were living here in Pointe-à-Pitre. That was his mother's business.'

'What?' I stopped in my tracks and turned around. 'That old place?'

'When she and Jérôme left Guadeloupe Mrs Dumas sold the business to that woman. Then last year an earthquake broke the pipes from the hot water tank. Wasn't any money to fix them. So the place went out of business. It's a common enough story in this part of the world. Life's hard here, Scott.'

'I had noticed that, Grace. It beats me why anyone without family left here would want to come back at all.'

'He's got family here. He must have. I wouldn't be at all surprised if we've already met two of them.'

'That's a depressing thought. I mean, if I'd even thought that was possible I'd have—'

'You'd have done what? Asked them questions? In French? They wouldn't have told you a damn thing. You may be black and you may be handsome but you're not from around here. Take my word. The only way you're going to get anywhere in Guadeloupe is to say it in Creole.' She sighed. 'We may have to come back here, so it would be best to take things slowly. In case you didn't notice, that's the Creole way. No one here's in a hurry except you. So why don't you remember that there's not a ball at your feet and slow down.'

'All the same, in the future, I'd like to know things like this, please. Otherwise I'm just a substitute.'

'Fair enough. But look here, there's something that *I'd* like to know. You said that you thought Jérôme Dumas might have been in trouble, back in Paris. What kind of trouble did you mean, Scott?'

'He was depressed and taking meds. His girlfriend

had dumped him because he was fooling around with other women.'

I thought about what that meant for a moment; I was fooling around a bit myself.

'Hookers mostly. He was on loan to another club – no player likes to be on loan. It really plays with your head.'

'I said "trouble", real trouble, not the ups and downs of normal life.'

'I was coming to that. You know, you could learn a bit of patience yourself, Grace.'

We walked up the street a way, back to the Yacht Club where we were hoping to find a taxi. The heat was at its most intense now so we sought out the shade of the buildings. For some reason I kept thinking that this was only in the high twenties, low thirties. In the Qatari summer the temperatures reached as high as forty-seven degrees; 2022 was going to be fun, but only if you were a local.

'Jérôme also liked to hang out with some Paris bad boys. To smoke some weed. I've done a bit of that myself in my time. But it's also just possible he was involved in a murder. A man named Mathieu Soulié was shot not long before Jérôme left Paris. A satin patch torn off a designer T-shirt bearing a Gothic letter D was found in the dead man's hand. Unfortunately for Jérôme I think the patch came off a shirt which he'd been modelling in a magazine.

'It's possible that Jérôme wasn't involved at all – he certainly doesn't strike me as the type who would shoot a man – but that wouldn't matter if he was scared that someone might tell the police he was. I don't know. He's not actually wanted for questioning by the police. I mean, the police haven't yet made a connection. But sometimes that doesn't stop someone from running away. I'm sure a lawyer would understand something like that.'

'Sure. That's my bread and butter.'

'I think maybe he'd actually given the T-shirt to the real killer who might have blackmailed him to get rid of the murder weapon. It's just a theory. But it would certainly explain why he was reluctant to go back to Europe.'

Grace nodded but she didn't look convinced.

'I'm here to help him, Grace. Not to get him into trouble. But then you knew that, otherwise you wouldn't have told your client about me. And he wouldn't be helping me now. If that's what he's doing.'

The Guadeloupe Tourist Board stood near the Yacht Club on a large square that was dotted with mango trees and royal palms. It was a handsome two-storey white stucco building with Ionic colonnades and a handsome portico and, except for the fact that it was closed, it was unrepresentative of the rest of the buildings in Pointe-à-Pitre. Out front was a taxi rank with just one battered blue taxi. The driver, who smelt of last week's sweat and probably the week before's too, agreed to take us to the next address on the search list that was in my companion's beautiful head. Overcoming our disgust at his body odour, Grace and I sat in the back seat and held hands like a couple of young lovers while he chattered away in Creole.

'He says those are the brothels,' said Grace, as we drove through a shanty town of squalid wooden shacks that were patrolled by the most unlikely-looking prostitutes I'd ever seen. 'I think maybe he's got your card marked as someone who might like to come back here on your own.'

'Thanks.'

'All part of the translation service.'

'Let's hope they're not on your list,' I said, staring out of the window at probably the ugliest pair of whores I'd seen in my life. 'I'd hate to think we'd have to go looking for him in there.'

'Why? Because these poor women are less glamorous than the hookers in Paris?'

'Actually I was thinking that the area doesn't look very safe. But probably that, too.'

'A hooker's a hooker. It's just that some are more expensive than others.'

I smiled. 'There's a reason for that.'

'Ah. You're a beauty fascist.'

'If you want to call it that, yes, I suppose I am. Most men are, I think.'

'Not around here they're not.'

'If I told you I had a real thing about ugly, fat women who wear too much make-up, how would that make you feel now?'

Grace smiled a quiet smile. 'Since I'm neither ugly nor fat I'd feel exactly the same way as I do now. I'm just trying to understand you a little better.'

'Good luck with that.'

'I'm teasing you. Most men like being teased a bit, don't they?'

'Only in strip clubs.'

'This girlfriend he had in Paris,' said Grace. 'What was she like?'

'She wasn't a hooker, if that's what you're driving at.'

'No, but you have met her.'

'Why do I feel like I'm being cross-examined in the witness box?'

'I expect that's a fairly common sensation, for you. And nothing at all to do with me.'

'No? I wonder.'

'So tell me about her. I'm interested.'

I shifted uncomfortably on the back seat. It seemed wrong to be describing one woman with whom I'd recently slept to one I was sleeping with now. Especially when the woman was as obviously intelligent as Grace. But I tried anyway:

'Her name is Bella and she's French. She's a model. Nice girl, I think. Lives in Paris. Tall, blonde and willowy. She has a hairdryer that looks like a gun. And a little painting by Pierre Bonnard on the sideboard.'

'Attractive?'

'The Bonnard? It's exquisite.'

'Her, of course.'

'That name. It's a bit James Bond, isn't it? Like Pussy Galore. Or Fiona Volpe.'

'I think a lot of these fashion models have names that strike normal people as daft.'

'What's she like?'

'Very beautiful. As you might expect with that name.'

Grace laughed. 'Men. They're such suckers for cars. I never get that.'

'You might understand why men like cars so much if you met her.'

'Maybe. Why do you ask, anyway?'

'I'm just trying to figure out what your type is.'

'I don't have a type.'

'Really?'

'Having a type has always seemed to me to be a little too restrictive. You could say you only date black women and then you meet a fabulous redhead. So, what, you're going to ignore the redhead because of some stupid, exclusive rule you've created for yourself? I don't think so. Men who say they have a type are usually trying to excuse their own failure to pull anything at all.'

'Hmm.'

'What does that mean?'

'I've generally observed that men who say they don't have a type are usually tomcats who will fuck anything they can.'

'That's a little harsh.'

'Is it?' She smiled. 'I doubt that.'

'As I recall I was lying quietly in my basket until you invited me to step through the cat flap.'

'That's right. I did. But now that I have I think I'm entitled to make a few conclusions about the feline company I'm keeping.'

'And what conclusions have you made?'

'None yet.' She smiled and squeezed my hand. It was

supposed to make me feel better only her nails seemed quite sharp. 'I'll let you know when I'm ready to make my summing-up.'

'I can't wait, your honour.'

Grace opened her handbag, found a handkerchief, dabbed her forehead and then produced a bottle of scent with which she deodorised herself and then the car.

The driver laughed and said something in Creole.

'Where are we going now?' I asked.

'The beach. In Le Gosier.'

'We were in Le Gosier before lunch, weren't we?'

'Yes. And now we're going back there.'

'Because it's preordained by your client that we should.'

'Yes.'

'I remind you of a cat, you said.'

'Yes. Why?'

'Well, you remind me of a cat, as well. But for entirely different reasons. The fact is, you're quite inscrutable. I look at you and I have no idea what you're thinking.'

'Good. I'd hate to think I could be so easily read.'

'Lady, I couldn't read you if you'd hired the Red Arrows to write your name in the clouds.'

'Maybe I'm not such a mystery.'

'No. But everything else to do with you is.'

'Trust me. All will be revealed.'

I pulled a face.

'What?' she asked.

'When a lawyer says trust me, I need to check I still have my wallet.'

'Go ahead. I think I know every cheap lawyer joke there is.'

'Except that there are no cheap lawyers.'

'And yet it was me who bought your air ticket from Antigua to Guadeloupe. And whose credit card is lodged with the hotel.'

'Believe me, I've wondered about that, too. And I've come to a conclusion. Actually, it's still more of a theory.'

'Oh? Might I hear what that is?'

'I don't think any of the people we've met on Guadeloupe are related to Jérôme Dumas at all. I think it's probably your client in jail who's related to him. Who's maybe at least as worried about him, if not more, as FC Barcelona or Paris Saint-Germain are. I think that maybe Jérôme's disappearance has something to do with your client being in jail. If I knew the name of your client I bet I'd find that Jérôme's disappearance follows on from his imprisonment like Sunday follows Saturday.'

CHAPTER 21

The taxi took us to a gravel car park at the furthest end of the beach at Le Gosier and dropped us near the town hall, an improbably large, ultra-modern building that was out of all proportion to the rest of the sleepy little town: it was as if someone had commissioned Richard Rogers or Norman Foster to design a scout hut.

I paid the malodorous driver and we walked down a quiet road where an old man straight out of the pages of Hemingway was wrestling a big, dead barracuda into the boot of a Renault Clio while another, younger man was manhandling lobster pots out of a small boat. We stepped onto a white sandy beach where Grace kicked off her shoes and I did the same. The sand felt good under my toes and, for the first time since our arrival on the island of Guadeloupe, I started to relax.

Lots of lardy-looking French people were lying on the beach, or floating in the water like so much white plastic flotsam. The sea lapped energetically at the sand and but for the ugliness of the cheap swimwear that was on show you might have thought you were in paradise.

That was me being a beauty fascist again. In my time as a football manager I've been called a lot of things – a cunt, mostly – but a beauty fascist certainly wasn't one of them. It was true, of course. I tend to think fat people ought to keep it covered. That or go on a fucking diet. Not that it was easy to see how anyone could put on weight in Guadeloupe. The place seemed like an ideal place to begin a crash diet.

Fifty yards off the beach was a small desert island and on the island was a lighthouse, although it was hard to see the necessity for warning any shipping to keep away. A simple Google search could have persuaded you of the absolute necessity of never going anywhere near Guadeloupe at all.

We walked about thirty or forty yards until we came to a wooden door in a wall of rocks and banana leaves. We stepped carefully between some Frenchies who were enjoying a little shade and whose grumbles indicated their resentment at our disturbing them, and Grace pressed an intercom button on the doorpost. Eventually a man's voice answered, in French.

'Yes? Who is this?'

'My name is Grace Doughty and with me is Scott Manson, from FC Barcelona. We're looking for Jérôme Dumas.'

'I'm Jérôme,' said the voice. 'Come on up,' he added, and buzzed us in.

'I don't believe it,' I said.

'Why not?'

'Jesus Christ,' I said, as Grace pushed the door open

and we walked through it into a nicely tended garden.'

'Ye of little faith,' said Grace.

'I used to play for Northampton Town, so that can't be true.'

The door closed neatly behind us and we walked up a long, sloping lawn towards a modern two-storey house constructed of red concrete and glass with a metal terrace and a big picture window. What resembled a set of large canvas sails covered the flat roof like several sun umbrellas. It was very private in that almost none of this could be seen from the beach and the house was shrouded with royal palms and red bougainvillea. Music by Stromae – who is almost as good as Jacques Brel, and a recent and happy discovery of mine, thanks to Bella – was blaring out of an open window while emerging from a tinted glass door was a barefoot young man wearing a Barcelona team kit and whom I recognised immediately as Jérôme Dumas. Around his neck were a pair of PSG Beats; on his wrist was a large gold Rolex and, in his earlobes, were the diamond Panther studs that Bella told me he'd bought from Cartier in Paris. I felt my jaw drop for a second.

'It's him,' I murmured. 'I'm sure it's him. I recognise the earrings.'

'You can thank me later,' she said as we neared the man in the Barca shirt.

'Jérôme Dumas, I presume,' I said, happily. 'Scott Manson. I've been looking for you everywhere. In Paris, Antigua and now here in Guadeloupe. You're a hard man to find, Jérôme.'

'I guess so.'

There was a football on the lawn and seeing it, out of sheer exuberance that my mission now appeared to be over, I kicked it to him playfully.

'Well, thank God for that, anyway,' I said. 'Although we do have a lot to talk about.'

'If you say so.'

He trapped the football with his left foot, flicked it up, bounced it off his knee and onto his head, nodded it twice and then headed it back to me as if hoping to see what I was made of.

'Your new employers are very anxious that you return with me to Barcelona as soon as possible,' I said. 'You've an important match coming up.'

I fielded the ball on my chest, and then up onto my head again, let it roll over my scalp, dropped it onto my knee and then my bare foot, and kept it up again a couple of times, before tapping it back to him. Between us it felt like a kind of language, a sporting Esperanto, and in a sense it is; where two or more men are kicking a football they're in a dialogue.

'Sure, and I'm sorry for all the trouble I've caused,' he said, grinning sheepishly. 'I know you've come a long way to find me, Mr Manson.'

Jérôme had the ball in the small of his back now. After a second he shrugged it off and onto his own head and let it bounce five, six, seven, eight times before catching it on his instep and playing it back to me again with perhaps a little more venom than was necessary.

'Scott,' I said, controlling the ball with my head.

'Call me Scott. I'm glad to see you've been keeping up your skills.'

I could feel the sweat breaking out on my head and chest as I tried to match his abilities with the ball, which were considerable and much superior to my own; even fifteen years ago I'd have been struggling to keep up with this guy. Now at the age of forty-one I was almost out of breath. I tucked my hands back against my wrists and concentrated hard to keep the ball just an inch or two in the air above one foot. I almost didn't notice when someone inside the house turned the music off.

'You're not so bad yourself, Scott. Not bad at all. For an old guy.'

'Thanks. And less of the old, if you don't mind, sunshine.'

'You were at Arsenal once, weren't you?' he said. 'Before you went into management?'

'That's right. I was a centre back.'

'I eat them for breakfast,' said Jérôme.

'Funnily enough, I've heard that one before. I think it was Paul Raury, from West Bromwich Albion, who said something similar to me just before I broke his ankle.'

'When you two are quite finished showing off...' said Grace.

I flicked the ball to Jérôme who played it off his knee, caught it in his big hands and tucked it possessively under his arm.

'This is Grace Doughty,' I said. 'She's a lawyer from Antigua. She's been helping me to find you. Although to be more accurate it's me who's been helping her, I think. Given that she seems to know the island and speaks Creole.'

'I've heard a lot about you, Mr Dumas,' said Grace. 'Too much, really. He's been obsessing that we were on a wild goose chase. I told him that you have to be patient with wild geese, but I don't think he believed that until now.'

'Can you blame me?' I said.

'Pleased to meet you.' Jérôme shook her hand and then mine. 'Come inside and have something to drink. You've come a long way, I expect.'

'Do you speak Creole?' I asked Jérôme.

'Yes. A bit. But when I answer the bell to the door on the beach I always speak French since it's nearly always French people who are ringing it. Usually they want to know if there's a toilet nearby. And I have to tell them, otherwise they piss on the wall.'

Inside, the air-conditioned house was very *Architectural Digest* – all open-plan with upper galleries of book-shelves and other rooms. A bank of white leather armchairs were arranged in front of a matching right-angle sofa, like so many sugar cubes. Lying by the sofa were several days-old copies of Antigua's newspaper, the *Daily Observer*, and a copy of Guillem Balague's excellent biography of Lionel Messi. On the wall was a big plasma television and on the screen was FIFA 15, with the sound turned down; Chelsea against Barcelona. In the middle of the room was a glass table and a couple of PS4 controllers, and everywhere there were vases of flowers and jugs of iced water, almost as if Jérôme had been expecting us. He poured us each a glass of water that was flavoured with elderflower cordial.

'Nice place,' I said.

'Yes,' said Grace. 'I didn't know it was possible to live as well as this on Guadeloupe.'

'It belongs to a friend of mine,' said Jérôme. 'Gui-Jean-Baptiste Target.'

'Why does that name ring a bell?' I said.

'He's the centre forward for SM Caen. Used to play for AS Monaco.'

I nodded. 'I remember. Wasn't he involved in that match-fixing scandal involving Caen and Nîmes Olympique in November 2014?'

'He was questioned, I think. But not really involved at all. No charges have been brought, anyway. He lets me borrow this place from time to time.'

'Is he from Guadeloupe, too?'

'Yes.'

'There's quite a crowd of you,' I said.

'Not a crowd, my friend,' said Jérôme. 'A *team*. If only the French would remove their objections to our FIFA incorporation then we could compete in the World Cup. Perhaps not in Russia, but certainly in Qatar. And you know something else? We could win. Especially if we were playing France. In fact I think I could guarantee it.'

'It's the same in England. There's nothing like sticking one to the mother country. Just ask the Scots, or the Irish. I think there's no one they'd rather beat than England. I should know. I'm part Scots myself.'

Jérôme grinned. 'Forgive me, but you don't look much like a Scotsman.'

'I'll take that as a compliment. Besides, people in Scotland have been saying that to me all my life. Which is one reason I live in England, I suppose. The English are a lot more tolerant of black people than the Scots. Anyone can look English, I think. But it takes a Scot to look like a Scot. And you know, whatever people say, the French aren't so bad.'

'I dunno. Some of them. Maybe.'

'I saw your apartment in Paris. Met your ex-girlfriend. I'd say you'd enjoyed pretty much all that France has to offer. And then some. From what I've read in your file, you were making fifty thousand euros a week at Monaco when you were just sixteen.'

'How is Bella?'

'She's well. Misses you, I think.'

'I doubt that very much. I wasn't very nice to her.'

'Not too late to fix that, I'd have thought. If it was me I'd try to mend my fences with her. I've rarely seen a more beautiful girl.'

'You think so?'

'You and she made a very handsome couple. She showed me the pictures in *Marie Claire* and *Elle*.'

'We did, didn't we? But she made her choice. And now I'm alone.'

None of the pictures I'd seen on television or in the magazines did the man's beauty justice. He was astonishingly handsome with a long nose, a full sensuous mouth and a shaven head. It was a strong, almost Egyptian head in that it reminded me of one of those huge granite carvings of the Pharaoh Rameses II that can be seen in Egypt's Valley of the Kings. He was tall and wiry, with legs as long as a crane fly's and when you saw him you realised that his was a perfect footballer's physique – not small, like a Messi, or as tall as a Crouch – but more felicitously proportioned, and just to see him was to picture him running at speed with the ball, or curling an improbable shot into the back of the net. Equally, it was plain to see why magazines and Italian designers were falling over themselves to sign him up. Paolo Gentile had not exaggerated. Except for the fact that his body was unmarked by tattoos it was easy to imagine this young man as the next David Beckham and getting rich beyond the dreams of anyone's avarice. But if I had an early criticism it was that he seemed a little sulky; like a spoiled child.

'Are you alone here now?' I asked.

'Yes, there's just me and the housekeeper – Charlotte – who comes in every day and cooks and cleans for me.'

'On the strength of the lunch we just ate I'm not sure there's a great deal of difference between cooking and cleaning on this island.'

'Where did you eat?'

'The Yacht Club in Pointe-à-Pitre,' said Grace. 'If you go, don't have the Creole Plate.'

'We're staying along the beach,' I said, 'at the Auberge de la Vieille Tour. But neither of us is very optimistic that it's going to be any better.'

Jérôme pulled a face. 'It's true. There's nowhere good in Pointe-à-Pitre.'

'This is quite a little hideaway you have here, my young friend. Very private. You could live in a place like this for months and no one would find you.'

Jérôme nodded. 'I certainly believed so.'

'I must say you don't seem to be very surprised that we did.'

He smiled. 'I heard that you were looking for me. I've been expecting you all day.'

'Was it the guy in Le Gosier who told you we were here in Guadeloupe?' I asked. 'The one with half the gift shop from PSG and who looks like a length of ebony? Or Queen Creole from the hairdresser's salon in Pointe-à-Pitre?'

'Both. I'm happy to say I still have lots of good friends in Guadeloupe.'

'Oh, I'm sure. And what about relations?'

'Sadly, I've no family on the island now. Not any more.'

'What about on Antigua?' I asked. 'Any family there?'

'No. Why do you ask?'

'No reason. Well, now that I'm here, I think it's best we put our cards on the table.'

'Such as?'

'Such as the company you've been keeping. If I'm going to be travelling with you, I'd like to know if there's anything important I should know about. You see, I wouldn't like to aid someone who's wanted by the police. Especially when I'm in a foreign country. I'm cautious like that. So why don't you tell me everything?'

'Does it really matter?' said Jérôme.

'You're joking, aren't you?'

'Look, Scott, I'll gladly return to Barcelona whenever you like. Pay whatever fine they impose. You've accomplished what you set out to accomplish, haven't you? So why don't you just leave it be? Give them a call and tell them to send a jet to the airport at Pointe-à-Pitre and we can be back there in no time.'

'All right. I'll put it another way. I'm afraid there are some things I need to know, and know now. For example, and most importantly: why didn't you get on that plane from Antigua to London and report for training at Joan Gamper in Barcelona, like you were supposed to do?'

He smiled, a little self-consciously. 'Maybe I didn't feel like it.'

'You don't want to talk? That's fine by me. I can understand your reluctance to tell me about this. After all, it's embarrassing to tell someone how you fucked up when you've only just met them. But what you've just told me so far won't be good enough for the people at PSG or Barca who sent me here to find you. Not by a long chalk. If either of the two clubs get so much as a whiff of ill-discipline or someone with a bad attitude then they can fuck you up good, my son. You're an investment and no one likes to see their investment just disappear without so much as an explanation. If Barca decided they didn't want you after all – which yet they might – PSG could put you up for transfer and sell you to the highest bidder..'

I sipped my elderflower water and waited for him to

say something but all he did was stare at the game on the screen as if he wished he could just carry on playing.

'Everything will be fine just as soon as I score my first goal for the Blaugrana,' said Jérôme. 'You'll see. They all will.'

'Sure it will. Just like it was after you'd scored your first goal at PSG. No, wait, you never scored a goal for PSG, did you? Correct me if I'm wrong but I thought that was why the French agreed to loan you to the Catalans. In the hope that you might do better in Barcelona than you'd done in Paris.'

Jérôme sighed loudly and, leaning back in his chair, shook his head.

'I think you're going to have to talk to me, son. Tell me, Grace, you're a lawyer, would an employer be within their rights to dismiss an employee who didn't turn up to work for the best part of a month, without an explanation? Not only that, but to sue him for breach of contract?'

'He's right, Jérôme,' Grace told him. 'You're going to have to tell him something.'

'It's complicated,' he said finally.

'It always is.'

'No, man, really fucking complicated.'

'Look me up on the internet sometime. You're looking at someone for whom complicated has been a pretty consistent career choice.'

'Really?'

'I don't know a better way to explain how I've been to prison for something I didn't do.'

'You did?'

'I served eighteen months for rape before I was acquitted. How's that for complicated?'

'I didn't know. Christ. That's really fucked up, man.'

'Look, I can help you, kid. The fact is I'm not just here to fetch you home, I'm here to save you from yourself, if you need it. Which I happen to think you do. You see, I gave my word to Paolo Gentile that I'd do this. He seems to think your arse is worth saving, although frankly I remain to be convinced by that.'

'Paolo. How is that old crook?'

'Coin-operated. Same as ever. He has big plans for you. He's convinced that he can make you the richest young man in football since Cristiano Ronaldo. Provided you're willing to toe the corporate line, of course.' I paused. 'Is that one of the reasons why you funked it?'

'A little, perhaps. But look, man, this is all very personal. It's not easy to tell a complete stranger why I didn't think I could go back.'

'You know, I did quite a bit of digging around in your life before I flew over here. I've sat around in your lovely apartment with Mandel, and with Alice. She's very loyal. I liked her. I've had dinner with Bella Macchina. I like her, too. I've been through your closets and your drawers. I've even been through your bathroom cabinet. I think I can safely say I know a lot more about you than you probably think I do. At the moment it's just me who knows this shit. Not PSG and not Barcelona. If they did they'd run a mile, so you can thank me later.'

Jérôme gave a very Gallic shrug. He didn't look very thankful. 'What do you think you know?'

'I know everything, from why Bella gave you the push, to your fondness for sex games with the Twin Towers, to your run-in with the Paris police. I know you're on meds for depression. I know that you used to have a gambling problem. I know about your friends in Sevran-Beaudottes, that you used to go there to smoke a little weed and buy some blow, and how one of those hoods gave you a gun. You might be surprised to learn that's the kind of thing that alarms a football club. And which can drive away a potential advertiser. Take it from one who's already been there.'

'Yes, but do you know *why* he gave me a gun?'

'I think it may have been something to do with the death of Mathieu Soulié.'

Jérôme nodded, unhappily. 'Those guys. They're bastards. I used to go to the Alain Savary Sports Centre and give them clothes and money, trying to put something back in, you know? I figure I've been lucky and I want to do something for people who've not been as fortunate as me.'

'That's very laudable of you, Jérôme.'

'Anyway, one day I gave them some stuff I'd been wearing on a shoot, with Bella. Some clothes from Dries Van Noten. There was this one T-shirt with a satin square and a letter D—'

'The one they found in Mathieu Soulié's dead hand.'

'That's right. Chouan – he's the gang leader – he must have been wearing it when they killed him. Either Soulié

tore it off or they deliberately put it there in his hand
to incriminate me. Anyway, Chouan said that if I didn't
do what he told me he'd make sure the police got the
T-shirt and a picture of me wearing it. I had nothing
at all to do with his murder. I even had an alibi. But
I don't think the cops would be too interested in that.
They'd still have me in for questioning on account of
how I've pissed them off already with my politics and
my big mouth. Just to give me a hard time.'

'And the gun?'

'That was what Chouan wanted. He told me to get
rid of it. To throw it in the river. Said he thought the
cops were watching him. I'm sure it was the gun that
killed that guy.'

'And did you?'

'No. I kept it in the apartment for a while until I
figured out what to do with it. Then I decided to hide
it. I figured it was evidence that might actually help to
clear me.'

'Sensible boy. Where did you hide it?'

'In a left luggage locker at Gare du Nord.'

'But there's an X-ray check on left luggage at all
French stations.'

'I put it in a bag full of old cameras I bought from
a junk shop. It's taped to the underside of an ancient
Canon with a long lens. On the X-ray machine it just
looks like it's part of the camera. Besides, those guys
at the station are more interested in talking to a PSG
footballer than in checking through his bag. Especially
when there's an autograph to give.'

'And the key is where?'

'In my bag upstairs.'

'You can give it to me later. We'll have a lawyer in Paris sort this out when we're back in Europe. I'm sure if you make a statement under oath this can be made to go away.'

'You really think that's possible?'

'Sure. Leave it to me.' I nodded. 'And that's it? The sole reason why you didn't want to go back home? What this was all about?'

'Yes,' said Jérôme. 'Maybe I lost my nerve for all that shit with Cesare da Varano, the designer, and then the Zaragoza Bank. It's not who I want to be, you know? It's not football, right?'

'Thank you.' I smiled. 'And yes, I agree, it's not football. But you're a bloody liar.'

'Why do you say so?'

'Oh, I don't doubt your story about the gun. However, I don't think it's why you didn't go home. Not for a minute. Call me a suspicious bastard but I think it's got more to do with something that happened here than something which had already happened back in Paris. You see, I think you were about to catch that flight back to London when something happened here to change your mind, or you found out that something happened. Something you read about in a newspaper at the airport, perhaps.'

'Believe me, if possible I try to avoid the French newspapers.'

'And so do I. So does anyone who's in the newspapers'

line of fire. But if it isn't possible to avoid them, then what do you do?'

'I don't understand.'

'Sure you do. Let me tell you why. This morning, Grace and I flew from Antigua's airport and while I was there I saw the local newspaper, the *Daily Observer*, prominently displayed at the newsagent.' I picked one of the newspapers off the floor and tossed it onto the table. 'This newspaper.'

'What of it? It's a rag. There's nothing in it.'

'The man who drives the boat from Jumby Bay and takes the guests back to the airport is named Everton. Everton told me that on the day you were supposed to go back to London you seemed fine until you got to the airport when something happened that appeared to change your mood. He says his last sight of you was at the newsagent reading a newspaper. Although he doesn't remember which one, he told me you seemed to be upset.

'I've already checked the editions of all the French newspapers they sell at the airport, *Le Monde*, *Figaro*, *Libération* and *L'Equipe*, from the same day that you were supposed to fly back. The ones you said you choose to avoid. And I believe you. And the fact is that I found there was nothing in any of those papers that would have caused you to change your plans so abruptly. Nothing at all. But the story on the front of that day's edition of the *Daily Observer* just might have done. Why? Because it was something recent, something which had happened on the island the previous night, something wholly unexpected and something violent.'

'Like what?'

'I'm coming to that. The newspaper reported that following an altercation on a boat in Nelson's Dockyard two men were found unconscious in one of the cabins. One of the men subsequently died and the other was under police guard in the Mount St John's Medical Centre. Neither man was named but it was reported that the boat belonged to a local man known as DJ Jewel Movement.

'I think when you saw this story in the newspaper you decided to delay your departure first, to find out exactly who was dead and who was still alive. Then, after later editions of the paper reported that DJ Jewel Movement had died and the other man was named as John Richardson and was being transferred to Her Majesty's Prison in Antigua facing a possible murder charge, I think you decided to remain in the area indefinitely so that you could offer him legal assistance in the person of Miss Doughty here. My guess is that this John Richardson is someone you *are* related to. Or at the very least a good friend. Ever since then I think you've been following the case in the papers and with the help of Miss Doughty.'

I smiled at her. 'I don't blame you for lying to me, Grace. And please don't be insulted. I know it's what lawyers do when they're being paid. Only they much prefer to call it client confidentiality.'

'I'm not insulted,' she said. 'And in point of fact I haven't actually lied to you, Scott. Not once. I've merely told you only what I'm able to tell you. I was just obeying my client's instructions. But you think what you like.'

'There's no need to call her a liar,' said Jérôme. 'It's not actually her fault. And she knows much less than she seems to know, perhaps.'

'So, why don't you tell me what's what here? And then I can be the judge of that.'

'How do I know I can trust you not to tell anyone else? I mean, you could spoil everything. My sponsorships. My deal with the bank—'

'Yes, I thought that was bollocks.'

'Everything.'

'You don't know that I won't spoil it. But I'm sick and tired of all this. I just want to go home to London, to try to find a proper job, not play nursemaid to someone who doesn't know how well off he really is. And frankly I can do without any more bullshit, too. The fact is I will certainly tell PSG and FCB what I do know if you hold out on me any longer. If you want to wreck your fucking career completely, that's up to you, son, be my guest.'

He pulled a face.

'I won't say the truth is always best,' I added. 'Sometimes a lie is kinder. But this isn't one of those times. I love the game. And I love the people who are good at the game. I saw the way you played against Barcelona back in September and I honestly thought you were the best player on the pitch.'

He nodded. 'You're right. That was the best I ever played for PSG. If only I'd scored that night things might have been different.'

'Football is hard like that. Very hard, sometimes. Talk about survival of the fittest. Sometimes it seems positively Darwinian. As unforgiving as Nature itself. A career can end in just five minutes with an ill-timed tackle, like the one that finished Man United's Ben Collett. On football's scrapheap at the age of just eighteen. But you're still in the game, son. Never forget that. And just because it doesn't happen at one club doesn't mean it won't happen at another. People never seem to remember that when Thierry Henry left Monaco he didn't go straight to Arsenal, he had a dismal eight months at Juventus.'

'You're right. He did, didn't he? Christ, I'd forgotten that, too.'

'The Italians played him on the wing but he was largely ineffective and I think he scored only three goals in sixteen appearances.'

'It's the same with me,' insisted Jérôme. 'PSG kept playing me on the wing when I'm a striker. In that game for Barcelona I was a nine, but a false nine. That's my best position. Same as Messi.'

'Barcelona clearly think the same way. That's why they're keen to have you playing for them ASAP. I want to help Barcelona because they were good to me when I was just out of the nick and I needed a coaching job. And you should know I'll always put them first. But I want to help you, too, Jérôme, because I respect your ability. I genuinely think you can be one of the best players in the world.'

'Thank you for that.'

I stood up, straightened the crease on my trousers and glanced around. 'I'd like to use the toilet if I may. While I'm out of the room I suggest you make a decision one way or the other.'

CHAPTER 22

Jérôme Dumas showed me to a lavatory on an upper floor. I washed my hands in a stone shelf basin and on my way back downstairs stuck my head around a couple of doors because I'm nosy that way. Jérôme's master bedroom was home to several Louis Vuitton bags and, strewn across the floor, a whole wardrobe of clothes and accessories; it certainly didn't look as if the cleaner was doing very much in that house; then again, it was a cleaner from Guadeloupe.

On the wall of another bedroom was a painting of a pumpkin by Yayoi Kusama, very like the one Dumas had at his apartment in Paris. They must have been selling a job lot of them to footballers that year.

Back in the treble-height drawing room, it seemed that Jérôme was finally ready to spill his guts. It was about time. My patience with him was growing very thin. If there had been a boot or a pizza at hand I might have thrown it at him.

'All right,' he said, 'I'll tell you everything. Everything. I just hope I'm doing the right thing.'

'Then it's lucky you've got your lawyer to advise you,' I said. 'Tell him, Grace. Tell him it's got to be like this. My way or the highway.'

'You're doing the right thing, Jay,' said Grace. 'Scott really is here to help. I wouldn't have brought him here if I didn't think you could trust him.'

'Thank you,' I said.

I knew Jérôme was serious because he turned off the PlayStation while he said this and you know something must be about to happen when someone under the age of twenty-five turns off one of those idiot-boxes voluntarily.

'So. Why don't you tell me what happened?'

'All right. I will. The guy in prison, in Antigua, Grace's mystery client – he's my father.'

'I see.'

'He lives in Antigua now. But he isn't from there. And he hasn't lived with my mother since the whole family left Montserrat, way back in 1995. That's where we're from, see? I'm not from Guadeloupe at all. I'm from Montserrat, which is the island between here and Antigua. When the Soufrière Hills volcano exploded in July 1995, it ruined not just Plymouth – which is the capital city of Montserrat – but my whole family. And not just ours. Two-thirds of the island's population were forced to flee their homes. A lot of them went to Guadeloupe. But my dad always hated Guadeloupe, which was where my mum was from, originally. Anyway, he refused to come here with her and it didn't help that they weren't married. Dumas is my mother's name. So,

I came here with her and he went to Antigua to live with his sister, and her daughter.'

'That's me,' said Grace. 'John Richardson is my uncle.'

'Jesus,' I muttered.

Jérôme grinned. 'I told you it was complicated.'

'It was my cousin here who paid for me to go to Birmingham University,' said Grace. 'But for him, I'd probably be cleaning floors at Jumby Bay. He's the most generous man I know.'

'And she wasn't lying, she really didn't know where I was,' insisted Jérôme. 'I didn't tell her. I didn't tell anyone. Even my dad didn't know for sure.'

'In which case, I apologise,' I said. 'I was out of line, I can see that now.'

'That's all right,' she said. 'You weren't to know.'

'I still don't know very much,' I added, pointedly.

'Whenever I went to Antigua I'd see my dad. He'd arrange a trip on board a friend's boat. We'd sail down to Montserrat, just to take a look. But I don't think things are going to get better there any time soon. There's still a lot of pyroclastic activity in and around the south part of the island. People are not allowed into the exclusion zone but me and my dad still go when we can, and see for ourselves. The boat's owner – DJ Jewel Movement – was another guy from Montserrat and a friend of my dad's. Or at least he was. The day before I was supposed to fly back from Antigua, we went out on the boat. Took a trip to the island, as was usual. Got high. A bit too high, actually. My dad and Jewel Movement quarrelled about something. Money, probably. They were still at it when I got off the boat in Nelson's Dockyard. But I never thought they'd try to kill each other. The first thing I knew about that was the morning I was supposed to fly back. Like you said, I was at the airport and I saw it in the newspaper. I didn't know what to do. But I knew I certainly couldn't leave the area. Equally, I didn't want the publicity of staying in Antigua and turning up at the police station and trying to bail him out, or whatever you do when that happens. I thought it might jeopardise all of Paolo Gentile's work in getting me all those endorsement deals. So I called Grace and told her. Then a friend of GJB – Gui-Jean-Baptiste – took me here on his boat until I figured out what to do. I'd hoped the police would accept his story – that it was self-defence – but instead they charged him with murder.'

'It goes almost without saying,' said Grace, 'that being charged with murder is always a serious matter. In Antigua, however, it's worse than serious. We have the death penalty in Antigua. My uncle is facing the gallows, Mr Manson. If he's found guilty he might easily be sentenced to death. As things stand now, it's unlikely he would be hanged; the Judicial Committee of the Privy Council would almost certainly prevent an execution. But the Labour Party, which took power in June 2014, seem to want to break away from the Commonwealth. And its legal system. If that happened we might soon start hanging people again in Antigua. Like in St Kitts and Nevis. And the Bahamas. By the time a verdict is reached in John's trial there's every chance that Antigua might have started to carry out executions again. It seems to be what the people here want.'

'Christ, I didn't know.'

'Oh, yes. That would mean I'd have to leave the island, of course. I couldn't continue to work in a society that hanged people.' She glanced at her cousin. 'Sorry, Jay; you were saying.'

'At first I intended to be here for just a couple of days,' said Jérôme. 'A week at the most. But the longer I stayed, the harder it seemed just to leave him and go back to Barcelona and play football. I mean, you can imagine how worried I was? I couldn't think about sport. Not for a minute. Someone once wrote that the immediate prospect of being hanged focuses the mind wonderfully. I'd agree with that except for the word "wonderfully". The last few weeks have been hell. I was already depressed but this made everything seem even worse. I've been following the case on TV and in the papers but I haven't been able to contact Grace. I gave her my numbers in Paris and Barcelona but of course I haven't been there. And there's no landline here; GJB likes it that way. Not even internet. As you've probably gathered by now, the mobile signal on the island is virtually non-existent. I didn't like to go into Pointe-à-Pitre even at night, in case I was recognised. So I've just been laying low here, hoping something will turn up. My dad would have been furious that I'd stayed on here, of course, instead of going back. For Dad my career comes before anything. Anything at all, including him. The family needs money, see? It's not just him. It's my aunt, too. She's been sick. My dad actually thought I was back in Europe until you showed up asking questions about my whereabouts. He only learned about that because Grace overheard you talking to that stupid cop in St John's. Anyway, Grace told my dad, and he was furious and said she had to get a message to me insisting that I go back to Barcelona with you, and that he'd be all right. And here you both are.'

Sinking back into the big white sofa like a collapsing balloon Jérôme uttered a deep and despairing sigh as if at any moment he might fall to pieces and give way to a flood of tears and the insupportable weight of a very large black dog. He shrugged, and then rubbed his scalp as if acutely self-conscious that I was looking critically at him, narrow-eyed, trying to judge the veracity of his story.

'I don't know what else to tell you. Really I don't. I can't say that my actions could make sense. But, I've been depressed. For several months, really. And I can't honestly explain why.'

'You don't have to,' said Grace. 'That's the nature of depression. The only true cause is physiological.'

'Maybe. But I know most guys would look at my cars and my house and my girlfriend and think such a thing impossible. How could a guy like me be depressed? But I am. And the fact is it's getting worse. I ran out of Seroxat a couple of weeks ago, which was all that was keeping me afloat really. Since then I've done nothing but stay in bed, play the PS4 and stare out of the fucking window. Frankly, I'm glad you're here as I really don't know what would have become of me otherwise.'

It all sounded plausible enough, and yet there was something about his story that didn't quite ring true. It was nothing I could put my finger on. Maybe it was just the fact that like a lot of rich young footballers Jérôme struck me not as someone stupid or lacking in intelligence, merely precipitate, a little unwise perhaps. Which was why most young footballers these days had someone like Paolo Gentile around; someone to advise them anyway. But I felt I had to push the door and see that there was nothing hidden behind it.

'What are you not telling me?' I asked.

Jérôme shook his head.

'Come on. There's always something people keep back right to the end. Something they don't want to give up.'

'Like what?' asked Jérôme.

'I don't know. But that's just how it is when you've been in prison like I have. You spend enough time with enough liars, you get a feeling for when there's more to tell.'

'I think you're being a bit unfair,' said Grace. 'It sounds to me like Jérôme's made a clean breast of everything. He was worried about his father. Any man can understand something like that, surely.'

'Now I know you're lying. You've got your lawyer speaking for you.'

Grace laughed. 'Here we go again. It's lucky I've got a sense of humour.'

'But I've told you everything,' insisted Jérôme. 'Honest.'

'Believe me, that's a word you never use when you're trying to tell someone the truth. Not that the football field is much different from prison, mind. The bullshit you hear when you're out there on the pitch. I wish I had five quid for every lie I've heard during my twenty-odd years in football. I never meant to hurt him. It was a fair tackle. I never dived. Who me? I played the ball, not the man. It was a fifty-fifty ball. That was ball to hand, ref, not hand to ball. I am ten yards back. And that's to say almost nothing about the lies you hear in the dressing room when you're a manager. The leg's fine, boss, it doesn't hurt at all. I can play the next half without any problems. I couldn't hear what you were saying, boss.

'Jérôme, do I look like a dick? All footballers are fucking liars. Lying is just part of the game now, like ice packs or isotonic energy drinks, or a chunk of Vick's VapoRub on your shirt front. I honestly think that if a team suddenly started to tell the truth, everyone would think they were on drugs. So, what is it that you're not telling me?'

'Nothing,' he protested. 'I've told you the whole story. And that's the truth.'

But I was swiftly wrong-footed by what happened next. Jérôme Dumas began to cry.

'That's it,' said Grace. 'I think he's had enough.'

'Now you really sound like his brief.'

Grace stood up. 'I think it best that we finish this discussion for now. We can meet again later. This evening. When Jérôme is feeling like himself again.'

'Suppose he goes walkies again? Then what? I'll have summoned the Barcelona jet here for no reason.'

'So wait a little,' said Grace. 'A few hours' delay until you're satisfied everything is as it should be won't matter very much now, will it?'

'No, I suppose not.'

She sat down next to the weeping footballer and put her arm around his heaving shoulders.

'You're not going anywhere, are you, Jay?' she said. 'Not now that we've found you.'

He wiped his face and shook his head. 'No, I'll be here.'

'We're going to walk back to the hotel,' she told him. 'We'll come back at around seven when perhaps we can go somewhere for dinner. That is, if we can think of anywhere they serve something that's actually edible.'

CHAPTER 23

Our two-roomed suite at the Auberge de la Vieille Tour was, we were told, the largest that the hotel had to offer, although that didn't make it seem any more comfortable. The dressing room at Stoke City was probably better appointed.

There was a long, split-level terrace with a table and couple of sunloungers, a nice view of an amethyst-green lawn and beyond this the sea, and in the blue sky a wide variety of bird life. Mostly these were mockingbirds whose sharp mockery possibly related to our choice of hotel. It certainly felt that way. There was no carpet, only a marble floor, and the suite was furnished with but the one armchair, a cheap-looking sofa that you might have found in any cut-price bedsit, and a TV with all the main French and Italian channels, which at least meant I wasn't going to be deprived of football. The minibar was about as well-stocked as a student's refrigerator and the Wi-Fi signal was weaker than a signal from the Mars Rover. One night in Guadeloupe's best hotel looked like it was going to be quite enough. I couldn't wait to get back to Jumby Bay and then London.

After the emotional energy of the conversation with Jérôme Dumas I was feeling a little tired and the bed looked comfortable enough so I had a quick shower in the tiny bathroom and climbed under the crisp white sheets. I fell to reflecting on the events of the afternoon. If there's one thing I hate in football it's a snivelling crybaby. Some of these pampered kids don't know how well off they are and quite a few of them need a fucking good slap. João Zarco hit a few City players in his time and probably the only reason I haven't decked one myself is because I haven't been in the job for long enough. Believe me, it happens a lot more than you think. In evidence I give you Brian Clough and Roy Keane. Unthinkable, isn't it? That's probably one reason why Keano is such a hard bastard today. I got decked myself when I was playing at Southampton, and rightly so.

But Dumas was different. He seemed genuinely depressed and there's no telling where something like that can end up, especially when the happy pills have run out. Hanging yourself on Wembley Way like my old mate Matt Drennan, or trying to head-butt a lorry on the A64 like poor Clarke Carlisle. In spite of what he'd said I reflected that there was still some careful handling to be done if I was going to get Jérôme Dumas on a plane to Barcelona.

Soon after I closed my eyes I found Grace lying naked next to me and smelling lightly of perfume and body lotion. I lay silently for a minute or two, enjoying the relaxing sound of the ocean through the open window.

I love the sound of the sea. Maybe it's because I'm a Pisces, but I think it has more to do with the fact that having been born in Edinburgh – which has in Leith a proper sea-port – the sea and the sound of seagulls wheeling over Edinburgh Castle were probably the first ambient noise of which I was ever aware. That and the sound of a few Hearts supporters carousing home along the Gorgie Road after a successful local derby. Relaxation was slow in coming, however; I was feeling a little guilty about the way I'd spoken to the woman now occupying the same bed as me.

'I owe you an apology.'

'Debatable.'

'Jérôme's father. John Richardson. What are his chances?'

'John will certainly plead self-defence. There's plenty of evidence that DJ Jewel Movement gave almost as good as he got. The trouble is that Jewel Movement was popular in Antigua. Finding an impartial jury might be difficult. Lots of people knew him and liked him. So, a jury might easily convict just because of that. Of course, John does have a very good lawyer.'

'I certainly wouldn't disagree with that.'

'I'm glad.'

I turned around and put my arms around her. She laid one long leg across my hip, gathered me closer and licked my chest as if it was the choicest morsel.

'It's my considered opinion that she's a very fine lawyer indeed.'

'Mmm-hmm.'

'All the same, I just want to say that I didn't mean to insult you back there at your cousin's friend's house. And I hope you weren't offended.'

'No offence taken. I think I'm a lot thicker-skinned than you imagine.'

'So we're all right, then,' I said.

'Better than all right. Wouldn't you say?'

'I'm certainly not about to contradict you while we're in bed.'

'We could do with more people like you in England,' I said, teasing her a little now; I was going to make her wait for it after the way she had kept the truth from me. 'People there are increasingly quick to take offence about almost anything. In evidence I give you the Twitter storm caused by something I tweeted a few days ago. For which I shall probably get fined by the FA and for which I shall have to apologise. Otherwise they could take away my coaching licence.'

'What did you say?'

I sighed. 'It was a stupid joke. A throwaway remark.'

'That's why it's called Twitter, isn't it? Because it's not supposed to mean anything important.'

'And yet it does. A Brazilian player called Rafinha came off during a football match in Barcelona and I suggested, humorously, or so I thought, that maybe he had his period.'

'I get it. Like the cranberry juice scene in *The Departed*. Ray Winstone and Leonardo DiCaprio.'

'S'right. Anyway, the Twitter sisters thought it was in poor taste and sexist and reported me to the FA who are now investigating the matter. It used to be that it was all right to be a sexist in football. Now everyone is obliged to sound as reconstructed as Ed fucking Miliband. What makes it doubly irritating is that my father had told me to stay off Twitter. And until then, I had.'

'I like you being a sexist. Especially right now. I wouldn't have you any other way.'

'I'm pleased to hear you want to have me, anyway.'

'But seriously, Scott, why don't you tell everyone on Twitter to fuck off and then close the account?'

'Is that your advice as a lawyer?'

'Yes. It is.'

'I never thought of that.'

'Your father's right. You should listen to him. Twitter is just a hostage to fortune. You stay on it long enough you're bound to slip up. So. Take the FA's fine, say sorry, and then say bollocks to Twitter.'

'You know, I think I will.'

'And being described as a liar is nothing new to me, Scott. I hear much worse than that in court. No, what I'd find more offensive is if you decided that just because I was a little economical with the truth, you didn't want to fuck me again.'

'Oh, there's very little chance of you saying anything that would achieve a result like that. In fact, I think it makes for a more interesting situation in bed, don't you? If I were to take charge of you, now.'

'What I think you're saying is that you'd like to show me who's the boss here.'

'It certainly beats getting screwed by my lawyer if I fuck you, don't you think?'

CHAPTER 24

From the hotel we walked back to the villa in the dark, along a main road that was busy with cars and mosquito-like scooters. There was an evening market in the car park at Le Gosier and we paused for a while to inspect the local fish, exotic fruits and vegetables, jars of honey, fresh-baked bread, jars of spices, sweets and candy, meats – raw and cured – and bottles of rum. There were even a couple of hamburger vans serving food that actually smelt appetising. It was all very colourful and just a little bit puzzling.

'Maybe we should just have dinner here,' I said. 'We certainly couldn't do any worse.'

Grace pulled a face.

'No, really,' I insisted. 'Some of the best meals I've ever had have been snatched at vans parked in front of English football stadiums.'

Ignoring the vans we walked on. The locals seemed friendly enough but we might easily have been somewhere in West Africa and it was hard to believe that we were in a part of the EU, although the prices were almost as high as if we'd been at a tourist market in provincial France. I wondered how the people of Guadeloupe – who looked as if they didn't have much money – could afford anything at all. But we bought some things and walked on, hand in hand.

'You know I'm going to need your help, Grace,' I said. 'The kid seems like a nervous wreck. There's no telling what he'll do. And if, when we go back to the house, Jérôme says he's changed his mind about returning to Barcelona with me, I'm going to need you to help me persuade him that his father has a reasonable chance of acquittal.'

'I know.'

'So, are you with me?'

'Let me tell you something about my cousin, Scott. I know you think he's a bit of a wastrel. But I owe him everything.'

'Is that a no?'

'No. Not exactly. But you have to understand how much I owe him. It wasn't just my university education he paid for. It was my apartment, too. And my offices. And my car. He also paid for his father's apartment, in Antigua. And his car, too. And Jérôme will certainly be paying for John's legal defence. That man we met this morning – the one on the sunlounger? He's the former football coach at the local lycée here in Pointe-à-Pitre. Gerville-Réache. To which Jérôme also regularly gives money. The woman in the hairdresser's? Jérôme sent her money when he found out that the earthquake had closed her business. He's the most generous man I know. Without him a lot of people on this stupid island would have nothing.'

'I appreciate that. And believe me, I think it's good that he looks after his friends and family. But surely you can see that he needs to earn money. Without a big salary from PSG and FCB all that could come to an end. If the goose stops laying the golden eggs it's not just bad for Jérôme Dumas, it's bad for everyone.'

'I understand that. But you see Jérôme and John, they weren't always close. And now they are. Very close. Especially since Jay's mother died. Since that happened they're even closer. So it's natural that he should be worried sick about all this.'

'I'm a football man, Grace. I'm not a sports psychologist. My job is to represent the club and to make sure he understands the club's position.'

'Just as long as you understand mine.'

'Oh, I do. But look, all he has to do is come back with me, have his medical and then explain why he went AWOL. He could even ask for some compassionate leave and return to Antigua for a while. If I endorse that request they're bound to say yes. Because they'll owe me big time for finding the kid.'

'You really think they'd allow it?'

'Why not? They've been very understanding of Messi while his whole life is being turned upside down by those bastards in the Spanish tax authorities. So I'm pretty sure they can extend a little of the same understanding to Jérôme Dumas and his father.'

'All right. I'll back you all the way. One thing's for

sure; he can't stay here in Guadeloupe. Spending all day hunched on the PlayStation isn't good for anyone. Least of all someone who's depressed. He needs to be doing what he's good at again, and that's playing football.'

We reached the house which was almost as private from the street as it had been on the beach – just another door in a wall that led into a lushly planted garden. This time Charlotte, the housekeeper, admitted us, and in person. She was a large, smiling woman in her forties who said almost nothing, but it was clear that dinner had been prepared at home; something delicious was well under way in the kitchen. Grace and I looked at each other and breathed a sigh of relief. We were both famished.

'Mr Dumas will be with you shortly,' she said, showing us into the drawing room. She pointed at a bottle of expensive rosé chilling in a wine cooler next to some glasses. 'Help yourself to some wine.'

I poured two glasses, sipped the excellent wine and then we went to inspect the beechwood bookshelves.

'Who did he say owns this house?' said Grace.

'A French footballer. Gui-Jean-Baptiste Target.'

'He seems to like reading about the game as much as he likes playing it,' she said. 'Nearly all of these books are about football.'

'That would certainly explain the PlayStation 4.'

'Oh my God. This one is by you. *Foul Play*.' She took it back to the sofa and opened it. 'Did you write this or did someone else do it for you?'

'No, I wrote that myself. Which probably explains why it didn't seem to sell very well. I should have got myself a ghost. Like Roddy Doyle or Phil Kerr. Kerr's more expensive, I hear. But then he doesn't look for a credit. The rumour is he's done quite a few famous footballers. Probably because as ghosts go he's more transparent than most.'

'Mr Target bought it. And from the condition of the book I'd say he read it too. There are passages here that have been heavily underlined.'

'Really? Such as?'

'"Football has become the new Esperanto. A modern lingua franca in the true meaning of that phrase: it is a bridge language, a trade language which facilitates cultural exchange throughout the world. A friend who was in a remote part of Vietnam told me that in the two weeks he was there he got by with just two words: David Beckham. Everyone has heard of Becks. And everyone likes him. Just to mention his name is to create some kind of bond. So let's forget Prince Andrew. It's Goldenballs who should be given a job as Britain's special representative for trade and investment; not to mention a knighthood and anything else that will show our appreciation for a man who is one of our best exports. Frankly, the royal family needs the lambent glow of Beckham receiving a knighthood more than the man needs this gewgaw himself. And isn't it time Beckham was asked to join the FA's board of directors? With all due respect to Heather Rabbatts – a non-exec-utive director of the FA board – it's not racial diversity that the existing board lacks, it's bloody footballers. If I can borrow a phrase of the England rugby captain, Will Carling, speaking of the RFU commission, the FA are just fifty-seven old farts. If the England team is ever going to matter again we're going to need footballers to make decisions about the English game. Because the national team is becoming increasingly irrelevant. If, with apologies to E.M. Forster, any football fan had to choose right now between not watching his country and not watching his club, it is more or less certain that he would have the good sense not to watch his country."'

I winced. 'I'd forgotten that. Oh shit. I don't think that's going to help me when I face an FA disciplinary panel for bringing the game into disrepute with my tweet about Rafinha's period. Do you?'

'Probably not. Could be you're going to need a lawyer there to do the talking for you.'

'It sounds like it, doesn't it?'

'Unless you can persuade David Beckham to represent you.'

Grace turned several dozen pages, read some more and laughed.

'What?' I said.

'This isn't much better. "The game is truly egalitarian in that it has something that appeals to everyone. It is the last bastion of tribalism in an otherwise civilised world. As such it is a refuge from all politically correct thinking. Those who preach politeness, orthodoxy, toleration and the socially homogeneous can be safely ignored; witness the hostile reaction of Tottenham fans to the FA's cloth-eared proposal to make using the phrase 'Yid Army' subject to legal sanction. Men and women feel safe within the world of football. It is an enclave from the self-righteous values of the BBC, the *Guardian*, the Labour Party, the fifty-seven farts and all the cares of the world and you try to breach its walls at your peril. Going to football is like saying 'fuck off' to all of the above. When you go to football you don't need to give a shit about your country's economic travails, bird flu, AIDS, gender equality, the war in Iraq, Afghanistan, the Troubles, Africa's starving, Islamic terrorism, Islam, 9/11, the Palestinians – in fact you don't need to think or care about anything very much except the game itself. Not only that but a football stadium is perhaps the last place in the world where a grown man or woman can behave exactly like a child without anyone really noticing or caring very much. It's like fishing in the way it clears the mind of everything except catching a fish, with this important difference in these socially fractured times that we live in: when you go to football you are part of a family. A family that doesn't ask questions about who or what you are because it's the colour you wear that counts; it's the scarf that matters, not what you say, or think, or do, and to hell with everything else."'

Grace put the book aside for a moment.

'How much did you say they can fine you?' she asked.

'That bad, huh?'

'No, really how much?'

'I'm not sure if there's an upper limit, actually. I think

the highest fine ever imposed was on Ashley Cole for calling the FA a bunch of twats on Twitter. True of course. But that cost him ninety thousand quid. No, wait. It was John Terry. Yes, of course. How could I forget? In 2012 he got fined £220,000 for calling Anton Ferdinand a fucking black cunt.'

'Two hundred and twenty thousand – pounds?'

I nodded. 'Frankly, I've been called a lot worse. And I've racially abused more than a few myself. It's swings and roundabouts, really. I think it's a complete nonsense that there's language you're forbidden to use on the pitch when half of the players in the Premier League can't even speak fucking English. Who says what – it's all bullshit. How is it even possible to police something like that when, for example, the Spanish word for the colour black is "negro"?'

'It would take me almost five years to earn that kind of money.'

'That's ten days' pay for John Terry. It's lucky he didn't bite Anton, as well.'

'I don't understand. How have you got away with this until now?'

'I told you nobody read that book. It was remaindered almost immediately. Most of the copies are in my attic, I think. Nobody reads fucking books in England. Not any more. But put something on Twitter and this is something very different. They treat a tweet like it's a letter from Emile fucking Zola.'

'They will read your book now, don't you think? The FA, I mean.'

'You're right. I'm going to need a brief to represent me, aren't I? So. The job's yours if you want it.'

'Really? You'd fly me over for the hearing? To London?'

'Why not? Just as long as I get to fuck you again, Grace. I ought to get something out of this hearing, don't you think? Besides, it will look good me having a black brief.' I grinned. 'I always did like black lingerie.'

'Scott, my dear, I think I'd better start thinking of your defence right now. Tonight. You're going to need every word of mitigation I can find in the thesaurus.'

CHAPTER 25

When Jérôme came downstairs he was wearing a pair of G-Star RAW jeans that looked expensively ragged and a message T-shirt which read *SCORES UNDER PRESSURE*. I'd once seen Mesut Ozil wearing one at the Chiltern Firehouse and thought he was taking the piss; scoring under pressure wasn't something he'd done a great deal of at Arsenal. Jérôme was also sporting his Cartier panther earrings and a gold Tourbillon watch that had more bling than the Kimberley diamond mines. We gave each other a homie handshake and then he helped himself to a glass of wine.

'This is a nice wine,' I said, politely. 'Domaines Ott. I must remember that one.'

'It's Gui who knows about wine,' said Jérôme, 'He's got a wine cellar downstairs that looks fabulous. Me, I just order from the expensive end of the wine list and then hope for the best.'

'Living in Paris, that could be costly.'

'It is. Maybe wine will be cheaper in Barcelona.'

'They make some pretty good wines in Spain. Perhaps as good as anything made in France.'

'What's the book?' he asked Grace who was still reading.

'I found it on Gui's shelves. It's by Scott.' She held it up to show him the cover which featured a moody picture of me. What else do you put on the cover of an autobiography? I remembered when the book first came out how unnerving it was to see my own face staring back at me off the shelves of my local Waterstones. Like seeing a poster of some wanted criminal.

'By Scott. Hmm. Gui likes to read.'

'From the number of underlinings it seems to be a favourite of his.'

'Then you must sign it for him,' said Jérôme. 'A lot of the others are signed. Fergie's book. Roy Keane's. Mourinho's. He loves having them signed. Here, let me find you a pen.'

Jérôme pulled open a drawer and produced a Mont Blanc fountain pen which he handed to me.

I tried to write my name, but without success.

'It seems to have run out of ink,' I said, handing it back.

'I think there's some more in the desk,' he said, sitting down at a modern-looking table near the window. He pulled at the barrel of the pen and then frowned. It was clear he didn't know how it worked.

'It's a piston-filler,' I said. 'I've got one at home. You unscrew the end, stick it in the ink, then screw the end back up, which sucks up the ink.'

'Shit,' said Jérôme looking at his hand. 'It seems there was maybe some in it after all.'

He wiped his hand on the back of his jeans.

'I've lost a lot of white blouses like that,' said Grace. 'Here, give it to me.' She took the pen, filled it with ink, wiped it carefully on a tissue from her handbag – but not without getting some ink on her own fingers – and then handed it to me.

'There you go.'

I opened the book's title page and wrote my name and an anodyne little message for Gui about how lovely his house was and wishing him good luck with his career. Books are hard enough to write but the dedications are even harder. Especially in football. The number of times I'd written *It's a funny old game*, or *This is a book with two halves*. Somehow *good luck* never seems quite enough. I handed the book to Jérôme who turned the pages as if the book had been an artefact from a time capsule. Maybe all books are. I mean, who the fuck reads any more?

'Perhaps I can read this on the plane to Barcelona,' he said. 'But why's it called *Foul Play*?'

'You remember I said I'd been in jail, for something I didn't do?'

He nodded.

'The full story of what happened is in here. How I got fitted up by the British cops for something I didn't do. There's that and the fact that I had a reputation on the park as a bit of a hard man. Until Richard Dunne I think I held the Premier League record for the most red cards. No, that's not quite true. I think he holds the record jointly now with Patrick Vieira and Duncan Ferguson. Honestly, though, I was never a dirty player. Just fully committed, as they say. I never set out to injure anyone. But I do think football's a man's game that's in danger of becoming just a little tame.'

'Oh? How?' He laid the book on the table and picked up his glass.

'I watched Messi up close twinkling his toes at Camp Nou the other week and I was thinking in the old days, someone – Norman Hunter, Tommy Smith – would have taken his legs off at the knees. I'm not saying that's a good thing, mind. Just that maybe the balance has gone too far the opposite way. Actually, I think that this is why a lot of European players struggle in the Premier League. Because the game is much more physical in England than it is in Spain. With one exception. Cristiano Ronaldo. I think he's probably the most physical player I've ever seen. I met him once and it was like shaking hands with fucking Xerxes. The king in that movie 300 about the three hundred Spartans? The one who Leonidas tells to go and fuck himself.'

Jérôme nodded. 'Good movie.'

I shrugged. 'Had its moments.'

'You know, I've been thinking of writing a book myself,' admitted Jérôme. 'Oh, I don't mean another boring autobiography about how I first got picked for Monaco and what it was like to pair up with Zlatan. No, I mean a proper book. Like the one your Russell Brand wrote?'

'Oh, you mean a booky-wook.'

'What's that?'

'It's like a book but it's written by Russell Brand. Which makes it a little bit different, I suppose.'

Jérôme nodded. 'Have you read his latest book?' he asked. 'It's called *Revolution*.'

'No,' I said. 'Have you?'

'Not yet. But I'm going to when I can get hold of a copy in French. I'm really looking forward to it. In fact, if you see one at the airport in Pointe-à-Pitre maybe you could buy it for me. So I can look at it on the plane.'

'Sure.' I noticed he said 'look' not 'read'; there's a crucial difference that's little appreciated by a lot of people who still buy books.

'I've even got myself a title,' he proclaimed.

'Yeah?'

'I'm going to call my book *The Electric Tumbrel*. Like the cart that they used to transport people to the guillotine during the French Revolution. Only this one's electric? Because we're in a hurry to get rid of some of these people, right? The bankers and the politicians. Plus it's modern and better for the environment, too.'

I smiled, thinly. I hoped I wasn't going to have to endure much of this boring lefty-crap on the private jet. If there's one thing I hate in the world it's a lefty with a mouth on him. Or her. Especially when they're sporting a pair of diamond earrings and a massive gold watch.

'I mean, where does it say that footballers can't be politically engaged?' he said. 'And it's not like Spain doesn't have severe economic problems. Did you know that youth unemployment in the country is fifty-five per cent?'

'Yes, I did. And it's a tragedy.'

'That's second only to Greece. The fact is we need to politicise this generation if anything is ever going to change. We have to see past the politics if we're going to establish a new way of governing ourselves. We need to overthrow the governments the way they did in Iceland. By mass civil disobedience. It's the only thing that works. Because I really believe that inequality is man-made and what we can make we can also unmake. The politicians we have now are part of the problem not the solution. So, into the electric tumbrel with them, that's what I say.'

'Sure, sure, but if you don't mind me saying so, what matters more right now is that you put this recent difficulty behind you. If you take my advice you should resume your career as quickly as possible and let your football do the talking for you. For a while, at any rate. There will be time enough for you to publish a book.'

'Yeah, you're probably right.'

'I know I'm right. You can say what you like when you start putting the ball in the back of the net.'

'You live in London, right? Like Brand?'

'I'm not sure he doesn't live in Hollywood now,' I said. 'Or Utopia, for that matter.'

Or perhaps cloud-cuckoo-land.

'But yes, I live in London. In Chelsea.'

'Chelsea. One day, I'd like to play for Chelsea perhaps. I think José Mourinho is probably the greatest manager in modern football.'

'I wouldn't say that at Camp Nou, if I were you. Although I happen to agree. I think in terms of matches and trophies won he's the most successful manager of the twenty-first century. Not to mention the most glamorous. Until José came along all managers in the English game were angry-looking Scotsmen in ill-fitting tracksuits, but he was the first one to look like he could walk from the technical area straight onto the pages of *GQ*. Like me, he's the son of a professional football player so I've always felt that we have something in common. But there's not a lot of love for José in Barcelona. Not since he was the manager at Real Madrid. Certainly not since he poked poor Tito Vilanova in the eye. Anyway, José said sorry. Which is probably just as well in the circumstances.'

'What circumstances do you mean?'

'Because Tito Vilanova died.'

'What, from a poke in the eye?'

'Not from the poke in the eye. But from cancer. That's why I say it was just as well that José apologised. Tito was just forty-five. They're still grieving about that at Camp Nou.'

'Thanks for telling me. Hey, it sounds like there's a lot to learn about playing in Barcelona.'

'That's probably true of anywhere. But it's especially true of Barcelona. I think you'll like it a lot there. Catalans – they're a little less reserved than Parisians. They're certainly more passionate about their football. *Obsesivo*. About everything, I think. Politics, especially. You'll make a lot of friends there if you say you're in favour of a referendum on Catalonian independence.

But that's all you should say about this. They'll ask you but don't ever let on which side you'd vote for. Best to keep your powder dry on that one.'

'What else?'

'You'll read a lot of crap in the newspapers – or online – about how the club is unhappy and going through a difficult phase. Actually, I don't think that's true. Yes, they lost a couple of key players in January; and there's a transfer ban until 2016 that's to do with some kids having the wrong documents. Which is bullshit. And who knows if Messi gets on with Luis Enrique or not? But they're only a point behind Real and getting better all the time. Financially, the club is better off than it's ever been. Annual revenues are more than five hundred million euros. Only Real does better with just over six hundred. There's no tyrant king who needs keeping sweet. They're even opening an office in New York to sell the club abroad. About the one thing I'd do is try to bring Johan Cruyff back into the Barca fold. At the moment he's having a protracted sulk at his home in Sarrià-Sant Gervasi. Like Achilles I think he's the key to future victory.' This time I didn't wait for him to look blank. 'A Greek hero. *Troy*. Brad Pitt.'

'Oh, right. Of course. Great movie. Things never clicked for me at Parc des Princes in Paris the way things worked in Monaco. Believe me, it certainly wasn't for lack of trying.'

'I know.'

'I just hope it can work out for me at Camp Nou.'

'Of course it can. You're still young. Listen, Gerard

Piqué was just twenty-one when he left Man U to play for Barca. Now there's a player who hardly ever made the team back in Manchester. But within months of starting work under Guardiola he was one of the best defenders in the world. Guardiola would probably tell you that Piqué was his best signing. In the World Cup squad at twenty-three. Married to Shakira. He even has his own video game. Man U let him go for just eight million euros; they'd have to pay six or seven times that now. Maybe more. That kind of success can be yours, too, Jérôme. I'm convinced of it. In a year's time, with any luck, PSG will feel the same way about you that Man U do now about Piqué.'

'You really think so?'

'I know so. I can smell it. The sweet smell of success for you.'

'I'd like my own PlayStation game,' said Jérôme. 'There's millions to be made in the games industry.'

I nodded. It was increasingly clear that Jérôme Dumas was a man of contradictions. It was equally clear it was going to be a long flight back to Spain.

'Me, I can smell dinner,' said Grace, changing the subject. 'And I'm starving. I feel like I haven't eaten since breakfast.'

Jérôme grinned. 'After what you said I thought I'd ask Charlotte to make something for us. She's a very good cook. Doesn't touch alcohol but loves food. We've got foie gras, lobster and everything. She was trained in Paris so she knows just how fastidious French people like Gui and me are about food.'

'Which makes me wonder why so many of them bother to come to Guadeloupe at all,' I said. 'You'd think that this was a place to be avoided.'

Jérôme led us into the dining room.

'It's cheap to get here,' he said. 'That's why. The French government subsidises the air fares and the cruise prices to make sure the tourism industry here is thriving. It costs a lot more to travel from London to Antigua. That way they think they can keep the locals happy. More or less. And it satisfies those French who want some winter sun but are too cheap to go to St Barts.'

'Why didn't you come here in the first place?'

He grinned. 'You're staying at Jumby Bay and you need to ask? Guadeloupe has got nothing like that. Besides, my dad lives on Antigua. There's all that and there's Sky Sports. Jumby Bay has got Sky. And that means football on the telly. Whenever you want it. Almost.'

I had to admit he had a point there.

Charlotte served a superb dinner which put us all in a very good mood. And afterwards Jérôme made us some excellent coffee and then helped us to some of Gui's vintage Armagnac. He was a good host like that but probably a bad house-guest for the same reason.

'So,' I said, 'are you ready to travel back to Barcelona with me and face the music?'

'I'm still a bit worried about my dad. But yes, I am.'

'That's good. I'll try to send a text to them tonight and have a private jet sent here within twenty-four hours to fly us back to Spain.'

'Good luck with that,' said Jérôme. 'Sending a text, I mean.'

'You're right. Perhaps I'd better call them from the hotel. Look, I have to go back to Antigua to collect the rest of my stuff from Jumby Bay. I'll do that first thing in the morning and then be back here to fly to Spain with you, tomorrow night. I'll tell them, in confidence, about your father and arrange for you to have some compassionate leave as soon as possible. You can take your medical, do the press conference and be back here to visit your dad in a week or two.'

'In the meantime, don't worry,' said Grace. 'I'm quite hopeful that as soon as Antigua's director of public pros-ecutions has had a chance to review the police evidence they'll see this was a clear case of self-defence, and agree with my submission that this doesn't warrant a murder charge. Once that has happened I'm very confident that we can get your dad bail.'

'Thank you. Both of you.' He shook his head.

'What?' asked Grace.

'I feel such a fool, really,' he admitted. 'To have over-reacted in the way I did. It's just that I've grown very close to my father.'

'Forget about it,' I said. 'A lot of people would prob-ably have done the same as you. I'm very close to my own father, myself. If he'd been facing a murder charge I'm not sure I could have left him to sweat it out on his own.'

'I'll come with you, Scott,' said Grace. 'Back to Antigua.'

I looked at her narrowly. 'Maybe you should stay here in Guadeloupe. It might not be such a good idea for Jérôme to be on his own too much until he's on his meds again.'

'I'll be all right,' said Jérôme. 'Really. You don't have to worry about me, Scott. I'll see you tomorrow afternoon.'

'Good. I'll come here in a car from the airport and pick you up myself. Okay?'

'Okay.'

On our way out of the door again, Jérôme took my hand and held onto it tightly. There were tears in his eyes and for a moment he seemed unable to say anything. I squeezed his hand back and smiled.

'I just want to say thanks, Scott. Thanks for helping me like this, man. I don't know what I've have done if you hadn't turned up.'

I shrugged.

'I guess that you'd have carried on staying here. This is a nice house. It's very comfortable. You've a fine cook here in Charlotte. And there's a copy of my book as well. I really don't know what else anyone could ask for.'

CHAPTER 26

I kissed Grace and then her fingers, still inky from the night before and smelling strongly of me. Taking advantage of our last chance for a fuck before I flew back to Spain, neither of us had had much sleep. Every time I'd opened my eyes I'd climbed on top of her bones.

'I'm exhausted,' she admitted. 'You must be, too.'

'I'll sleep on the jet,' I told her. 'In fact I'm kind of banking on that. It'll be a good way of escaping from Russell Bore's half-baked theories about the future of global capitalism.'

'He means well.'

'So did Robespierre. Seriously though, how much influence do you have with your cousin? Because someone needs to tell him to button his lip for a while. Catalans are a generous-hearted people but they don't much like it when people start telling them where to get off. There's a good reason that Spain had a civil war.'

'I'll speak to him.'

'Do. And while you're at it tell him to lay off the hookers and the weed.'

'Yes. I will. I must say the gun thing still worries me a bit.'

'You can leave that to me.'

We left the hotel and went to the airport in Pointe-à-Pitre to get on the Diamond Star I'd chartered for a return flight to Antigua. It turned out that Guadeloupe's airport had the best mobile signal on the island. As soon as we were there I started to receive texts and missed call messages. Most of them were from Jacint Grangel at Barcelona, Charles Rivel at PSG and Paolo Gentile, but there were one or two from Louise Considine, in London. To her I sent a text saying that I missed her and that I was looking forward to coming home: both of which were true. I'd already spoken to Jacint from the hotel, the night before.

It was a bumpy flight that had us both groaning like a couple of pensioners on Blackpool's Big Dipper, and I was glad I'd hired a twin engine light aircraft; there's something about having two engines instead of one that reassures me – even if they are propeller engines.

When Grace and I landed in the airport at St John's and had recovered our nerves we said our goodbyes in the terminal.

'I'll see you in London,' I told her.

She said nothing for a moment.

'The FA? My disciplinary charge? Remember?'

'No.' Grace shook her head. 'I don't think so.'

'What do you mean? I'm going to need your silver tongue, Grace. My own has a habit of getting me into trouble. That and my thumbs. But I've taken your advice and binned my Twitter account. I should have done it months ago. It's been nothing but grief.'

'Look,' she said, 'the last few days – they've been nice, very nice, but frankly I'm going to have my hands full preparing my uncle's defence. In spite of what I told Jérôme back in Guadeloupe, there's still a long way to go on this one. Any optimism you might have heard from me was calculated to help you get him back to Spain for his medical. Until the DPP says that this is a case of manslaughter he's still facing a capital charge.'

'Yes, I had wondered about that.'

'Before you spoke to him last night you asked me to back you up and I did. Not because I was anxious to please you, Scott, but because I don't see that anything's helped by him staying here. So, let's just agree that we had a great time and leave it at that, can we? Maybe you'll come back here to Antigua and maybe you won't. We'll just wait and see, okay? For the record I hope you do. But I think I told you I wasn't looking for anything serious right now. And I meant that. I might not have mentioned this before but I'm thinking about going into politics and I don't want anyone on the island thinking that I'm not a serious person. Which it could easily look like if I go to London to defend something as trivial as your sexist tweet.'

I grinned. 'Well, that's telling me.'

'Oh, but you'll easily find a brief to look after you. Hire yourself a QC. There's plenty of them doing not very much. Better still, hire Amal Clooney. I'm sure that this is just the sort of high-profile case she's looking for.

It seems to me strange that the English law I studied and learned to love has nothing better to do these days than pay attention to a long line of stupid people who are just waiting to be offended by someone's else's opinion. I used to think England was the home of free speech. Thomas Paine. The rights of man. Speaker's Corner. Now I tend to think it's just the home of wimps, wallies and witch-hunts.'

'I can see you were made for politics,' I said.

She was right, of course. I knew that. But as Everton ferried me back to the hotel I felt just a little sad that I wasn't going to see Grace any time soon. I hadn't told her – it wasn't perhaps what she wanted to hear – but she was the first black woman I'd ever been with and I'd liked it; I'd liked it a lot. I don't think there's anything Oedipal about that but maybe, just maybe, I'd fallen for her in a way I hadn't expected.

'Did you find him, boss?' said Everton. 'Your missing footballer? Monsieur Dumas.'

'I found him. He's been hiding in a house on Guadeloupe.'

'Hiding? From what? Or who?'

'I think he probably had a nervous breakdown.'

I was trying out this explanation just to hear how it sounded. It sounded a lot better than saying Jérôme's father killed someone. That never plays well.

'I'm going back there this afternoon. I've returned to Jumby Bay to settle my bill and fetch my bags. Barca are sending a jet for us. To Pointe-à-Pitre.'

'They must be pleased.'

In truth 'pleased' hardly covered it. Jacint Grangel had been ecstatic.

'I knew you were the man to find him, Scott,' he'd said when I called him from the hotel in Le Gosier the previous night. 'This is fantastic news. And very timely. We have weeks to get him fit for *el clásico*. Oriel is going to be delighted. And Luis. As for Ahmed, well, he had his doubts that you could pull this off. I'm really going to enjoy watching him hand you a cheque for three million euros. But is he fit? Is he all right? And where the hell are you? I've called you several times.'

'Just charter a private jet. And send it to Guadeloupe as soon as possible. There's a company in England I use sometimes called PrivateFly. They're pretty good. It's a little complicated so if you don't mind, Jacint, I'll explain everything in an email.'

'Sure. I can't wait to read it. Will you please copy it to Paolo Gentile? I think he's phoned me every day since you left Paris. Have I heard anything? What's happening? Would I be sure to call him back the minute I had any news? He said you'd ignored all his texts. If it comes to that you've ignored mine as well.'

'Mobile reception isn't so good on Guadeloupe. Nor is the food. The food is lousy. As a matter of fact, nothing is very good. Except the weather, of course. No complaints about that.'

'It's better than here, I can assure you. It's been cold in Barcelona. We've even had some snow in the mountains above Tibidabo.'

I was going to miss the weather, but probably not much else. I wasn't looking forward to meeting the FA, but I was very much looking forward to getting back home to London and seeing Arsenal at home to London City – although that was going to be a difficult match for me to watch. Who was I going to support? The last time I'd seen the two in action against each other I'd favoured the Gooners, only because I'd once played for them and because I was still angry with Viktor Sokolnikov; but time had softened my anger, not to mention my principles. I missed the team. I missed them more than ever I could have admitted to almost anyone.

I tried to give Everton some more money but he wouldn't take it.

'You done give me enough already, boss.'

'All right. But if you're ever in London – to see Tottenham Hotspur – make sure to look me up. We'll go together.'

'For sure.'

At Jumby Bay there was already a message from Jacint saying that a Legacy 650 – a long-range jet – would collect us from Guadeloupe at seven o' clock the following morning, Atlantic Standard Time. This meant I was going to have another night in the Caribbean whether I liked it or not. I would have preferred to have spent my last night at Jumby Bay, which is a beautiful hotel. But I didn't want to risk leaving Jérôme on his own for too long; in spite of everything that had been talked about and agreed I still worried that he might go walkies again. Without his meds anything was possible. So I packed my bags and flew back to Pointe-à-Pitre in the Diamond Twin Star that had brought Grace and me to Antigua.

I paid little or no attention to the spectacular view you get in the back of this aircraft. I'd realised there was something about the Caribbean – anywhere in the Caribbean – that I didn't like. Probably the fact that it's so very far away from anywhere else. I used to be jealous of people who went there during the winter while I was stuck at home playing football, but actually I think I was better off. Going to the Caribbean every winter is a kind of curse. It made me feel a little bit like Napoleon exiled on St Helena.

At the airport I bought Brand's book and tossed it into the back seat of the white Mercedes limo that was to ferry Jérôme and me back to the airport. Then it drove me to the house in Le Gosier. I was banking on staying the night there and not La Vieille Tour which, without Grace to keep me company, would have been too depressing. I told the driver to pick us up at five the next morning and then rang the doorbell.

Charlotte let me in the door just as the Queen Creole hairdresser I'd seen the previous day seemed to be leaving. Charlotte told me that *le maître* was in the front garden. A heap of Louis Vuitton luggage lay in the hall which I found reassuring. At least it looked like he was ready to leave. I tossed my own cheaper overnight bag on top of the pile and went to find Jérôme.

He was lying on a sunlounger with a pair of red Beats on his ears. He was wearing the same clothes he'd been wearing the previous night, including the earrings and the watch. It was almost as though he hadn't been to bed, and the minute I started speaking to him I knew something was wrong. It seemed that he'd developed a cold – a box of fresh tissues lay on a glass table by his arm, while under the sunlounger was a cloud formation of used ones – and, perhaps understandably, he seemed very morose. His hair was shorter and I concluded that the hairdresser must have come there to cut it but it didn't seem worth mentioning.

'Have you got a cold?'

He sniffed loudly and nodded back at me. 'A cold. Yes. It came on this morning. I just hope a cold is all it is and not something else. Like flu.'

I tried not to wince; the Embraer Legacy 650 seats thirteen which, as private jets go, is a good size, but the cabin is still small – small enough for a sneeze to carry his cold germs to me. I'd had a flu jab in the UK but there are so many different strains of flu you've no way of telling if that covers you for whatever flu they get in a tropical climate like that of Guadeloupe.

'That's too bad,' I said. 'But I don't think it will affect your medical. These days sports doctors know how to take that into account. They're looking for something a bit more serious than a cough or a runny nose. Take a sleeping pill, get plenty of sleep on the plane and you'll probably be fine.'

He nodded again.

'Here, I got you a present from the shop at the airport.'

'What is it?' He eyed the paper bag suspiciously and then held out his hand.

'The book.'

He looked blank.

'Russell Brand's magnum opus.' I took it out of the bag and handed it to him.

He stared at the cut-price Karl Marx on the cover almost as if he'd never seen him before.

'The one you asked for?' I said.

'Oh, right. Thanks. Thanks a lot. I'll read it on the plane this evening, perhaps.'

He didn't even open it; instead he just laid the book under the lounger on a bed of snotty tissues. It's keeping the right company, I thought.

'Which reminds me. The plane is going to be a little later than I said. We won't be leaving until seven o'clock tomorrow morning.' I glanced at the Hublot on my wrist – a present from Viktor Sokolnikov. I shrugged. 'I thought I could stay here with you until then. I'd already checked out of that hotel when I found out about the plane.'

'Sure. Be my guest. Tell Charlotte to pick out a room.'

'All right. Thanks.'

'How long does it take? To fly from Pointe-à-Pitre to Barcelona?' His voice was rusty with cold.

'Eight or nine hours, probably. Which gives you even more time to recover from whatever it is that you've got. So that's good.'

He grunted and stood up, almost as if he wanted to get away from me.

I followed Jérôme onto the lawn, collected the football still lying there under my instep, toed it into the air, dropped it onto my knee, bounced it a couple of times, let it fall onto the grass and gently kicked it to him.

Without much enthusiasm he trapped the football with his right foot, tapped it off the laces on his pink shoe six or seven times, flicked it up into the air, nodded it twice, headed it back to me, and then turned away. Game over.

He retreated indoors and for a while I left him alone; I wondered if he was upset about having to leave Guadeloupe in order to fly back to Spain to face the music. And I had to remind myself that I was dealing with someone who was a depressive; whose mood swings made him seem unpredictable, not to say a pain in the arse. So slapping him was not an option. Besides, he was more muscular than I had realised earlier; his upper body made him seem as muscular as Cristiano Ronaldo, who has probably the best physique in the game today. I don't doubt that he could have hit me as hard as I could hit him; maybe harder.

A little later on I went into the kitchen where Charlotte was polishing marble work surfaces and generally avoiding my eye.

'Our plans have changed a little,' I explained. 'We're leaving first thing in the morning. So, I'm going to need a bed. For tonight. It's just one night.'

She nodded. 'Just pick yourself out a room, sir. All of the beds are made up.'

'Thanks. I will.'

I went out and put my overnight bag in the spare room with the painting of a pumpkin by Yayoi Kusama, very like the one Dumas had at his apartment in Paris. Then I went back to the kitchen. I'd seen a Krups bean-to-cup coffee machine and was now intent of making myself a cup. I did, and it tasted delicious.

'Is this coffee local?' I asked Charlotte who was still there. 'It's fantastic. I noticed it last night after dinner. This stuff makes the coffee in the hotel taste like mud.'

She nodded. 'That's Bonifieur you're drinking,' she said. 'It's the local coffee here in Guadeloupe. Bonifieur is the ancestor of Jamaican Blue Mountain coffee, and very rare. Very expensive, too. That is, anywhere else except this island. Here, I'll make you some more.'

'Bonifieur,' I said. 'I never realised. I wonder if it's too late to go and buy some beans.'

'There's no need, sir. I'll give you a bag before you leave. We've got lots of it.'

Charlotte made a pot of coffee, put it on a tray with a cup and a jug of hot milk and I carried it through into the drawing room where I sat on the sofa, turned on the TV, hunted down a sports channel and started to watch some golf while I savoured what I was drinking. I loved watching golf more than I enjoyed playing it. I especially like those plush American courses like Augusta where even the fairways look like they've been uphol-stered with green velvet.

After a while I noticed Jérôme standing on the level above.

'At last,' I said. 'I've found something I really like about Guadeloupe. The coffee. It's Bonifieur. Fantastic. You want some? I'll fetch a cup.'

'I don't like coffee very much,' said Jérôme.

'Me, I love it. Coffee's my thing, you know? I mean, after football.'

'I prefer fruit juice.'

'You should watch that. A lot of fruit juice, it's just sugar. People think it's good for them and it's not.'

'Okay.'

'You know, I think it's really good the way you support people on this island. The local school's football team. Grace told me that you even sent money to that hairdresser who was here earlier.'

Jérôme sneered. 'Yeah, I'm a real saint, aren't I? Everyone loves me. But I'm not such a great guy, you know. I can be difficult. A selfish prick, you know? In fact, there are times when I fucking hate myself.'

He was off his meds all right; his mood seemed to be the exact opposite of the one I'd seen last night.

'I think we all get like that sometimes.'

'Maybe.'

I finished the cup I was drinking and went up to join him on the upper level.

'You and Gui must be great friends if he's prepared to lend you this lovely house.'

'He's all right, I guess.'

'You know him from Monaco, you said.'

'Yes.

'I don't recall seeing him play. Is he good?'

'I guess so.'

'Well, there's nothing wrong with his taste anyway.'

Jérôme shrugged moodily.

'That Spanish teacher I was telling you about last night,' I said. 'The one who taught me? I found her address. I'll text it to you.'

He nodded. 'Thanks.'

'And I was thinking. You know what would really make them love you in Barcelona? If you took the trouble to learn just a few words of Catalan, for the press conference. I don't speak much Catalan myself. But I can give you a few words. For example, you could say something like *Estic encantat de ser aquí*, and *Tinc moltes ganes de jugar per al miller equip del món*. You can learn it like a parrot. If you can say all that I just said then I swear they'll think you're the next Messi.'

'You think so?'

'Sure. They love people who make an effort to speak a bit of Catalan. It's important to them. Part of their national identity.'

Jérôme looked doubtful. 'Whatever you say, Mr Manson.'

'Scott. Call me Scott. I can see I caught you at a difficult time.'

'Meaning what exactly?'

'You're in a mood.'

'I've a cold.'

'No, it's a little more than that.'

'If you say so.'

'Are you angry with me, Jérôme? Did Grace say something, perhaps?'

'Like what?'

'About me? About us?'

'Such as?'

'I don't know.' For her sake I thought it best not to mention that she and I had been intimate. 'It's just a pity she's not here now. To help reassure you that everything is going to be all right.'

'Look, I'm just a bit nervous, that's all. I'll be glad when all this is over.'

'Sure.'

Jérôme went into his bedroom and closed the door behind him. By now I was quite sure he was avoiding me. The previous evening I'd gained the strong impression that he liked me. But now I had the impression that he couldn't bear to have me around.

I went into the room I'd chosen for myself. Something was wrong, all right. But I wasn't exactly sure what it was. And then, seeing the painting of a pumpkin by Yayoi Kusama, I had an idea. On closer inspection it turned out to be just a print. I lifted the frame off the wall for a moment and then replaced it carefully.

I went back downstairs and poured myself some more coffee. The sports channels were all in French but finally I found a football match – Chelsea versus Burnley, which is a very different experience when you have a French commentator who almost manages to make Burnley sound like it's somewhere exotic.

A few hours later I heard Jérôme moving around upstairs and went to find him.

'There's something I've been meaning to ask you,' I told him.

'Oh?'

I pointed through the door of the room I'd picked out for myself.

'This picture,' I said, pointing at the Yayoi Kusama. 'It's a copy of the one that's in your apartment in Paris, isn't it?'

He shrugged. 'I don't know. It might be. I have an art advisor who buys all my pictures. As investments mainly. To be honest I know nothing about art.'

'It's the same one,' I said firmly.

'If you say so.'

And then he walked out again.

By now I knew there was something strange happening in that house. The picture was upside down. I knew this because it was me who'd hung it like that.

And if that had been the only strange thing about Jérôme Dumas I might have excused his behaviour. Quite apart from his offhand manner there were a number of things I'd noticed about him which didn't seem quite right. For a start there was the way he had favoured his right foot when playing keepy-uppy earlier; I knew Jérôme was famously left-footed. Then there was his declared dislike of coffee when after dinner the previous evening I'd seen him drinking several cups. And after all his declared interest in Russell Brand, why hadn't he been a little more pleased to receive a copy of his book – a book which he'd told me himself he was very keen to look at? And what had happened to the ink stain on his fingers? The same ink had still been on Grace's forefinger at the airport in Antigua when I'd said goodbye to her that morning.

I stood up, turned the picture the right way up and lay down on the bed to think. After a while I got up and went into the bathroom and stared at my reflection in the mirror, almost as if hoping the guy looking back at me might say exactly what was wrong. He said nothing helpful; and yet it was almost as if he could have told me the answer. As if I was actually already in possession of the solution to the mystery which was confounding me.

'Why is Jérôme Dumas behaving strangely?' I asked the person in the mirror.

'I've no idea,' said Scott Manson. 'Perhaps it's just that he's a cunt.'

'But you do admit that there's something peculiar here?' I said.

'Yes. Very definitely. But look, all of this strange behaviour can be easily explained, surely. You've said it before. He's off his meds.'

'That only explains the observable behaviour, not the physical details. For example, did you ever know a lefty who instinctively played the ball with his right?'

'No,' said Scott. 'But lots of lefties are good with both feet.'

'That's not what I'm asking,' I said. 'I passed him the ball when he wasn't expecting it and without thinking about it, he trapped the ball with his right. That's reaction. Not choice.'

'All right. I'll concede that.'

'What about the picture?'

'The picture? I think that's weird, yes. But I don't

know that you can infer anything from that. Perhaps he just didn't notice the picture was upside down? Perhaps he's just a philistine.'

'If it was any old painting, I'd agree. But even a print by Yayoi Kusama costs a lot of money. The one in his apartment must have cost at least a million dollars. I know because I checked it out when I was in Paris. But he didn't turn a hair when he was looking at it the wrong way round.'

'He's got a cold,' said Scott. 'So, he's not seeing straight. I've had a cold and I didn't know what day it was.'

'You've never had a cold that meant you didn't know what day it was. You're exaggerating.'

'Yes, but to make a point.'

'What about the inky finger?'

'He washed his hands.'

'Grace washed her hands. Since last night I estimate she washed her hands at least three or four times. And the ink was still on her fingers this morning.'

'So, maybe he's just the fastidious type.'

'In which case why is he wearing the same clothes he wore last night? I can still see the traces of the ink on his jeans from when he wiped his hand on them. That's not very fastidious.'

'Good point. The book by Russell Brand can be easily explained. It's just a fucking book you gave him. Not a big deal. Besides, he's ill-mannered. You already know that about him.'

'And not liking coffee?'

'Perhaps he was drinking coffee last night for a reason. To be sociable. To stay awake for some reason. I've met people who drink coffee who aren't as crazy about it as you are.'

'Perhaps.'

'Of course, anyone overhearing this little chat with yourself would conclude that there's nothing wrong with him. That you're the one who's fucking crazy. A schizophrenic.'

'True. All right. We've got until seven o'clock tomorrow morning to figure this out, all right? After that we'll be on the plane back to Barcelona. And it will be too late.'

'Mmm hmm. How many engines does this plane have anyway?'

'It's twin-engined.'

'Would you call yourself a nervous passenger?'

'Yes, Scott. I would.'

'Then maybe he is, too. Did you think of that, Sherlock? Maybe he doesn't like to fly any more than you do.'

'I never thought of that. But still, it would only explain the moody behaviour. Not the details. And aren't you forgetting something? When I was giving him a couple of Catalan phrases? I never suggested a Spanish teacher to him last night. Nor before. That was just bullshit. A bluff. To see what he'd say.'

'You're a suspicious fucker, Manson. Do you know that?'

'Yes. I am. Let me know if you think of anything, okay?'

'You know where to find me. I'll be right here whenever you need me, pal.'

I went back into the bedroom and lay down. I hadn't slept much the night before and so I closed my eyes and, for some surreal, peculiar reason I started to dream of Manchester United and a League Cup game they'd played against Barnsley back in 2009.

The way you do sometimes.

CHAPTER 27

I sat bolt upright on the spare room bed as if a powerful current of electricity had been conducted through my body, and swore, loudly, several times.

'Fucking hell. Fucking hell. Fucking hell.'

Okay, it's not exactly '*eureka*' and I'm no Archimedes but suddenly the solution to the problem that been occupying me earlier now seemed so bloody obvious that it shouldn't have been a mystery at all; in fact, the very ordinariness of the answer now seemed to be in inverse proportion to the apparent difficulty of the original question. It was simple. And it was brilliant. And nobody but me had guessed it until now.

'Fucking hell. The sneaky little cunt. The duplicitous bastard.'

I jumped off the bed, went into the bathroom, splashed some water onto my face and then stared into the mirror at my ruefully smiling double. The man I knew almost as well as I knew myself.

'You look very pleased with yourself, Scott Manson.'

'You have to admit. It's the only possible answer.'

'Go on then. You're dying to tell me what I already know, of course. But don't let that stop you.'

'It's not him,' I said. 'The kid downstairs. It's not Jérôme Dumas. It can't be. It looks exactly like him. Almost exactly. It sounds like him. Almost. Even behaves like him.'

'Almost.'

'Precisely. But it just isn't him. It's some other sod. I'm looking at you in the mirror and I'm thinking this is what he sees. Only he doesn't need a fucking mirror to do it.'

'You mean...'

'Exactly. He's got a brother.'

'Like Gary and Phil Neville.'

'More alike than them. Identical. And probably a lot more amicable than those two bastards.'

'Fábio and Rafael da Silva? The Brazilian lads.'

'Yes. Monozygotic twins.'

'Did you say psychotic or zygotic?'

'You probably need a bit of both to get away with a scam like this. I was trying to work out why the fuck I was thinking about Manchester United before I went to sleep, and that's the reason. Them. The da Silva boys. Old Trafford's Cheech and Chong.'

'They were good. Rafael is better than Fabio, who's now at Cardiff City, I think. Which says all you need to know. And don't forget the Bender boys in Germany.'

'Jérôme has got a secret twin.'

'Or Frank and Ronald de Boer. Rene and Willy van de Kerkhof. Except that they're not secret twins, of course. Everyone knows about them.'

'This would certainly explain why Jérôme didn't know about Russell Brand's booky-wook, about the picture, or the Spanish teacher, and why the brother I met this afternoon isn't quite like the one I met last night. There's no ink on his forefinger and he plays with his right foot instead of his left. Because he's not the same man. Apart from that they're identical.'

'Fucking hell, you're right, you know.'

'Exactly.'

'But why? Why would you do something like this?'

'I don't know. But when you think about it, it could be the basis of a very nice racket.'

'I see what you mean. If one brother ever gets injured, the other can take his place. Like *The Man in the Iron Mask*.'

'Yes. Just like that. I wouldn't be at all surprised if Jérôme Two is almost as talented a player as Jérôme One. Only not quite. Which makes a big difference in football, of course. I mean, there are lots of lads with plenty of talent but only a few with the extra five per cent of ability you need to carry you into professional football at the highest level.'

'That could be it, yes.'

'Which would explain this whole weird scam. One twin supports the other. They probably shared everything. The same job. The same girl.'

'You mean?'

'Why not? Bella Macchina. It's what twins do, isn't it? Shag each other's girlfriends.'

'It's what you'd do if you were a twin, Scott, which

isn't necessarily what most normal people would do. Not everyone is a bugger for the hole like you.'

'Maybe you're right. But it also explains why he – they – liked to hire those two French hookers he called the Twin Towers. Because he, they, were into twins in a weird way that no one could ever have suspected.'

'Fucking hell. That's right. So. What the fuck are you going to do now?'

'I don't know. Have it out with him – them – I guess. Here and now. I think I'll have to tell the one who's here to go and fetch the other from his hiding place so I can hear them out.'

'That could be tricky.'

'Tell me about it.'

'Suppose they don't want to play?'

'Then I'll have to leave them here and fly back to Europe by myself.'

'And the clubs? What are you going to tell PSG and FCB?'

'I don't know that either. I think a lot depends on what the twins have to say about this. But if this has been going on for a while, and I rather suspect it has, then there are an awful lot of people in Paris and Barcelona who are not going to be happy. Not to mention Paolo Gentile.'

'Do you think Grace Doughty knew about all this? She was pretty economical with the truth before, wasn't she?'

'Yes. I do. The bitch. I think she knows everything.'

'A good fuck, though.'

'Yes, a very good fuck. And I'm going to miss that.' I paused and thought for a second. 'But it might explain why she didn't want to come back to London to represent me before the FA. Because she didn't want to be involved with this little scam any more than was absolutely necessary. The plain fact of the matter is that it's fraud, pure and simple.'

'And the father? John? Where does he fit into this picture?'

'I'm not quite sure. My brain is still a bit puffed out after thinking of this answer.'

'You didn't exactly think of it. I mean, it sort of arrived in your subconscious mind, while you were napping. It's not like you deduced it while smoking your favourite pipe, is it?'

'Where does it say that all your best thinking has to be done consciously?'

'True. But don't think this makes you a fucking genius. It doesn't. Not by a long chalk.'

'Maybe so, but if two big clubs like Barcelona and Paris Saint-Germain thought that I was the one man in football who could solve this fucking problem for them then you have to admit they were bloody clever, because that's exactly what I've done, isn't it?'

'Good for you. But where does that leave your three million euro bonus? Have you thought about that? Will they still pay it if all this comes out into the open? They never said anything about paying you if it turns out that Jérôme's disappearance was related to some wrongdoing. Did they?'

'I don't remember. But look, that hardly matters right now. All that matters is the truth, surely?'

'Don't be too sure about that. Lies and lying are the oil that keeps the wheels of civilisation turning smoothly.'

'Who said that?'

'I did.'

'Well, you should know. The amount of lies you've told. Or maybe I should say that you are planning to tell.'

'To who?'

'That nice policewoman. Louise. You are going to lie to her, aren't you? When you get back home. About what you've been getting up to here and in Paris with that other bird. The lovely Bella.'

'I don't know that I'm planning to lie to her, exactly.'

'No, you're just going to do what Grace Doughty did. Which is to be economical with the truth.'

'Touché.'

'You know it's not fair to her, don't you? Louise. She's a nice girl. Too good for a bastard like you, probably.'

'Agreed. But what can I do? Grace handed it to me on a plate. And so did Bella Macchina, more or less.'

'Would you Adam and Eve it? What a load of bollocks. "And the man said, The woman thou gavest to be with me, she gave me of the tree and I did eat."'

'Yeah, all right. Guilty as charged. I'm feeling bad enough about that as it is without you making me feel even worse.'

'Are you? Are you really? I doubt that. I really do.'

'It's not like we're married or anything.'

'And that would make such a big difference to

someone like you, wouldn't it? Need I remind you of how you behaved when you were married? You were shagging someone else's missus, that's what you were doing. Paolo Gentile was right, you know. For you, this is a weakness. An Achilles heel. Which is a nice way of saying that you're just a cunt. A clever cunt. But a cunt nonetheless.'

I sighed and turned away from the bathroom mirror. You can take only so much from your own conscience.

Feeling a little cross with myself I went to find Jérôme 2 – or whatever the hell his name was – and then have it out with him.

CHAPTER 28

As I passed the master bedroom I saw the door was open a few centimetres and, peering through the gap, I glimpsed Jérôme 2 lying fast asleep on his bed. For a second or two I contemplated barging in there and waking him up with my hands wrapped around his neck to demand an immediate explanation but a few moments of reflection convinced me that it was probably best to adopt a slightly softer, more laid-back approach than half-throttling him first. Nobody reacts well to being rudely awakened and while I thought I could probably hold my own in a fight with him, I saw little point in exacerbating what already promised to be a delicate situation. And, thinking it might be better if I waited for him to wake up on his own, I went downstairs to search Gui-Jean-Baptiste Target's extensive drinks tray for a bottle of oak-aged bourbon I'd seen the previous night.

I was about to help myself from a bottle of Elijah Craig when I glanced out of the window and, in the garden lights, caught a glimpse of Charlotte leaving the house with a laden tray in her hands. Given her size she would have been hard to miss. It was like watching a Swiss ball float through the garden. I quickly followed the housekeeper in time to see her place the tray on the lawn and unlock a door near the bottom of the garden before picking the tray up again and going through the door. She closed it carefully behind her and running after her I was just in time to hear the sound of the key turning.

Was the tray for her, I wondered, or for someone else? Maybe she was a live-in housekeeper and these were her quarters. Perhaps she locked the door to ensure some privacy for herself. You could hardly blame her for that. Then again, I remembered her saying goodnight to everyone during dinner last night, and having gone out by the front door. Besides, there was a bottle of beer on the tray and I seemed to recollect Jérôme Dumas saying something about her not touching alcohol. So the beer could not have been for her but for someone else.

As I pondered these circumstances the thought now occurred to me that, perhaps, I had misjudged the situation. It wouldn't be the first time. Was it possible that Jérôme 1 was being held prisoner, just like the man in the iron mask? Far from being in cahoots with Jérôme 1 perhaps Jérôme 2 was intending to take the place of his twin brother whom he'd incarcerated in order that he might enjoy a taste of the Lamborghini lifestyle himself. Having seen Guadeloupe you could hardly blame him for that. And who would ever know? Even if he wasn't as talented a player as his twin, Jérôme 2 might even manage to play a couple of games for Barcelona before they concluded he simply wasn't up to scratch and returned him to PSG. Meanwhile, Jérôme would still be on a hundred grand a week – six or seven times as much as an islander's average yearly salary. Only a few months earning this kind of loot would probably be enough for any young man living out his days in Pointe-à-Pitre. It might easily leave him set up for life. That's a lot of temptation for anyone to resist, even a brother. Perhaps especially a brother.

I took a few steps back and surveyed the low, flat-roofed building into which Charlotte had disappeared. It seemed to be a large garage or perhaps a small house that was the twin of the larger one, and, thinking I might gain access to this building more easily from the beach, I walked to the very bottom of the lushly planted garden and used the door through which Grace and I had first entered the house, the previous day.

The beach was clear of French tourists now; a cheap foam mattress lay abandoned; further up the strand I could hear a guitar being strummed and some laughter, and there was a strong smell of dope in the air. I wouldn't have minded a toke myself. My heart was throbbing in my chest like a squid in a net. Squadrons of pelicans were still hitting the waves in the moonlight like feathered harpoons in search of unwary fish. You had to admire their skill; they seldom came up short. The turbid sea crashed onto the shore and drew back again in a grating, melancholy roar of sand and shingle while the blackening night sky was regularly pierced by a ruby red beam from the island lighthouse that was more than enough to illuminate my new purpose. I walked a few yards along the beach and turned a corner onto some large wet rocks that seemed to cover a long sewage pipe that led into the sea. There I found a steel gate padlocked several times, yet which could easily be mounted provided there was something to cover the no mans' land of barbed wire that festooned the top.

I went back and fetched the abandoned mattress – but not without getting thoroughly wet from a particularly vigorous wave – and bent it over the coils of barbed wire. With this simple precaution I easily climbed over the gate and dropped onto a concrete path that led up to a series of steps. Near the top of these was a low rectangular building from which emanated a flickering blue light. A few seconds later I was standing beside a sliding glass door. I peered around the edge to see Jérôme i watching a movie on television – *Goodfellas* – and eating a meal off the tray brought to him by Charlotte who now seemed to have gone. He wasn't wearing an iron mask but a large set of Beats headphones which adorned his unwitting skull as if he'd hoped to prevent the sound of the TV from reaching my inquisitive ears.

I paused to observe his demeanour. It was almost astonishing how alike the two brothers were. But for the absent earrings and watch I would have sworn that this was the same man I had just seen asleep in the master bedroom. He was wearing a Barcelona football shirt and a pair of white jeans. He didn't look like a prisoner, however. He was laughing; Joe Pesci was in the middle of his 'I'm funny how?' scene. Jérôme was too relaxed, too much at home in his comfortable surroundings to look like he was in any kind of trouble. I pushed gently on the polished steel handle of the sliding glass door, just to see if it was open. It was, which proved simultaneously that this man was certainly no prisoner.

'Fucking bastard,' I muttered.

The headphones Jérôme 1 was wearing now served my purpose, and a minute or so later I had crept into the room and seated myself silently in an Eames chair immediately behind the sofa on which, deeply absorbed in his movie, he was still ensconced. I could even hear the dialogue in the Beats. I smiled bitterly to myself. I was going to enjoy this moment; no one likes to be hoodwinked. I now had the irrefutable evidence of the existence of Jérôme 2's twin brother. Evidence I was now determined to make the most of, like Hercule Poirot in the big reveal scene at the end of some crappy movie.

Finally, he took off his headphones, dropped them onto the sofa and just sat there, quite still, as if he suspected he was no longer alone; my aftershave, probably. Creed. It is, as James Bond observes to Mr Wint in *Diamonds are Forever,* 'rather potent'. A few seconds more passed like this and then he turned slowly around and met my eyes. For a moment I thought he was going to shit himself.

'It's not how it looks,' he said, quietly.

'I suppose I should have suspected something like this, given that your name is Dumas,' I said. 'What, is your dad related, perhaps? To the famous French author of *The Count of Monte Cristo, The Three Musketeers* and yes, *The Man in the Iron Mask*? Is that where you got this idea, do you think? By the way, Alexandre Dumas was a proper author. Not like that irritating velvet-rope revolutionary you seem to admire so much. Now that we're all out in the open I can tell you what I really think about Russell Brand. I can't stand him. All the same, I wonder what he would make of this situation. Are dishonest bankers any worse than dishonest footballers?' I sighed. 'Anyway, Dumas would certainly have loved this story. It's got everything.'

Jérôme 1 said nothing.

'Incidentally, he was black too. Dumas. His father was from Haiti. A little-known fact that people often tend to forget. Or perhaps they're just not aware of it. The black count, the French used to call him. At least I think that's what they called him. Lucky that he wasn't playing for Queens Park Rangers against Chelsea, eh? John Terry might have called him something else. What do you think? I mean, you'd be the man to ask.' I smiled thinly. 'Forgive my manners but I'm just a bit pissed off to discover that you and your twin brother have been playing me for a cunt. And after all your earlier protestations of honesty. That hurts. I mean, I really did come here to help you and now I find that you've been taking advantage of me.'

'It's not how it looks at all,' he repeated.

'Isn't it?' I grinned. 'Oh, I'm sorry, you mean there's actually a plausible explanation that makes this all right? At the risk of being played for a cunt again, why don't you tell me what that is? Fess up, son. Or is telling the truth just something that's just way beyond your abilities? Only I feel I should warn you. My patience is almost gone. If what you tell me sounds or smells like bullshit I shall walk out of here, get on that plane and go home by myself. And you can stay here and rot on this grubby little island. Like fucking Napoleon.'

'It's like this,' said Jérôme. 'You see—'

'No, wait a moment. I'd like Tweedledum to be there when Tweedledee starts to talk. I mean, I've no way of knowing which of you is the real deal. Come on. Let's go and wake him up. I want to make sure I get more than fifty per cent of the story. Maybe he'll contradict you. Who knows? I somehow got the impression earlier that Jérôme Dumas is not such a great guy. That he's a selfish prick.'

We left the beach house and walked up the lawn to the main building.

'By the way, what's your brother's name? Is he Jérôme Dumas, or is that you?'

'I'm Jérôme. His name is Philippe. Philippe is older than me by about five minutes. And wiser, too, probably.'

'That makes us practically related.'

Jérôme was about to go upstairs and fetch his twin brother when I caught sight of the Mont Blanc on the table where I'd left it last night.

'Wait a minute,' I said. 'Let me see the palm of your right hand.'

He hesitated.

'It's all right,' I said, picking up the pen. 'Much as I'd like to, I'm not going to stab you with this. I just want to make sure who I'm talking to.'

He held out his hand; there was still some ink on his forefinger. But I still wrote a large letter 'J' onto the back of his hand blew on it to help dry it off, and then inspected my handiwork.

'There. That should keep things straight for a while. I wouldn't like you two bastards to work a switch on me again. Now go and get your doppel-fucking-ganger and let's see what's what. And don't take long about it. I'm in no mood to be patient here. Come on, move it. If I had a football boot in my hand I'd throw it at you, kid. I really would.'

CHAPTER 29

Oddly, I hadn't met many twins since leaving school, but I'd never met twins who looked as alike as these two did. Two peas in a pod just about covers it, provided you could find two peas that were also perfect specimens of pea. There's something weird about some twins – but not these twins, who were both perfect physical specimens. My earlier, conceited confidence ebbed away more than just a little as the two men came downstairs and faced me silently, as if intent on convincing me that I might be seeing double.

In spite of all this it didn't go unnoticed by me that Philippe Dumas was holding a large hunting knife in his hand. There was a line of sweat beads on his forehead and the muscles in his neck and arms looked about as tense as steel hawsers. And there was a meanness in his brown eyes I hadn't seen before.

Suddenly I began to perceive the obvious difficulty in my situation. Apart from Grace Doughty, no one knew where I was. Barcelona had sent a jet to meet me at the airport, in Pointe-à-Pitre, but other than that they really hadn't a clue as to my exact whereabouts. My email to Jacint had informed him only of the circumstances surrounding Jérôme's disappearance – which bore no relation to the present facts. I hadn't thought to give them an exact address for the simple reason I didn't know what it was. For all they and PSG knew I could have been anywhere on the islands, which have a land area of more than sixteen hundred square kilometres, much of it jungle-covered hills.

It was only now that I remembered why the father of these twins was in jail. *He was accused of murder.* Maybe murder was not something brother Philippe was unfamiliar with. And I began to feel afraid, like I was back in the nick and facing down some racist bastard with a home-made shiv. As close to the sea as this there would be no problem getting rid of my body; they probably knew a boat they could borrow to take my corpse out beyond the island and dump me over the side. The local fish would eat me and I'd probably never be seen again.

But if there is one thing I've learned in football it's never to show your fear, because it's a mistake to think of it as just a game; football is about mental toughness, about saying and doing whatever you need to help your team win. I guessed that I was going to need a lot of that now.

'What, are you going to kill me? Is that it? I should be easy enough to kill. Two of you, one of me. That's one way of making this problem go away, I suppose. How about it, Jérôme? Are you ready to add a stabbing to your list of crimes and misdemeanours?'

'You don't speak to my brother like that,' said Philippe, grabbing hold of my shirt collar with his empty hand. I took hold of his thick wrist and tried to twist my collar from his grasp but he was much stronger than I had supposed. 'You don't know him. You only think you do. He's not a criminal. He's a good man.'

'I don't doubt it, since you're the man with the knife in his hand. But his career is over if you kill me. That much is certain.'

Jérôme looked at his brother carefully. 'No one's going to kill anyone,' he said, which seemed to be as much for Philippe's hearing as for mine. 'All right? We're cool here. So, put the knife down, Philippe.'

But Philippe's grip merely tightened on my shirt collar and on the handle of his knife, which was one of those with a black blade and a serrated edge – the kind you expect Rambo to pick his teeth with. I expect there was a useful compass in the handle, just in case you got lost at the local supermarket. I started to look for the exits, wondering if I could make it to the bottom of the garden before the twin with the knife caught up with me and cut me a new smile.

'I don't think Grace will be too happy if she finds out that she's become an accessory to a murder,' I said. 'How's that going to affect her chances of running for political office? Not well, I'd have thought.'

'Shut up,' said Philippe. 'Leave her out of this. You've done enough talking, Englishman.'

'Oh, I agree,' I said. 'But consider this before I shut my mouth. Or before you do it for me. Barcelona and

PSG know where I am. I sent them an email from Jumby Bay telling them I was at the house of Gui-Jean-Baptiste Target. Not to mention the limo driver who'll be back here at five a.m. wondering where I've got to. I bet that even the Guadeloupe police could solve that crime. If I disappear, this address is the first place they'll look. And it won't just be your father who goes to jail, it will be the two of you. If you're lucky they'll give you twin beds in the same stinking cell. And in twelve months' time the only balls you'll be kicking are each other's for being dumb enough to kill me.'

'He's right,' Jérôme told his brother. 'It's not worth it. So put the knife down, eh?'

Philippe glanced at his brother and then pushed me away. There were tears in his eyes. 'He shouldn't speak to you like that, Jay. He has no idea what you've been through. Better for us both that we get rid of him. He's going to spoil everything. For you, me, Dad, everyone.'

'No, no. It's okay. It's okay. You'll see, Philippe. Everything is going to be fine. We'll sort this out, I promise. I'll make him understand. All right?'

'Better listen to your brother, Philippe. For once he's talking complete sense. You'd be making a very big mistake to kill me and think you could get away with it. But there's still a chance to salvage something from this mess if you both level with me now.' I nodded. 'That's right. Tell the truth. The whole truth. And maybe we can fix this mess.'

Jérôme put his hand on Philippe's arm, and then on the hand that was holding the knife. Finally he managed to take the blade away from his brother. He laid the long, black knife on the table next to the Mont Blanc. From where I was standing the pen didn't look like it was mightier than the sword but there was no doubt that my prospects had improved, a little. I let out an unsteady breath as fear gave way to nervousness.

'Shit, I need that drink,' I said, and returned to the tray where this time I poured myself a large glass of twenty-one-year-old Elijah Craig bourbon with a shaking hand, and drained it in one noisy gulp.

I knew I wasn't completely out of the woods yet. And I figured my best chance of preserving my safety was to get hold of the knife before they changed their minds about cutting my throat. I poured another drink and walked to the table where the knife was now within my grasp. I sipped the bourbon, put the glass down, picked the knife up and examined it objectively, almost as if it had already been used to commit a crime and there was an evidence tag attached to it.

'This would certainly get the job done, I suppose,' I remarked coolly. 'Saw a man stabbed in prison once. With a shank made from a toothbrush and piece of glass. I don't think the guy who stabbed him expected him to die because the victim was stabbed in the thigh. But the femoral artery was cut right through and he bled to death before anyone could do anything about it. That's the one thing they never get right in the movies. The blood. There's a lot of blood when someone bleeds out. A whole gallon of the stuff makes a hell of a puddle.'

I looked at the twins, neither of whom seemed bothered that I was the one now holding the knife. I put it down, collected my drink and sat on the sofa.

'I'm all ears, gentlemen.'

Which was hardly true; there was my chest to consider; my chest felt like I'd just played on the losing side in a cup final.

The twins looked at each other for a moment as if exchanging some telepathic remark – they did a lot of that, I was to observe – and then sat down opposite me. For a moment neither man said a thing but then Jérôme held his hand up in front of my face as if to indicate his true identity and started to speak, albeit with some difficulty.

'I've never talked about this to anyone except my family,' he said.

'Don't tell me,' I said, wearily, 'you're the true king of France.'

'Jay,' said Philippe Dumas. 'Why take a chance? He's a prick. You can't trust this guy to keep his mouth shut. And once it's out in the open it's out. There's no going back with something like this.'

'I have to tell him, Philippe. You heard what he said. If I level with him there's still a chance for me.'

'That's right, Jérôme,' I said. 'A good chance, I'd say. You're a top player. With everything going for you. But if I have to get on that plane by myself, it will be because of your bullshit. It will be over. I can promise you that. No football team will ever touch you again. I'll make fucking sure of it.'

Jérôme nodded. 'All right,' he said. 'I'll tell you everything. The whole story.'

I sipped some bourbon and waited, patiently.

'Have you ever heard of a footballer called Asa
Hartford?' said Jérôme after a long pause.

'Yes,' I said. 'Of course.'

Almost everyone in English football has heard of Asa
Hartford. Back in the early seventies he was a Scottish
international who played for West Bromwich Albion. A
good one, too. I think he even knew my dad. He also
played for Scotland. Then – in 1971, was it? – Leeds
United bought him in a high-profile transfer that fell
through after it was discovered that Hartford had a
hole in the heart.

'He has a ventricular septal defect,' said Jérôme.
'That's the proper medical term for the condition.' He
paused. '*For my condition.*'

I frowned as the implications of what he was telling
me began to sink in.

'Holy shit. You mean—'

'There's a tiny hole in the septum – in the middle
wall – between the left and right ventricle in my heart.
In a normal heart all of the blood that is pumped out
from the left ventricle goes into the aorta. In people with
VSD, when the heart beats, part of the blood in the left
ventricle flows back into the right ventricle through the
septum hole. So, the heart works harder as it has to
pump not only the blood entering the heart normally
from the rest of the body, but also an extra amount of
blood flowing through the VSD.'

'Jesus, I think I'm beginning to guess what's been going on.'

'No need. You've done enough guessing, Mr Manson. This is a condition that affects only me, not my brother, Philippe. We're identical twins in almost every other regard. I discovered I had a hole in my heart at a clinic in Marseille about eight or nine years ago, just before I was going to start playing for AS Monaco. And it was pointed out to me that this might prevent them giving me a contract. So we hushed it up. My mum and my dad. Grace. Everyone. You understand, because of the chance that this gave my whole family we couldn't afford to do anything else. My father arranged for my twin to come over from Guadeloupe and take the medical on my behalf. We did the same thing again in Paris when I went to join Paris Saint-Germain. Only that time I went back to Guadeloupe and for a while my brother took my place in Paris. To have a taste of the good life himself. He's a good footballer, you see. Very good, actually. Just not as good as me. It's not every pair of twins who are as good as the Da Silvas.

He plays for a part time local team called CSC. But because he normally wears a beard nobody notices that he looks like Jérôme Dumas. Besides, his name isn't Dumas, it's Richardson, Philippe Richardson. No one ever knew we were twins because how many twins live apart like we did? Me living with our mum in Marseille and Philippe living with our dad in Monserrat and then here in Guadeloupe.'

'I can see that,' I said. 'But Asa Hartford had a

successful career. The transfer at Leeds fell through, yes. But he went on to play for Manchester City, didn't he? Nottingham Forest? Everton? And for big money, too. He was a great player. He even played for Ally's Tartan Army in the 1978 World Cup. And he's still alive. I think my dad still sees him from time to time. VSD is mostly asymptomatic. A lot of people go through life without even knowing that they have it. And certainly there are plenty of sportsmen who have it. Aren't there?'

'Perhaps that used to be the case, in Asa Hartford's day,' said Jérôme. 'Frankly, it's never once given me a problem. Not once. Not so much as a twinge. It's a very common heart condition. It's estimated that lots of kids are born with a VSD. But insurance companies have changed everything since football became a billion dollar business. Also, VSDs can cause strokes in some people – it's the condition that nearly killed Fabrice Muamba – so its very hard to get insured to play when you have VSD. So you see my dilemma,' said Jérôme. 'I make a lot of money. And the way things are going I'm likely to make a lot more thanks to Paolo Gentile. There's even talk of me becoming the black Beckham. But all of that ends if it becomes known that I have VSD. On the other hand, if Philippe goes to Barcelona in my place, then everything can proceed as normal.'

'You mean if Philippe here flies back to Barcelona to take the club medical on your behalf? If he deceives the club into thinking he's you? I can see why that's attractive. The money. The cars. The women. Sure. It makes perfect sense.'

'But you know it's not just me who stands to benefit from all this money. Surely you can see that. I know you think I'm what the English call a champagne socialist, yes? But I really do believe in giving something back. To the people here in Guadeloupe. To my father. My brother. The local lycée. A new wing for the local hospital.'

'All right, all right. You're a saint. I get that. But what I don't understand is that none of this would have been a problem if Philippe had just flown home from Antigua in your place like he was supposed to do. I wouldn't be here now. You could have done all this and no one would have been any the wiser. What the fuck happened?'

'You're right. What happened was this. The night before I was due to fly back to London I left Jumby Bay to come here on a boat owned by a friend of my dad's, DJ Jewel Movement. I got off the boat, Philippe and I swapped clothes and he got back on the boat and they sailed back to Antigua. But somehow DJ worked out that we'd switched and demanded money from Dad. He thought we were working some kind of confidence trick and he wanted a share of the profits.'

'They were still arguing about it when I got off in Nelson's Dockyard,' said Philippe. 'DJ was a crook. A violent crook. That knife on the table is his. I took it with me when I got off the boat. Because I was afraid for my dad.'

'It's just like I told you before,' added Jérôme. 'More or less.'

'When I got to the airport I saw the newspaper and

guessed what must have happened,' said Philippe. 'Or at least part of it. The newspaper didn't say who was actually dead. My dad or DJ. So I got a ride back here to sit it out until I knew for sure. But I don't know, the stress of that got to me, I guess. I got pneumonia and couldn't travel. I'm only just over it, really.'

'So we were stuck,' said Jérôme. 'I could hardly fly to Spain and take the medical myself. Not without risking everything. Then you turned up and we thought that you wouldn't notice. That there wouldn't be time for you to notice. We thought that you'd be so pleased to have found me that you wouldn't suspect anything was wrong. Why would you notice? Even here on Guadeloupe nobody seems to have worked it out. And you wouldn't have noticed, probably, if the plane hadn't been delayed. By now the two of you should have been airborne and all of your suspicions allayed with a sleeping pill and an in-flight movie.'

'Then what?'

'Like you told me,' said Jérôme. 'I'd have asked the team for some compassionate leave and when Philippe came back here, I'd have taken his place.'

'Very neat. I have to hand it to you, it's a great scam.'

'Like I said, I didn't have a choice. I'm still a good player, Scott. I can still make it to the top of the game. You've seen me play. You know what I can do. You said yourself, I can go right to the top. And you know the Asa Hartford story. A high achiever. A Scotland inter-national, like you said. So, you have to let Philippe go back in my place. Otherwise it's not just me who suffers, it's a lot of other people, too. This game we love – it's the only real social mobility that exists in the world. It's the only chance people like me from a small island like Guadeloupe have of moving up in the world. For some genuine wealth redistribution.'

'That's hardly fair,' I said. 'You're putting this on me.'

'What's fair got to do with it? This is football, Mr Manson. And you do what you have to do in order to win. We're part of an entertainment industry that's now worth billions, thanks to the likes of Sky and BT. What's the difference between me hiding the fact that I have VSD and a Hollywood studio concealing the fact that the romantic leading man in their latest movie is secretly gay? Answer me that.'

'You could die. That's the difference, surely.'

'And if I'm willing to take that risk? Whose business is it except mine? If I'd rather die than give up football? Who should mind but me? And who better than a player like you to understand something like that? How do you like not playing football any more? Do you miss it? I'll bet you do. But at least you had your chance. You had your chance. At least you played, and for as long as you could. Don't take that away from me, Mr Manson. Please, I'm begging you. You take football away from me now, you'll be taking away everything I've got and everything that I'm ever going to have.'

'Don't put this on me,' I said again.

'Who else should I put it on? The pilot of the jet? I'm not asking you to lie for me. I'm just asking you not to say anything to PSG or to FCB.'

'To be economical with the truth. A lie by omission.'

'If you want to put it like that, yes. But where's the harm? Who's injured by your silence? Surely that's what really matters. Who gets hurt?'

'You're asking a hell of a lot, son. I told you before I owe a lot to Barcelona. More than you know.'

'And I repeat the question: who is hurt? Look, just assume for a moment that I go to Camp Nou and score lots of goals. Which is a fair assumption given the number of goals I scored at Monaco. It never really clicked for me at PSG because they kept playing me on the wing, when I'm a natural nine. You can see that.'

'A false nine,' I remarked. 'I can see that all right.'

'Perhaps. But you said yourself, I'm still a top player. Assume that during the remainder of the season I score... let's say ten goals. How is the club damaged? Or, assume I play in *el clásico* and score just one goal and that goal is an equaliser, or even the winning goal, perhaps. How is Barcelona damaged by my condition? Suppose they sell lots of shirts as a result. Suppose all that. How is PSG damaged by Barcelona profiting from my loan to them?'

'Suppose I just tell Barcelona and let them decide.'

'You know that won't work. They're a big company and they have big company rules. It's not people like you and Luis Enrique who decide things at clubs as big as Barcelona. Not any more. It's accountants and lawyers and management consultants and actuaries. Medical actuaries. I've looked into what might happen in considerable detail. Don't think I haven't agonised about this myself. I have. A medical actuary is a physician who puts a number on the risk incurred by a medical insurance company when a company like PSG or FCB employs someone like me. A doctor with a calculator and a set of tables who knows nothing at all about football but who makes a bet on whether or not his medical insurance company would have to pay out in the possible event of me keeling over in the middle of a game.'

'I know what a medical actuary does, thanks.'

'Right. Then you know how that works. No one likes to bet on a horse when they think there might be something wrong with it. That's all I'm asking you to do. Make a bet on the man you see, not on the man you can't see – the man with a hole in his heart. I'm a sure thing, Mr Manson. I can feel it. I'm no crock.'

I glanced at my wristwatch. There wasn't long before the jet was supposed to take us to Spain. And it seemed I now had to decide the future of Jérôme Dumas, not to mention his whole fucking family and possibly – if Paulo Gentile was to be believed about the commercial possibilities for their futures, together – Bella Macchina, too. I could certainly have done without that responsibility.

'I'll think about what you've said. And let you know – well, as soon as I've arrived at a decision. In the morning, probably.'

I collected the bottle of Elijah Craig off the drinks tray. I don't normally drink spirits; then again, I'm seldom put in fear of my life.

'I'm going to change my clothes because I'm soaking wet, and then I'm going to finish this bottle.'

CHAPTER 30

In my time as a football manager I've had to make some tough decisions. Who to drop from a team; who to sell. I remember having to break it to the guy who was my captain at London City that an injury meant he was never going to play for the team again, and it would probably spell the end of his career. And it did. I remember hearing the sound of him weeping in the bogs afterwards – him, a real hard Scots bastard. He took to the bottle after that and I felt like shit for weeks. More than a few weeks. It felt like I'd ruined his life and it's been a skidmark on the porcelain of my soul ever since.

But choosing between two players was easy compared with the dilemma that Jérôme Dumas had landed me with. How do you decide something like that? How do answer a question that might result in the end of a young man's career? There was that and then there was all the excess fucking baggage he'd managed to attach to my decision: the kids' school in Pointe-à-Pitre, the hospital wing in Le Gosier, his brother's welfare, his father's legal defence, his cousin's legal practice in

Antigua. I told myself that a hole in the heart was one thing but that I'd have to have no heart at all to rule against him playing again.

In a way I actually admired him. His determination to play the game at all costs was something I could easily understand. You had to hand it to the lad, the idea of sending his twin to take his medical was cheeky and ingenious and just the sort of thing my old mate Matt Drennan would have done. The game was different then, of course, and that was only ten or fifteen years ago. It's true, the money has changed everything. Jérôme was right about that. And why *was* it all right to conceal the true sexuality of a leading man in Hollywood – not mentioning any names, of course – and yet somehow unacceptable to cover up something like VSD? Why is there a higher standard expected of football clubs than movie studios? I don't get that. All the crap from the Labour Party in the wake of the so-called 'obscene' Premier League television deal, about clubs not paying the living wage to some of their employees, had really pissed me off. Why the fuck stop there? Why not slap a windfall tax on the clubs and give the money to fucking Palestine, or to find a cure for Ebola? Cunts. The BPL is one of our most successful exports and there's nothing obscene about that.

He was also right about VSD. More than he knew, perhaps. He probably didn't realise it but only a week or so ago I'd read a very relevant story in the sports pages of newspapers. An English court of law had ordered Tottenham Hotspur to pay £7 million in damages to a promising star of the youth team, Radwan Hamed, who suffered cardiac arrest days after signing his first professional contract for the club, since when he had been unable to live independently. An ECG screening before he signed showed his heart to be 'abnormal' but he was not stopped from playing by team doctors with the result that Hamed's family had sued Spurs for negligence. Spurs were indemnified by the doctors' insurers in respect of these damages but it underlined that there was no way that any insurance company was even going to countenance the possibility of allowing a man with a hole in his heart to play top-flight football. The days when an Asa Hartford might have enjoyed a full fifteen years at the top of the game were long gone.

By now I was just a little bit pissed. But that was good. I was going to need to be a little bit pissed to tell Jérôme I wasn't going to participate in his deception, which was the decision I was always going to have to make. Because the plain fact of the matter is this: I owe Barcelona a lot. I owe them everything. It was them who took me on when no one else was prepared to give me a chance. And you don't forget that in a hurry. Not in football. In spite of what I'd told Jérôme, I knew I would have to decide in favour of the club. That's what loyalty is. I couldn't have decided any other way. Not in a hundred years. Naturally I felt really sorry for Jérôme Dumas but the way I saw it I didn't have any real choice in the matter. Choosing between the club that had nurtured my managerial ambitions and a player who was prepared ruthlessly to deceive it at all costs was, if I'm honest, never a choice at all. But that didn't make it *feel* any better. Which was why I'd grabbed the bottle of anaesthetic.

In truth, most of the time I was sitting in my room with the bottle I was trying to think of a way of salvaging something of Jérôme's career. Nobody likes to throw someone on life's scrapheap. Least of all me, who knows a few things about being on the scrapheap. When you're in prison you realise that the scrapheap looks like a step up from where you are now.

I might have called someone with whom I could talk this over – my dad, perhaps – but the signal on my phone was, predictably, non-existent. So I was on my own. And those are the toughest decisions of all.

I slept for a couple of hours, woke around four, took a shower and went downstairs. The Louis Vuitton bags were still piled in the hall and the twins were where I'd left them on the sofa, wearing expressions of deep concern and anxiety. I glanced around. The knife was gone, thank God. I went into the kitchen, brewed some Bonifieur coffee and came back into the drawing room. Both of the twins stood up, expectantly.

I saw no point in beating around the bush so I took a deep breath and said, 'I've decided. I'm afraid the answer has to be no.'

'I told you,' said Philippe. 'He's their man, not yours. You should never have trusted him, Jay. Now what are you going to do? It's over, do you hear?'

He stared balefully at me for several seconds, as if he dearly wanted to hit me.

'You bastard,' he said. 'All you people care about is money. None of you gives a damn about the people who play the game. Real people. And the real people who depend on them.'

And then he walked out.

'Sorry about that,' said Jérôme. 'He's upset, that's all.'

'I can see. Look, I'm sorry. But that's just how it is.'

He sat down again and stared at his hands. 'Yes, I understand.'

'Actually no, I don't think you do. I may be English but Barcelona – this club is like family to me, Jérôme. And you don't lie to your family. I agree with everything you told me last night. It all makes perfect sense. But I can't get over the fact that if I allowed Philippe to take your medical I'd be letting the club down badly. I'm sorry, Jérôme, but it's a bridge too far, I'm afraid.'

He nodded silently.

I sat down, poured some coffee, and hoped that the sofa would swallow me up; either that or that the limo driver would ring the doorbell and I could leave. I don't like flying all that much but this was a flight I was really looking forward to.

'Tell me, what kind of football player is Philippe?'

'Are you making polite conversation? Because I'm not feeling very polite right now.'

'Humour me. What kind of player is he? A defender? A goalkeeper. Describe him.'

'Honestly?'

'You can certainly give it a try.'

Jérôme grinned. 'He's a natural winger,' he said. 'A good one, too. Right-footed. A good passer of the ball. His range of passing is excellent. He sees gaps in defences from a long way off. And he runs with the ball almost as fast as he does without it. Very strong, very fast, and very, very fit. Well, you can see for yourself how fit he is. If he'd had an earlier start in the game he might have been a professional, too. Probably at a top club. That's why it was so easy for him to take my medicals. He looks the part already and he has some good ball skills. Enough for the cameras. And, in spite of what you've seen of him since you've been here, he is a very calm sort of individual. Steadier than me.'

'So why didn't he start earlier in the game?'

'The opportunities here are, as you've probably observed, limited. It's not like footballing scouts come to Guadeloupe as a matter of course, although perhaps they ought to given the way the island supplies footballers to the French national team. Besides, Philippe was always more interested in his school work than in sport. He wanted to go to university, to go his own way. We've never been the kind of twins who always did the same things. When we were living together, almost always he tried to do different things from me. And then of course we were separated. Which is a weird thing to do with twins. But in a way he didn't mind. Neither of us did. Which makes us much more individual than you might think.'

'And did he go to university?'

'Yes. He studied agriculture at the University of the

French West Indies and Guiana in Martinique. Paid for by me, of course. He now works for the Guadeloupe and Martinique Banana Growers' Association.'

'Does he like that?'

'Not really. It's only lately that he's come to wish he could have been a footballer, too. And to realise what he's missed. When he saw the way that I live in Paris – my cars, my apartment, my girlfriend – I think it was pretty hard for him to take all that on board. What might have been, you know?'

'I can imagine.' I left unasked the question I wanted to ask, which was if he'd slept with Bella Macchina. 'Is it a well-paid job? With the banana company?'

'By local standards, yes. But not by French standards. Most of his money comes from me. What I give him and my father enables them to have a pretty good lifestyle out here. But for that he'd like to come to France more often and look for work there.'

'And is he married?'

'Married?'

'That's right. You know? A woman with a ring on her finger and a rolling pin in her hand.'

'No. Look, Mr Manson, if all of these questions about my brother are because you're going to suggest that he could take my place at Barcelona or Paris Saint-Germain on a permanent basis, we both know that isn't going to work. There's no way he could survive the pace of the game in Spain. Or for that matter in France.'

'You think I don't know that? I'm not that naïve, son. That isn't what I'm suggesting. I told you, I'm not going to be a part of your very forgivable fraud; equally I'm not going to tell Barcelona anything about your VSD. Since you were only on loan, I figure it's not their business.'

'What are you going to tell them?'

'You can leave that to me,' I said, without having the least clue. 'But I will have to say something more to PSG, who hold your contract, although I'm not yet exactly sure what. I need some time to work out some things in my head.'

'They'll sack me. You know it. And I know it.'

'That's right. They probably will. The real trick is going to be to get them to sack you for all the wrong reasons.'

'What the fuck are you talking about?'

'Look, Jérôme, I think I already told you that I know one or two things about being dumped. A lot of what happened was my own fucking fault, on account of how I've never been able to keep it zipped. But believe me when I tell you that however low you're feeling at this present moment in time, I have felt much much lower. Which is why, against all my better judgement, I'm determined to try and help you.'

'If you really want to help me, Mr Manson, then let Philippe go to Barcelona to take my medical.'

'I think you need to clean your bloody ears out. I've told you why I can't do that. So, I suggest you put FC Barcelona out of your tiny mind for good, and place every ounce of your trust in me. That's right. You're going to have to trust me on this for a while. But first

I'm going to ask you a very important question to which I want a straight fucking answer.'

'I'm listening.'

'Then here it is. And think about it before you open your trap again. Is football still the most important thing in your life? Don't answer yet. *Think about it.* I don't mean all that off-the-field shit that comes with being a top footballer – the deals and the endorsements and the commercial bollocks – I mean the game of football, pure and simple. Is it the pre-eminent thing in the life of Jérôme Dumas? *No, really think before you answer.* A Saturday afternoon and a big match with you playing in front of fifty thousand fans. *Think.* Is that what still floats your boat?'

'I don't understand.'

'It's not a difficult question, son. It's really very fucking simple. Is it football you really like or the prospect of being the black Beckham? Is it the dressing room that's important to you or the photographic studio? The sports pages or a spread in *G* fucking *Q*? Liniment or hair gel? Vaseline or aftershave? A jockstrap or an Armani suit? Some dolly birds or your team mates? The roar of the crowd or the squeal of some totty you're banging up the arse in a nightclub? Playing keepy-uppy or footsie with a hooker? Because I'm not going to waste my time helping you, young man, if all you really want to do in life is help yourself. You see, I love this game and I love people who love it as much as me. Those are the only kind of people for whom I am prepared to take risks and make sacrifices. Do you understand?'

'Yes. I love the game. I can't imagine life without football. Without my team mates. It wouldn't be worth living. It's what gets me out of bed; and it's what I'm still thinking about when I go to bed. What I dream about when I'm asleep. Every night, since I was a small boy.'

'Is the right answer. That's all I wanted to hear from you, Jérôme. Very well then. I shall certainly need to speak to some people first before I tell you anything more about what's on my mind. All I will say at this stage is, don't give up hope. Not just yet. There may be a way to make sure that you can still play professional football. So, please, try to be patient.'

CHAPTER 31

'So, let me get this straight,' said Charles Rivel. 'You found Jérôme Dumas, in the French Caribbean, on the lovely island of Guadeloupe—'

'I can see you've never been there, Charles.'

'You found him. But the loan agreement we made with Barcelona has fallen through. Why? I don't understand. You brought the player back to France, didn't you?'

'Yes, he's back at his apartment here in Paris.'

'But surely you could just as easily have taken him to Barcelona. They paid for the plane, after all. So why isn't he there now, in Spain? Why isn't he at Camp Nou getting fit for the match against Real Madrid?'

'Because I told them he'd had a nervous breakdown. And that he didn't want to play in Spain any more. That, for the moment, he wanted to stay in France. But none of that is true. They know it isn't. But they're happy with the story I've given them for now. The fact is, I thought the fewer people who know the real reason why he's not going to be playing there the better.'

'Better for who?'

'For you *and* for him.'

'Forgive me, Scott, but shouldn't all this have been our decision at PSG? We sent you to find a missing player, not scupper a good deal. It's true there was no transfer fee but need I remind you that the Catalans were going to pay all of Jérôme Dumas's wages? Which are not inconsiderable. Not to mention a loan fee of several million euros.'

We were meeting for breakfast in the restaurant at the Bristol Hotel in Paris, which is where PSG likes to do its business. The cheapest room at the Bristol is more than nine hundred euros a night, which makes business as comfortable as it gets. It's where the club's sport director, Leonardo, did the deal with Edinson Cavani, when he joined from Napoli in July 2013, for a fee of about forty-eight million quid, then a Ligue 1 record. And it's where the club paid for David Beckham to stay when he was playing for PSG; in the Imperial Suite to be exact, which, at £14,500 a night, costs rather more than the cheapest room where I was now staying. But then it is easily large enough for a game of indoor five-a-side. Becks was worth that much in just his shirt sales. It was nice to be in a really good hotel again but most of all it felt good to be back in a country where they take food seriously. Especially the humble croissant. With butter and apricot jam and hot coffee it is the cornerstone of a civilised breakfast.

'Believe me, Charles, I've done you a very big favour. An enormous favour, in fact. And I'm about to do you another. When I've told you what I've done you'll want to upgrade me to the David Beckham suite and throw in a free football.'

'So tell me. I'm listening.'

So I told him, everything – I even told him about the gun, and the murder in Sevran – and it was fun watching the Frenchman's smooth jaw drop onto his silk Charvet tie.

'Jesus Christ,' he said.

'Is he staying here, too? I'm surprised he can afford it.'

'Are you serious? Dumas was using his twin to trick our doctors? And was planning to do the same at Camp Nou? I don't believe it.'

'I'm perfectly serious. It's true. I guess the boy isn't called Dumas for nothing.'

'Beating Chelsea in the Champions League. Overtaking Olympique Lyonnais in Ligue 1. These would be good for PSG. These I understand. And I can see how all this is good for FCB. But how is any of what you're telling me good for PSG? We'll get to how it's good for the player later.'

'While it's true that you won't ever be able to sell Jérôme Dumas, you will have avoided any significant legal problems that might easily and expensively have resulted if Jérôme and his twin had managed to pull off this little scam. For example, you might have been held legally liable to FCB. As might have been your medical insurers if he was to suffer some sort of problem during a match. Like the lad at Tottenham who suffered a heart attack? Radwan Hamed? That just cost Spurs' insurers the best part of seven million quid. Although I dare say they'll pass that cost onto the club when the next premium comes to be paid.'

'Yes, I see.'

'Also, given the fact that the twins undoubtedly pulled the same trick when he came here from AS Monaco who, incidentally, had no idea of what was going on either, it means your contract with Jérôme is null and void. In other words, you don't have to pay him any more. So, the player's wages don't even come into it. That's how it's good for PSG. Although I expect you will have to repay the loan fee to Barcelona.'

'Could we recover our transfer fee from ASM?'

'I doubt it. It was your doctors who, through no fault of their own, pronounced him fit to play. I'm afraid that's why medicals take place under the auspices of the purchasing club, not the vendor. I'm not a lawyer but I should say that this is a simple case of caveat emptor. Let the buyer beware. Of course, they weren't to know that Jérôme had a twin. And of course ASM will rightly argue that he conned them as well. So I don't think there's much mileage in it for you by trying to hold them legally accountable.'

'I suppose we could sue Jérôme Dumas, couldn't we?'

'That would only make you and your doctors look like mugs. And nobody wants that. Legal action is best avoided here, I'd have thought. Besides, it's not like he didn't actually play for the club. And play well, on occasion. In the first round Champions League Cup tie you played against Barcelona in September he was man of the match, remember? In all respects but the medical he's functioned perfectly well. And could easily continue to do so, but for the lawyers and the doctors and the medical lawyers.'

Rivel sipped his coffee and nodded as I continued speaking.

'Sack him by all means, Charles. In fact, I recommend you do sack him. But it won't play well in the press if the reason you're getting rid of him and perhaps even contemplating legal action is because he has a hole in the heart. If you'll pardon the expression, it makes you guys look heartless.'

'That's true.' His eyes narrowed for a moment. 'You are telling me everything, Scott, aren't you?'

'Yes. Everything. Which is a lot more than I told my friends at FCB. And I owe them in a way I don't owe you. Which reminds me. I've decided to waive my bonus. The finder's fee that your Qatari friend offered if I found the boy.'

'Why? As I recall you are entitled to a reduced fee. A million euros. So why not take it? You've earned it. You've done what we asked.'

'Because I've been well paid for what I've done. And because I don't like to profit from someone else's loss.'

'Isn't that the nature of capitalism?'

'Perhaps. But there are some varieties of loss when capitalism must stand quietly in its technical area with its hands in its pockets, just watching the game. And this is one of those.'

'I thought he was the lefty, not you.'

'He is. I'm not. And after what the Labour Party said

about the Premier League and its television deal I'm never voting for them again. I'm just trying to do what's right here and, in my opinion, that's something which has no politics. This now brings me to the reasons I think you ought to give to the press when you *do* sack him. And this is very important, Charles. Not just for you. But for Jérôme Dumas.'

'And why should I give a shit about him, Scott? The bastard made a fool of us.'

'He'll never ever play football again at the highest level. On account of a serious medical condition he'll have to live with for the rest of his life. That's why. Very likely he will continue to live a perfectly normal, active life. But as we both know, medical actuaries deal in numbers, not in people. And to be fair to them there is always the possibility that all of this might become a much larger problem.' I let that sink in for a moment and then added: 'Besides, he's just a kid. Like most kids he thinks he'll live forever. Frankly, it's the sort of thing any young player would do in order to keep playing. The sort of thing I'd have done myself, if I'd been in his boots. When people are desperate to escape grinding poverty, this is what they do. Think how that will play in a newspaper like *Libération*.'

'When you put it like that...' said Rivel.

'Charles, if you saw what he'd come from – on the island of Guadeloupe, I mean. It's a dump. But it's a dump that's full of beautiful people. Most of whom haven't got much money and are starved of opportunities to better themselves. Honestly, if you knew where he's been giving some of his money – local schools and hospitals – you'd realise that he deserves to have some kind of a future. Preferably in football.'

'I thought you said he'd never play football again.'

'No, I said he'd never play again at the highest level.'

'Oh, you mean he can play in another league. Actually, Scott, I can't honestly see how that's going to work out either. Unless you allow the twins to practise the same deception on another club. Which can't happen.'

'You let me worry about that.'

'For legal reasons PSG would certainly want an undertaking that the Dumas twins never pull this kind of stunt again.'

'And you'll certainly have that. I guarantee it. And they won't be pulling any kind of stunts again. At least not of a medical kind. Look, all I need PSG to do is to sack him, like I said. I think you should sack him for misconduct. Specifically because of the political comments he's made to the press which you regard to be incompatible with his employment at PSG. Specifically the interview he gave to *Libération*. Take him at his own word. He's a communist who advocates Maoist revolution, isn't he? How does that play with your team owners? The last thing they want in Qatar is a revolution. Of course, everyone will think there's a lot more to it than that. And then maybe you can get your PR people to hint that he was involved with some bad boys in the *banlieues*. Which he was. Of course, in the long run, none of this will do Jérôme's reputation any harm at all. Much better to be sacked for being a bad boy than for having a hole in the heart. In fact, I rather think the Maoism might even go down well with his new employers.'

'What do you mean, his new employers? We haven't even sacked him yet.'

'But you will sack him. Because you have to. Because he can't play for you any more. Like I said, your insurers won't let him.'

'For Christ's sake, Scott. Why do I get the feeling I'm being bounced into something? And who are his new employers? It's not London City, is it?'

'No, it's definitely not London City. In view of what's happened you can be absolutely sure about that.'

'Yes, I saw the news.'

'No, it's someone else, Charles. And I spoke to them an hour ago. Before I came down here to have break-fast with you.'

'So, who?'

'I'll tell you. And I can safely say that provide you agree to everything I've told you just now, then I've solved all of your problems, Charles. And Jérôme's. Not to mention one small problem of my own.'

CHAPTER 32

Skype. To my mind it's not the fact that calls are free that they should be selling, it's the fact that they're calls *you see*. Somehow, when you're doing an important business deal, you need more than just a voice assuring you that everything will be as promised. You need to see a face. That's what it means to stay in touch. Almost. The day you can seal a deal on Skype with a virtual handshake will be the day that Skype is actually worth the 8.5 billion dollars that Microsoft paid for it back in 2011. Of course, 'face' – *miàn zi* – is very important to the Chinese, especially in business, and it means a lot more than respect and knowing one's place. It's about courtesy and trust and the recognition that the time of someone as rich as Jack Kong Jia is valuable and that he could always do business with someone else.

'Thank you for taking my call, Mr Kong Jia. I know you're a very busy man.'

He was seated in a room that was almost all white and in stark contrast to the black sky and neon lights of Shanghai I could see through the window behind him.

His tattooed arm was heavy with bracelets and charms. Around his neck was a shark's tooth, which was enough to remind me that the man might be dangerous. It's a rare billionaire who doesn't have some extra teeth.

'And thank you for your kind gift, Mr Manson. How did you know that I am so very fond of movie posters?'

'Sir, it's in an article about you in *Forbes* magazine.'

'Yes, but it was clever of you to know that I like James Bond movie posters best of all. And that the UK *Dr No* poster was one I did not yet have.'

'I noticed that you'd invested in the last Bond movie, sir. It was on the film's credits. Therefore I assumed you might be a fan, like me. I'm afraid it was just good luck that I chose that particular one. Although since it is particularly rare it was perhaps a reasonable assumption that you might not have it.'

Rare and also expensive. The poster had cost me £5,000. That was the upfront cost of doing business with Jack Kong Jia.

'I'm glad you called, Mr Manson. I've been thinking about you. Especially in view of what's happened today.'

'What's happened?'

'You haven't seen the news?'

'I'm in Paris, sir. I haven't been paying much attention to the news. And it's still pretty early here.'

'Viktor Sokolnikov has been found dead at his estate in Kent. It looks as if he was murdered by the Kremlin.'

'Oh. I see. No, I didn't know. Jesus.'

A hundred thoughts crowded into my mind for a second; thoughts about Viktor and our time together at London City; concern for his family; and a question mark about the stewardship of an important football club. What was going to happen to the team that João Zarco and I had helped nurture?

'I'm watching it on the TV news now. But then we are ahead of you here. We get everything before you get it.'

'So I believe. Sir, about those two football players who were supposed to come to China to join your club.'

'Chad Yekini and George Mboma. Yes, it's a pity they decided not to come. We could certainly have used them. There's a big match with Shanghai Taishan coming up in three weeks. Not that they would have been here by then, of course. They were going to come only at the end of the European season. But all the same, it's nice to dream, isn't it?'

'Might I ask what kind of money you were prepared to pay them?'

'Each of them had a three year deal worth two hundred thousand pounds a week.'

'Christ.'

'Plus whatever they could make from their image rights. Under my guidance, of course. Which would also be quite a lot. CSL players are very much in demand to sell almost everything in China. Especially when they've been playing at top clubs.'

'I didn't know players in China got paid so much.'

'The Chinese Super League is going to be the wealthiest in the world, Mr Manson. You can take my word for it.'

'What would you say if I told you I could replace them both? And in time for your match with Beijing?

If I said that one of them is a very long way off the end of his career, while at thirty-seven years old Chad Yekini is very close to the end of his. I take it you've heard of Jérôme Dumas. He's just twenty-two.'

'Dumas. Of course. He's a top player. He plays for Paris Saint-Germain, does he not? But I read in the sports pages that he was now on loan to Barcelona.'

'Not any more. The loan isn't going to go through. I happen to know that PSG are about to sack him. Among other things, for his Maoist revolutionary views.'

Mr Jia laughed. 'That's hardly a problem here in China. In spite of what happened during the Cultural Revolution a great many people in this country still revere Chairman Mao. So he might play for us, is that what you're suggesting?'

'Provided you could agree to waive his medical I can guarantee that I can bring him to Shanghai, sir. And to have his signature on a contract by the end of the week.'

'You interest me a lot, Mr Manson. And the other player?'

'His identical twin brother. Not famous like Jérôme. But he's an excellent footballer. Which is why I'm offering them both to you as a two for one.'

'Hmm.'

'I'm right in thinking that twins are considered to be a sign of good luck and good fortune in China, aren't I?'

'You are. They are especially prized in sport. A lot of Chinese people even touch them for luck.'

'Then their image rights ought to be worth quite a lot to you.'

'That's true. In fact, I know just the brand I could interest in using them. Identical twins, you say?'

'Like two peas in a pod, sir.'

'There's a brand of cigarette called Gemini. Made by Shanghai Tobacco. Which I own. We could use them to sell Gemini Cigarettes. Or Twopenny. That's an internet company I also own. Much cheaper than Tencent, our main business rival.'

'You could use them for anything you like. I happen to think Jérôme's Maoism is only skin-deep.'

'Obviously I have to ask. What's wrong with Jérôme Dumas if you want me to waive his medical? I assume that this is the real reason that PSG want to be rid of him. And why he isn't going to Barcelona.'

'It's not that Jérôme's not good enough for Barcelona. He is. I think you'll find that he's actually playing at the very top of his game. I advise you to take a look at the first round cup tie PSG played with Barcelona in September last year. Jérôme Dumas was the man of the match. But since then it's been discovered that he has a VSD. A hole in his heart. And now he's finding it difficult to get cleared to play by the club's insurers.'

'I know what that's like.'

'By the way, the other twin, Philippe – he's fine. There's nothing at all wrong with him.'

'VSD is much more common than people realise. It's ridiculous that people think you're going to die because of a tiny defect like a hole in the heart. There are almost three million people in China who have this condition. And who are living perfectly normal lives.'

'I'm glad you think so.'

'But is it because I told you that I have a hole in my own heart that you think you can bring me a player who isn't good enough for Barcelona? Perhaps you calculated that this would make me weak?'

'Not weak, sir. Understanding. Sympathetic, perhaps. And I owe you, remember? After my stupid mistake last month which you were generous enough to overlook, temporarily? We agreed that we should find some service I could perform for you in order to make amends for my error. I would humbly suggest that this is it. In spite of his condition, which as you say is a minor one, Jérôme Dumas is still a top player. It's also my impression that in any team he and his twin would make two thirds of a very formidable attack. Enough to win the Chinese Super League, perhaps. But if you disagree then it may be that I have to fly to China and look for another team owner who can give these young men a chance. Who could overlook such an inconvenient thing as a minor heart defect.'

'Hmm. And this has only just come to light?'

'I'm afraid so.'

'What's wrong with doctors in France and Spain?'

'I don't think it's the doctors who are at fault, sir. It's the insurance companies they advise.'

The Chinese billionaire paused and looked thoughtful. That's the other good thing about Skype. You know when it's time to shut up and let silence be your friend.

Then I said, 'When we met, you said you thought it was probably Shanghai Taishan FC who stitched me up, didn't you?'

'Yes. It was. I have had very good information to this effect.'

'It would be good to get some payback, wouldn't it? To stick it to those bastards. I'd like to get a piece of that myself.'

'It would be brilliant,' said Mr Jia. 'You really think this could work, Mr Manson?'

'Yes, I do.'

'I'm not asking for your optimism, Mr Manson. I want your honest, hard-headed opinion as a professional football manager. No sentiment, now. What does your own experience tell you?'

'It's not without some risk, sir. I should think the chances of something serious happening to the boy are perhaps five hundred to one. But a one in five hundred chance is probably just too high for a European medical insurer to take the chance. The payouts are too big when things go pear-shaped.'

'Take my word for it, Mr Manson. Five hundred to one? Those are very tempting odds for a Chinaman. That's a good bet. Anything else is a sure thing, and they don't exist. A player can score a hat-trick in one game and in the next break his leg in a way that finishes his career forever. How do you insure against something like that? You can't. Not yet. In a few years' time we may be able to measure bone density and estimate the probability of a player fracturing a limb in a tackle, and then where will we be? All sport contains risk. That's why we enjoy watching it.'

I let him think some more.

'Frankly, sir, I think the Dumas twins could become an important figurehead for any Chinese team. Especially Nine Dragons. Perhaps the best thing to do would be for you to meet with them and me, and then, if you are in agreement, we could make a contract for one year. We can see how things work out.'

'You mean suck it and see.'

'Something like that. And of course Shanghai Taishan wouldn't be expecting something like this. Not at this stage of the European season. All of the best players have contracts in Europe until the end of our season. So, just imagine if the Dumas brothers came and you beat Shanghai Taishan. Can you imagine it?'

'Just to see the look on Xu Yi Ning's face. I'd give a million dollars for a moment like that.'

I guessed that Xu Yi Ning was probably the owner of Shanghai Taishan FC and a bitter business rival of Mr Jia's.

'Then it sounds like we have a deal. Because I can't believe it's money that's going to stop this from happening. After all, a million dollars is four weeks' pay for these boys.'

'Yes, we have a deal.'

'I'm delighted to hear it, sir.'

'Might I ask what's in this for you, Mr Manson? Are you representing these twins as an agent? Will you take a cut of their fee? Where's your interest here? I'd like to know, please.'

'I'm not getting a penny from either of them, sir. They have a football agent, but he's out of the loop on this one. The fact is, it was me who uncovered the fact that Jérôme has a VSD. And I'm feeling a bit guilty about it.'

'All this is to your credit. In China we say that the selfless can be fearless.'

'Yes, well there's all that and the fact that, like I said before, I owe you a big favour.'

'It's good of you to recognise that. And if we pull this off you'll find that I'm not ungrateful, Mr Manson.' He grinned. 'Because you're absolutely right, of course. I hate those bastards at Shanghai Taishan. I've kept quiet about what happened to me and you. But you're right – we should have our revenge. And I will love it if we beat them. Love it.'

I grinned as I recognised an echo of what Kevin Keegan had said about Manchester United when he was still the Newcastle United manager, back in 1996.

'What?' he asked.

'I just realised something, sir.'

'What's that?'

'How much you love your football. You're the real deal, sir. And no mistake.'

'Coming from a man like you, Mr Manson, I take that as a real compliment.'

As soon as the Skype call was over I switched on the television to watch the Sky News report on Viktor Sokolnikov's death. The whole of his five hundred acre country estate in Hythe had been closed off by police while government nuclear scientists searched poor Viktor's house for radioactive material, although this seemed merely a precaution as the TV journalist had already reported a rumour that the Ukrainian billion-aire had been found hacked to death with a sword – a *kindjal*, which is used for bear-hunting in Russia.

I composed an email to Viktor's wife and grown-up daughter, but didn't send it – I wasn't sure if an email was appropriate in the circumstances; later on I wrote a letter and sent that instead – and then went down to breakfast with Charles Rivel, from PSG.

CHAPTER 33

After breakfast I went shopping, bought some presents for Louise at Galeries Lafayette – I was feeling guilty, of course – carried them back to the Bristol Hotel and then took the Metro out to Sevran-Beaudottes to meet with the mother of John Ben Zakkai, who was the fifteen-year-old footballing *wunderkind* I'd first seen playing keepy-uppy on the artificial pitch near the Alain Savary Sports Centre. Since I'd met him I'd been keeping in touch with him on What'sApp and we'd become friends. I was now about to become his patron and benefactor.

I'd been thinking deeply about what Mr Jia had said, how the selfless can be fearless. I'd decided to make this my maxim in all my dealings with Madame Zakkai and her son. The truth was I might have gained something for myself if I'd obeyed my instinct, which was to take the boy and his mother to La Masia – in English, it means 'the farmhouse', which is the name often used to describe the youth academy for FC Barcelona – and there to introduce young John to Jordi Roura and Aureli

Altimira who would undoubtedly have seen what I had seen in the boy: a prodigious footballing talent.

But there was a small part of me that would have been brokering this introduction in order to make it up to FCB for the disappointment I'd seen in Jacint's face when I'd told him that Jérôme Dumas would not be coming to the club after all. Because that was what I'd planned to do ever since the moment I'd seen John Ben Zakkai play football and felt my heart skip a beat. Was that what it had been like when Bob Bishop went to Belfast and discovered a fifteen-year-old genius named George Best – a boy whose local club Glentoran had previously rejected as too small and light?

Sometimes the only way you can be sure that you're doing the right thing is when your actions run against all that you hold most dear; and when you know that there are people you call good friends who might believe that what you're doing was disloyal and an act of ungrateful treachery.

A couple of days later, and at my own expense, the three of us – Sarah Ben Zakkai, John and I – flew from Paris to Madrid, to keep an appointment I'd made for us with Real Madrid and the manager of Cadete A.

Covering approximately 1,067 hectares of land, and a short distance from Madrid-Barajas Airport, Real Madrid City is probably the most advanced sports training facility in the world. That is no exaggeration. Designed by the architect Carlos Lamela, the Valdebebas Park complex is ten times bigger than the old Real Madrid Sports City and forty times bigger than the

Santiago Bernabéu. Small wonder that it cost almost half a billion euros.

From the airport we drove straight to the facility and through three levels of security, which is perhaps why it is better known to locals as the secret city. Groups of fans stood on a roundabout just off the motorway and peered into our car as we approached the main buildings, hoping to catch a glimpse of their footballing heroes. Convinced that we belonged to the club, a few of them even waved at us. John waved back.

'They're going to be doing that just for you, before very long,' I told John. 'That is if things work out the way I think they'll work out.'

'This is fantastic,' said John. 'I can't believe we're actually here. This place looks amazing – like a temple to football.'

'That's fair,' I said. 'But don't ever call this place the spiritual home of football. Nor any other except London. Got that? And specifically the Freemason's Arms which is a pub in London's Covent Garden district. Because that's where the rules of football were laid down by the first football association back in 1863. If there's one thing that bugs me it's when ignorant stupid people talk about places like Brazil, or Spain, or Italy, as the spiritual home of football. That's just bollocks. The game we play today is an English game, and don't you ever forget it, son.'

'Understood, Mr Manson.' John grinned back at me. 'But I still can't believe we're here.'

'Nor can I,' I said, hardly wanting to explain to the fifteen-year-old just why I felt so ambivalent about being there, in Madrid. It would hardly have been fair to have told him that for me it was like changing sides in a war, or becoming a Roman Catholic after years of worshipping in a Protestant church. Not that I was changing sides – just trying to do something that was in John's best interests rather than my own.

'Perhaps we'll meet Martin Ødegaard,' said John.

'Don't you want to meet Cristiano Ronaldo?' I said. 'Or Toni Kroos?'

'Oh, sure, but Martin is who I dream of becoming, you know? He's only sixteen. The youngest guy ever to play for his country. He just signed for Real. And now he's in the reserves, and being managed by Zinedine Zidane, and making fifty thousand euros a week. I mean, that's any kid's dream, isn't it?'

I had to admit all this did sound pretty good and helped to persuade me that maybe Madrid was still the best choice in spite of my reservations about what I was doing.

We parked in front of the entrance hall, which was like the lobby of a very modern hotel, where we were met by some people from the youth academy who led us to 'the white house' – the area reserved for the youth teams. Here were several dressing rooms, and seven pitches each with their own stand and the very same natural grass as that used on the pitch in the Santiago Bernabéu, which comes from Holland. Or so we were informed.

I wished the boy luck and then left him to get changed while Raul Serrano Quevedo from the club's public relations department gave Madame Zakkai and me a tour of the main building.

This giant, T-shaped building is huge and contains dressing rooms, gymnasiums, classrooms, conference rooms, offices, a hydrotherapy pool and medical centre, press area, etc. on both sides of the complex. There are ten grass and AstroTurf football pitches surrounded by stands with a capacity for more than 11,000 spectators.

After our tour, Raul took us to the café-restaurant called La Cantera. He was a handsome, good-humoured man wearing a blue shirt and tie, and a blue quilted jacket, and his English was impeccable. Through the enormous windows the players' friends and families could watch training sessions on the nearby pitches; members of the public were forbidden to watch however. Everything was brushed steel and white wood. A waiter brought us coffee, fresh orange juice and some delicious, sugar-free carrot cake.

'Frankly, this is the most amazing training facility I've ever seen,' I told Raul Quevedo. 'I've stayed in some five star hotels that weren't as good as this place. In fact, I think I just did.'

Raul nodded. 'It's taken a long time to get here, but we like it,' he said, modestly.

'You must like coming to work here.'

'I love it. Every day I arrive I tell myself I'm the luckiest guy in the world.'

For obvious reasons my arrival had been scheduled so that I wouldn't see an actual training session. Just in case. We were watching the kitman collecting each player's boots from where they had left them beside the door to the dressing room a little earlier.

'But then everyone who works here thinks the same,' said Raul. 'Even him. The kitman. He'd probably do the job for nothing if we asked him.' He shook his head. 'Actually, he'd probably pay us to do the job. Lots of guys would. That's what this team means to people.'

I nodded. 'I get that.'

'It's hard to see this place and not believe that you're not going to win an eleventh Champions League title this year.'

'Coming from a man with your Barcelona connections that's high praise indeed, Mr Manson.'

We went to watch the game – Real Madrid's Cadete A team versus the Cadete B team. John played for the Bs, which is as stern a test of a fifteen-year-old there is. I was nervous for him, as I wanted him to do well. John didn't try to showboat, which is what happens to a lot of kids, but he was very strong and creative on the ball and when he chipped the goalkeeper from outside the box to score a goal, I knew he'd probably earned his golden ticket.

Almost as soon as the ball was in the back of the net Santiago Solari from Cadete A came to find us. Jokingly nicknamed the little Indian, Santiago was a tall, powerful-looking Argentine who was probably the same age as me. Back in the early years of the century Solari had been an effective midfielder for Atlético and then Real Madrid, before ending his playing career at Inter Milan. But like Zidane with whom he'd played

– Solari had passed the ball to Zidane when he scored that famous wonder goal in Real's 2–1 defeat of Bayer Leverkusen – he'd chosen to come and coach at Real. And when you saw the secret city it was easy to see why.

'Where the hell did you find this kid?' Santiago had been educated at Stockton University in New Jersey, USA, and his English was as good as my Spanish. 'He's excellent.'

'So you will take him?' I said.

'Are you crazy? Of course we'll take him. He's the best kid I've laid eyes on since the first time I saw Lionel Messi play for your cadets at FCB. I've never seen a boy with better control of the ball than him. Balance, agility, confidence, and a ferocious shot. And what's more he's strong. Very strong. He can mix it with the best of them. With a physique like that he could be playing for the first team within two years. Like Martin Ødegaard. I just don't understand how he's not been on anyone's horizon. There were thirty different clubs vying for Martin's signature.'

'He's a Jew, that's why,' I said. 'Since *Charlie Hebdo* it's not so easy to be a Jew in Paris right now. Most of France's Jews are keeping their heads down, or even leaving. And who can blame them?'

'Jewish, huh? Then he could be the best Jewish player since José Pékerman.' Santiago wagged his finger as I looked blank. 'Argentine player. Coached the national side in the 2006 World Cup.'

John's mother, Sarah, began to weep when I told her the good news. I took her hand and squeezed it.

'All of this means you can get away from the *banlieues*,' I said. 'That you and John can come and live here in Madrid. You'll like it here. What's not to like?'

'Sure,' said Santiago. 'You'll love Madrid.'

'Thank God,' she said.

'Come with me, please,' said Raul. 'I'll have someone show you around the place where the families live.'

They got up and went away to get someone from the accommodation wing to show Madame Zakkai where it seemed she was now going to be living.

'But I don't get it,' said Santiago. 'You're a Barca man, Scott. At least you were before you went to London City. Why would you bring him to us and not to the Catalans? They've got an excellent youth academy of their own. You know, I'm still half-convinced that this is some kind of cruel joke. That you're going to take him to FCB after all.'

'You can sign him this afternoon, if you like,' I said. 'His mum's here. And me to give him advice. So go ahead and draw up a contract. In fact I insist on it. But I'm not his agent. He doesn't have an agent. Yet. But he soon will. As soon as you've signed him I'm going to call Tempest O'Brien in London and have her look after his interests from now on. However, just so as you know, I'm not making any money from being here. And I don't intend to, so please don't spoil it for me by offering. Perhaps you can cover my expenses and we'll call it quits.'

Santiago nodded.

'But you've still not explained why you brought

him here to us. Does this mean you've fallen out with
Barcelona? Please. I'd like to know.'

'No, I haven't fallen out with them. And if you don't
mind I'd like to keep it that way. My bringing John
Ben Zakkai here to Madrid must remain confidential.'

'Now I'm more puzzled than ever. No money. No
kudos. I don't get it.'

'Oh, I thought about taking him to Camp Nou. Believe
me, this wasn't easy for me. I suppose I wanted to make
sure that what I was doing was right for the boy and
not me. I couldn't have been sure of that if I'd obeyed
my first instinct, which was to take him to my friends
in Barcelona. It would have bothered me, you know?
We're born selfish and the game of football encourages
us to be that way. To be tribal. To win at all costs. I'm
surrounded by it. Infected by it. And that's all very well
but it's not what makes us human. I guess I wanted to see
if it was still in me, to perform an act of pure altruism.'

'I see. At least I think I see.'

'You might say that the pleasure of helping this kid
get into football is sufficient reward for me. There's not
much room for religion in my life, Santiago. Maybe
doing something like this is all the religion one really
needs.'

'Paying back. I get that.'

'No, it's not about paying back. It's about paying
forward, I suppose. I think the game needs a bit of that
right now. Don't you? If it's going to continue to be
the game we know and love? I was lecturing the poor
kid in the car about the importance of recognising the

game's past, but the future's even more important. This is going to sound bogus coming from someone as well-off as me, but when we think about the people who are investing in the game – the Qataris, the Emirates, the Glazers, the John Henrys, the Ortegas, the Pinaults, the Abramoviches – it just seems to be about money and nothing else. That's all people seem to understand by the word "investment". But there has to be a different kind of investment – an investment in the future. We have to do something for how we want football to be, not for how it is. As soon as I saw this boy I realised that my greatest fear was that somehow he'd slip through the net, and remain undiscovered. Which would have been a tremendous loss to the game. After all, you don't have to be a Manchester United fan to appreciate George Best; or a *cul* to appreciate the skill of Lionel Messi. Who knows? Maybe one day John Ben Zakkai will do something similar for a promising boy he talent spots. I'd like to think so.'

Santiago nodded.

'There's all of that,' I said, 'and then there's this: lately I've been behaving like a shit. You know? With women? Well, you might excuse it and say that I'm a man and sometimes I behave like any other man. But I can't seem to stop myself from doing it or even to admit it – at least, not without hurting someone. So. You might say that bringing John Ben Zakkai here, to you guys – that this is my penance. This is how I get to look at my face in the mirror again. This is how I manage to live with myself. Does that make any sense at all?'

'Scott. I'm a Roman Catholic. I'm named after St James the Great. The first disciple and the patron saint of Spain. What you say makes perfect sense to me.'

'Of course, now that I've been here I know that I was right to come to Madrid after all. This place is amazing.'

We shook hands because in football – especially in Spain – I'm happy to say it's still important.

CHAPTER 34

London was cold and grey and wet which was fine by me. I'd had enough of living out of suitcases for a while. I just wanted to draw the curtains, switch on the telly and stay home for a week. Chelsea were top of the Premier League – José was on his most brilliantly provocative form ever – Arsenal were third and London City were in the drop zone. In spite of City's desperate travails it felt good to be back home, even if that meant a trip to an FA independent regulatory commission hearing into my alleged misconduct.

The FA headquarters used to be at Soho Square and before that in Lancaster Gate but, since August 2009, it's been at Wembley. It cost the FA £5 million to leave the eight-floor building at Lancaster Gate, a not insignificant sum given the £10 million it had already cost to relocate, and at a time when the FA was struggling to find a sponsor. But then the FA has always been very good at wasting money and ripping off football fans. Why else are the FA Cup semi-finals now played at Wembley? To make money for the FA, of course, and to hell with the cost and inconvenience for the fans. But they can't even find a sponsor for the FA Cup since the Budweiser deal ended. For all the good these bastards do, the home of English football might as well still be the Freemasons Arms in Covent Garden. Very little seems to have changed since 1863 in the way these goons think. About the only way they're better than FIFA is that they're probably too dumb to be corrupt.

Wembley. Whenever I think of it now I think of Matt Drennan, who hanged himself on Wembley Way because he couldn't bear to be out of the game. That and a whole lot of other things – booze, pills, depression, divorce. The trouble is that when we play football professionally we're too young to know how lucky we are. Unfortunately by the time we know how lucky we are, it's too late and we're on the cusp of retirement. Football is the cruellest sport. I watched a telly programme about bees, and the way drones are kicked out of the hives at the end of the season reminded me of the way we treat footballers who are similarly considered to be past it. The drones fly off and try to figure out what to do with themselves but in the end the result is always the same; they die. Football is almost as bad as that.

I drove to Wembley in my Range Rover. You know what the outside of the place looks like: it's a big, modern, overpriced stadium with a carrying handle like a shopping basket at your local Tesco. You've seen it often enough when England are scraping a 2–2 draw with Switzerland or 1–1 with the fucking Ukraine. Thank God for Frank Lampard. Not so much three lions that night as three pussies.

That's not a joke I'd make on Twitter. I was glad I'd closed my Twitter account. I wish I'd done it sooner.

I nudged my way through the waiting newsmen and into the car park. It was a Friday and there wasn't much to write about, obviously. A few die-hard feminists had rolled out the red carpet for me. Literally. On the carpet was written: *This is what a real period looks like.* And there were banners which I slowed down to read. It seemed the least I could do. *MENstruation: as usual the problem begins with a Man.* And *You'd think a big c**t would understand about periods.* I kind of liked that banner. I even winked at the cute girl holding it in front of my windscreen.

Wembley. Inside the offices of the Football Association, things are a mess – some wanker architect's idea of what the future looks like, with the kind of brightly coloured, essentially uncomfortable furniture you might have expected to find in a Stanley Kubrick film of the early 1970s. Whenever I'm there I half expect to see Malcolm McDowell strolling around with a blackthorn stick in one hand and a bowler hat on his head. And without doubt I was expecting a solid kick in the balls. Not to mention a hefty fine.

Wembley. As if the place wasn't already hopelessly opaque, all of the windows have 'privacy panels' made of frosted vinyl, presumably to stop disgruntled England fans with sniper rifles getting a bead on any of the cunts who work there; meanwhile the carpets in the so-called 'breakout areas' – I think I know what that is on a football pitch, I'm not so sure what one looks like in a suite of offices – are grey, red and green like some hideous piece of abstract art that's been entered for the Turner Prize. And why not? A fucking carpet is no worse than any of the crap that wins the prize, year on year. Everything about the interior of the FA at Wembley jars like a bad LSD trip and seems to confirm exactly why England football is in such a parlous state; as you walk from one eyesore office to another, you tell yourself that if they can't get something as simple as the interior decor right, how can they possibly expect to be any better with the management of English football?

Wembley. The wall in the tiny room where my barrister and I were asked to wait until the actual hearing began had a full-length picture of the England Ladies' football number 10, Jodie Taylor. A nice-enough-looking girl if you like women in football kit but it was as if someone was trying to remind me that women play football too, and that a tasteless Twitter joke about a man who couldn't stay on the pitch and finish the game because it was his period was not going to be tolerated. I pointed this out to Miss Shields, my brief.

'I'm sorry some women were offended by my joke,' I said. 'In defence I should say that my social media offence was committed in Barcelona, where people have a sense of humour, and not in England, where apparently they don't. But at least now I know why having a period is sometimes called the curse.'

'An offence allegedly committed on social media renders all such national borders meaningless, I'm afraid,' said Miss Shields, who'd been selected by my solicitors. 'The fact remains that lots of women in the UK were offended. And that's the substance of the FA's charge against you, Mr Manson. You might almost say that it's an offence of strict liability. You said something. Lots of people were offended by it. Therefore the comment brings the game into disrepute. It's really that simple.'

'They *said* they were offended. That's not quite the same thing as *being* offended. Sometimes I think there's a special Twitter feed that's there to round up the kind of people who have a pitchfork handy so that they can go straight round to Frankenstein's castle and burn it to the ground. There ought to be a special equation used to compute the speed with which people in Britain now take offence at almost anything. Like the hedge funders have, to calculate shit about financial futures. The Clarkson Ratio. Or the Rio Ferdinand Formula. Or the Ashley Cole Calculation.'

Miss Shields nodded patiently. 'It's best you get it all off your chest while you're in here with me now, and not in there where you'll only talk up the fine.'

'I guess you're right.'

'Now then. You've been charged under the terms laid down in relation to media comments and social network in FA Rule E 3(1). In that you made a comment which was improper, which brings the game into disrepute, and which is insulting.'

'I deleted the tweet,' I said. 'And closed my account. Doesn't that count for anything?'

'Sadly not. I have read the written observations you provided to explain the context of why you said what you said but I now think it's best we don't use those. Just in case we aggravate the original offence.'

I nodded. 'You're probably right.'

'So,' she said. 'What *do* you want me to say?'

'Plead guilty. Offer some mitigation. You know the kind of thing. Take the fine.' I shrugged. 'They've got to raise the money for English football somehow. Sure as hell no one's going to be interested in a friendly against the Republic of Ireland. The moth-eaten blazers at the FA don't seem to understand that there's no such thing as a friendly in football these days. Not at over a hundred quid a pop. There's nothing friendly about England ticket prices. And no one gives a shit about an under-23s match between England and China. Or a disability eleven versus the Russian Blind.'

Miss Shields frowned.

'You think I'm joking, don't you?' I said.

'Yes,' she said, flatly.

'Well, I'm not.'

She nodded. 'You know, I think it's probably best that you leave *all* of the talking to me.'

'I agree.'

They called us into a room and you could have cut the atmosphere with a pair of plastic scissors. The four-man hearing was actually three men and a woman. I guess the dog couldn't make it. The chairperson was a man but it was the woman who did the talking and she seemed a little disappointed that I'd decided to plead guilty. The pencil she was holding in her tiny fist looked as if she'd sharpened it especially to stab my cock with it.

Miss Shields did her best but in spite of her eloquent arguments to the effect that most normal women wouldn't take offence at the tweet I'd made, the FA still felt inclined to fine me twenty-five thousand quid. Which is a nice round sum and the same fine they gave Mario Balotelli for his infamous Instagram post about Super Mario and the Jews. It will probably keep them in expense-account lunches and dinners for about a month. FA independent regulatory commission hearings are like speed cameras; if you drive in London, you're bound to get a fine and three points eventually. It's the same with being in English football. The pain in the arse is the lecture you get, especially when it was obvious the chairman thought the whole thing had been whipped up by the media. But of course the FA is terrified of the media and is more likely to pay attention to some idiot's tweets – and that includes me – than the fact that we can't seem to win international matches against anyone who matters, when it matters most. Scoring goals and winning trophies used to be the proper province of the FA; now it's all about adjudicating petty grievances on social media, or punishing managers who say what everyone in the game knows: that referees are making too many mistakes.

Ignoring the press who were waiting in the car park like a pack of scavenging dogs, I drove back to my flat in

Chelsea and made a cup of Bonifieur coffee and watched my ugly mug on Sky Sports News. Always good for a laugh. There was a famous sportswoman in the studio who called me a dinosaur and said she hoped I would not be welcomed back into sports management any time soon. Which seemed to be a fairly safe expectation. To my relief she was cut short by the news that London City's manager, Stepan Kolchak, had resigned with immediate effect, ahead of the big game with Arsenal. A minute later my landline started ringing. I was going to ignore it until I noticed that the number identified the caller as Viktor Sokolnikov. Momentarily unnerved by this call from the dead, I picked up the handset and found myself speaking to Viktor's Russian-American daughter, Yevgeniya. I'd met her once before; ferociously smart, and famously beautiful, she was studying for an MBA at Harvard. Or so I had thought.

'I was very sorry to hear about your father,' I said. 'In spite of all our differences I always liked him.'

'Thank you, Scott.'

'Is there any news about his killer?'

'No. And there won't be. But everyone knows who ordered his death. He wouldn't pay the Kremlin the protection money they were demanding. And so they killed him. That's how it works, these days. Since Berezovsky. Since Khodorkovsky. You pay up or you find yourself dead or in prison. This is something I'm going to have to get used to myself, since I inherited the bulk of my father's fortune. Not to mention his football team.'

She sounded more American than Russian.

'I take it that Stepan Kolchak's resignation had something to do with you.'

'That's right. He was useless, of course. Couldn't manage a team of painters and decorators. I asked him to resign. To give him a little dignity. But I was much more inclined to sack him.'

'It sounds like you're going to be taking an active role in the club, Yevgeniya.'

'Very active. I'm given up Harvard and I'm back here permanently. To manage all my father's affairs. Including London City. My father always liked you, Scott. Admired you very much. I believe that he would have asked you to come back to manage the club at the end of the season. Of course by then it will be too late. We'll have been relegated and we can kiss goodbye to a hundred million pounds' worth of television money.'

'I wouldn't be too sure that he would have asked me back. And I'm not so sure I'd have wanted to go back to City.'

'I'm not my father. So. Mr Dinosaur. Mr Sexist Pig. What do you say? I will pay you what Arsenal pay Arsène Wenger: £7.5 million a year, plus a five million pound bonus if you keep us up. A three-year contract. And here's your chance to prove all those women wrong who were calling for your head today. I think it would actually do you good to have a woman boss. Come and work for me, Scott. Come and work for a woman. Only please, come soon. As I'm sure you know we have a very important game against Arsenal on Sunday. Perhaps the most important game in our season. So, just don't keep me waiting, okay? I have the curse right now and I become very irritable when I don't get what I want.'